DOROTHY GARLOCK

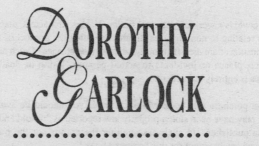

The Searching Hearts

WARNER BOOKS

A Time Warner Company

WARNER BOOKS EDITION

Copyright © 1982 by Dorothy Garlock
All rights reserved.

Cover design by Diane Luger
Cover illustrations by Michael Racz
Hand lettering by Carl Dellacroce

This Warner Books Edition is published by arrangement with the author.

Warner Books, Inc.
1271 Avenue of the Americas
New York, NY 10020

Visit our Web site at
http://warnerbooks.com

W A Time Warner Company

Printed in the United States of America

First Warner Books Printing: October, 1997

10 9 8 7 6 5 4 3 2 1

BJ / *Karen*

❧❦❧❦❧❦❧❦❧

Dear Reader:

If THE SEARCHING HEARTS is a title that seems familiar to you, then you may have read this novel back in 1982 when it was first published. This new edition is a re-publication of one of my first novels.

My books were not widely distributed at that time because novels from new writers seldom are. But though I've written thirty-five other books in the intervening years, THE SEARCHING HEARTS is still one of my favorites. The Western atmosphere is authentic, with grit as well as glory; and the love stories are passionate but possible because the people I write about are very real to me. I'm delighted that Warner Books is able to bring you this new edition of THE SEARCHING HEARTS.

My next book, SWEETWATER, will be published in March of 1998. If you're curious about it, turn to the back of this book, where you'll find the first chapter. I hope you enjoy it as much as you enjoy THE SEARCHING HEARTS.

Dorothy Garlock
Clear Lake, Iowa

❧❦❧❦❧❦❧❦❧

Turn this page for praise for Dorothy Garlock and her latest romance, *Larkspur*.

The Searching Hearts

Books by Dorothy Garlock

Annie Lash
Dream River
Forever Victoria
A Gentle Giving
Glorious Dawn
Homeplace
Lonesome River
Love and Cherish
Midnight Blue
Nightrose
Restless Wind
Ribbon in the Sky
River of Tomorrow
The Searching Hearts
Sins of Summer
Tenderness
The Listening Sky
This Loving Land
Wayward Wind
Wild Sweet Wilderness
Wind of Promise
Yesteryear

Published by WARNER BOOKS

To my son Herb, who would have been a great wagon master, and to Jacky, who would have seen beauty along the way.

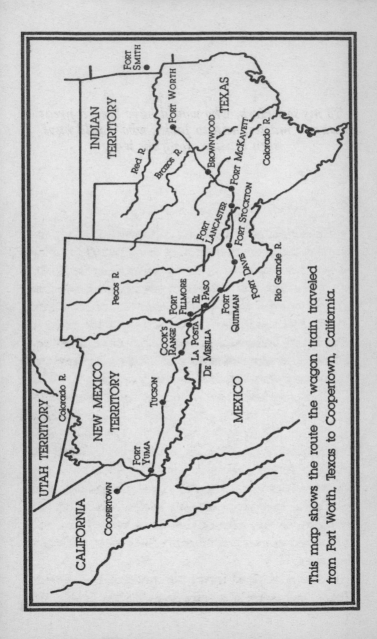

This map shows the route the wagon train traveled
from Fort Worth, Texas to Coopertown, California.

One

Tucker Houston stood in the drifting dust and listened to the jingle of the harness and the soft, cajoling voice of the teamster as he hitched fresh horses to the stage that had just deposited her here. Despite her present worries, the sounds brought back memories of her childhood. The weekly arrival of the stage in Fort Smith, Arkansas, had been an exciting event for the dozen or more children who lived on the farm, the "throwaway farm" as it was usually called.

Tucker reached out a hand and tugged on the calico bonnet tied beneath the chin of the girl standing beside her, tilting it forward so the fair young skin was shaded. Laura Foster stood patiently with her hand on Tucker's shoulder. Anything Tucker did, any decision Tucker made was all right with her. It always had been, ever since the day Tucker had found her clinging to the gate of the throwaway farm, too frightened to move, with tears rolling from her sightless eyes.

After a week of travel, the town of Fort Worth, Texas, had come as a surprise to Tucker. It was just there, rising abruptly out of the flat land. It was larger than she had expected it to be, considering its newness. The stage to Yuma started here, and the town had grown by leaps and bounds. Shops lined the rutted track: blacksmiths, wagon repair shops, mercantile stores, and saloons. All seemed to be doing a thriving business. A man on the stage had said there was even talk of making Fort Worth the county seat.

The departing driver climbed back onto the seat of the stagecoach, ignoring the girls because they were no longer his responsibility, and waved to the man standing beside the tired team of sweating horses.

Tucker half closed her dust-rimmed eyes against the brilliant glare of the surrounding sunlit plains that now looked so desolate and awesomely lonely. The sound of the stage was soon lost to her, but she could still see it snaking its way over the flat land. Perspiration oozed from every pore in her skin. She knew it was hot, but not that hot. She was sweating from fear! Fear of the unknown Lucas Steele and what he would say and do when he discovered she was just a nineteen-year-old girl—with very little in the way of education to recommend her as a teacher and with a totally blind seventeen-year-old girl in tow.

"Why are we standing here, Tucker? Why are you so quiet?"

"I was waiting for the dust to clear. I don't see anyone who looks like he's expecting us. Pick up your valise and let's get in out of the sun."

Tucker led Laura into the shade of a brush arbor

that fronted the stage station, if it could be called a station. It was a long building with a dirt floor and a network of pole corrals behind it.

"Phew! It's hot. Take off your bonnet, Laura, and fan yourself with it."

"Is this a very big place? Tell me about it, Tucker. Do you see the wagon train?"

"It's not as big as Fort Smith, and it's rough and new-looking, and it's just squatting right out here on the prairie," she explained. "I don't see any sign of a wagon train, but there's an awful lot of men around, and some of them are giving us the eye," she added crossly.

Laura giggled behind her bonnet. Her unshakable faith that Tucker would take care of them never allowed her a moment of worry. Tucker had been her friend and protector from the time she was a scared six-year-old and Tucker a mature eight. When she was left at the gate of the farm, she had been blind for only a short while and could remember what many things looked like. Tucker had taken complete charge of her and immediately started teaching her how to take care of herself. Having Laura to care for had given new meaning to Tucker's young life.

Tucker had no memories of her childhood before the farm, but she knew there had been a time when she was loved. It would be lovely if she knew what her name had been in those days. She had been found beside a burning prairie schooner that had been attacked by renegade Comanches, according to the cattle-driving outfit that had chased them off. A young cowhand had offered to "tuck 'er" into his coat and, after being tucked into first one coat and then another, she was given the unlikely name of Tucker by the time they reached the farm. The overseer at the orphanage had been an admirer of Sam Houston and had added Houston to complete her name.

When Tucker left the farm at age sixteen to work for Mrs. Rogers in her dressmaking establishment, she took Laura with her. The farm had a new manager by that time, and, from the way he watched Laura, Tucker knew he intended to put her to work—flat on her back, servicing him and anyone else who had the price. That would never happen to Laura as long as she, Tucker, could prevent it.

She looked at Laura now as they stood beneath the shady, yet breezeless, bower. Laura was so pretty, so sweet and cheerful, despite her blindness. She was eager to learn and could do many things sighted people could do. She could even make better biscuits than Tucker could. She did their washing and kept their room in order, and she could stitch in a hem after Tucker had pinned it for her. And . . . she was pleasant company. If Lucas Steele didn't want Laura, he could darn well send them both back.

A June bug buzzed around under the brush arbor. Tucker brushed it away before she pushed a tendril of hair from her damp forehead. It was curly hair of a remarkable copper color, and it was often inclined to be unruly. She was resigned to its contrariness in much the same way she was resigned to her orphan status in life. Her skin tones were pale and fine, and she had learned to protect herself from burning by wearing a bonnet when in the hot sun. The unbrushed tangles of her coppery hair now hung about her face, thick and cloudy and glistening in the sunlight, accentuating her green eyes, deepening them to brilliant emeralds.

Her face was beautiful. Most men stared at it, as well as at her long, supple swaying body, with riveted attention. Once that had unnerved her, but her attitude had changed, leaving her with a residue of ready hostility toward a certain sort of man.

"I'm nervous, Laura," she admitted.

"Don't be nervous. Mr. Steele will like you. You can be awfully nice when you put your mind to it." Laura's face brightened and dimples appeared in her cheeks. She was a small, softly rounded girl with lovely white skin, rosy cheeks, straight dark brows and curling eyelashes. Her hair was the color of light honey and she wore it tied at the nape of her neck with a colorful ribbon.

"A man on a black horse is coming toward us," Tucker said softly. "Put on your bonnet, Laura, and face your left. We might be about to meet our Mr. Lucas Steele."

He was a big, lean, broad-shouldered man with a ruggedly handsome face. He wore a black hat pulled low over his forehead. He sat easily in the saddle and studied them carefully as he approached. He rode up to within a few feet of the arbor and sat looking at them. He stared at them for so long that his level gaze took in the faint but unmistakable hostility in

Tucker's expression. His eyes were of a gray so light as to be almost colorless at times; but as he moved his head and the sunlight glinted on them, Tucker saw them take on a startling blue gleam. His hair was blue-black, thick and smooth, and dark sideburns framed a cleanly shaven face. His nose had a classical line, straight and faintly arrogant. Tucker's eyes did not linger on his mouth, nor on the deep creases on both sides of it. She did not like the faint, amused smile it wore as he watched her.

"Who are you?" he asked as he threw a leg over the saddle horn and continued his lazy inspection of them.

Tucker regarded him coolly. "Who are you?" was her response.

Taking his time in an infuriating way, he ran his narrowed eyes over her face, down her slender figure in the dark cotton dress, and back up to the flame-colored hair that framed her forehead and cheekbones. Tucker stiffened as his eyes roamed. When they came back to her flushed face, there was amusement in them, and she wanted to snap at him, ask him what was so all-fired funny. Instead, she did what she had done in similar circumstances. She controlled her temper, took a deep breath, and eyed him in exactly the same way he had eyed her. In most cases it embarrassed even the most blatant of men. This time, however, it didn't work.

"Handsome, don't you think?" The gray eyes mocked her.

She stared at him without a hint of amusement.

"I've seen better sights riding behind a team of mules."

He grinned. "She's just got to be Tucker Houston, the schoolteacher." He spoke as if he was thinking aloud; his voice was smooth. He watched her all the time as though trying to gauge some reaction to what he was saying. "If she's such a sour old maid, I wonder what curdled her sweetness."

"You can wonder till the cows fly!" Her temper crept up as she spoke, clouding her reason.

"You're waspy." He gave her a wicked, teasing smile. "And after all the trouble I'm going to to get you to California. You just might find yourself a husband out there, if you're lucky. 'Course you'll have to sweeten up some." He slid from the saddle and came toward Laura. "Lucas Steele, young lady. Are you as waspy as your sister?" He held out his hand, and when Laura simply smiled up into his face, Tucker's heart stood still. "Come on, shake hands. I'll not bite."

Laura put out her hand. "I wasn't sure, Mr. Steele." Her small laugh was open and friendly. "Tucker isn't waspy when you get to know her."

"I'll have to work on getting to know her then, Miss Laura, but in the meantime I'll get a buckboard to take you to the camp. We're about a mile away. We'll be heading out in the morning, so if there's anything you need, you better get it now."

"There's nothing we need," Tucker said in a tight voice. "Mr. O'Donnell gave us a list, and we outfitted ourselves before we left Fort Smith."

"Got stout shoes?" His face altered slightly. "You'll be doing some walking."

"Of course." Not for anything would she let this man know that they had less than five dollars and couldn't buy anything even if they needed it.

"Of course," he echoed. "Well, sit tight. I'll be back." He looked at Tucker and grinned. "Bet you can hardly wait."

Tucker kept her lips pressed firmly together and glared at his back as he left them.

"What did he look like, Tucker?" Laura whispered.

"Well . . . he had two arms and two legs . . . and I suspect two horns under his hat!" Tucker's face was still burning from the way he had looked at her. "I've seen his kind before. A blowhard, that's what he is. I don't like him!"

"I thought he sounded . . . nice."

"Nice? He sounded to me like he thought an awful lot of himself."

Laura giggled. "Hold onto your temper, Tucker. Wait till we get started to California before you explode. Besides, I think he was just teasing you."

Tucker swung her bright head around so she could see Laura's flushed cheeks. Seldom did she see her when she wasn't calm and cool. She was excited now. Tucker reached for her hand and squeezed it. Come to think about it, she reflected, I'm all aflutter myself.

A flatbed wagon driven by a Mexican came rumbling around the corner.

"Here comes the wagon. Lucas Steele, too, darn it!

Look down, Laura, like you're real bashful." Tucker picked up her valise.

Lucas dismounted and let the hanging reins ground-tie his horse. "I'll take that, Red." He took the valise from Tucker's hand and bent to scoop up Laura's. He set the bags up on the wagon and lifted their trunk, set it on the tailgate, and gave it a shove.

Tucker moved with Laura to the end of a wagon.

"Here you go, little gal." Lucas seized Laura by the waist and swung her up onto the end of the wagon. He then moved so fast Tucker had no time to protest. Hard hands gripped her waist, and effortlessly he lifted her. Automatically her hands went to his shoulders when her feet left the ground. He held her there for a moment and looked deeply into angry green eyes before he sat her down on the end of the wagon beside Laura.

"Don't expect that kind of service all the time, Red. From now on, you're on your own. Everyone on this train will pull his own weight. That means you, too, Laura."

It was Laura's giggle that caused Tucker's temper to snap.

"I didn't ask for your help. From now on you can keep your hands to yourself." And as usual, once her tongue started, she didn't know when to stop it. "And my name is *Miss* Houston."

"*Miss* Houston? O'Donnell said you were a widow." Sharp eyes searched the face that was now flooding with color.

"I am!" Tucker's defenses were not what they

should be. She was tired, and his infuriating presence was too distracting.

"Liar!" His grin more than the word infuriated her. "See you at camp, Red. You, too, Laura." He wheeled the horse and was gone.

"He wasn't mad, Tucker," Laura said as soon as the wagon was in motion. "He just likes to tease you." Laura's keen perceptiveness was always a surprise to Tucker.

"He's crazy as a bedbug if he thinks I'm going to be his amusement all the way to California!" She was shivering with suppressed agitation.

"Then don't rise to his baiting, Tucky."

"It's hard not to, darn it. It's just our luck that Lucas Steel would be *that* kind of man."

Laura's laugh was a little shaky. "Don't worry, Tucky. We'll be all right."

The sun was sinking and the sky was hazed over. A wind kicked up a sudden gust that flapped the brims of their bonnets. For as long as she could see them, Tucker kept her eyes on the sparse buildings that made up the town. The driver cracked the whip and the wagon picked up speed, stirring up a cloud of dust. They rounded a curve in the trail and left the town behind them.

Events of the last few weeks had crowded in on Tucker so fast she found it hard to believe that she and Laura were actually sitting here on this buckboard that was carrying them out to the wagon train bound for California. Of course, none of this would have happened if she hadn't pricked one of Mrs.

Rogers's richest customers with a pin when the woman had angrily slapped her hand away from the sleeve she was working on, or if she hadn't hit Mrs. Rogers's husband across the face when she caught him peeking into the room while Laura was undressing.

It had taken being fired from her job to jar her out of the dull life she was leading as Mrs. Rogers's seamstress. The dresses she made were always for someone who needed them in a hurry and didn't care a whit if she sat up all night sewing by the light of the kerosene lamp. She hated the job, but it paid the money she and Laura needed to live on.

Their savings were almost gone, and Tucker was beginning to get panicky when she saw the advertisement in the newspaper.

WANTED:

Women of good moral character to travel to California. Hardworking men are seeking wives. Teacher also wanted. Apply Logan Hotel on Tuesday.

Almost desperate because she had looked so long in vain for work, Tucker read the advertisement to Laura. The two girls talked long into the night about the possibility of going to California. The idea of accepting transportation on the premise that they would marry unknown men at the end of the journey—no matter how hardworking they were—was simply out of the question. Yet their circumstances in

Fort Smith were grim. Laura, with her unfailing confidence in Tucker, insisted that Tucker could teach school. Hadn't she taught all the younger children at the farm after she had been allowed to go to school? Hadn't the teacher said that Tucker was the best student she had ever taught? After long, whispered discussions it was decided that Tucker would apply for the teaching job and, if she was hired, would insist on taking her younger sister with her. They would conceal Laura's blindness for as long as possible in the hope that, when it was discovered, it would make no difference.

Later Tucker relayed every word of the interview to Laura.

Mr. O'Donnell turned out to be a lawyer hired to recruit the women. He stood in the airless room at the hotel and talked in quick, jerky sentences, as if hurrying to get the interviews over with.

"I have been commissioned to select six ladies from Fort Smith to travel to Coopertown, California. The town was established fifteen years ago in eighteen forty-three and is located in a green valley where warm sunshine and gentle rains raise crops beyond your imagination. There are twenty unmarried men in this valley who live in comfortable cabins, some with artesian wells and established grape arbors. They want wives and have raised the money to bring them to California."

"You mean . . . six of us can choose from twenty? I like them odds. I'll go!"

Tucker looked around to see who was speaking. It was a plump girl with hair on her upper lip.

"There will be twenty women, plus a teacher, making this trip. Only six from Fort Smith, the rest from Texas. Mr. Cooper, the man who founded the town, thought it best to provide women from different areas, since not all the men are Texans. The train will form in Fort Worth, Texas, and be led by Mr. Lucas Steele. He will be in complete charge, and should he not be pleased with any one of you he will pay your fare back to Fort Smith." The man was nervous, sweating, and he mopped his brow with a handkerchief. "Now I'd like to speak with each of you privately." He motioned to the woman in the first chair, and she followed him into another room.

Tucker was almost the last woman to be interviewed. She walked into the room on shaking legs. The man looked harassed; the interviews before had obviously been trying. She sympathized with him. She wouldn't have picked any of the women except the one with the small boy, and she looked too frail to withstand the journey.

"I'm applying for the teaching job," Tucker announced before she sat down.

The man looked surprised. "Mr. Cooper hoped for an older, experienced teacher, but he did say that if one couldn't be found who was willing to make the journey, a female of marriageable age would do."

It was pure desperation that caused Tucker to say she was a twenty-four-year-old widow and had taught school. That wasn't such a big lie, except that she was really only nineteen. But she *had* taught the younger children at the farm. The man laid down his pencil and gave her his rapt attention, and from there on she lied brazenly.

She had gone to school until she was sixteen, she told him, and after that she had taught for two years until her marriage. Now that her husband was dead, she wanted to leave Arkansas and all her sad memories. No, she assured him, she didn't fear the long trip to California. And yes, she was a strong, healthy woman. The lawyer looked doubtfully at her slender frame, and she was tempted to flex her muscles for him.

"Perhaps I should make something clear at this point, Mr. O'Donnell. I have a young sister and I will not leave her behind." Tucker held her breath while she waited for his answer.

"Is she a stout, healthy child?"

"She isn't a child. She's . . . fourteen." Tucker hoped her small laugh wasn't too forced as she lied about Laura's age.

"Give her a year or two and she'll be of marrying age," he said tiredly. "I don't see any problem in taking along a girl of that age. And frankly, you are the only applicant I've had for the teaching job. Not many teachers want to cut loose and travel to a new, raw land. If you want the job, it's yours. No doubt you'll be the prettiest woman on the train and will have no trouble at all getting another husband when you get to California." His eyes were smiling.

Tucker tried not to let her elation show. "I'm not

interested in remarrying at this time in my life. I only want a job so I can support myself and my sister."

He pulled at the mustache that curled down on either side of his mouth. "I wish it was as simple to select the other women as it was to select the teacher. There are but two here I'd even consider sending to Coopertown," he told her confidentially. "I'll have to wire Lucas Steele to find the others elsewhere." He stood and held out his hand. "I'll be in touch with you, Mrs. Houston. You and your sister will leave on the Friday stage if you can be ready by that time."

"We'll be ready." Tucker shook his hand, then walked out of the hotel, dazed that it had been so easy.

Two

The camp stood out clearly against the skyline. It looked small out there on the prairie, the wagons scattered around a spreading oak. Tucker suddenly remembered to describe it to Laura.

"We're almost there, Laura. The wagons aren't the big Conestogas, but a lighter type of covered wagon. There're a few people standing together looking this way." She groped for Laura's hand, to reassure herself as well as Laura. "Here comes Lucas Steele again! What are you giggling about, Laura Foster?"

"It's the way you say it, Tucker. I can tell you're just fit to be tied."

"Thank goodness he's only motioning for the driver to come around to the other end of the line. It'll be all right with me if we don't see him again during this whole trip."

Tucker looked at each of the women as she passed. Some answered her smile, some waved. She saw two young children clutching their mothers' hands and a boy who looked to be ten or twelve years old.

When the wagon stopped, Tucker jumped down

and then helped Laura. Lucas Steele was there beside them and pulled their trunk out so he could lift it down. "Lottie," he called.

The woman who came toward them was large without being fat. She had a dark, straight-brimmed hat crushed down on her head and a black apron tied about her waist. She was plain, her face so weathered it was impossible to tell her age.

"This is Lottie, Lottie Fields," Lucas said without ceremony. "Do as she tells you and you'll make out all right. This is Tucker Houston and her sister Laura Foster."

Laura murmured, "Ma'am."

Tucker said hello in answer to the woman's nod.

Lucas let his eyes slide over them briefly before he mounted his horse. "We'll have a meeting after supper."

Tucker looked after him. He was all business now. That was the way she preferred it. She turned and found Lottie looking at the way Laura was standing so patiently, holding her valise. Tucker started talking nervously.

"What do we do first, Lottie? We're both dog-tired and hungry."

"First we ort to get this trunk up inta the wagon."

Tucker took one end of the heavy chest, Lottie the other. They lifted it up onto the wagon bed, and Lottie sprang up to tug it into a space that seemed to be reserved for it. Her eyes kept darting curious glances at Laura.

"Laura. Come to me, honey." Tucker held out her

hand and Laura came toward the sound of her voice. "We'll have to tell Lottie. I can see now that it was foolish of me not to tell Mr. Steele." She put her arm across Laura's shoulders. "If we can't go to California, we'll just have to do something else. I just bet we could get laundry work at the Fort." They were brave words and she almost choked on them.

"Mr. Steele will let us go, Tucky. You worry too much." Laura's voice was soft and gentle and trusting, and Tucker wanted to cry.

Lottie jumped down from the wagon and stood with her large, work-worn hands on her hips, plainly puzzled. Tucker tried to blink back the tears, but they kept on coming.

"Laura's blind, Lottie. I didn't tell Mr. Steele. We need the teaching job and decided to wait until we were on our way and it would be too late for him to send us back."

"Land-a-Goshen! If that ain't the most outlandish thing I ever heard of. If Lucas didn't want ya, he'd put ya on the stage and send ya back if ya was almost to Californey! He sent two outta here a'ready for havin' a cat fight. Ya better tell 'im, that's what ya better do."

Tears were streaming down Tucker's face. They were tears of weariness and frustration. She didn't want Laura to know about them, so she forced a laugh and made her voice light.

"I'll tell him after supper. But right now, I'm hungry as a family of buzzards."

Laura's fingers came up and touched Tucker's wet cheeks.

"Lottie, can Tucker get in the wagon and have a good bawlin' spell? She hates for anyone to see her cry."

Lottie nodded indifferently and ambled away.

"Oh . . . you—" Tucker sputtered.

"Go on. I'll wait right here in the shade," Laura insisted. She took her hand from Tucker's and waited until she heard her crawl into the wagon before she felt her way around to the side where a water barrel was attached. She stood there until she heard Lottie coming back toward her and held out her hand to stop her.

"Lottie?" she whispered. "Lottie, will you take me to Mr. Steele?"

Lottie's big hand enfolded hers. "Come on."

The first thing Lucas did after he left Tucker and Laura with Lottie was to ride to the supply wagon where he kept his personal belongings. He lifted out the pair of saddlebags he had stashed with his bedroll, dug into the pockets, and pulled out a bundle wrapped in doeskin. Carefully he unwrapped a small velvet box and opened it. He hadn't looked at it for a long time. The soft leather had protected it well. The little portrait looked as bright and as fresh as it had years ago when his father had bartered it from an unsavory comanchero who said he had taken it from a dead Indian. The miniature was one of the few material things his father had left him, and Lucas had cherished it since his death.

The catlike eyes looked back at him, glowing with heady brightness, set deep and slanted beneath full, curving brows. Many a night he had lain in his bedroll and dreamed of the girl with the green eyes. He felt a twinge of something he had almost forgotten, and his dreams once more led out down the trail. Tucker Houston could almost be the woman in this portrait, the woman he felt he'd come to know and want. Her hair was brighter, her eyes greener. This woman's face was rounder and her chin not quite so pointed. She wouldn't have been as tall as Tucker, but her head was tilted in the same proud, defiant way. The instant he had set eyes on Tucker he had seen the resemblance and felt, in some strange way, that she should know him, too.

What had caused him to speak to her the way he had? It was as if he was compelled to provoke her, make her aware of him. He couldn't remember ever trading sallies like that with a woman before. It was no wonder she'd taken the attitude she did. He wrapped the box and was tucking it away, almost guiltily, when Lottie came walking up with Laura.

"Lucas, the gal here wants to talk with ya."

"Talk away."

"Will you walk me back to the wagon, Mr. Steele?"

"I doubt if you'll need me, Laura, if I point you in the right direction."

"You know?"

"I suspected. Sure, I'll see you back to the wagon. Things going all right, Lottie?"

"Tolerable, Lucas."

Lucas took Laura's arm and led her over to a box. "There's a seat behind you if you want to sit."

"Thank you. How did you know I couldn't see? Tucker and I thought we had fooled you."

"You would have, but you smiled at me and ignored my hand. I thought it was strange. Then I remembered a man in California who is blind; he does the same thing. Why were you keeping it a secret?"

"We were afraid you wouldn't give Tucker the job if you knew about me and . . . she'd never go away and leave me." She paused to give him a chance to speak. He didn't. "Mr. Steele, I'm not her sister, either. Tucker and I are orphans and we don't have anyone but each other, but we're not sisters. I feel I should be honest about that, too." To her surprise he laughed. "You suspected that, too?" she questioned innocently.

"I didn't really think about it, but there's no family resemblance," he pointed out.

"I know. People have told me that Tucker is beautiful. Very beautiful. Is it true?"

"Yes," he said simply. "Yes, she's very beautiful, but so are you."

"I am?" She said it with disbelief. "Tucker said I was, but Tucker loves me."

"She's right about that, anyway."

"I came to ask if Tucker still has the job. She's awfully worried and I asked Lottie if she could get in the wagon and cry. She'd just die if she knew I said that! She hates for anyone to see her cry. She's real proud."

"I could see that," Lucas commented dryly.

"Well? Are you going to send us back?" Laura pressed.

"What for? Have you another terrible secret to tell me?"

Laura giggled. "Well . . . I could tell you about Tucker getting fired 'cause she whacked Mrs. Rogers's husband with a razor strap."

Lucas chuckled. "That sounds like something I'd like to hear about."

Tucker's tears dried up as soon as she got into the wagon. She had let them all out in front of Lottie and had felt like a ninny. She sat for a while and tried to convince herself that Lucas Steele wouldn't be angry because she had been less than honest about Laura. How would a man like Lucas Steele know what it was like to be a woman and alone? No, not alone; she had Laura. If not for Laura she might have given up long ago and taken the easy way out, hired out to a farmer or plantation owner, or ended up working in a saloon. That was the usual fate of the girls from the throwaway farm. She'd had a taste of the pawing and the pinching. The very thought of it made the hair stand up on the back of her neck.

She sat thoughtfully. A big green horsefly buzzed in under the canvas and she watched it buzz out again. A woman's voice, scolding a child, reached her. A mockingbird sang in the tree above. Somewhere during this time her ambivalence left her.

She smoothed her hair with a few quick, artful movements and realized how stiflingly hot it was in the airless wagon. She wiped her face on the hem of her dress and climbed out. She had never before felt so physically and emotionally wrung out.

Tucker circled the wagon before her eyes began to search the camp for Laura. Her heart started to pound as it always did when Laura wasn't where she expected her to be. She began to walk rapidly down the line of wagons, but stopped when she saw Lottie coming toward her.

"Where's Laura?"

Lottie took her time answering. "Over yonder." She jerked her head back over her shoulder, a habit Tucker was to become used to.

"Over where? She can't wander around till she gets to know a place," Tucker cried desperately.

"She's with Lucas. Leave 'er be." The big woman said the words flatly, leaving no room for argument, and walked on.

Tucker was stunned speechless for a moment, then resentment took over. She followed after Lottie.

"You took her to him? I said I'd talk to him after supper."

"Yup. I took 'er. He'll bring 'er back."

"Lottie!" Tucker's heart was racing even though it felt as heavy as lead.

"The little gal knows what she's about." Lottie kept on walking.

"She doesn't! She's only . . . fourteen."

Lottie stopped. "If'n she's fourteen, so am I. And

if'n she is, she's got more gumption than some *teachers* I've met up with."

"Well . . . !" Tucker felt the color drain from her face.

"I might not ort to of said it jist like that." Lottie's face softened just a fraction. "What I mean is, you ort to give the little gal more rein. It's her what's causin' the ruckus. Let 'er try 'n fix it."

For the second time that day tears sprang to Tucker's eyes. What Lottie said made sense. All these years she had been so protective of Laura she hadn't stopped to think that Laura was a grown woman.

She sniffed. "I think I'm going to like you, Lottie."

"Humph! Mebbe. Mebbe not. Come on 'n let's figger out the sleepin'. You'll be stayin' the night anyhow."

The longer Laura was away, the more anxious Tucker became. She was almost to the point of taking action of some kind when she saw her, her hand on Lucas's arm, moving toward the wagon. Lucas was looking down and his face was unreadable, but Laura was beaming and talking as usual. Tucker stood with her hands clenched behind her and waited for them to approach. Lucas looked up and pinned her green eyes with his gray ones. He looked at her long and deeply. Laura couldn't know, so she kept up her breathless stream of chatter.

"We hadn't been in the coach an hour when a man moved over by Tucker. He said she sure was pretty and then he said did we want to look at what was in his case, 'cause he was a drummer—you know, a peddler—and he had things that would sure be pretty on Tucker. I heard him get down the case and open it, and then Tucker slapped him. He fell back in the seat and later she told me that he—"

"Laura!" Tucker was almost choking with embarrassment.

"Tucky, are you there? Are we back already?" She held out her hand and Tucker took it and drew her close, as if together they would face the enemy.

"Are you settled in, Miss Houston?" Tucker opened her mouth to say something, but Lucas turned and said, "Lottie, I told Mustang to come over and put some wire around that spoke. Glad you told me. It might mean the difference between having to put in a new one." The sound of a shot rang out and Tucker was startled. "That's the call to supper." Lucas looked amused, and the sight of his lips twitching caused her to grind her teeth. He walked away after saying, "Take care of big sister, Laura."

Tucker's back stiffened at his knowing tone.

Laura waited to speak until the quick pressure on her hand told her they were alone. It was a signal they had used since childhood.

"It's all right, Tucky. He knew anyway. He said he knew when he met us in Fort Worth, but was waiting for us to tell him. He said I would be expected to do whatever I could and that he'd have no one lazying. He's got a friend in California who's blind, and he said he'd take me to meet him when we get there.

He's like me. The friend, I mean. He's not always been blind. He's married and has two little boys."

"Oh, Laura, honey!" Relief was all the emotion Tucker could feel. "I was so scared. I didn't know what we'd do. But whatever possessed you to go to him alone? I said I'd talk to him."

"You always have to do everything, Tucky. You've taken care of me for eleven years. I want to make things as easy for you as I can. I may not be able to do a lot of things, but I can talk."

Tucker hugged her briefly. "Yes, you can, you blabbermouth! What were you telling him about that traveling salesman for?"

"I like to talk to him. He's interested in every-thing, and he listens. Not many people really listen, but he does. I like him, Tucker. I like him a lot."

"Well, I can't say that I really like him, but as long as he lets us go with the train to California, I guess I like him better than I did."

Lottie handed each of the girls a granite plate, a tin cup, and a spoon. She jerked her head toward the other end of the camp and started off at a brisk walk. Tucker decided that Lottie knew no other way to move. They followed her. Women were coming out of the wagons in front of and behind them. Laura, with her hand on Tucker's shoulder, walked confi-dently, and they took their place in line behind Lottie.

A woman was dishing out stew from a large iron kettle. Another removed a pan of corn bread from a portable oven and was slicing it with a broad knife. A squat, bowlegged man, his face covered with whiskers, and a dilapidated hat on his head, was poking sticks beneath a black pot suspended over a blaze. Coffee boiled over and he cursed.

Tucker turned and smiled at the woman standing behind her. She was a tall, handsome woman, with dark hair pulled back severely and fastened at the nape of her neck. The beautiful gold earrings she was wearing didn't seem to go with her worn clothes. She nodded, but didn't smile. A tall boy stood silently beside her. He had her dark eyes and hair and her quietness.

The woman dishing out the stew took Laura's plate from her hand, filled it, and put it back into her hand. She smiled shyly when Laura thanked her. Tucker led her to the far side of the campfire to sit beside Lottie and went to get coffee for the two of them.

The drover looked out from beneath his tattered hat and grinned at her. His smile was almost toothless, but his blue eyes were bright.

"Howdy. Name's Mustang. We been a waitin' on ya and the little missy to get here."

"Tucker Houston."

"Figgered it. Ya got the purtiest hair I ever did see. Comanches'd give six ponies fer ya." He gave her a sly, mischievous wink.

"Only six? I think I'll hold out for ten," she said in a confidential whisper.

The old man chuckled and tilted the pot to fill the cups. Tucker looked over his head and saw Lucas standing at the end of the grub wagon. His eyes were on her, and she looked away quickly.

Tucker attacked the meal with relish. The stew was surprisingly good, the coffee strong and bitter. She emptied her plate and sat quietly watching the women. They were in groups of two, three, and four, all except the woman and the boy who had stood behind them in line. They sat alone.

"Where are the rest of the men?"

Lottie eyed her sharply. "Why?"

Tucker bristled. "Not for the *why* you're thinking. I just wondered. I know Mr. Steele can't take us to California by himself."

Lottie grinned, if you could call it a grin. Her weathered face wasn't used to smiling.

"Got yore back up, don't ya?"

"Maybe," Tucker admitted.

"No maybe about it," Laura said and giggled.

"Someday I'm going to wash your mouth out with soap, Laura Foster." Tucker's mood could switch from resentment to tenderness to teasing all in a matter of seconds.

"The men is comin' in now. They been out with the remuda. The horses 'n mules done et up all the good grass 'round here, we been a waitin' so long," Lottie finally explained.

Tucker heard the sound of running horses. The riders pulled their mounts to a sudden halt, leaped from the saddles, and draped the reins over a rope that had been stretched between two trees. There were eight of them, some older, whiskered, range-toughened, and a few were young Mexican boys. They crowded around the grub wagon, filled their plates, and squatted down on their haunches to eat. They ate swiftly and went back for second and third helpings. It was comforting to hear the quiet rumble of masculine voices keeping up a steady stream of talk while they sipped at the hot coffee Mustang poured from the squat black coffee pot.

Everyone was quiet and waiting. Tucker found it hard to believe she, Laura, and the others were seated out in this field on the edge of nowhere. They sat with their backs to the darkness, looking at each other's faces in the flickering light of the fire. There was a certain tension, and all eyes turned to Lucas as he stepped out and away from the other men.

"Ladies." He had removed his hat and the white streak across his forehead stood out in bold relief from his suntanned face. "Ladies," he said again after he was sure he had their attention. "The last of our party arrived today, and we'll be heading out in the morning. Some of you have heard this before, but I'll say it all again. This is going to be a hard, fast trip. I'm hoping to make it to California in fifty to sixty days. I'm thinking if the Butterfield stage can make it in thirty, we can do it in fifty. We'll be going over a well-traveled trail and will have army escort for part of the way. Now I don't reckon anybody has gone across country before with twenty-two unmarried women. We would've had twenty-four, but two have been sent back. I'll not put up with cat fights, shirking, or whoring. I want that understood right now. If any of you get the notion to make eyes at the Army, you better forget that, too. The men in Coopertown raised the money to send me back here to fetch you. They paid to outfit this train to bring you back and, by God, that's what I'm going to do. They'll at least get a chance to see you and to court you. The rest will be up to you and to them." He put his hat back on his head and pulled the brim down over his eyes. He was facing in Tucker's direction, and she could almost feel the impact of his sharp, gray eyes.

"This trip will be no picnic. It's the middle of April, and we need to get going before the water holes dry up. It's going to take guts and grit to get there. We'll cross the Pecos at Fort Lancaster, then move on to Fort Stockton. We'll travel through a dreary, desolate country, where nothing lives but Indians, snakes, and renegade traders usually called comancheros. You can expect to see some dreadful things. We might not all make it. You'll never go to bed without a thorough search for a snake, a tarantula, or a scorpion. The wind will blow, the sun will cook your skin. We may run into a cyclone or a hailstorm. For certain we'll run into hostiles."

For the first time a nagging doubt, or rather apprehension, clouded Tucker's mind. What had she brought Laura into? Lucas gave her no time to think; he was speaking again.

"I know I'm painting a grim picture, but I want you all to know what to expect. If any of you want to back out, now is the time to do it." He stood with his arms folded, his feet spread. "I've put together a good bunch of experienced men. We'll have the best scout west of the Pecos. I've ridden many a trail with Buck Garrett and would trust him with my life. Mustang will lead out each day in the grub wagon. The rest of the wagons will rotate so one isn't eating the dust all the time. Chores have been divided up. Some of you will cook. Those of you who are going to drive a team will not be expected to cook or gather firewood. Later we'll put a couple of slings under the wagons and firewood can be picked up along the way. It's scarcer the farther west we go. There's no need for any of you to be sprucing yourselves up to look pretty. Save that until you get to California. If any of you have britches, wear 'em. Those of you who don't have britches, make some out of an old skirt. I want all of you in pants by the time we leave Fort McKavett. Put your hair up under a hat. I don't want some Apache Indian or renegade comanchero finding out this is a train of women; I don't think I need to tell you why. If any of you have anything to say, now is the time to say it."

For a while the scene around the campfire was suspended in silence. The people seemed to be mesmerized by the man standing before them. Tucker glanced quickly at Laura. She was facing Lucas, her lips parted, an excited look on her face.

"We'll be up an hour before dawn," Lucas said, "and leave at first light. We'll noon on cold . . . tucker." Tucker thought he hesitated just a fraction before he said that. "We don't stop till sundown. That's all."

It was a quiet, subdued group of women that got to their feet. Each was thinking her own thoughts and wondering at the enormity of the step she was taking. A child cried; its mother picked it up in her arms. Tucker reached for Laura's hand.

Three

"Tucker Houston." Lucas was by her side.

"Yes?" Tucker couldn't see his face and was glad he couldn't see hers. Damn! Why did she have to turn beet red every time he looked at her?

"I want you to keep a journal. Here is a list of every woman and child on the train. Copy it off and give it back to me. Keep a daily diary of everything that takes place from tomorrow on. Later on I'll give you a map so you can mark our course, designate our camping places, where we pick up the Army and where they leave us. This shouldn't be too difficult for a teacher. Can you drive a team?"

"Of course," she said tightly.

"Do you have britches?"

"No, but Laura and I will make some."

"Laura sews?" he asked after some hesitation.

"Of course."

"You and Lottie can trade off driving the team or leading a string."

"Don't like to sit a horse, Lucas. I done told ya that." Lottie spoke strongly. "I'll drive the team."

"Then we'll teach Laura to lead a string."

"No." Tucker said firmly. "I'll do Laura's work."

"Oh, yes, I want to, Tucker. I loved it when I rode the pony at the farm," Laura piped up.

"A pony and a horse leading a string are two different things," Tucker said sharply.

"She can do it. Stop coddling her, Red."

"How do you know what she can do? You only met her today. You'll get her killed, that's what you'll do!" A fierce, defiant glint glittered in Tucker's eyes.

"Lottie, take Laura back to the wagon." The softness of Lucas's tone carried more menace than if he had shouted. "Red and I have got to come to an understanding."

With a grip so vicious she only just withheld a pained cry, his fingers closed around her wrist and they were walking rapidly into the darkness.

They were well away from the camp when Lucas jerked her to a halt. Her pulse was hammering wildly, and the fingers that circled her wrist tightened their grip. They stood like that for several seconds, saying nothing.

"Don't question my orders again! Is that understood?" His teeth were clenched with barely suppressed anger.

Coldly she stared at him, taking her time, her disapproval obvious. "Then don't be giving orders where Laura is concerned. I know better than anyone what Laura can do. I've taken care of her since she was six years old."

"That doesn't give you the right to own her."

"Own her?" she said furiously. "I've more right to tell her what to do than you have!"

He threw her hand from him in a gesture of contempt. She would have walked away, but his hand shot out and gripped her shoulder.

"Are you afraid you're going to lose her, Red? Are you afraid she'll get to where she won't need you and will want a life of her own without you?" he jeered.

Her control snapped, her hand flashed up, and she struck him a resounding slap across the face. It was the last thing she'd ever expected to do, and something she would regret, she knew instantly.

"Damn you!" His face was the picture of fury. Before she had time to move, much less apologize, his hands whipped out and shook her by the shoulders until her teeth fairly rattled.

Tucker's unbelieving eyes looked at him as she sought to regain her composure. She was speechless with surprise and hot anger.

"I don't take to being slapped, you redheaded cat!" he whispered harshly as his arms pulled her forcibly against him even before he finished speaking. One large hand entwined itself in the hair at the nape of her neck and pulled her head back. Using the hand in her hair to hold her, he suddenly covered her mouth with his, hard and angry.

Tucker struggled for only a moment, then breathlessness forced her to abandon her wrestling and yield to the hands that held her and the fierce, cruel demand of his mouth. His arms pinned her so tightly against him she could feel the wild beating of his heart against her breast. The tangy smell of him was in her nostrils as her nose pressed against his cleanly shaven face. His mouth, as it ground into hers, tasted of tobacco. At last he released her lips, and for a moment she stood locked in his embrace, breathing deeply and erratically like someone who has run too far and too fast.

"Let go of me!" she demanded in a husky voice.

Slowly he let his arms slide from around her. She saw a hint of a smile twitch at the corners of his mouth as she moved away.

"Think about that before you strike me again. Next time it might not end there," he said softly.

Tucker's throat felt choked with a bitterness that made her say rashly, "Find another teacher. Laura and I won't be going with you!"

His laugh was short and dry and owed little to humor, but it did more than anything else to make her heart throb under her ribs in a strange and urgent way. Almost unconsciously she raised her hand and rubbed its back across her lips, still warm and tingling from his kiss.

"You're going, Red. And if you get it into that stubborn head of yours to run off, I'll come and get you. You're like a spittin' barn cat. All you need is for someone to rub your ears," his fingers gently fondled her cheek and looped a strand of hair behind her ear, "and to slap you down once in a while."

Tucker caught her breath sharply. This was something else she hadn't expected. She tried to move away, but he held onto her.

"I'm no man's plaything!" she hissed at him, and the soft chuckle that followed infuriated her. "You try it again and you'll find a knife in your back!"

She could feel the laughter in him. His eyes rested on her face for a long time, and at that moment, given the strength, she felt she could have killed him! The murderous impulse increased the longer he held her prisoner between his powerful hands.

"I wouldn't have missed meeting you for anything, Red."

"Stop calling me that!"

"Want me to call you sweetheart? You're anything but sweet."

"No!" She was afraid she was going to disgrace herself and cry. She braced herself for another mocking jibe, but when he spoke it was without amusement in his voice.

"The safety of this train depends on every one of you doing what you're told. That means you, too, Red. Don't question my orders."

"I didn't!"

In the stillness that enclosed them after her words she looked her bewilderment. His statements moved sluggishly through her mind even as she battled the violent storm of emotions that pounded inside her and threatened to accelerate beyond control and send her hurtling past all bounds of reason. She had to do something; she tried to jerk her arm away, and instilled all the coolness she could command into her voice when she stated: "I think we have said everything we need to say to each other."

Instead of loosening his grip, he moved forward to imprison her other arm and pulled her up against him. After a tense second, his rigid frame relaxed and his anger gave way to reluctant amusement.

"I never did like a tame horse, Tucker Red." He spoke admiringly and laughter spilled into his words.

"If you don't mind," she said, carefully blending in a touch of sarcasm to give credibility to her words, "I'd like to go back to the wagon."

"I don't mind at all, Red."

With his hand firmly clamped to her arm, he guided her around the camp so they would approach the wagon from the outside. Tucker's teeth caught her bottom lip in an agitated nip as she stumbled along beside him. The evening was warm and alive with the soft music of cicadas and crickets, and the moon cast a pale light on the white tops of the wagons.

"I trust you've brains enough not to do anything foolish," he said as they neared the wagon.

"I haven't completely lost my mind," she snapped. "I imagine you know our circumstances as well as I do. But Laura hasn't had much experience with men like you!"

To add to her irritation, he laughed. "Neither have you," he said softly.

"Enough to know a jackass when I see one."

"You are the most willful, balky, pigheaded woman I've ever met, but I still think you'll do nicely when I get you broken in."

Tucker allowed his words to wash over her, knowing full well he was trying to provoke her. They walked the last few yards in silence, and as soon as he released her arm she went quickly to the end of the wagon.

Lucas watched her go, a peculiar emotion moving through him. There was something about this one that goaded him to anger her. Why did he go out of his way to make her hate him? And why in the hell had he kissed her? He certainly hadn't meant to. But never had he touched lips so sweet, or flesh so soft, and never had he had to force himself to allow a woman to leave his arms. He scowled to himself. It was that damn portrait he had carried so long.

Lucas stretched out on his bedroll beneath the freight wagon. A poignant loneliness possessed him for the first time in a long while. Far away a coyote called to his mate and her answer echoed in the stillness. He was filled with a quiet unrest; his thoughts raced. For a moment he speculated on how it would be if the redheaded woman responded to him out of love. How would it be if she whispered words of love in his ear, and there was a softening in her eyes when they stared up into his? He suddenly felt the desire to recall all the details of that time long ago when for a few short weeks he had known love. He turned restlessly in his bed and wondered about the strange, twisting feeling that was churning inside him.

The first trip he made to California was in '44 when he was twelve years old. That was fifteen years ago. He and his father had left his dear, gentle, Scottish mother and his sisters buried beneath the pines behind the farmhouse in East Texas after the scarlet fever had taken them. They made it all the way to the Pacific coast, and there they found the same kind of people they had left in Texas—people with tawdry dreams of making a fortune—possessive, crowding in, taming the land.

William Steele took his son to the mountains, and it was there, by his father's side, that Lucas killed his first bear, wrestled Indian boys, and learned to wear black, oiled buckskins and moccasins. He had hunted with Gray Eagle and tumbled his sister, Little Dove, in the bushes. It was a happy, carefree time of his life. He was twenty years old when he and his father made another trip over the trail. Texas had changed; towns were springing up, county lines were being drawn, settlers were moving in.

They returned to the mountains of California. William Steele had seen Texas for the last time. He died swiftly, an arrow in his throat, and his son buried him beside a mountain stream. It was during that first lonely winter Lucas found Shining Star. She was a Crow, a white Crow. Somewhere on the Oregon Trail a train had been raided, and Shining Star had been taken from her family and passed farther and farther west and then south. She had become more Indian than white. But she was not an Indian and she was not white.

When Lucas found her, she was second wife to Running Horse. Running Horse was old, he was not happy: he had no sons. Shining Star hoed and weeded the rough fields, rubbed fur for dresses, pounded clothes by the stream. She had not understood why other girls went to sleep with the warriors and enjoyed it, had not understood why she bore no children to make her life more comfortable.

Lucas traded a pony and a knife for Shining Star, and she came to live with him in the lonely cabin. She took pride in belonging to the mountain man and in time came to love him. He, too, came to love the gentle girl with the soothing hands and the soft brown eyes who held him to her breast and crooned to him. It had been long ago and far away, and time had dulled the pain of finding her crawling to the cabin, an arrow in her breast. She had gasped her last breath and died in his arms, and he had buried her beside his father. He sought out Running Horse and killed him with the arrow he had pulled from the breast of his beloved. Running Horse had feared Shining Star would give sons to the mountain man, and he would be shamed because he had none.

Lucas rode out of the mountains but returned as often as possible. He could make his way there from any part of the West. The years had not been kind to the cabin, but beneath the tree beside the stream the wildflowers he had planted grew in riotous profusions.

He thought about it now. It would be spring in the mountains. The air would be fresh and cool. He would go back. He would always go back and keep going back from wherever the trails over the years would take him.

The only man who knew anything about that part of his life was Lone Buck Garrett. Buck had wrestled with him when he was a boy, had hunted with him, had trekked back to the Big Pineys with him and his father, had been with them when they visited the graves of his mother and sisters.

Now, Buck Garrett, lying in his bedroll a dozen steps away, wondered at his friend's restlessness. He had been surprised to see Lucas walk out from the wagons with the redheaded woman. Later, when he came to his bedroll, he seemed to have things on his mind, so Buck didn't speak out. Buck was not a talkative man. He had never addressed a group of over five people in his life. His quietness had nothing to do with being shy; he simply didn't have much he wanted to say. He was a realist. He had never held the grand illusions about the country that other men held. He expected to work hard and live hard, and, in time, to settle down. But where? When? With whom? He hadn't settled these questions in his mind yet. Only one thing was sure. This was his last trip to Texas. He longed for the cool mountains of his boyhood and the cabin beside the stream, where William Steele was buried and where Lucas had laid Shining Star to rest.

Buck was tired of a life among people who held you at arm's length, accepted you on sufferance because you had a good eye for tracking and a fast gun. He was twenty-five years old, and he had not yet found his place. He was not white because he had Indian blood. He was not Indian because he had white blood. Resentment smoldered in him when he remembered not being asked to stand guard like other men because the whites didn't trust him. Yet he actually had more white blood than Indian. Lone Buck, he had become. Lone Buck, scout, hunter, and hired gun. Only Lucas knew who he was. Only for Lucas would he have signed on to take these white women to California.

Four

"H'yaw! Hee-yaw!" Lottie shouted at the team as she cracked the whip over their backs. The wagon began to move.

The camp had been stirring since an hour before daylight when Mustang had banged on the iron pot and hollered, "Come 'n git it!" While Tucker had helped Lottie hitch up the team, Laura had taken up the sleeping mattresses and arranged the bedding so they would have room to sit during the day and a place to dress. This would be their place, their home, their sanctuary until they reached California. Lucas Steele had been up and down the line, talking, advising, directing since the camp was astir. He'd tipped his broad-brimmed hat in answer to Tucker's nod, said something pleasant to Laura, and passed on.

Several riders were now in the trail ahead, some beside the train, and a few were leading strings of mules, obviously replacements for the mules hitched to the wagons. Nothing was said about Tucker leading a string, so she climbed up on the seat beside Lottie and Laura.

The train moved out at a fast pace. They were third in line behind the grub wagon. Tucker leaned out and looked back at the curve of wagons following. The canvas tops glowed white in the early morning light.

"I wonder why they didn't send us out on the stage, Lottie. I doubt it would have cost as much as outfitting this train."

" 'Cause they kin sell the wagons 'n teams 'n the rest of the stuff when we get thar, and the profit will pay fer most of the trip." She gave Tucker a contemptuous glance. She had filled her lower lip with powdered snuff, which was now trickling down the corner of her mouth.

Tucker untied the strings of her stiff-brimmed sunbonnet and took it off. The breeze ruffled her hair. The sun was climbing higher over the horizon, promising a warm day as only a Texas day could be in the middle of April. She watched the rhythmical steps of the mules, each hoof kicking up a tiny puff of fine white dust. The miles stretched before them, endless and timeless.

Laura's hand found Tucker's. "We're on our way, Tucky. We're on our way to California."

"We're on our way. I pray to God we get there."

"Humph!" Lottie said, and spit over the side. "Ya got a better chance gettin' thar with Lucas Steele 'n Buck Garrett than ya'd a had with anybody else."

"Do you know much about them, Lottie?"

Tucker smiled her relief that Laura had asked and she didn't have to.

"Know of 'em? Both ain't got no quit atall when it comes to fightin'. Both got enough gumption not to fight if'n thar's a better way. They can track 'n palaver 'n fight if'n they got to. Can't ask no more of a man."

"They must be about perfect then." Tucker said it under her breath, but Laura heard.

"Tucker! Are you all right? You didn't sleep good last night. I heard you turning and turning. I lay awake, too, and listened to the coyotes and the owls."

"I was too tired to sleep," she answered absently. And had too much to think about, she added silently to herself.

"Where are you from, Lottie?" Laura asked.

"Indian Territory."

"Did you leave a family behind?"

"Yup. In the ground."

"Are you going out to find a husband?"

Lottie spat into the dust, shifted the heavy reins, and glared at Laura, her leathery face grim. Laura sat smiling, unaware she had found a raw spot with Lottie.

"Ya ask a powerful lot of questions, missy. Ain't none of yore business why I go, but I'll tell ya and get it settled. I ain't got nothin', not a pot to piss in, I ain't got nobody, not a human. I come to hate these prairies, ever' inch of 'em—and they stretch a million miles. I got nothin' to look forward to, and I got nothin' to look back at."

Silence followed while Laura drew a deep quivering breath. "Lottie!" She put her hand on Lottie's arm. "You're alone, like me and Tucker. But you've got us, now. And we've got you. We've got to look forward to something. We'll look forward to California. Our searching hearts will find love and peace in California."

Tucker turned to stare at Laura. Her face was radiant with happiness, her lips smiling. What she said was beautiful.

Lottie said, "Humph." But it didn't have the same force behind it that it usually had.

Tucker put her arm around Laura and gave her a hug. Suddenly she was almost happy. The sky was bluer, the breeze cooler, the country more golden and beautiful. Things would work out. They were just bound to.

Now that they were moving, she could even watch Lucas roaming up and down the line of wagons without feeling rattled. She felt detached from him this morning, as if it had been someone else he had held in his arms and kissed last night. She had spent half the night thinking about that kiss, such a new experience for her. He had bent forward before she could move, and his mouth had crushed down on hers demandingly, almost hurting her. She had put her hands on his chest to push him away, but she had not stood a chance against his strength. Her hands had flattened against him, feeling the warmth of his body under her palms, hearing the beat of his heart as he forced back her head and deepened the kiss to hot, insistent possession.

She began to tremble now, thinking about it again,

and stared out over the greenish-gold sea of grass, its emptiness broken only by a small grove of deeper green trees in the distance. When Lucas rode up beside the wagon, she looked at him with dazed eyes and smoothed her dress down over her knees with a nervous motion. His eyes, gray slits between thick dark lashes, rested on her face for a moment, then passed on to Lottie.

"Creek ahead, Lottie. Won't amount to much, rock bottom and about foot of water. Incline on the other side's got deep ruts; try and stay in 'em."

"Sure, Lucas."

"It's a lovely day to start a journey, Mr. Steele," Laura said.

The gray eyes flicked back to Tucker's set face. "It sure is, Laura. I'll be around tonight, Miss Houston, to bring that map. You'll not be expected to lead a string until we get to Fort Stockton and pick up more stock."

Tucker started to say something but didn't trust her voice, so she nodded coolly and looked at the trees ahead that seemed to advance on them. Lucas rode up to the next wagon, and Tucker cursed herself for being a tongue-tied fool.

The first day on the trail went quickly. The sun followed an arc-shaped course overhead and then went on its relentless path until it was a glowing red orb hung low over the shadowy western edge of the world. When it disappeared, only a faint rosy tinge remained to remind them of its passing. Lucas was waiting to guide the wagons into a loose circle for the night.

Lottie pulled the mules to a halt beneath the fanning branches of an old pecan tree. Tucker leaped down, stretched, and helped Lottie unhitch the team. They led the animals to a shimmering shallow creek where they were allowed to drink before they were turned in with the other stock to roll in the dust and eat the short prairie grass. By the time the women got back to their wagon, a fire was built in the center of the circle and over it hung a huge iron pot. On one side of the fire the squat, very black coffee pot was already sending up a plume of steam.

Laura had wash water and towels waiting for them. She had already washed herself and brushed and plaited her honey-gold hair into one long braid with a colorful ribbon tied on the end of it.

"Lottie said we can have fresh water to wash in now, but later on if we have wash water at all we'll have to share it." In a surprisingly short time Laura had become familiar with the wagon and its contents, and she moved about with easy assurance. "Do you think that skirt I brought from the farm would do to make britches, Tucker?"

"I don't see why not. I'll cut them out tonight and you can start sewing. Maybe Lottie's got a pair we can use for a pattern."

"I like Lottie. She wants you to think she's full of meanness, but she's really soft as mush inside. Something's happened to hurt Lottie," Laura commented thoughtfully.

"I like her, too. I'm glad we're with her and not some of the others." Tucker was thinking of the silent woman with the gold earrings.

"You don't like Mr. Steele, though, do you, Tucker?"

"What makes you say that?"

"Were you mad at me last night for wanting to ride the horse?" Laura could never stand to have a shadow of misunderstanding between them.

"No, you smarty-pants brat!" Tucker used the term affectionately. "I was afraid you'd get hurt."

"Mr. Steele said you coddle me. I never thought you did."

"Maybe I do, Laura. But it's hard not to." The words Lucas said last night came blaring into her mind. *You're afraid she can get along without you.* Am I really that selfish? she wondered. No, dammit! I've only given Laura as much as she's given me.

"You mean everything to me, Tucker. I know what would've happened to me if not for you. I'd be in a whorehouse, that's where I'd be."

The tip of Tucker's tongue came out and moistened her dry lips. Laura's words upset her more than she wanted to let on, so she hid behind obvious foolishness.

"Well, if the worst comes, we'll both go to work in a brothel . . . but it'll have to be one with velvet drapes and thick carpeting on the floor and a Chinese cook and a—"

"You always say crazy things, Tucker Houston,

when you don't know what else to say," Laura interrupted.

"Maybe. But between now and supper I've got to work on that journal."

"How many steps to the next wagon, Tucker? I'll walk along here until Lottie comes back."

"About twenty-five steps from the back of ours. Here's your cane. The ground is uneven, so be careful." Tucker handed her the walking stick and watched pensively for a moment as Laura walked away, tapping the cane in front of her.

Inside the wagon Tucker got out a bound book, pen, and ink, and settled down to write.

April 16, 1859.

My name is Tucker Houston and today we started our journey to California. At dawn we left our camp on the Trinity River, a mile from Fort Worth, and set a fast pace in a southwesterly direction. There are nineteen women and three children in our party. I will list their names and ages, also the names of the men accompanying us, below this entry. Our train is made up of ten covered wagons, two supply wagons, and a grub wagon. Mr. Lucas Steele is in charge of this expedition, and Mr. Buck Garrett is the scout. Mr. Steele rides at the head of the column and at times down the line of wagons trying to keep them close together. Today we traveled over rolling prairie land and crossed one creek, the name of which I will

supply later as well as the name of the creek
where we are camped for the night.

Tucker read through the entry and closed the journal. She would have liked to add that she was dead
tired and not at all sure she had done the right thing in
bringing Laura into this rugged and untamed land.
But she knew the journal was meant to be a strictly
factual account of their journey.

She stretched her arms high over her head. She
ached in spots she hadn't even known she had.
Before leaving the wagon, she brushed her stubborn
hair and firmly twisted it into a burnished copper knot
on the top of her head.

The banging on the iron kettle announced supper
just as she was stepping down from the wagon. She
looked around for Laura and found her talking to the
tall, dark-haired woman who drove the wagon behind
them. "Laura," she called to let her know she was
coming for her.

"Come meet Marie and Billy, Tucker."

"Hello," Tucker said and smiled, but when the
woman didn't smile back Tucker thought, who cares,
I'm tired, too.

"Hello," she finally responded in a voice that was
low and cultured.

Tucker smiled at the boy. "I bet he's a big help to
you."

"He is."

Tucker decided the woman wasn't going to say

anything else, so she took Laura's hand and they walked toward the cook wagon.

The daylight disappeared while they ate, replaced by the tongues of color licking up from the glowing logs of the campfire into the surrounding darkness. Most of the women were resting beside their wagons, the two with children were putting them to sleep. Laura and Tucker sat on a quilt and listened to the crackle of the fire. The warmth was inviting and the smell of the smoke was pleasant, but Laura was tired.

"Did Lottie come back, Tucker?"

"No. And I don't see her at the cook wagon."

"I heard the men come in to eat. Are they still there?"

"There's no one around the cook wagon. Everyone must be as tired as I am." She shivered and hugged herself with her arms. "I'm starting to get cold, too. How about you?"

"So am I. And tired. But Mr. Steele said he would bring you the map. Do you want me to wait up with you?"

Tucker got to her feet, stiff and sore. "No, you go on to bed. I'll see if I can find him."

She stepped over the wagon tongue and walked alongside the outer circle of the wagons. The ground was uneven, and in her tiredness she stumbled once or twice. She could see the light of the drovers' fire ahead and their shadowy figures around it, but before she reached it she saw, silhouetted by the red glow, a tall figure coming toward her. She recognized the lithely moving man instantly. Walking close beside him was a woman. An overwhelming desire to melt into the darkness gripped her. She bitterly regretted her impulsive decision to come looking for him. Uncertainty delayed her until it was too late to do anything but stand and wait.

The woman had her hand on Lucas's arm. "Thank you, Mr. Steele," she was murmuring.

"Go on over to her wagon. Mrs. Hook will see that you get settled in." The shadow that was his face turned to Tucker. "We have another name to add to the list, Miss Houston. Cora Lee Watson. I'm putting her in with Mrs. Hook and her boy for the time being."

Cora Lee was still standing very close to Lucas and looking up into his face. "Where will I find Mrs. Hook?"

"Over there." He pointed toward the right wagon. "Lottie already went ahead to talk to her."

"Thank you again," she said with a soft purr, and Tucker could almost see the demure sweep of her lashes. " 'Night."

" 'Night." Lucas watched her as she walked away. "How did it go for you today, Red?"

The tone of his voice nipped at her temper, which was already aroused by her indecision and discomfort, and she clenched her teeth together angrily.

"Well enough," she snapped. "I came for the map."

He took her arm and propelled her toward a clump of trees. "I said I'd bring it to you."

"When? Midnight?" She tried to pull her elbow from his grasp, but his fingers tightened.

"Couldn't wait to see me again, huh?"

His teasing made her writhe in helpless fury. "Would you mind letting go of my arm?"

"Make me," he said in a soft voice deliberately calculated to infuriate her.

"What's the point? You're bigger and stronger than I am."

"Smarter, too." He knew he was goading her, but couldn't seem to stop.

"What do you mean by that?" She spun around to face him.

"I know you like my hand on your arm, even if you won't admit it," he told her with a flick of his lashes that sent his eyes skimming over her tense, slender body and back to her flaming cheeks.

Tucker stared into his face with bitter distaste. "You're quite the dandy, aren't you? You should have a very enjoyable trip to California, but don't expect me to be any part of your pleasure."

The gray eyes stared down into hers, narrowed and amused, as though he could read the rebellion inside her head.

"You're going to be *all* of it, Red." There was a world of meaning in his voice.

"You are out of your mind!" She choked the words out.

"Temper getting away from you?" he teased.

"In about a half a minute you're really going to feel my temper, because I'm about to lose it!"

He laughed, and hard, brown fingers came up to close around her throat and tilt her head up to him. "I can't help it, Red. I can't help teasing you. You rise to the bait like a bear after honey."

The note of patronizing superiority made her spine prickle the way it had the day they'd met. She started to pull her arms away from his grasp, but it was undignified and humiliating to struggle against his easy strength.

"I don't like you! I don't like anything about you."

"You liked my kiss last night." He shook her gently.

"I didn't! I hated it!"

"That's the second lie you've told me. Why did you tell O'Donnell you're a widow?"

"Because it suited me at the time!"

His hands tightened. The gray eyes were sharp. "Don't ever lie to me again, Red." He sucked in a deep breath. "You've never had a man, have you."

Tucker's face flushed with color. She bit her inner lip. His words were not really a question, and she was startled by her reaction to them. Her stomach tightened with nervous apprehension at the open mention of such intimacy. It was merely a form of tension she had not felt before, she told herself, but it made her strangely uneasy. It threatened the safety of the guard she had had to place around her feelings.

"Sit with me while I smoke."

The gentle request caught her unaware, and she moved with him to a downed tree trunk. The constant sniping at each other was tiring, and her heart was beating twice as fast as it should have been. It was a relief to get off her shaky legs, and she let out a sigh as she sank onto the log.

"Tired?" Lucas asked as he began to construct a smoke between long, slim fingers.

"I expect I'll get used to it."

The match flared and he held it between cupped hands until it blazed, then raised it to the cigarette in his mouth. The light outlined his face and turned it into a bronze mask.

Far too handsome, Tucker thought. Her eyes clung to the smooth skin and hard cheekbones. Suddenly she felt an inchoate fear of this man, a fear of the completeness she felt when she was with him. She wanted to rid herself of the sensation. The black lashes lifted and the gray eyes looked into hers. Oh, my God! Why was she being so docile? Why was she sitting here?

He blew out the match. "Don't run, Red."

Did he know her every thought? Her green eyes were bits of sparkling ice. "It's impossible to like you," she spat at him.

"You were thinking about hightailing it."

"Run? From you? Why would I run? I'm not your prisoner."

"No." He began to laugh, shifting the lines in his face. "We sure strike sparks off each other, don't we, Red?"

In spite of her determination not to, she laughed. "I guess so. But for some reason you make me . . . mad!"

"Yeah, I guess I do." The laughter was still in his

voice. "Have you ever had a smoke?" He drew
deeply on the cigarette and the end flared briefly.

"No!"

"Want to try a puff?"

"No." She shook her head vigorously.

"There've been a few times in my life when I
would have given a year of it for a smoke." He held
the cigarette between his thumb and forefinger and
held it toward her mouth. "Try it, it's sometimes
relaxing. Draw the smoke into your mouth, but don't
let it go down your throat."

She put her hand on his wrist and bent her head
until her lips found the end of the cigarette. It was
damp from his lips. The shock of finding it so—and
the sudden realization of what she was doing—
caused her to draw in more smoke than she intended
to. She coughed, her eyes watered, and his hand
moved down her back, gently thumping.

"You got too much. Want to try again?"

She shook her head and coughed again. Remotely,
as if she watched another person, Tucker registered
the fact that she was sitting in the dark with a strange
man and had taken a puff from his cigarette. For the
rest of her life she was to remember this moment, but
for now she was consumed with a variety of emotions: guilt, for the surge of joy that went through her;
fright, because what she was experiencing was so
strange; and regret, because she didn't know how to
handle her feelings.

"You feel it, too." Ordinarily Lucas would not
have revealed this crazy thought, but there was some-

thing about her that made him reckless. The words were out and he could not take them back.

Tucker tried to absorb what he said. "I don't know what you're talking about."

"I believe you do," he said quietly, his eyes intent on her face.

She felt an unreasonable flash of resentment that he could read her thoughts so clearly. "I must get back. I shouldn't have come out here." She got to her feet, feeling giddy and uncertain. "I'll get the map later."

He was on his feet, towering above her, and he pulled her into his arms, holding her so tightly she could hardly breathe.

"It's too soon for you, isn't it, Red?" he murmured, his voice muffled in her hair. He lifted her chin, forcing her to look at him, and gazed down into her face.

All her newly discovered feelings swirled around inside her until finally they burst from her in the form of a moan. "I don't understand you!"

"I don't understand myself, either, Red. I just know that all day I've waited for now. I want to kiss you again, hold you again. I'd crawl inside you, if I could."

"I don't understand," she repeated in breathless amazement even as she raised her lips to meet his. There was no thought to what she was doing. Instinct alone guided her. She lifted her hand to the hard contour of his jaw and held it there while the pressure of his mouth threatened to whisk her into the edge of blackness.

The bittersweet taste of tobacco on his mouth, the smell of smoke as her nose was pressed against the roughness of his cheek, did nothing to quench the slow-burning fire inside her that kept growing and growing. Finally he dragged his mouth from hers and buried it in the softness beneath her ear.

"Red, Red! Oh, Tucker Red!" His voice was a tormented whisper. His pulse was racing as wildly as hers. His skin was hot to her touch, and the heat seemed to fuse them together. She made not a whimper of protest when his mouth found her parted lips again, and she felt his tongue exploring the inner surfaces. She was enveloped in a whirling velvet mist of sensations. It seemed right and good that his hand was caressing her breasts and her nipples were straining to reach the source of their arousal.

She was clinging to him weakly. The seductive movements of his hands across her hips and back, molding her closer to the granite strength of his body, were setting off explosive charges. His lips left hers momentarily, then hungrily returned to capture them in a soul-stirring kiss as an insidious, primitive desire grew inside her and she became helpless to stop it. These wanton, abandoned feelings were strange to her, she was powerless to control them. Instead, they were controlling her, taking over and making her want the physical gratification of his possession.

It was Lucas who drew back and held her away from him. In trembling caresses his hands moved over her back and shoulders as he peered down into her flushed face.

"I never intended to kiss you like that, Tucker Red." She bent her head and refused to look at him. His arms enfolded her once again, but tenderly, and her arms went about his waist and she stood with her face in the curve of his neck. "I'm just as confused as you are." His voice was close to her ear. "Since the moment I saw you I've not been able to get you out of my mind. But I've got to. I've got to keep my mind free because I'm responsible for all those women. I can't let anything interfere with that. I thank God you're not one of the intended brides. I think if you were I'd grab you up and run off with you. You understand, don't you, that there can be nothing between us on this trip?" His arms drew her close again. "But when we get to California, Red, I want to show you the mountains. They are cool and green and a man's got room to breathe." He lifted her face with a finger beneath her chin and kissed her gently on the lips, then opened them with his own, tasting their sweetness to the fullest.

Mindless, unconscious of time or place, Tucker let him lead her back down the row of wagons. She had let him carry her away into unknown caverns of desire, never dreaming she could be so totally abandoned in the giving of herself—or so hungry to receive all that was given back. At the end of her wagon they stopped. His hand left her arm and shifted to her jaw, his thumb tracing the outline of her lips.

" 'Night, sweetheart." It was a mere whisper, and with a disquieting glitter his eyes roamed her face.

"Good night." Frustration throbbed in Tucker's throat, making her words sound like a sob of despair.

She tried to turn her face away, but her head was already being lifted to his descending mouth. She resisted, only because of this mindless power he had over her. His mouth opened over hers in a series of long, drugging kisses, and she surrendered to the inevitable flash of wildfire raging through her veins. Then it was over, and he held her away from him.

"I don't know when I'll get to kiss you again," he said in a voice husky with emotion. He stood silently, his eyes searching her face, then he pivoted on one heel and walked swiftly away from her.

Tucker stood there dumbfounded, her fingers pressed to her lips, glad there was no one to see her, glad she had the night in which to get her feelings for Lucas Steele under control.

Five

There was someone who saw Lucas walk Tucker back to her wagon, someone who saw him kiss her but didn't hear the words he whispered to her.

Cora Lee Watson lay in her bedroll beneath the wagon she was going to share with Mrs. Hook and her son. Not for anything was she going to sleep in that crowded space inside. She couldn't endure that closed-in feeling between the boxes or the quivering gray canvas between her and the sky.

Cora Lee was pleased with herself. She had managed, quite easily, to join the train. Lucky for her the drummer she was traveling with was in Fort Worth at the same time Lucas Steele was. From the moment she saw Steele, she knew she had to have him. The town was buzzing with news about the train of brides he was taking to California, although he was camped a mile out of town and was closemouthed about it. Each time the stage came in and brought more women for his train, Cora Lee itched to join them.

Early this morning she had taken a horse from the corral behind the blacksmith shop and had ridden out after the train. When the wagons stopped for the night, she had turned the horse loose, knowing it would find its way back to the Fort, shouldered her belongings, and walked into the camp.

Lucas had listened to the partially truthful story about the brutal stepfather who mistreated her, and she had slid the neck of her dress down, showing him the deep, rough ridges made by his whip. Those scars had smoothed many paths for her over the last few years and were almost worth the pain she had suffered getting them. This time it had been amazingly easy. Lucas Steele was no different from any other man faced with a pretty, tearful girl with whip scars on her back. Cora Lee knew she was pretty, beautiful in fact. She doubted if there was another woman on the train half as pretty as she was, unless it was the redheaded woman Lucas walked back to the wagon.

Lying in the bedroll with her arms folded behind her head, she felt warm and beautiful and confident. And, as always when she felt like this, she thought about men.

Cora Lee hadn't always known she was attractive. Her family was poor. Her father, a brutish man, had been eternally angry at a world that had given him so little. Perhaps because she was a girl and of little use on the farm, or perhaps simply because she had been blessed with beauty while he was cursed with poverty, he seemed to resent Cora Lee deeply and tended to make her the scapegoat for all his ills. Her father's attitude and actions, combined with her mother's ineffectualness and her sister's indifference, had convinced the young girl that she was worse than use-less—and that likely no one else would ever want her around either. And at that tender age, she had no way of knowing otherwise.

Then another man had come into her life. . . . Her first lover had been almost as big as her father. She had not been a small girl herself, only a young one at the time—barely fifteen. He'd stepped out from behind a tree and told her how pretty she was. After a lifetime of abuse, Cora Lee was enchanted by his flattery. Sensing this, he'd continued chatting amiably until he was sure he'd won her completely. When he finally touched her, she melted and he bore her to the ground to have his way with her. That had been the beginning, and before long the kind words of several other hungry men had found their way into her heart. After a while, her covert activities had become a habit, almost an addiction, and finally men's actions came to mean far more to her than their words.

By the time her father found out about his daughter, she was beyond caring about any morality he might belatedly try to force upon her. It was the summer she was sixteen when she got the beating that left the ridges on her back. A drifter had stopped by the house to get a drink of water. Her father was out, and her mother and sister were in the garden. Cora Lee found the man appealing in a coarse kind of way. He lingered, eyeing the bodice of her immodestly unbuttoned dress. She reached out and drew him into the house.

She was lying on her back on the floor when her

father came into the house. Satisfied and languorous, she was barely aware that the man had skulked out the door while her father was snatching the bullwhip from the pegs on the wall.

Now, lying beneath the wagon, Cora Lee shivered and stirred restlessly while remembering the whip on her flesh. She had no doubt that her crazed father would have beaten her to death if her screams had not reached her mother and her sister and they had not come to hang on the arm that wielded the lash.

She was forbidden the house. Her father said if she would rut like a bitch in heat, she would live like one. She slept on the hay in the barn until her back was healed enough so she could cover her nakedness, and then she left her home in a peddler's wagon.

Cora Lee had some regrets, but not many. She had managed quite well over the years. There had been a procession of men, none of whom were ultimately important to her. It was only important that she have a man when she wanted him. She had become a little more selective when she'd realized she had something men wanted—and that she could afford to choose among them. It amused her to let them think they were winning something from her, subduing her, even while she was heartily enjoying the act—practically living for it. It was also exciting for her to know that some men even feared her because she showed them so plainly what she loved.

It had been a satisfactory way of life until she saw Lucas Steele. Just thinking about him, Cora Lee felt desire grow in her like a living thing.

* * *

Cora Lee's eyes had not been the only ones to observe Lucas and Tucker. Buck Garrett had seen Tucker come to meet Lucas, had seen them walk away together, and had been awake when Lucas walked softly to his bedroll and lay down. He had never known Lucas to spend so much time alone with a woman. Could it be he was tired of being lonely and without female companionship? Was that the reason he had been so easily persuaded by the girl with the turquoise bracelet on her arm? He had expected Lucas to send that one on her way, for he had seen the desire in her eyes, and the way her lips had parted enticingly even while the tears were running down her face. It wasn't like Lucas to be so easily taken in.

Lone Buck lay with troubled thoughts. He had always been alone, always lonely. He didn't have the memories of a woman to warm his thoughts as Lucas had of Shining Star. He had never even known a *nice* white woman. His companions and the women he'd known had been mix-matches, trash, like him, and with them he had been locked into a certain pattern of behavior. He had been rowdy and wild and had fought and whored. It was expected of him. He was a half-breed.

Only with Will and Lucas Steele had he ever been himself, and even with them he felt separated by some of the things he felt and thought. To no one, not even these two men, had he ever confided all his innermost dreams—dreams of a quiet life, and respectability—or his deepest fears and emotions.

Since his return from the year in Yuma Prison, the loneliness had consumed him. Most of the time he accepted it, hardly noticing his isolation, but sometimes, like today, it enfolded him like a dark blanket, smothering him. Lucas depended on him, had hired him over the protest of the men financing the train. But they—like most folks—saw him as merely an insolent, wild rebel, a lazy, shiftless half-breed who should have been left to rot in prison.

Lone Buck swallowed against the bitter taste flooding his throat and turned his thoughts to the golden-haired girl he saw sitting on the wagon beside the red-haired woman.

The girl was blind! She couldn't see! Oh, God, what must that be like? Never to see the mountains, the prairie, a herd of wild horses, a sparkling stream, a flock of ducks soaring beneath the clouds. Yet each time he saw her, she was smiling, her voice full of laughter. How could she be happy? He would like to talk to her, learn the secret to her cheerfulness. He would like to be near her, look at her, hear her voice. What did one say to a nice girl like that? Certainly not the sort of things one said to a whore, nor the hard, rough talk of hunting and drinking men.

Thinking about her made him feel all mixed up and shaky inside, bursting with surprised happiness and yet scared to death of having her find out about his past. No doubt she would think him a worthless half-breed. Still . . . he could not keep his thoughts away from her.

* * *

It had started raining during the night, a steady, gentle, but persistent, spring rain. By the time the mules were hitched and breakfast was finished, the ground was already slick with mud. The downpour, urged on by a chilly wind, continued all morning. But seldom did anyone complain about rain in this country; it meant not only water in the water holes and basins, but also grass on the prairie.

Lone Buck took up his position in front of the train. Lucas moved up to ride beside him. Neither man spoke; there was nothing to be said. Both knew that every day, every hour, every mile, would make the difference between finding water in the barren, wild country ahead or suffering the torture of being without it.

It was past noon when Lucas held up his hand signaling the slowly moving wagons to stop. He and Lone Buck rode ahead to a creek swollen with the sudden rain. They rode into the middle of it and looked upstream. A few dead, twisted branches came tumbling toward them.

"We can make it if we get a move on," Lone Buck observed.

Lucas nodded in agreement and put his fingers to his lips, giving a shrill whistle. "Mustang will start 'em rolling."

The rain had slowed to a fine drizzle. Lone Buck looked at the stream and back to Lucas. "Can the women handle the mules in this?"

"Lottie can. I'll put the drovers on the other wagons."

Together they rode back down the straggling line. Lucas called to the drovers to leave their mounts and climb up onto the wagon seats. Lone Buck led Mustang and his wagon across the creek, and Lucas fell back to urge the drovers to keep the other wagons moving.

"Keep moving! Keep moving!" he yelled. "We cross now or we'll have to wait here for a couple of days."

Buck came back down the line with Mustang riding on the rump of his horse. He took him to the rear of the train where Mustang swung up onto the seat and took the reins from Mrs. Hook. Lucas swung her son Billy off the seat and onto the back of his horse.

"Get Laura," he shouted to Lone Buck. "It's going to be rough going for these last two wagons."

Tucker heard the orders and moved over so Laura was sitting on the outside of the seat.

"I'll be all right, Tucker. I'll be all right here with you."

"Do as Mr. Steele says," Tucker said, and she hardly glanced at the man who rode the big bay horse up beside the wagon. Arms reached out to take Laura while she was still trying to reassure Tucker.

"Don't worry. I'll be all right. You be careful and hold on. I'm afraid for you, Tucky."

"Oh . . . go on with you! I'll handle the whip for Lottie. Gee-haw!" she shouted, and the whip cracked over the backs of the straining team.

Trusting, as always, Laura relaxed in the arms of the man who settled her on his lap. Her own arm went around his waist. She had never felt so wildly excited in her life. She was flushed with elation. The trip had surpassed all her cheerful expectations. And now this! She was riding on a horse with a strong, silent man who held her as if she were some fragile thing that would fall apart if she received the slightest jar. She turned her face up to his and could tell he was looking at her. His breath was warm on her face. It smelled clean and slightly minty, as if he had been chewing mint leaves. There was something loud and determined thumping between them. Was it his heart? Of course it was. The exertion of lifting her and seating her across his lap would cause even a strong man's heart to pump faster.

"Please tell me what's happening." It was at times like this, more than any other, that she wished she could see. The man didn't say anything, so she said, "What's your name?"

He waited so long to speak she began to think he wasn't going to, and then he said, "Buck."

"Buck Garrett, the scout?" Laura's smile was enormous. "Lottie told us about you." A groan of pain almost escaped his lips. "She said we had a better chance of getting to California with you and Mr. Steele than we would have with anyone else." She waited, but not a sound came from him. "Lottie said you didn't have no quit atall when it came to fighting."

Here it comes, Buck thought. He didn't want to hear what she was going to say. But he didn't want to take his eyes off her face, either. He wanted to record every little detail so he could remember it and what it felt like to hold her.

Laura chattered on. "She said you had enough gumption not to fight if there was any other way."

The relief he felt was almost painful, and he couldn't think of a word to say.

"Do you want me to hush up, Mr. Garrett? Am I bothering you? Tucker says *I've* got no quit atall when it comes to talking." She giggled like a little girl and brought her hand out from beneath the slicker to wipe the rain from her face. He bent his head over her so the brim of his hat gave her some protection.

"No, don't stop. I'm . . . just watching the horse." My God, she was pretty! More than pretty. She was as soft and sparkling as the early morning sun.

"Are we to the creek yet? Will I be too heavy for your horse?"

A chuckle escaped him. "Horse don't even know you're on it."

His voice was low and soft, and she had felt the vibration in his chest when he'd laughed. She wished he would do it again. She also wished she dared place her hand on his face so she could know more about him. He was slender, she knew that much, and the thighs she was sitting on were rock hard. Tilting her head against his shoulder she laughed a soft, trilling sound, and tightened the arm she had put around his waist to support herself. Was it the thrill of this unexpected ride that was causing this feeling of exhilaration? Or was it the feeling of being in the man's encircling arms as he held the reins? The horse's movements brought her into rhythmic contact with his chest. There was no way she could escape his closeness, not that she wanted to.

The horse was making its way carefully now, and she took her hand from the slicker and grasped his arm.

"Don't be afraid," he murmured. "You might get splashed a bit, but that's all."

"I'm not afraid, Mr. Garrett. I'm not a bit afraid. Oh, I'd like to ride sometime when the horse could run. It would be wonderful to feel the wind hitting my face!" She felt the vibrations again.

"We'll have to try it sometime." The words came out so easily, he was hardly aware he'd said them.

The splash of the water kept her silent. She felt the horse slip once on the rocky bottom of the creek, and she tightened her arms around Buck, hugging close, her face resting against him. The arms that enclosed her also tightened, and she felt the heavy pounding of a man's heart against hers for yet a second time. She leaned against him as the horse climbed the bank. When they were on level ground, she raised her head and could hear the men shouting at the excited mules.

"Hee-yaw . . . ya bastards! Hee-yaw . . . ya goldurned ornery, stubborn jackasses!"

Laura's pounding heart released a flood of happiness that was reflected in her brilliant smile. Buck feasted his eyes on her face, her cheeks pink with excitement, her tumbled hair as gold as a prairie sunrise. Now that he had moved back from the creek and stopped the horse, he could look at her, really look at her.

"Do you think the mules understand those cuss words, Mr. Garrett?"

Her delight in everything astounded him. "They seem to," he said slowly.

She laughed again, and he thought it was the sweetest sound he had ever heard. He liked the feel of this small, trusting girl clinging to him. God! What would it be like if she were his own?

"Have Tucker and Lottie crossed yet?"

"They're about to."

"Oh! Tell me about it, Buck," she said, using the familiar name for the first time.

His name came from her lips so easily. He could only think her name in his thoughts . . . Laura, Laura, Laura. "They're coming down the bank a slippin' some, but it don't make no never mind to Lottie." He stopped, thinking he had said enough.

"And Tucker? Is she still in the wagon? Is Tucker all right, Buck?"

"She's all right. She's standin' behind the seat a crackin' the whip." He laughed. It wasn't a chuckle this time but a real laugh, the third one in the last ten minutes. That was more than he'd laughed in the last ten months! "She sure can handle that whip."

Laura grabbed his hand and held onto it. "Yes, she can. She taught me to use it. I can snake it out and make it crack. Are they in the creek yet?"

"Yes. Lucas is alongside. He won't let nothin' go wrong." His hand turned over and clasped the one lying on his own, and the unexpected grip of her small hand made his heart gallop.

The wagon rolled up the bank and onto the level trail, and Buck had no choice but to move his horse toward it. Tucker was waiting to guide Laura's feet to the wheel and her hands to the frame so she could pull herself over onto the seat. The horse stood patiently, and the hands at her waist lifted her. She was laughing as she turned to sit down.

"That was exciting, Buck. I almost hope we have more creeks to cross."

"Ma'am." Buck lifted his hand to the brim of his hat and touched his heels to the horse.

"Thank you, Buck," Laura called.

Tucker watched the scout move away. It was the first time she had seen him up close.

"What does he look like, Tucker?" There was a funny tremor in her voice. "Tell me what he looks like. He's young, isn't he?"

"I'd say so. Somewhere below thirty. It's hard to tell."

"He was nice," Laura said. "And . . . shy."

"You talk enough for two," Tucker teased.

"I had to drag every word out of him." There was a gentle smile on her face. "Tell me what he looks like," she repeated softly.

"I've not seen him out of the saddle, but I don't think he's real tall. Not as tall as . . . Mr. Steele. He's got dark hair and . . . there's no whiskers on his face. His brows are straight and his lashes are thick, so I didn't see the color of his eyes. His nose is in the right place. I'd say he's not the most handsome man I ever saw, but he's not the ugliest either."

"I liked his voice. He has the softest voice I ever heard."

"Humph!" Lottie snorted. "He's a breed. Ever'body knows Lone Buck Garrett is a breed."

The smile left Laura's face, and she turned toward Lottie. "And . . . what does that mean, Lottie?"

"It means 'is pa or 'is ma was part Injun, that's what it means."

"I knew that. It also means his grandma or his grandpa was part Indian. But what's that got to do with him? I suspect all of us are part something or the other."

"I ain't a holdin' it agin 'im. I was just a tellin' ya, that's all."

"All right. So you've told me."

Tucker looked with surprise at Laura's tight features. It wasn't like her to be so belligerent. "Lottie didn't mean it was anything against Mr. Garrett, Laura. She thought it might help me to describe what he looks like."

"She could have said he had one feather in his hat instead of two!"

"Laura!"

There was silence among the women for several minutes before Laura said, "I'm sorry, Tucker. He was kind and gentle and . . . I liked him. I don't care if he's a little bit Indian or all Indian!" The stubborn look was back on her face.

"Get down off your high horse, Laura. That's what

you say to me. No one said it wasn't all right for you to like him."

The familiar light smile touched Laura's lips. "I'm sorry, Lottie."

"What fer? Speakin' yore mind? Ain't no call to be sorry for speakin' yore mind."

Laura didn't answer; she hardly heard what Lottie said. She was reliving the time she had spent held close in the man's arms, the gentle rain wetting her cheeks, and her heart thumping against his.

Six

April 17

Today was the second day of our journey and we traveled in a heavy spring rain. Past noon we crossed Timber Creek and shortly after the drovers reported it was swollen out of it's banks. I was told to add the name of Cora Lee Watson to the list of women going to California. She joined us last night. I do not know how she came to be on the prairie miles from Fort Worth.

April 19

We have scarcely made ten miles a day for the last two days. Other wagons we passed are bagged down and waiting for the ground to dry. We are wet and cold, but Mr. Steele pushes on. Today we passed an unmarked grave of piled stone.

April 20

More of the same, but this evening the clouds are thinner. We passed a sod house. A woman and children came out to wave at us. They looked so lonely standing there.

April 21

Sunshine today. Even the mules had more spirit. The prairie is covered with small blue flowers that resemble bells. Among them, in patches of orange and red, is another type of flower. Everything looks fresh and clean, but the ground is still soggy underfoot. I don't know where we are, but we are coming into hilly country. Mr. Steele has not brought the map he promised.

Tucker made the entry in the journal, closed the book, and put it away. She wasn't exactly pleased with what she had written, but without the map she could record only her observations. It had been a frustrating few days since Lucas had walked her back to the wagon and left her with his kiss burning on her lips. She had gone to bed filled with wonder that he had singled her out of all the women on the train and as much as declared his love for her. It all seemed to have happened so fast! She hadn't spoken to him since that night, but she had seen him.

Nervous and excited, she had waited the next morning for him to come riding down the line. She had searched his face, her eyes bright with her secret happiness, and his had slid over her as if nothing had passed between them. She had sat stock-still, tears biting at her eyelids, her stomach churning. His rebuff was the most painful experience of her life. Now, after several days had passed, all that was left was embarrassment. She had been foolish and gullible. She tried not to think about it, but when she did it was as if it were someone else he had held in his arms that night. Now pride forced her to return his gaze coolly when they met.

As if materializing from her thoughts, Lucas was striding toward her as she came out of the wagon. Every evening he and Mustang came walking by, checking the ironbound wheels. She usually managed to be away from the wagon or in it when the inspection was made. Tonight Lucas knelt down as he came to each wheel and looked with care at the metal strip that bound the wood circle together. Mustang commented on each; being a wagoner and a blacksmith by trade, he was performing one of the tasks assigned to him.

After nodding a cool greeting, Tucker moved toward the small campfire Lottie had built. Several such fires blazed in front of the wagons where the women rested before going to bed. Despite her cordial nature, Tucker was no nearer becoming friends with any of them than she was the day she arrived. There was not the camaraderie among them she had expected. Each woman kept to her own small circle with her own thoughts to occupy her.

She went to stand beside the fire after passing behind Laura and placing her hand on her shoulder so she would know she was there. She stood with her back to the wagon, very aware of the male voices behind her.

"Is that Mr. Steele and Mustang checking the wagon, Tucker?"

"Yes." Tucker wished Laura hadn't said anything. It would give Lucas an excuse to stop and talk if he heard her say his name. He did.

" 'Evening, Laura. 'Evening, Lottie. You making out all right?"

" 'Evening, Mr. Steele. We're doing fine now that the rain has stopped. Tucker says we're coming into hilly country," Laura responded.

"We are, Laura. They're mostly rolling hills, but in some places we'll have to make our own tracks. We're traveling a bit askew till we get to the San Antonio–El Paso Trail." Lucas spoke to Laura but his eyes were on Tucker, and she moved out of the firelight to hide the color that was creeping up into her cheeks.

"Is . . . Mr. Garrett still scouting ahead?" Laura asked with a breathless flutter in her voice that no one but Tucker would have recognized.

"He rides ahead, but not too far out now. It's after we cross the Colorado and head for the Pecos that we'll be glad we've got Buck with us."

"It was nice of him to take me across the creek."

Lucas stood silently, his eyes on Tucker, who was edging toward the darkness. He had a notion to grab her by the hair and jerk her away from the others and ask her what the hell was the matter with her. She was looking at him like he was something lower than a snake.

Tucker was tense and nervous and suddenly very tired. A movement caught her eye and the soft glow of a woman's face came into view. Cora Lee was waiting for Lucas to walk her way. A desperate anger filled Tucker, and she made an abrupt move back toward the fire. She felt sick. Her supper was rolling round and round in her stomach. This was the third night in a row the girl had waited for him to finish inspecting the wheels. Oh . . . she hated him for making her feel this way, for making her wonder if he had held Cora Lee in his arms and kissed her! Was Cora Lee as intoxicated by his kisses as she had been? Did Cora Lee quiver with rapture when he whispered, "I've waited all day for now."

"Miss Houston." Lucas was suddenly at her elbow, and she turned to him, her green eyes glowing with anger.

"Yes, Mr. Steele?" she snapped, her voice reflecting her agitation.

His gaze narrowed at the resentment smoldering in her eyes. His mouth thinned, and he pulled a folded paper from his shirt pocket.

"The map. Perhaps you'll make a copy of it so I can have this back." She took the paper from his hand, and still he stood there. He knew the others were watching, and he knew Cora Lee was waiting in the darkness. Damn that girl! She always had some half-baked, yet plausible, excuse for waiting for him. He faced Tucker calmly, his expression giving away nothing of what he was thinking. Her head was tilted defiantly, her red-gold mane of hair glistening in the firelight, her eyes flashing, venomously over his face. He was moved by her obvious anger.

"I think we should discuss the journal, Miss

Houston." He waved his hand toward the outer circle of the wagons for her to precede him.

Tucker's compulsion was to defy his order; she trembled with the force of it. Lucas gave her a menacing look, and, with a whirl of her skirt, she pivoted and walked proudly and stiffly between the wagons and out into the darkness.

A desperate anger stopped her before she had taken many steps, and she turned to face him. His grip on her arm set her feet in motion again, and she was propelled over the uneven prairie until the glow of the campfire and the outlines of the wagons were but dim images to her.

He finally pulled her to a halt. She refused to struggle, but he continued to hold her arm as if his hand were glued to it. Hatred and contempt coursed through her. Her gaze darted to the object of that disdain.

"I don't wish to speak with you alone. There's no reason why we can't discuss the journal in front of the others," she hissed.

Lucas looked at her in silence. Her catlike green eyes shimmered moistly with her anger. When he finally spoke, it was lazily, as though he were thinking aloud, the way he had done the day they had first met in Fort Worth.

"She's as mad as a brindle steer with one horn. I wonder what put a burr in her blanket this time?"

"While you're wondering you can turn loose my arm," she snapped, "unless you intend to break it."

He laughed softly in arrogant satisfaction, but he didn't release her arm. He gazed at her flawless face, her flashing emerald eyes lit with the fire of her hostility. Dear God, she was lovely! The hunger to be near her, to touch her, had been with him for days while he'd foraged for an excuse to be alone with her. Now he had reached the end of his endurance, and a painful restraint in him broke. He reached out and pulled her to him, wrapping his arms around her as though she were life itself.

Now she struggled. "Damn you, Lucas Steele! Get your hands off me!" Thoughts whirled about her brain like wind-whipped tumbleweeds. "Let go of me, dammit!"

The arms tightened, crushing the breath out of her. "Be still! What changed you, Red? What the hell is the matter with you? You let me think we had something for each other, and then all I get from you for the past week is the back of your head!"

"What did you expect?" she gasped when she could catch her breath. "You looked at me like I was . . . nothing!" Her breath now came in heated spasms. She kept her body rigid with determination to prove she could resist his embrace, yet she wanted to yield, wanted to strip the last vestiges of reserve from her mind and body and be carried away on the flood.

"I told you, Red, that I—"

"You told me plenty, but if you think I'm—"

"Hush up! Let me finish. I told you that I've got to give all my attention to getting this train to California. After we get there I want to court you, Red. I knew the moment I saw you that you were my woman."

"Ha!" She renewed her effort to leave his arms.

"Is that what you told Cora Lee Watson?" She spat out the words before she could stop them.

"Cora Lee?" His eyes were as bright as midnight stars when she looked at them. She felt him take a deep breath, and when he released it the stern mouth was twitching and the hollows on each side of it were already slowly deepening. "You're jealous, Red! By God, you're jealous!" He lifted her off the ground and whirled her around. When he set her back down, he allowed his lips to brush hers, lightly, like the wings of a butterfly, but it wasn't enough. "Dammit, Red!" It was a groan that ended as his mouth, hard and intense, found hers again, bruising its softness.

Oh, why couldn't she think? Now his lips were playing at the corners of hers, tracing a path to her eyes and then back to close over her mouth, making it his own. His tongue was insistent, demanding that she meet it with hers. She responded hesitantly at first, then with welcome, and finally with passion. It didn't matter that he was undermining her control; she clung to him, her hands sliding over him, feeling the strength of his muscles, the smoothness of his back. A little whimper escaped her lips and a small warning crept into the back of her mind. He was seducing her into complete submission, and every particle of her being was responding to his touch. She knew she should have found his blistering kiss distasteful, but it was wildly exciting. Her sanity argued, this is madness! Her passion whispered, give up, give up!

Tucker felt as if she were drifting. Euphoria spread throughout her taut body, relaxing her painfully tensed muscles. Tomorrow she would probably hate herself and him, but that was tomorrow. Right now she felt a wondrous warmth suffusing her. His mouth was persistent, ardent, relentless, snatching away her breath as well as her poise. There was a rightness to the sensation of his hands on her buttocks pressing her closer, and to the feel of her arms entwining themselves about his neck. Why hadn't she realized how long she'd been wanting to feel these sensuous, seeking lips on her own?

"Ahhhh, damn!" Lucas groaned again in frustrated agony as he buried his mouth in the hair behind her ear. "I can't take you here in the wet grass . . . but God, I want to!" His mouth, hard and rough, came back to hers, and his hands, urgent in their quest, sought the softness of her breasts beneath the loose top of her dress. Pink-tipped and ripe, they trembled beneath his warm caress.

"Lucas . . ." she protested softly.

"Red. Tucker Red," he murmured, his breath hot against her neck. His hand inside her dress roamed over her naked breasts, hungrily seeking the taut nipples and touching them with fire. He tugged at her skirt, all the while kissing and caressing her. He pushed her down until they both fell to their knees and toppled over onto the wet grass.

Tucker came out of the trance of pleasure he was working on her and realized that her skirt had been pulled from beneath her. She could feel the throbbing hardness of him through his clothes as he shifted his weight to come into closer contact with her thighs.

She pushed against his shoulders, but he was adrift in his passion.

"No, Lucas! You must stop!" she whispered anxiously, but he hardly heard her. She tugged at him until he drew back and looked into her face.

"I've got to love you," he said simply, his voice pitched just above a whisper. His mouth opened over her lips, raking his teeth over their soft, generous curves. The ravaging kiss set a fire in her blood that blazed uncontrollably. The tormenting touch of his hand on her bare flesh brought her to an ardent, fevered frenzy. She made no protest when his mouth moved to her naked breast.

She was so beautiful! Here was everything he had ever dreamed of having. He was almost dizzy with desire, and he wanted to take her immediately, thrust himself into her, and satisfy the hunger that gnawed at him. But he knew he couldn't do it. She was so soft and sweet and virginal. He couldn't take her here on the prairie! The ground was soaking wet, and he was dirty, sweaty, and stinking of horses. She deserved for him to make it as beautiful as possible, to be soothed, aroused, so she could taste the full pleasure of it. He forcibly held himself back and withdrew his hands from her body, pulled down her skirts, and cuddled her in his arms. His skin was cool and moist with sweat, his breathing ragged and uneven. She could not guess the depth of torture it put him through to stem the tide of his passion.

"Heaven," he whispered, his voice strangely broken. "Your body is heaven, but I can't take it. I can't do that to you, my sweet and beautiful Red. When I do take you, it will be long and sweet and wonderful . . . and you'll have no regrets."

For a long moment he simply lay there with his eyes closed. Reason dissolved the hunger that tormented him. She was his . . . the long length of her, the beautiful green eyes, the lips, breasts, and small round buttocks . . . all his. He felt he knew her as he had never known anyone before. He knew her mind, her soul, her spirit. She had never known the touch of another man, and he had never known a woman who hadn't. He alone would possess her. The thought sent a quiver of desire through him, and he stroked the hair back from her face and kissed her tenderly time and again.

Abruptly he pulled away from her and got to his feet in one fluid motion, pulling her up beside him. She stood with bowed head while he straightened her dress and smoothed the grass from her hair. He lifted her face with a finger beneath her chin. Their eyes locked, hers moist with a faint trace of confusion, his tender with regard for her.

"You're mine, Tucker Red. You belong to me. I can wait, my love," he said softly. "When the time is right, both of us will know it and there won't be any holding back. I'll have all of you—heart, mind, and body."

Tucker's eyes wavered beneath the intensity of his. She was suddenly like a small girl in a fully bloomed woman's body. His words echoed to the very core of her being. She summoned all her determination to speak, but her voice still came out thin and weak.

"I don't know what possessed me to let you. . . ." Her lower lip quivered and, as she stared up at him, tears welled within her eyes. "I'm not . . . a loose woman."

Lucas lifted a finger and wiped away a tear that trickled slowly down her cheek. Then he murmured soothingly, "I know that. Don't tremble so, sweetheart." His arms held her with infinite care, gently, lest he destroy the moment.

Soon her trembling ceased and she lifted her head. "I should go back."

"Walk with me first." With his arm encircling her waist, they strolled slowly in the darkness. The moon was lost momentarily behind a wandering cloud. An owl hooted, a prairie dog barked, and the faint sound of a child crying reached them.

Tucker was agonizingly aware of the man at her side during the long period of silence that ensued. Finally Lucas's hushed voice came to her ear.

"What happened to your folks?"

"Killed . . . by Indians up in the Territory. My mama put me in a trunk and some drovers found me, gave me a name, and took me to the orphan farm."

"You've no kin?"

"No, but I've got Laura."

"Does Laura have kin?"

"No, but she's got me." She turned to look up at him. The moon lit her face. His steely eyes met hers and warmed as they searched within the shimmering green depths.

"You both have me now." The whispered words caused her heart to make a frantic leap. To cover her confusion she began to talk.

"I never had anyone of my own until Laura came. She was someone to look after and to fight for. I didn't have time to feel sorry for myself after that." Her voice trailed away, and they walked in silence for a while. Then, as if compelled to tell him exactly how it had been, she continued: "Someone had been awfully mean to Laura. She had marks all over her body, and she was half out of her mind with fear when she was left at the gate. She was like a cowering little puppy that had been kicked and beaten! Sometimes at night she would wake up screaming and hold onto me. Apparently she could see until shortly before she came to the farm. I think that man, Oscar, did it. All she could remember was that she hurt all over and didn't know if she was awake or not because she couldn't see. I used to be afraid Oscar would come back and take Laura away, and I'd plan on how I was going to kill him." She laughed lightly at her childish dream. "I'll always look after Laura."

"Of course you will," he said quietly. "Laura manages well for a blind girl. Has a doctor ever looked at her eyes?"

"After we left the farm we went to a doctor in Fort Smith, and he said a good whack on the head could have caused her to lose her vision. He didn't think there was anything wrong with her eyes beside that."

"Was Laura disappointed? Does she have hopes of seeing again?"

"She used to, but not anymore. She has such a happy, loving disposition. She worries more about me than she does about herself. And of course I worry about what Laura would do if something happened to me. I've been with her for so long I feel like her mother."

"Have you ever thought that Laura might want to marry someday?"

"No! There's not a man alive who would have Laura and . . . love her and take care of her. She'd be just a convenience to him! But she's not going to be . . . used by any man!"

Silence followed her outburst. They had walked in a circle and were nearing the wagons. The child was still crying.

"Mrs. Johnson and her little girl are leaving the train tomorrow," Lucas said. "The child isn't well and Mrs. Johnson has changed her mind about going to California. She didn't realize the trip would be so hard on the child."

"Will you take her back to Fort Worth?" Somehow the thought of his leaving set her to trembling again.

"Tomorrow night we'll camp near the town of Brownwood. It isn't much of a town, but I'll find someone there to take her to the stage line." They reached the end of Tucker's wagon. Only glowing embers remained of the campfire. It seemed everyone in camp was asleep except the two of them and the crying child. "I'll have to put Lottie in with Mrs. Schaffer, who'll be left with just her child. Can you and Laura manage your wagon alone? If not, I can move Cora Lee Watson from Mrs. Hook's wagon to yours. She can drive a team."

Tucker didn't answer immediately, and when she did speak it was calmly, despite the flash of resentment she felt on hearing Cora Lee's name. "Why don't you put Cora Lee in with Mrs. Shaffer?"

With his hands on her shoulders, Lucas stared at Tucker so penetratingly that she wished she hadn't asked the question.

"I mentioned it to Mrs. Shaffer, but she refused to share a wagon with Cora Lee. Well . . . can you and Laura manage?"

"Of course we can." They continued to look deeply into each other's eyes. The moment quivered with tension.

" 'Night, Tucker Red."

"Good night."

Still they stood there. Everything around them was so peaceful. This is happiness, she thought. His hands slid down to her forearms and slowly, haltingly, he lowered his mouth to hers. His lips were soft and deliciously gentle. They entrapped hers, igniting a fire within her whose sudden warmth was reflected in the color gradually creeping up her pearly throat to flood her cheeks with pink. When it was over, she looked into the gray eyes peering at her and wished this moment would never end.

She leaned against the wagon and watched him walk away into the shadows. Tonight she had lost the fumbling uncertainty of her feelings for him and was possessed with the glow of knowing she was in love. The warm, velvety darkness of the night hid the smile that curved her lips. She was almost ready to climb into the wagon when a soft voice reached her.

"Lose something, Miss Houston?" Cora Lee came

from around the wagon, her steps soundless, her pale face framed with hair that hung to her waist. Tucker was shocked into silence by the knowledge that the woman had been listening to her and Lucas, had seen them kiss.

"I can't say as I blame you for forgettin' this out on the prairie," the woman murmured insinuatingly. She jerked her head out and away from the wagons. "After all, Lucas is a real . . . man! Best I've ever had." She produced Lucas's map and Tucker's hand automatically reached for it while her moment of happiness died a quick death. "Don't worry," Cora Lee said with a light laugh. "He's man enough for both of us."

Tucker jerked the map from her hand. "You were spying on us!" she hissed.

"Sure I was. But I don't mind him havin' you, long as there's enough left over for me."

"Why you . . . you . . . you're just a—" Tucker floundered helplessly.

" 'Course, I am," she interrupted easily as she sauntered away, but she turned back to whisper loudly, "and what are you?"

Stunned and horrified, Tucker moved into the wagon, careful not to wake Lottie and Laura. Automatically she slipped into her nightgown, took the pins from her hair, and with shaking hands plaited the tumbling copper strands into one long braid. She lay down on the pallet Laura had fixed for her. Nothing in her young life had prepared her for the emotions that now churned violently inside her. Her slim body shuddered as she finally gave way to racking, silent sobs.

Seven

A mile outside the town of Brownwood, Texas, on Pecan Creek, Captain James Doyle and his men were bivouacked. It was a quiet little glade. A grizzly old sergeant squatted before the campfire cutting strips of bacon into a skillet. A faint trail of whitish smoke coiled up from the fire and dissipated in the greenery of the branches above. The sun, oblivious to the hunger in a man's stomach, hung over the western horizon, swollen and crimson.

Captain Doyle, a seasoned soldier of the plains, sat silently and thoughtfully, cradling his tin coffee cup in his hand. His scouts had reported that a ragtag train of ten wagons was coming in from the east. Green and ill-equipped, the scout had said, with thin strips of iron on the wheels of their wagons and small, inadequate water kegs attached to the sides.

Damn! This land was difficult enough to cross when you had plenty of time and when you didn't have the Comanches, the Apaches, and renegade Mexicans to worry about. Of course it was easier now than it had been a few years back: there were stage stations along the way, if they hadn't been burned out. But if you were late—not by months or even weeks, but days—you could die of thirst out there on the plains. If there's no water for mules, or grass to fill their bellies, they won't carry you far in search of water.

The captain looked to the east. The train, led by the lieutenant he had sent out to invite it to camp beside them on the creek, was coming in. The lead wagon stopped a respectable distance away, and the others spread out along the creek. Farmers all, the captain mused, and not even very good farmers, judging by the condition of their equipment. It was none of his business what kind of workers they were, he chided himself, but it did concern him that they had women and children with them. It would be time enough after supper to test their mettle and offer his assistance.

When the meal was finished, the men from the newly arrived train gathered around a flickering campfire. The captain sat on a wooden box, his back to the darkness, looking at the faces turned toward him. He himself had gone from wagon to wagon and asked them to gather here with him. They were a mismatched group if he ever saw one. Take Blanchet: the man's hands were those of a farmer, but from the sound of his voice and the words he used he might well have been a teacher. And Collins: he doubted if the man even knew one end of his horse from the other. He probably depended on brute strength and bluffed his way through life with a chip on his shoulder. Taylor, no doubt, had the finest wagon of those resting beside the creek. This evening his family had taken their meal on china plates. They were quality folk, and it was difficult for the captain to understand why they had joined up with this outfit.

Frank Parcher, the scout, a short, lean man about forty years old, was another misfit. He hadn't come to the meeting, although he'd been invited like everyone else. The captain didn't cotton to him at all, knew instinctively he was dangerous. It was the arrogant assurance of the man, as well as the unanswered questions about his qualifications for leading this train. Parcher was obviously a trailwise man, but somehow his being here with these folks didn't fit the pattern at all.

All the men were hushed and waiting. There was a tension in the group around the campfire, as if each expected the captain to come up with some miracle that would make this trip easier, some magic that would solve all their problems and assure them they would get to California in the morning.

Always a man to lay his cards on the table, Captain Doyle got to his feet and addressed the group with his usual brusqueness: "The army officially closed Fort McKavett last month. Some troops are still there, but from now on trains going west will be more or less on their own. However, my men and I have been assigned to Fort Stockton, and my orders are to wait at this point for a wagon train coming down from Fort Worth and escort them that far. There's rough country between here and Fort

Stockton and rougher country beyond. You're welcome to wait here for the other train, fall in behind, and take advantage of our escort."

Everyone was quiet, as if waiting for the next person to say something. Finally Blanchet spoke. "How long before the other train gets here?"

"Should be no more than three or four days, unless they got held up by the rains up north."

"Why be it us what's got to fall behind and eat dust. We got our own scout. He knows the country." The man Collins spoke from the ground.

"When I said fall behind, Mr. Collins, I meant join up with the other wagons. Your position in line will have to be worked out among you."

The farmer's face reddened at the slight rebuke. "We done paid Parcher to lead us," he said stubbornly.

"I realize that," Captain Doyle replied patiently. I'm merely offering our services."

"We ain't got no time to be a waitin' 'round. I heard the water holes dry up, then there ain't 'nuff grass to fill the belly of a jaybird. I say it's time fer us to go on and let them folks catch up."

"You're right about the grass. The country is extremely barren, just sandy sage plains. You'll camp many nights without water or grazing grass, and you'll scrounge for firewood to heat coffee. As cruel and unpredictable as the land is, the rivers are worse. They tumble violently through narrow gorges, and far more travelers have lost their lives crossing rivers on their way west than have been killed by Indians." Captain Doyle turned once again to the man on his right. "And you, Mr. Blanchet? Do you have anything to add?"

Rafe Blanchet got to his feet. He was a tall, thin, sandy-haired man. "I favor waiting and joining the other train, if they will be so kind as to let us. I have come this far and I want to go on, but the few days we may have to wait can be spent in repairing our wagons, resting our mules, and repacking our belongings. We know little or nothing about how to cross the desert or the mountains, much less the rivers. It's true we have hired Mr. Parcher to lead us, and he has assured us we have a good chance of avoiding hostiles and outlaws. Still, I believe for the sake of our wives and children we should wait." He sat down and all eyes turned to the hulking farmer on the ground.

"People is pourin' into Californey. All the good land'll be took up afore we get thar," Collins grumbled.

The captain turned to a sallow-faced man who sat nervously clenching and unclenching his hands. "Mr. Taylor?"

Mr. Taylor shook his head. "I'm with the others." The captain was surprised by the words, but no one else seemed to be. Then, almost as if he realized he should say something more, Mr. Taylor got to his feet and there was, for a moment, only the sound of the crackling fire. "Mrs. Taylor and I are in no hurry. We are willing to wait for the other train." He sat down and looked toward the captain for approval.

This man certainly wouldn't be any great asset on

the journey, Captain Doyle thought as he nodded to the next man.

Unnoticed, the scout, in oiled leather britches and doeskin shirt, stood in the shadows. He chuckled as he listened to the argument about whether or not to take the army escort. The fools hadn't learned a damn thing since they'd hired him on in Baton Rouge. All they wanted to do was get to the promised land!

Frank Parcher melted into the surrounding darkness. There was a woman waiting for him. She'd be there, right where he'd told her to be, a hundred and twenty paces south of the last wagon. He paused to look around the camp before he moved on. The women were cornered at the other end, straining to hear what was being said at the meeting. He laughed quietly to himself again. They'd still be hagglin' an hour from now, as if it was so all-fired important whether they got to Californey this year or the next.

Survival was the important thing. Parcher had learned this the hard way. Use what you can and destroy what you can't. This belief had served him well over the years. Parcher knew that no man was his friend when it came to that man having something he wanted, be it a woman or anything else.

He had watched Blanchet's woman—like a man watches an animal with its foot caught in a trap—for over a week before he'd pounced. It's been easy. He had her to the point now where she would lay down and let her throat be cut if he told her to. It had been good enough for a while, but he was getting tired of her lying there like a limp pile of hides while he had his way with her.

He walked into the clearing and there she was, standing with her back to him. He took her by the arms and pressed her to the ground. There was no resistance; there had been none since that first day two weeks before. Hell, *then* she'd fought, he remembered, savoring the thought . . . until he'd squelched her struggles with his insinuating threats. Frank considered the woman beneath him a slut, something less than a whore, more worthless than an animal. He slapped her across the face, trying to drive some life into her. She raised her arm to protect herself, but he pushed it aside and slapped her again. She lay still then, breathing heavily. He tore open the front of her dress and toyed with her breasts for a while, biting and scraping his rough, whiskered face across the tender nipples, then sucking them until strangled whimpers escaped her lips. He liked to hear the sounds that came from a throat that wanted to scream but didn't dare. He lifted his head and told her to kiss him. She did.

When he opened his britches and ordered her to lift her skirts, she did as she was told and said nothing, but she winced with pain as he plunged his hardened manhood into her softness, pinning her to the ground. He rammed her delicate body against the packed earth until he was finished, then got swiftly to his feet and stood there leering at her disarray.

When she tried to pull down her skirt, he reached for her and fastened his hand in what remained of her bodice, hauling her to her feet. As she gasped and fell into his arms, he plunged his tongue into her mouth, filling it. When she gagged, he hurled her away from him and watched her stumble back and fall to the ground. He turned to leave her, then looked back.

"Tomorrow night," was all he said as he walked away.

Frank was still unsatisfied. He wanted to get out into the hills where there was a small Mexican village. There was a little *señorita* waiting for him: she didn't know it, but she was waiting for him. He found his horse, saddled it, and rode south. He needed something young, something tight, something that would claw and scratch and bite and scream, something that would help him get rid of the demon riding on his back.

Sarah Blanchet stumbled from the bushes when she was sure Parcher was gone. She was crying. Behind her tears her thoughts pounded like a hammer in her head: *Bitch . . . slut . . . whore.* She walked up the line of wagons, seeing nothing, neither the starlit sky nor the whirling waters of the creek beside the wagons. She did not see the campfire or hear the voices around it. She made her way toward her own wagon, climbed in, and pulled out her husband's rifle. Then she sat down on the bunk. She wanted to find the strength to walk out into the circle and reveal what Frank Parcher had done to her. But Rafe Blanchet was the only decent thing that had ever come into her impoverished life, and she couldn't let him be shot out of the saddle. Parcher had vowed he would kill him as sure as he'd coldbloodedly killed their faithful old dog Queenie as a warning. He'd wait in the trail ahead until Rafe rode out, or he'd put the rattlers in the wagon. Rafe was deathly afraid of rattlers.

There was only one other thing to do. Sarah gripped the rifle between her knees, rested her forehead on the end of the barrel, and blew her brains out, bloodying the canvas of the wagon that her husband had built and outfitted with such care and hope.

Frank Parcher rode back into camp at dawn. Within minutes he knew Rafe Blanchet's wife was dead. He sat beside the fire drinking coffee and watching the preparations for the burying. There was no question in his mind that he hadn't evened the score with Rafe Blanchet . . . Blanchet, who had tried to make him look like a fool in front of the whole train, who had questioned his advice, who had tried to put him into a bad light. He had evened the score, and he had enjoyed himself while doing it.

Frank had no regrets about the dead woman: she was weak. Any man on the train could've had her after he found her weakness—caring for someone else more than she cared about herself. It had taken only a couple of little threats and she had spread her legs. For a brief time she had been handy, had served his purpose. He moved and flexed his shoulders so his shirt wouldn't stick to his sore back. That *señorita* last night had almost clawed the hide off him. He'd had to hit her, hard, to take some of the fight out of her. He chuckled thinking about it. God, but she'd been a pistol!

It was more than an hour later when Frank noticed he was being avoided. The women had always been skittish, but the men had accepted him, soaking in the yarns he spun about Californey. None of them knew doodly-squat about anything except farming, and they hung on every word he spewed out. Some of them, he knew, had seen him coming out of the bushes after he'd tumbled Blanchet's wife. But there were things these men did and did not do according to tradition, a moral code they lived and died by. One of them was not to tell a man his wife was a whore. He didn't think they would tell Blanchet even now.

Frank watched one of the men enter the wagon, hand out the blanket-wrapped body, and place it in the arms of her husband. Rafe headed out toward the open prairie, the others following, somber and quiet.

Alone in the silent camp, Frank wasn't sure why he didn't just fork his horse and skeedaddle. He didn't like that army captain butting in, and there could be trouble if anyone took the notion to tell Blanchet he'd been plowin' his wife. Yet he wanted to wait around and look over the other train that was heading this way. A curiosity had been working on him since he'd heard the captain talking about it.

He stretched and winced. Goddamn, his back was sore. He grinned: his back wasn't the only part of him that was sore. He needed sleep, but not here. He'd ride up into the hills, find a place where he could catch a few winks, then ride out and meet the train coming from Fort Worth.

Midafternoon came. Frank got up from the grassy spot where he had napped, and mounted his horse. He pointed it north, crossed a stream a half mile farther, and rode on. Finally he stopped and dismounted and climbed a small tree, confident that what he was looking for should be nearby. After several minutes in the scrubby pine oak, he swung himself back to the ground and mounted up again. A half hour later he sat amidst a clump of cedars and looked at the broad expanse of valley stretching below him. He rested comfortably on his horse, knees up in Indian fashion, knowing that, among the trees, he himself made no changes in the skyline if anyone should be watching from the train inching along below.

The wagons were small and light, and the only stock being driven were mules and horses. He studied the slowly moving teams, and a sudden excitement gripped him. Goddamn! Those were women driving the wagons, unless the men were wearing dresses and sunbonnets! He could see a few men on horseback and one or two on the wagons, but that was all. For a long moment he debated with himself the possibilities of picking off this train. He could do it. He'd take the men one at a time from behind the rocks in the hills they'd have to pass through. And the women . . . Jesus!

What Frank didn't know was that Lone Buck was at this very moment watching him from behind, having trailed him for the last half hour. Had Parcher made one move toward his gun, he would have been dead before he hit the ground.

Frank sat staring at the wagon train, then boldly, letting the dust from his horse's hooves announce his approach, he rode down the hill. He passed a Mexican boy leading a string of mules and came up from the rear to the last wagon. A big, rawbones woman with a man's hat crushed down on her head was driving it, and sitting beside her was a young woman with a child on her lap. He tipped his hat to the young woman and she nodded. He set his heels to his horse and trotted up to the next wagon.

A serious-looking woman with straight black hair and gold earrings had the reins in her hands. Beside her was a girl with loose brown hair floating around her shoulders and a large turquoise bracelet on her arm. She gazed at him openly from his face down to his boots, and between them flashed an awareness of their affinity. He grinned at her and let his eyes dwell on her breasts. Her eyes glinted darkly at him, and they each knew what the other was thinking. He felt a surge of sexual excitement. She moistened her lips, her eyes still on his face, and he felt himself becoming more aroused. He reluctantly headed his horse to the next wagon.

The two women there barely returned his greeting, and he moved on. He glimpsed the copper hair glistening in the sunlight even before he reached the next wagon. He rode up beside it and his horse had to keep pace on its own, because Parcher could do nothing but stare at the woman on the wagon seat. She was the most beautiful creature he had ever seen. Her face was like the one he'd once seen on a cameo in New Orleans, and her hair was all curly and shining like a fire on a dark night. She glanced at him and quickly looked away. Her eyes were as green and as fierce as those of a treed wildcat.

"Howdy, ma'am."

Squinted emerald eyes flashed at him. "Howdy." She had a cool, no-nonsense voice. He chuckled.

"Who is it, Tucker?" Laura asked.

"No one we care to know, that's certain."

Frank had to drag his eyes from the redheaded woman to look at the other one. She was a queer one, kept looking straight ahead all the time. He looked back at the redhead.

"I ain't never seen so many women on one train," he commented. Tucker ignored him. "Ya ain't very friendly." Silence. "Ya got a man?" the anger that had been brewing in Tucker all day was almost to the boiling point. "Well, makes no never mind, sweetie, if ya got a man or not. You and me are goin' to get mighty friendly."

Tucker picked up the small whip beside her. Her hand flashed out, and the end of the crop stung the rump of his horse. The frightened animal leaped and danced, and it was all Frank could do to stay on it.

"Why you little bitch!" he exploded, but by the time he had his horse under control he was laughing. Here was the woman for him. Here was the woman he'd always been looking for and had known he would find some day. He reined his mount up beside the wagon to tell her so, but a large man on a black horse was charging toward him.

"Who are you and what do you want?" Lucas challenged.

Frank never spoke hastily. His eyes narrowed curiously as he decided what tactics he would use. There was something here he wanted, something he had to have.

"Frank Parcher," he introduced himself with a smile. "I'm from the train that's waitin' ahead with Captain Doyle. I was scoutin' so the folks'd know how long they had to wait up fer ya."

Lone Buck had followed Frank down the hill and was now moving along parallel with them. Frank began to have a tight feeling in his chest.

"Where is the captain waiting?"

Frank smiled easily. "Can't say as I blame ya fer bein' cagey, what with so many women 'n all. Captain Doyle's waitin' down by Brownwood. Say, did ya hear the army done closed Fort McKavett?"

"You don't say," Lucas said drily as he took in Tucker's set features. "Everything all right with you, Miss Houston?"

"Fine." Tucker snaked the whip out over the mules' backs with unnecessary force, keeping her eyes straight ahead lest she yield to the impulse to slash Parcher's lying face. Not once did she look right at him until the two men rode away, and then she glanced up in time to see the stranger looking back over his shoulder and grinning at her.

That night Tucker made a brief entry in the journal.

April 21.
Tonight we are camped with another wagon train on Pecan Creek, just outside the town of Brownwood. We traveled over twenty-two miles today. Mrs. Johnson and her little girl left the train tonight to return to Fort Worth, and wagon partners have been changed accordingly. For some reason I'm beginning to wonder if there will come a day when we'll all wish we'd gone with her.

Eight

Lucas was angry. "They're not joining up with my train. I don't give a damn if they get to California or not! We're moving out in the morning with or without your escort, Captain Doyle. You can do as you damn well please about the Louisiana farmers. I'm not giving them another thought." Lucas dropped his cigarette to the ground and carefully rubbed it out with the toe of his boot.

Captain Doyle knew Lucas Steele by reputation only. He had a name for being a hard man as well as a good one. He could understand Steele's concern; he had twenty-two women, two children, and ten men to lead across wild, barren country.

"There'll be no escort west of Fort Stockton, Steele. The most I can do for you is to send a dispatch to Fort Davis to be expecting you. It's very likely you might be grateful for the extra guns of those farmers."

"Every man on my train is worth three of those greenhorns," Lucas said cuttingly, "and Lone Buck Garrett is the best scout in the Southwest, bar none.

And don't discount the women. Each and every one of them's got grit, too."

"There's women and children on the other train, too, and I'm giving them my protection to Fort Stockton," the captain said firmly.

"You do that, but don't be expecting any help from me."

"Steele! Don't be a damn fool, man." Captain Doyle was losing patience. "There's some good folks on that train."

"Maybe so, but they're not my responsibility. Good night, Captain Doyle."

Lucas skirted the farmers' camp and walked quickly through the ironwood thicket to where his wagons were stretched out along the banks of the creek. He was more troubled by Captain Doyle's words than he had let on. He was well aware of the dangers of traveling from Fort Stockton to Fort Davis. The great Comanche war trail crossed the El Paso road just west of Fort Stockton, and the Mescalero Apaches from New Mexico Territory often raided the road west of Fort Davis. Still, he reasoned, there had been stagecoach service on the road for the last five years. He was confident he could make it with his train of light wagons. He wasn't so sure about the cumbersome, overloaded wagons of the Louisiana farmers.

He walked to the campfire, angry because of the unexpected problems forced upon him. He didn't know Captain Doyle, but he knew that any man who came to this country from West Point and stayed had to have strength of character and dogged determination. It also took fighting ability and, above all, sound judgment. He wasn't questioning Doyle's sagacity, only the part of it that applied to him and his train.

Lucas crouched beside the fire and got himself a slice of beef between two pieces of bread. He was hungry and ate quickly, being careful not to stare into the fire. Gazing into a fire was the mistake of a greenhorn. Lucas knew that a man who watches the flames sees nothing when he turns quickly to look into the darkness, and his momentary blindness could cost him his life.

Mustang joined him. The flickering light illuminated the lines in the old man's face and danced off the scattered silver in his beard.

"Folks over thar ain't too friendly." He filled the tin cup in his hand with boiling coffee. "They had a buryin' today, so I guess they ain't in no mood fer visitin'."

"One of the women killed herself last night. Captain Doyle said her husband told him she had been acting strange and hadn't talked much for the last couple of weeks. He figured she was homesick," Lucas reported.

"Some folks jist ain't cut out fer trailin'," Mustang observed solemnly.

"You told the women what I said about not leaving camp?"

"Yup. I tol' 'em. Don't think they'd of no how. They's a quiet bunch of females. Don't mingle much.

I tol' that Cora Lee not to go a prowlin' 'round. She's a traipser, that 'un."

Lucas glanced around the camp. Most of the women had gone to bed, but a few were gathered in little bunches beside their wagons.

"Guards set up?"

"Yup."

"Where's Buck?"

"Down at the creek skinnin' out a deer. Gonna bury it in the coals. It'll be mighty fine tastin' come mornin'."

"We're moving out at dawn. I'd planned on giving the women a half day to bathe and wash clothes, but the sooner we get out of these hills the better. Besides, we may have to raft the Colorado, and that'll take time."

Lucas got up and headed toward the brook. Once in the thick brush he stopped and gave the soft whistle of a night bird. He waited and the answering whistle came from his right. With soundless steps he moved toward the edge of the creek and the shadow that was the scout. Buck had finished skinning and gutting the animal and was tying its legs to a pole so he could carry it back to camp.

"Captain Doyle wants us to hitch up with the other train," Lucas said quietly.

"Figured it," was Buck's terse response.

"He's giving them escort to Fort Stockton. We'll be on our own unless he divides his troops."

"It's better this way, without them."

"What do you mean?" Lucas questioned.

"No thinkin' Indian would attack a fast-movin' wagon train if there was a slow one comin' down the trail."

"You're right. What do you think of Parcher?"

"Mean as a rattler with its tail tied in a knot."

"I don't want him with the train and I don't feel good about him following it," Lucas agreed.

"I'll put Chata to scoutin' the rear."

"That skinny Mexican kid isn't even dry behind the ears yet," Lucas teased.

Buck looked at Lucas with one of his rare smiles but said nothing.

"I only took your advice to hire him on because he knows horses and mules," Lucas continued in a joking vein.

The men worked silently for a few minutes.

"The boy's got eyes in the back of his head and he can shoot like a son of a bitch. He's quick, but not foolhardy," Buck defended, knowing it was unnecessary.

Lucas chuckled and picked up one end of the pole holding the deer carcass. Buck hoisted the other end, and together they carried it to the pit Mustang was digging beside the campfire, holding it until the old man could sprinkle a thick layer of hot coals in the hole. They carefully lowered it, and with two flicks of his knife Buck cut the vine holding the legs. Mustang shoveled the remaining coals in over the meat and covered them with loose earth. The camp was considerably darker now without the flickering fire. Lucas sank down on his haunches and refilled his coffee cup. His mind was restless and uneasy.

Buck left the two men without a word, as was his way, and walked around outside the line of wagons. The night seemed alive with movement: there was the sound of the breeze stirring the leaves on the giant cottonwood trees, the rushing of the creek, the restless pawing of a horse, and the sound of a woman coughing. Then there were other noises that only Buck's trained ear could hear. They were small sounds, but different sounds, like the footsteps of a very light person walking toward him. He stopped and waited. Cora Lee Watson emerged from the darkness and approached him.

She placed a hand on his arm and looked into his face. He looked down at the fingers that closed over the sleeve of his buckskin shirt and back up to her wide, glittering eyes. He knew what she wanted, and he knew he wouldn't take what she offered. It wasn't because he didn't want to, or that she didn't attract him, but rather because a sense of loyalty to the men who were paying him to bring their future brides to Coopertown prevented him. He loosened her fingers from his arm, shook his head, and released her hand. Her breath left her suddenly, anger tightened her features. He thought she was going to strike him and he waited, but her clenched fist remained at her side.

Buck stood quietly while Cora Lee battled within herself. At another time Buck would have liked to know this woman. She was beautiful and willing . . . and he was lonely. The anger on her face turned to pleading. He slowly shook his head again. She turned and quickly walked away from him. He stood still for a moment, listening to her footsteps until he was sure she was going back to her wagon. He walked on, and another slim shadow issued from the night. Buck dropped his hand to his holster.

"*Señor.*"

"*Sí,* Chata."

"He come, *señor.* Like you say. He look long at the *señorita,* and go back to camp. They post no guards. No one to watch."

"You're sure it was Parcher?"

"*Sí, señor.*"

Buck was not surprised that Parcher had come to spy on the teacher's wagon. He had expected it and had asked Chata to keep watch while he cleaned the deer. The young Mexican melted back into the darkness, and Buck went toward the wagon.

Someone was sitting on a blanket beside a fire that had burned down to a few glowing coals. He could see only the blur of white that was her face. She sat with her knees drawn up and her arms clasped around them. Her hair was untied and hung down to her waist. She looked so small, so helpless, so . . . lonely. His heart began to pound with a new rhythm and he stood stock-still, gazing at her. Hungrily his eyes slid over her slim figure, silky, honey-colored hair, and light face. He knew he shouldn't be here. It was unfair to stand and spy on her like this. He moved his feet restlessly.

Laura lifted her head and listened. She heard the sound again. Someone was standing quietly now.

Suddenly she was afraid and called out, "Who's there? Is that you, Mr. Steele?"

Buck cursed himself. He wanted to turn tail and get away, but he could tell from her voice that she was frightened, that she knew someone was there. He couldn't walk away and leave her to wonder who it was.

"No, ma'am." They were the only words he could manage at the moment.

"Buck!" She held out her hand. Mindlessly he went to her and took it in his. "Buck," she said again, and her fingers gripped his.

He dropped down on his haunches beside her. She was smiling at him, and he wondered if she would have given him the same welcome if she knew he had Indian blood. She refused to let go of his hand, and he continued to gaze at her face. She was beautiful! Sweet and beautiful! Some would say the teacher was prettier, but to him this small, soft creature was the loveliest thing he had ever seen.

"I was scared I'd not get to talk to you again. Oh! That's being brassy, isn't it? But flitter! I don't care. Tucker says girls shouldn't be forward. She says ladies wait and let the man make the first move to get acquainted. But . . . I don't know when a man looks at me, so I can't go by those rules. I'm glad you came, Buck. I was hoping you would. Can you sit and talk to me?"

"I can sit a spell." He eased himself down beside her.

Words gushed out of Laura's mouth like water

from a fountain. "I like to sit here and listen to the night sounds. I hear real good. I guess it's because I can't see and have to depend on my ears. I was listening to the water rushing down over the rocks in the creek and I was wondering where it was going. And I like to hear the owls, they sound so melancholy at times. My favorite, though, is the mourning dove, but then again, I like the mockingbird, too." She stopped talking suddenly and turned a stricken face toward him. "I'm making a regular jackass out of myself again." Her voice was almost a whisper. "But . . . I'm afraid if I stop talking, you'll go."

"I won't go. I like to hear you talk."

Her face broke into a smile, and she brought his hand into her lap, holding it with both of hers. "Then will you do some of the talking?"

"I'm not much of a talker."

"Tucker says I talk enough for two people." Her lips twitched and he watched, fascinated. "There's so much to talk about. What do you see when you're out scouting? Are you looking for a way for us to cross the hills?"

"I don't have to look for a way to cross the hills. There's a trail of sorts. Sometimes I look for a good crossing when we ford a stream."

"You don't watch for Indians?"

"Well, yes, but we're not likely to run into any that lift hair until we pass Fort McKavett. What we look out for here is renegades, outlaw bands. There's men out there that would steal the coins off a dead man's eyes."

"Really? And you're out there all by yourself? Oh, Buck! I didn't realize."

Her concern made him feel all mixed up and shaky inside.

"There's nothin' for you to be scared of."

"I'm not scared for me," she murmured.

The sad note in her voice whipped him into speech. "I found a patch of strawberries in the hills today. I picked some and sat under a tree and ate 'em," he said abruptly. He didn't know quite why he told her something so unimportant, except he knew he couldn't tell her he was trailing Frank Parcher and at one time thought he was going to have to draw and kill the polecat. He was so conscious of his hand in both of hers that he wasn't thinking clearly.

"Tucker and I used to pick wild strawberries. We'd fill our pockets and not tell the other kids where he found them." She laughed softly, remembering. "The bullies would want to take mine, but they didn't dare if Tucker was around."

"You been with her a long time?"

"Yes. She's more than just a friend. She's been like my sister, my mother . . . I love her very much."

Buck felt a flush of embarrassment. It was such a personal thing to tell someone! The girl was so open with her feelings, he didn't know how to handle his own when he was with her. He gently tugged his hand and she let it go.

"Is Miss Houston in the wagon?"

"Yes. She's tired tonight. I think she's kind of

under the weather. She tried not to be cross, but I could tell she was."

Buck got to his feet and reached for her arm to help her up. "Can you find your way to the wagon?"

"Sure. The wagon is to my back. Tucker never leaves me unless she makes sure I've got my directions straight." She bent to pick up the blanket, then reached for his arm and tucked her hand into the crook of it. "But I'd be glad if you walked me."

Buck was surprised at how confidently she walked beside him. They reached the end of the wagon, and Laura put her hand out and touched it. She seemed to know exactly where she was.

"Is there a moon tonight, Buck?"

"Yes, ma'am."

"My name's Laura."

"Yes, ma'am." He was tongue-tied again and absurdity of it made him half angry. Hell. . . .

"Would you mind if I touched your face?"

Buck stood frozen. The silence was long and breathless. Finally he said, "No, ma'am." It was scarcely more than a whisper.

Laura's heart fluttered, and she drew the tip of her tongue across dry lips. The blanket fell at her feet when she raised both arms, letting her hands move up his chest to his shoulders. The buckskin shirt was smooth and soft beneath her fingertips. Her hands reached his throat, moved up beneath his ears, and paused. She could feel soft, silky hair against her fingers, and moved them around to the back of his neck.

His hair came to the top of his shirt and was cut off bluntly as if he had used a knife.

The bold possessiveness of her actions, the sheer wonder of it, sent a thrill of excitement through her even while she made an effort to concentrate. Her fingertips wandered up to his eyes, traced the straight brows above them, then traversed the slope of his nose down to his lips. The moment crackled with unresolved tensions. Her palms caressed his cheeks and the firm lines of his jaw. Her senses were being led into open rebellion by the touch of her hands on his face.

They stood there for a moment, suspended in time. Then slowly, haltingly, she again slipped her hands behind his neck and let them remain there. It was a moment in which they both knew something had changed, forever. It was as sudden as that. She leaned against him. Buck could feel small firm breasts, warm clinging arms—and the intimacy of that contact sent waves of shock reverberating through him. Strange, tempestuous feelings were threatening to swamp him. As if compelled by forces stronger than he, he lowered his head and pressed a gentle kiss to her lips.

Laura had no time to wonder at this new experience because his arms wound around her, and she was held so closely against him she could feel the hard bones and muscles of his body thrusting against the softness of hers through her cotton dress. The first gentle touch of his lips had awakened the bittersweet ache of passion. A feeling, until this moment unknown to her, fluttered in her breast.

His hoarse, ragged breathing accompanied the thunder of his heartbeat as the realization of what he had done came to him. His hands grasped her waist to hold her away from him.

"Ma'am! Laura. . . ." He looked down into eyes that seemed to be looking into his. Her lips were smiling, and her arms refused to leave his neck.

"Thank you for kissing me. It was much sweeter than I imagined it would be. I never thought a man's lips would be so . . . gentle. Did you like it?"

"Yes, ma'am!" Oh God, yes, he thought.

"I liked it, too. But I don't think it would have been so nice with another man." She could feel the pounding of her own heart in her throat and temples.

Mesmerized, he watched her face. There was no coyness or pretense about her. Her thoughts and feelings were uttered honestly as they came to her. He trembled with the desire to wrap her in his arms and crush her to him. Only her endearing, trusting acceptance of him prevented it.

She moved her hands to his cheeks. They were warm; rough whiskers lightly scraped against her palms. She laughed, and it was only a whisper in the night.

"I've never felt a man's whiskers before. Well . . . maybe once before." She sobered, remembering. "A man at the farm grabbed me and Tucker hit him with the shovel. I don't like to think of that, but I'll think about this, Buck. I'll remember each feeling, each sound. I feel so strange, so light and giddy. Will you kiss me again?"

God Almighty! Didn't she know what she was doing to him? He couldn't have refused her if his life depended on it. Their breaths mingled for an instant before he covered her mouth with his. There was no haste in his kiss. It was slow, sensuous, languid. He took his time deliberately, with closed eyes and pounding heart. She offered herself willingly to his possessing lips. She felt as well as heard the raspy sound that came from his throat when his lips left hers.

"That was even better!" Her arms slid down from his neck and encircled his waist. She hugged him to her. "Oh, Buck! I could stay here all night with you, but I'd better go to bed. I'll not sleep a wink, though. Will you come and talk to me again?"

"I'll come," he breathed into her ear, and to himself he said, I'll come like a tame bear with a ring in my nose.

"I'll be waiting," she whispered and slipped from his arms. The wagon was behind her and she stepped up onto the box and through the canvas opening.

Nine

There was nothing about the day that was different from the day before except that the wind was stronger, flinging up fine particles of grit, and Tucker's hands, now in her best leather gloves, didn't hurt quite so much where the reins had rubbed blisters on her soft palms.

They had moved out of the camp beside Pecan Creek at dawn while the Louisiana farmers were still around the breakfast fire. After the wagons were strung out along the trail, a troop of soldiers led by a big, red-faced captain galloped past and slowed their mounts to a walk some distance ahead of the train.

"What was that, Tucker?"

"The soldiers. I'm glad I'm not trying to handle the flag in this wind. Their captain must be a stickler for regulations."

"Will they scout with Buck?"

"I guess so."

"I'm glad. I don't like to think of him being alone out there, even if he isn't likely to run into Indians that lift hair."

Tucker flashed her a dark look, but controlled her uneasiness enough to ask calmly, "Where did you hear that expression?"

"Last night. From Buck. He said we're not likely to have Indian trouble until we pass Fort McKavett."

This was the first time Laura had mentioned her meeting with Buck. Tucker had heard their voices last night and had feigned sleep when Laura came to bed. A feeling of disquiet settled on Tucker. Everything had gone wrong since they set out on this blasted journey. And now the scout, Buck Garrett, was after unsuspecting, childlike Laura. The fact that Laura hadn't mentioned him until now was proof that she was already smitten with him.

"What other words of wisdom did our great Mr. Garrett have to offer?" Tucker asked sharply. She glanced at Laura's face and saw her lower lip tremble. Instantly she regretted her unkind remark. "I'm sorry, honey! I didn't mean to sound so waspy. But at the moment I'm thinking if we threw all men into a snake pit, we wouldn't be able to tell them from the snakes!"

"It's all right. I knew yesterday that you had a bad case of the drearies. Did you and Mr. Steele have another set-to? I hope it wasn't over me this time."

"Of course it wasn't over you. You and I are just plain dumb when it comes to men, Laura. We simply don't understand how their devious, conniving minds work." Tucker drew a deep breath against the pain of remembering the whispered words that had set her heart to fluttering: *You're mine, Tucker Red. You belong to me. I can wait, love.* Damn him! Sure he could wait! He could wait for her because he had Cora Lee!

Tucker tried to put all thoughts of Lucas out of her mind. After all, there wasn't anything she could do about it. What had taken place under the cottonwood tree was best forgotten. But her mind kept straying back to it like a tongue seeking a sore tooth.

"Don't worry, Tucker." Laura reached for her arm and gave it a gentle squeeze. "I'm not falling in love with Mr. Garrett. I like to talk to him and think about him, but I'm not foolish enough to dream impossible dreams." Tucker dragged her thoughts back to Laura. "There's one good thing about riding in the wagon every day," Laura went on thoughtfully. "It gives you plenty of time to think."

"About what?" Tucker asked teasingly, not liking the serious tone of her voice. "About the time we put the frog in old Mr. Claiborne's coffee jar?"

"No, not that. I've been thinking about what the priest in Fort Smith told us about convents, and how they take care of girls like me. If there's one in California, I think I want to go there."

"What?" Shock and dismay made Tucker's voice sharp. "You can just stop thinking about *that*, Laura Foster! You're not going to leave me and go to a place like that. I'll never. . . ." She was going to say more, but the huge knot in her throat made it impossible to go on.

"Don't cry! Tucky, don't cry! If you do, I will, and I don't want to. Just think about it while we're riding along, and I'm sure you'll realize it's the best place for me. In the meantime, don't get in a snit if I talk to Mr. Garrett. Nothing will ever come of it, Tucker. I know that. And he won't take advantage of me the way you think. Somehow I think he's more scared of me than I am of him."

"Just don't ever mention that convent to me again, Laura. I don't want to hear another word about it!" Tucker wanted to say more, but her thoughts and emotions were tearing her apart. Damn that man for ever telling Laura the place for her was in a convent school where she could be useful! Useful! A willing worker bending over a washtub is what he meant. A drudge with nothing to look forward to! In just a few years she would be old and broken. Scalding tears stung Tucker's eyes. Laura's heart was the same as any other woman's heart, her dreams the same. Her blindness didn't alter that.

The day got no better as it wore on; if anything, it got worse. When they stopped at noon, Tucker and Laura carried water to the mules, then sat in the shade of the wagon to rest. Laura brought out the cold meat and bread she had wrapped in a cloth at breakfast. They fanned away the sticky flies with their sunbonnets while they ate.

When Lucas came riding down the line, Tucker wanted to get up and move into the wagon, but pride forced her to sit and wait.

He dismounted and squatted down on his haunches beside them and let his horse crop the green grass that edged the dusty trail. He watched Tucker's expressive face, puzzled at the hostility turning her eyes to sparkling green pools. Damn her! Damn all women! What had put the burr under her tail this time? He decided to force her to speak first.

She said the first thing that came to her mind. "What happened to the soldiers?"

"They rode on ahead and will wait up at Fort McKavett. Captain Doyle is annoyed with me because I won't join up with the other train." His eyes narrowed as he watched her.

"You don't seem to be disturbed by the captain's disapproval. Why don't you want them to join us? I can't see how it would do any harm."

With a tight smile, because he knew she was deliberately being obstinate, he pointed out: "They're overloaded, undersupplied, and ill-advised. They hired a scout. Let him earn his money."

"I didn't like him," she commented vehemently.

"Neither did I. That's the main reason I won't join up," he responded seriously.

"But what about the captain?"

"He gave me until we get to Fort McKavett to make up my mind."

"And?"

"It's made up."

Tucker sat woodenly, not looking at him, but glad that the scout who had looked at her as if he were seeing beneath her clothes wasn't going to be with the train.

"Are we making good time, Mr. Steele?" Laura asked.

"At the rate we're going, we'll be at the Colorado soon," he began absently, his thoughts elsewhere. Recovering himself, he continued, "When Buck and I crossed the last time, we found a place with a good rock bottom. We have it marked, and if the river isn't up we'll be able to ford it. We're going to set a faster pace this afternoon, just in case we can cross before nightfall. 'Course if the river's up, we'll have to wait till morning and raft it."

Tucker couldn't come up with anything to say, so she kept her face turned away. His presence, his voice, grated on her nerves. Dear God, how was she going to bear the rest of this journey? She looked at Laura's troubled face and knew she should say something friendly to Lucas, convince her there was no serious contention between them. She was desperately trying to think of something when Lucas's horse nickered and she heard the soft scuffle of hooves in the sand.

Buck rode up on his big sorrel, his hat in the crook of his arm, his eyes on Laura. He dismounted and went to where she was sitting beside the wheel.

"Hold out your apron, ma'am."

"Buck?" Laura got to her feet, her hands twisted in the blue apron tied about her waist. "Buck?" she said again, her face showing her pleasure.

"Hold out your apron," he prompted gently.

Laura grasped the sides of her apron and lifted it.

"What is it?" she asked when she felt the weight of something being dropped into it.

"Guess," Buck's voice teased her.

"I can't, and I'll drop it if I let go," she giggled happily.

"Then open your mouth."

She obeyed, and he reached into the apron and popped a large ripe strawberry into her mouth.

"Strawberries! Oh, Buck, it's been years since we've had strawberries."

Buck put his hat on and stepped back. Suddenly shy, and embarrassed that Tucker and Lucas had been watching, he raised his hand to his hat brim and nodded politely to Tucker. He took up his reins and turned to his horse.

"Buck?" Laura started toward the sound of his restless horse, and he quickly took his foot from the stirrup and came toward her, his hand reaching protectively for her elbow. "Thank you. Will you stay and help us eat them?"

"I ate my share while I was picking." He walked with her back toward the wagon. "I'll look for a patch down by the Colorado, and you and Miss Houston can go berry picking." He left her and went to his horse without looking at Tucker or Lucas.

"Thank you, Buck," Laura called happily. She stood quietly smiling until the sound of his horse was lost to her.

Lucas's eyes sought Tucker's, and he held them with his own in a question that had nothing to do with the two of them, but with what had transpired between Laura and Buck. It was obvious to Tucker that Lucas was more surprised than she was.

Laura turned back to the two and broke the silence. "Have a strawberry, Mr. Steele."

"Thanks, I will." He selected one from the pouch made by her bunched apron. "It's time to get moving." He glanced at the gloves Tucker was pulling on, started to say something, then changed his mind. As if snared, his gaze lingered on her bodice where the worn calico clung moistly to her breasts. Tucker's heart tripped and began to pound. He mounted his horse. A white grin slashed his brown cheeks. " 'Bye for now, Red. You, too, Laura."

" 'Bye, Mr. Steele," Laura called, then said to Tucker, "I don't know why I keep calling him mister when I think of him as Lucas."

Tucker hadn't realized how tense she was until Lucas was out of sight. She began to relax.

In the middle of the afternoon they passed a homestead. The house was built of limestone amid a stand of pecan and oak trees. It looked permanent and secure, with clothes hanging from a rope stretched between two trees, and a large iron wash pot boiling over a fire in the yard. A woman carrying a baby came out to stand beside the trail and wave as they passed. Her husband and son brought dressed smoked turkeys hanging from a rod to trade with Mustang for coffee and sugar. This was wild, new country—dangerous, yet beginning to be settled. Tucker wondered how the woman managed to live so far from society.

By the time the wagons reached the banks of the Colorado River, dark, heavy clouds were building on the horizon. A cool breeze fanned them, lifting Tucker's hair and tugging at her skirts. The wagons gradually slowed to a halt as the first ones in line began fording the river.

Laura laughed. Her spirits had been high all afternoon. "Do you think we'll cross today?"

"I don't know. The trail turns up ahead, so all I can see are several wagons and a red bluff."

An hour later they were still waiting. There was only one wagon ahead of them now. The wind, growing stronger, was pushing the thunderclouds swiftly toward them. Tucker would have liked to walk ahead and watch the crossings, but she was afraid to leave the restless mules in Laura's care. Lightning flashed and there was a distant rumble of thunder. Shortly after that Buck came galloping toward them.

"Lucas says for you to pull out and let the next wagon pass. He'll be back for you. I'll take you across, Laura." He wheeled the sorrel around and eased him up to the wagon. Laura stood on the wheel and waited for his hands to grasp her waist and lift her to sit across his lap.

Not even the excitement of riding with Buck could take the anxiety out of her voice as she called out to Tucker, "Be careful, Tucky. Lucas will take care of you, but be careful."

Buck's arms closed about her, and she hugged his waist with both arms. A great tenderness welled in him. She was so innocent and trusting in his arms.

"I'm so glad you came for me!" Her arms gripped him tighter, and her face found a place to nestle against his shoulder. "All day I've thought about . . . last night. It's something I'll remember forever."

Buck swallowed, fighting the constriction in his throat. Never had he wanted anything as much as he wanted to protect this wonderful creature, cherish her, shield her from life's cruel blows that could crush her bubbling spirit.

"Buck?" Laura said softly, suddenly worried because he wasn't saying anything.

"I thought about . . . last night, too," he said. Good God! He'd thought of little else. He was glad there was no one to see the naked longing on his face when he looked at her.

"I want to say this before we get to the river, because then I'll have to keep still. Don't think that I'm. . . . What I want to say is that . . . I don't take it for granted because you come and talk to me that you're courting me. Or that you're interested in me the way a man who likes a girl is. I like to talk to you, but I don't want you to talk to me because you . . . feel sorry for me. I've said this all wrong!"

"Tucker's right. You do talk too much."

"What?"

"I said you talk too much. Do you feel sorry for me?"

"Why would I do that?"

"Don't you know?" he asked in a voice that was low and choked.

"Know what?" she asked weakly, suddenly terribly afraid of what he would say.

Buck's stomach had twisted into a cold, hard knot. He felt a black pall of doom settling over him. Finally he spoke, his voice remote and toneless.

"I'm part Indian. I'm what's known as a breed."

"Oh, that!" She let out a sigh of relief, and when she turned her face to his shirt he could feel her shaking with silent laughter. "I was so afraid! I was afraid you were going to say you had a wife and six children, or you had a horn in the middle of your forehead."

He reined in his horse. She was still laughing and was such a pleasure to look at—warm, sparkling, and pretty. He wished he could enfold her warmth in his arms and kiss her. Sternly he put such thoughts from his mind. She must not have understood what he said.

"Didn't you hear what I said, Laura? I'm part Indian."

"I know that, Buck. Lottie told me the day you took me across the creek. You're lucky. At least you know what you are. I've no idea what I am. Does that bother you?"

"Good God! 'Course not!" He put his heels to the horse and it moved ahead.

"Well, then?"

For an instant Buck thought about spurring his mount and running away to some remote spot in the hills where he could have this soft, sweet woman all to himself. Years of frustration and pain dropped from his shoulders. She knew about him and didn't care! Surely she knew how much he ached to love her!

"River's coming up fast, Buck," Lucas shouted from the river bank. "Must have been a hell of a rain up north."

Laura felt an unexpected thrill as the animal moved under her. She felt its reluctance to enter the river and the muscles in Buck's thighs bunch as he urged it into the swirling water. The roar of the river increased as they moved out to where it gushed and broke over obscured rocks. Laura sensed the rise of the water and clung for dear life to the solid strength of the man who held her.

"Pull up your skirts so they won't drag in the water." Buck's calm, reassuring voice was close to her ear. "Just hold onto me and you'll be all right. Dolorido will swim." The horse slipped and swayed precariously. Buck's arms tightened around her, and she buried her face in his shoulder. So absorbed was she in her fear that she failed to notice when the horse's feet left the slippery river bottom. "Don't be afraid, *querida*. Don't be afraid, my love." Had she really heard those words, or was she dreaming them?

An eternity went by while she clung to him. Then she felt a jolt as the horse's hooves struck solid rock and began the climb up the bank. She could hear shouting and cursing as the men strained to help the mules pull a wagon up from the river.

"Pull, ya blasted jackasses! Pull, ya gol-durned buzzard bait!" the unmistakable disgusted voice of Mustang cursing the mules rang out.

Laura couldn't suppress a giggle and was rewarded by an answering chuckle from Buck.

"I'll leave you with Lottie now," he told her.

Fear for herself was now replaced with fear for Tucker. "Is the river too high for Tucker to cross?"

"She'll be all right. Lucas'll see to it. He'll bring her wagon over. You just stay with Lottie and quit worryin'." He lifted her down from the sorrel. She clung to his hand.

"Come on, Laura." Lottie's hand was on her arm and she reluctantly let go of Buck.

"Lottie, I'm scared for Tucker. What's happening now?"

"Wal, I ain't goin' to tell ya not to be scared. If'n it warn't fer the ropes, the last wagon would a gone down river. I don't see Lucas a riskin' another one. Let's git in under the trees. It's been rainin' pitchforks up north 'n it's 'bout to do the same here."

"Where's Buck?"

"He's down on the bank a motionin' to Lucas to stay over thar. I'll swear to goodness but that Buck's got gumption. He's a tellin' 'im that they'll have to raft it. Lucas'll have to stay over thar with Tucker while the men here git to buildin'. Them drovers is a'ready gittin' out the axes. Wal, that means we git a tarp stretched and a fire goin'. Them men'll be hungry as hosses when they's done."

"Isn't it getting dark? They can't cross in the dark." Laura suddenly felt the terror, the aloneness, of being separated from Tucker.

" 'Course they can't. They'll raft it come mornin'."

"But . . . Tucker!"

"Ain't nothin' goin' to happen to 'er. Lucas is thar." Lottie put her arm across Laura's shoulders, and a look of unaccustomed gentleness softened her face. "I'll be a lookin' after ya till Tucker gits here."

"Thank you, Lottie." Laura hugged her briefly in spite of knowing it would embarrass her. "Is it dark yet?"

"Jist 'bout. But I kin still see across. Lucas pulled the wagon back 'n is unhitchin' it. Now we jist can't stand here a jawin'. We gotta git the pot a boilin'."

"What can I do? I know how to peel potatoes."

"It would help a heap if you was to hold onta the little'n and her ma'll go huntin' dry wood. It'll take a heap of it if they's goin' to build that thar raft by the light from the fire."

"I can do that. I'll tell her a story."

Watching from across the river, Tucker saw Laura walk away with Lottie. Searching her soul, she found a feeling of gladness that Laura was enjoying Buck's attentions. But there was also a certain uneasiness about losing control over Laura's life, and thus the capacity to protect her from life's real, or imagined, dangers.

Ten

The rumbles of thunder grew louder and more frequent, a continuous muttering that exploded now and then into a crashing boom, and lightning stalked the horizon, leaping high into the sky with dramatic grace. Lucas unhitched, watered, and staked the team out for the night. Somehow Tucker could not make herself move away from the wagon—not while her heart was pounding at the realization that she was alone with Lucas, a roaring river between them and the rest of the train. With her face set and her hands clutching the skirt of her dress, she stood waiting.

He was so close she could have reached out and touched him before she knew he was there. Outlined against the flickering sky he stood tall, broad-shouldered, and hatless. The rising wind ruffled his dark hair, giving him a faintly satanic look. There was a tightly strung alertness about him, something primitive and menacing.

"I suppose you think I arranged this," was his quiet remark.

His voice and manner sent a wave of irritation over her. "Did you?" she demanded bluntly.

"I didn't arrange for the river to rise."

"No, but you arranged for me to be the last to cross."

"Only because I wanted to be with you and make sure you were safe." The soft drawl was in direct contrast to his stance and the biting grip of his hand that shot out and gripped her arm.

Tension hovered in the night while her thoughts and emotions raced and collided in wild disorder. Her words came bitingly. "After you saw Cora Lee cross safely."

"After I saw all the women cross safely," he corrected.

The lightning flared again, flashing gold sparks into the emerald eyes that stared up at him. It illuminated the pale oval of her face and was caught in her flaming, wind-blown hair.

"Of course," she said, and her words were almost lost in a deafening roll of thunder. Shielding the anger in her eyes with the dark screen of her lashes, she shook his hand from her arm.

He glanced up at the sky. The rain began, a scattering of drops shaken from the heavy clouds by the rumble of the thunder. "We'd better get under cover if we don't want to spend the night in wet clothes."

She stared at him with chilly dismay, unable to find any more words. He was looming over her, looking down into her face, and although he didn't touch her she felt his presence up and down the length of her body. She felt suddenly weak and liquid inside.

She climbed up on the wheel and into the wagon, conscious of him following her. In the dim gloom she fumbled for a candle and was about to light it when Lucas took it from her hand.

"We'll have no light or fire tonight."

The rain splattered against the canvas with loud plops. It was close inside the wagon, close and warm. Lucas seemed to fill the space that had been more than ample for her and Laura. Alarm shivered along her nerves, and her skin prickled with the chill of the stormy night. The canopy above her quivered in the wind, billowing, making the wood frame creak and moan sadly.

"Why not?" Her low-voiced query hung in the air.

"You know why not. This is wild country, and there's a river between us and the rest of the train." His hand was on her arm again, moving up and down in a caressing motion.

She shook it away and moved to the end of the wagon. The canvas end was laced securely against the rain, and she felt more hemmed in than ever. She stiffened in dismay: she could see the outline of him sitting on her trunk, his long legs making it difficult for her to get past him.

"Are you going to stand up all night? Sit down, Tucker." His voice held a tone of tiredness, resignation, that sounded strange coming from him. "I've no intention of spending the night in here with you, if that's what's worrying you."

Tucker's fear receded a fraction, and yet an unpleasant feeling remained in the pit of her stomach. "Where will you go?"

"I'll be around."

A match flared briefly in his cupped hands. He held it to the end of the cigarette dangling from his lips, then quickly blew out the flame. The familiar scent of the tobacco smoke reached her nostrils, and she wanted to weep for the wonderful time she had spent with him before she knew about Cora Lee. She moved to pass him, holding her skirts so they wouldn't brush his legs. She sat down across from him and stared into the darkness. She thought he was staring in her direction, but couldn't be sure. One thing she was sure of, however, was that he wasn't behaving like the arrogant, teasing man she had been alone with before.

The rain settled to a gentle patter and the thunder began to subside. The silence seemed to bear down on Tucker until she felt she had to say or do something. She reached behind her for the cloth with the leftover bread and meat she and Laura had had at noon. She put the largest piece of meat between two hunks of corn bread and held it out to him. "Mustang always gives us more than we can eat." She kept her voice steady only by sheer strength of will.

"You eat it," Lucas urged.

"There's more."

He took it from her, being careful not to touch her fingers. She sat, stiff and self-conscious, wishing she didn't have to eat the food in her hand but knowing she must because he was watching her. He finished eating and, while he was rolling and lighting another cigarette, she wrapped what was left of her portion in the cloth and tucked it away behind her.

"Why did you do it? Why did you let me think you felt something for me?" His questions were asked quietly. There was no trace of sarcasm in his voice, only a kind of sadness. She moistened her lips, but he spoke again before she could answer. "Twice now I've felt on top of the world after seeing you, only to have you give me the back of your head or look at me like I was some kind of varmint the next time I've been near you. I've gone through hell these past few days wondering how I could've been such a fool to be taken in by your playacting." Occasional lightning lit the wagon interior as he spoke, revealing his face creased in thought.

At first Tucker was stunned into silence by his words, then anger took over. "I was the one who was fooled!" she spat out scornfully. Her voice shook with rage and unshed tears. "I still don't understand what stopped you that night. I must have been out of my mind to . . . to . . . let you do what you did!" Now that she was started the words gushed forth. "How do you think I felt after she told me she'd been watching? Cora Lee had been watching and laughing about it, making it dirty. Making me feel like dirt! I made a complete fool of myself over you. I wish to God Laura and I had gone back to Fort Worth with Mrs. Johnson. But you knew we didn't have anything to go back to. We couldn't leave if we wanted to! You thought you'd have a little something extra to play with on the way to California, didn't you? Well, you'll just have to get along with Cora Lee, because you won't have me! And that scout, that friend of yours, Buck Garrett, won't have Laura, either!" Her anguish demanded release, but her heartache hid itself deep within her, beyond the reach of tears.

The silence that followed was unbearable. A sudden, heavier burst of rain battered the canvas roof over them. Thunder rumbled in the distance and, as though roused by the sound, a coyote howled, another answering.

"Are you waiting for me to tell you Cora Lee lied about watching us?" his voice came to her quietly. "I knew she was watching and that was why I suggested we walk. She'll not do it again, or she'll leave the train at Fort Lancaster."

"Liar!" The word burst from her in bitter rage. She was shaking all over and felt something inside her giving way. "Damn you," she sobbed. "Damn you to hell! She's too convenient, too willing, for you to get rid of."

"I think you'd better explain that."

"Oh, she offered to share you with me. She said you were . . . man enough for both of us!"

He did not speak or move. The silence pounded in her ears. When she thought she could bear it no longer, he spoke.

"You believed her!" Anger flared momentarily, but died in weary resignation. "I was ready to build my life around you. I thought I had found a woman to share my thoughts, my dreams, my future. Someone to love and cherish. I thought in time you would come to care for me that way." She sensed his eyes on her, willing her to look at him. she refused, and his voice continued bleakly. "But you folded under the first blow."

"But . . . she said . . ." Tucker's bewilderment temporarily surpassed her anger.

"I don't want to hear what she said." He stood up. "I guess the rain has let up. I'll take a turn around." There was no softness in the harsh lines of his face, no hint of warmth in the piercing gray eyes. The lips that had once kissed hers in tender passion now twisted in icy indignation.

"But . . . you can't sleep on the wet ground." She remained where she was, a confusing feeling of defeat settling over her.

"There's a tarp tied to the side of the wagon; I'll use that."

He was leaving! Well, what had she expected? Lucas would never fall all over himself denying Cora Lee's claims. He had too much pride for that. Her heart thumped, then picked up speed until it was galloping. Then something snapped in Tucker's aching mind and, to her horror, she heard herself say in a rapid, choking voice she almost failed to recognize as her own: "Lucas! Don't go!"

Then she was crying. Tears spurted to her eyes and sobs tore at her throat. She whirled to move away from him, but his arms went around her, holding her to him. For a moment she resisted the pressure of his embrace, then suddenly she hid her face against his chest in a rush of anguished despair.

"Red!" His voice was husky, tender. He was holding her fast and kissing her wet cheeks. "Red, don't cry," he murmured again and again. Tucker leaned against him, holding onto him while her head spun crazily. The pent-up tension of the past several days came flooding out in the form of tears that poured down her cheeks and seeped into her mouth.

"I didn't want to believe her," she sobbed. "I wanted to think she was lying, but she's so sure of herself and so . . . beautiful."

He stopped her words by lifting her chin and putting his mouth lightly against hers. "Hush." He was holding her tightly and speaking soothingly. "You're much more beautiful than Cora Lee. How could any man want her after seeing you?"

Her eyes sparkled through the tears spiked on her lashes. "I've been so miserable." She couldn't keep the pain from her quivering voice.

"No more than I." He hugged her even closer. "We've not spent much time together and I may have expected too much of you. I feel I've known you forever and didn't realize how little you knew about me." He sank down onto the trunk and pulled her into his lap. His hand began stroking her forehead, pushing her tousled hair back and smoothing it caressingly. She sighed and he kissed her gently, his lips lingering on hers. Held close against him, feeling his heart pounding heavily against her breast, her confidence gradually returned and pushed away the waves of despair that had threatened to drown her. She slid her arms about his neck and gave him a long, grateful kiss.

"I can't bear for us to quarrel," she whispered.

She felt laughter shake him. "But we will, my fiery redhead. We'll quarrel, we'll fight, and we'll make up." He paused, then said in a different tone, "You're my woman."

She lifted trembling hands and stroked the hair back from his forehead. Then, with her palms against his cheeks, she leaned forward and kissed his lips warmly before resting her head on his shoulder. This was bliss! He adjusted her on his lap and cuddled her close. She snuggled in the circle of his clutch, feeling his heart beating as wildly as her own, and wrapped her arms lovingly around his neck.

"I love you, Lucas. I love you, love you." Her voice was the softest of sounds.

He searched her face for confirmation of her words, and when she smiled radiantly at him he could see the love in her eyes. With a groan, like a wounded animal returning to the comfort and safety of its lair, he rested his cheek against hers. It was a moment removed from sexual desire; all that mattered was the need to be close to each other, to be unified and strengthened. He didn't seek her lips, but pressed his warm mouth close against her temple with a gentle reverence that stirred her heart. His hands caressed her, and he threaded his fingers through her coppery hair.

"I want to tell you about myself," he breathed

huskily. "I want you to know all about me, and I want to know all there is to know about you."

They sat on the trunk, Lucas with his back to the wagon side, Tucker held tightly in his arms. She told him in detail about the throwaway farm and about how lost and lonely she had been until Laura arrived.

"For the first time in my life I had someone of my very own, someone who loved me and depended on me. Can you understand that?"

Between kisses he told her about his home in the Piney Woods, about his mother and sisters buried there, and of the mountains in California. He told her about the cabin beside the stream, about his father, and about Shining Star.

"Did you love her?"

"Yes, I loved her. She was sweet and gentle and needed someone to be kind to her." He looked into her eyes for understanding. "She was like a lost little rabbit."

"And me?"

"A green-eyed wildcat!" His eyes teased her, and he chuckled happily before his lips found hers in a kiss of deep dedication that told her she was one of the truly fortunate women who had the exciting, turbulent, entirely devoted love of her man. Their lips met again and again, as if each kiss were sweeter than the one before. His hand moved down her back and over her hips, stroking, caressing. Gradually his kisses became more forceful, and she gave herself up to the awesome knowledge that it was she who was causing this powerful body to tremble so. He whispered endearments during the brief intervals when he was not taking the lips she offered so eagerly. They kissed and murmured to each other and were both lost in the wonder of the moment.

Finally Lucas lifted his head. "Red, oh Red. . . ." His voice was a groan in her ear. "I'm going to have to leave you, or I'll do more than just kiss you." His lips moved to hers as if he couldn't stay away from them, and he kissed her like a long-starved man. They clung together as waves of passion swept over them.

"Don't go!" She whispered the words in his ear, and the shiver of excitement that went through her was sheer heaven. She felt tremblingly alive under his urgent mouth, and she pressed her body to his in an abandonment of pure delight. As his mouth assaulted her lips, his fingers fumbled with the front of her dress. With a growl of impatience he moved away from her so he could remove completely the barrier between them. In the flickering light from the occasional lightning, her breasts were twin hills of pure white.

He looked into her eyes with great tenderness, then enfolded her in his arms. With a long, deep, shuddering breath he slid them both from the trunk to the floor and they lay down together, his heart thundering against hers.

"Lucas, Lucas. . . ." She stretched the full length of herself against him and wound her arms around his neck. The sweet burning pressure of his lips on hers fused them together, blotting out everything else. Then his mouth found her breasts and traveled over them, tantalizing her with the movement of his lips and tongue. She arched her body toward him and almost cried out in the urgency of her desire. She wanted to possess every inch of him and never be done with him. "Lucas, oh Lucas. . . ."

Half kneeling, half lying over her, his lips left hers for an instant as he pushed aside the last vestiges of her clothing and quickly shrugged out of his own. "Ssshhh . . . be quiet and let me love you."

She tangled her fingers in his dark hair and the strands fell across her breasts in an exquisite caress. His mouth and hands explored the hollows and curves of her body with sensuous roughness, as if compelled to know every inch of her. His fingers found the moistness between her thighs, and she lost all track of anything but the basic, primitive drive and the storm of emotions that surged through her.

What happened between them was wondrous, miraculous, incredible. His muscular body atop hers and his velvety touch between her thighs started a fire that surged through her, causing involuntary little shudders of delight. He spoke in snatches of tender words, soothing her, quieting her.

"Be still, my sweet love," he murmured. "Let me love you. Let me be yours. Oh, God! I knew it could be like this."

Now she would be forever his, body and soul. She could feel his powerful arms and legs twined around her, and yet she had the strange sensation of not knowing where his body ended and hers began. She was floating in suspended warmth.

When he entered her it was slowly and reverently, making no sharp or hard thrusts. Then he lay still for a while. She felt his great body tremble with the effort it took to hold back. He lifted his face to look at her. His gray eyes, dark with passion, burned into hers. He leaned his face closer to hers, his mouth over her mouth, his breath and her breath as one. He caressed her lips with his and then began, ever so slowly, to penetrate her deeper and deeper with a slow, sensuous motion. He had never before had a woman who had not yet had another man, and the miracle of the barrier that resisted his throbbing passion sent waves of delightful shudders through him.

His hands held her in a vise; his body, muscular and hard, delighted her senses beyond belief. She clutched him tightly and ran her hands over the warm skin of his back. Heat radiated from his body to hers, sending her into a rapture of love so exquisite it made her head spin with the desire to know all of him.

He kissed her without haste, feeling the most wonderful of all touches as the membrane thinned and yielded to his hardness. There was a sharp thrust of pain. The cry that escaped her was lost in his mouth. And then ecstasy! There were the strokes that came with a driving, primitive rhythm; there was the giving, the mutual surrender. They were one, belonging, possessing, and they soared higher and higher. They reached the highest mountain and the world exploded, lifting them up on a cloudlike formation that cradled them and took them spinning out into a warm, misty darkness. Tucker felt as if her soul were reeling somewhere above her as Lucas's seed erupted and spilled into her, filling her.

When they settled to earth once again, he lay still, breathing deeply, with his face nestled in her tumbled curls. At last he stirred and eased himself up on his elbows. He smiled into her jade green eyes and kissed both lids, one after the other, cradling her head in one strong hand.

He removed himself from her and covered her with his shirt. She stretched her legs, a powerful feeling of enchantment engulfing her. She had not noticed the cool air when her body was bared, nor the hard floor of the wagon. Lucas's warmth had covered her, cloaked her. They lay next to each other for a long time in a silent harmony that needed nothing to make it perfect. He turned her face toward him and looked into her eyes; they were solemn, and he lightly kissed the tip of her nose.

"You're mine, Tucker Red." He said the words slowly and carefully. "Nothing will change that."

Tucker, suffused with joy and wonderment, lay warm and secure in his renewed embrace, experiencing a strange sense of peace. There had been a little pain, but no shame. It had been the most beautiful experience of her life. She sighed contentedly and reached to kiss his neck and rub her palm against the roughness of his cheek. He raised a finger and leisurely traced a line down her neck and over the swelling curve of her breast. Her soft mouth parted with yearning, and he leaned to kiss her waiting lips, touch the tip of his tongue to hers. Her eyes grew dark, like two bottomless green pools staring up at him, and her face glowed as radiantly as the moon on a clear night. Their moist skins clung together, and he kissed her long and tenderly.

"Well, Tucker Red, that was the first of a million times for us." His voice in her ear was lazily teasing, but underneath there was a hint of determined possessiveness.

She laughed against his cheek and twisted her fingers in his thick, dark hair. He chuckled and nibbled at the soft flesh of her neck, and his hand found one small, firm breast. He trailed his fingers over the tender nipple, and she thrust it harder into his palm in eager anticipation. His wandering caresses made her quiver, and his kisses on her mouth were warm, devouring, fierce with passion.

"I'd better get up now or it may be quite a while before I do." He raised himself up on one elbow, a shock of dark hair falling across his forehead. "I've got to look around and make sure someone doesn't sneak up on us." He got to his feet and pulled her up beside him.

Tucker laughed when his head connected with the wooden bow that held the canvas cover over the wagon. He grabbed her playfully, happily, and his fingers found her ribs. She couldn't stop the laughter that brimmed up in her throat. They dressed quickly and she wrapped a shawl around her shoulders. Lucas strapped on his gun belt and lifted her down from the wagon with infinite care.

The storm had passed, leaving the land glittering

and clean in its wake. The night air was cool, the day's heat gone, and a faint breeze stirred. Lucas drew Tucker away from the wagon and deep into woods where the trees grew tall and the brush was thick. He took the shawl from her shoulders and draped it over her hair and around her, rebozo fashion, and backed her up against a large oak tree.

"Stay here while I take a look around. Stand still and don't move," he whispered. "I'll not be gone long."

"Indians?" she whispered fearfully, clutching his arm.

"I doubt it. Someone from the other train may have followed to see if we crossed the river. I pulled the wagon far off the trail, but even a poor tracker could find it. Wait here and I'll circle around." She nodded, and he placed a quick kiss on her mouth and left her.

Lucas moved cautiously through the trees, as silent as a shadow. The grove was still except for the usual night sounds. An owl hooted from a nearby tree before flying off on lazy wings. A pack rat cowered at the sound, nervously circled the small clearing, and scurried away on some nocturnal hunt of its own.

After several minutes of slinking through the woods, Lucas quietly changed direction and edged back toward the water, heading directly for the trail the wagons had passed over that day. Concealing himself behind a cottonwood, he waited and listened. And then he heard it . . . the soft sound of creaking saddle leather and hoofbeats muffled by the rain-sodden earth. The sound was almost inaudible save to one whose wilderness-honed hearing could distinguish the slightest unnatural noise from the roar of a rushing river. He hesitated until he could no longer hear it, then squatted low in the brush and eased out so he could examine the tracks in the trail: a lone horse headed toward the river.

Knowing now what he was looking for, Lucas moved back into the brush. Remaining within the bushy shelter, he circled back to the wagon, his ears alert for any sound at all. A movement some distance away caught his eye. He faded into the stand of trees near the wagon and waited silently, his buckskins only a shade lighter than the surrounding darkness. He concentrated all his attention on the shadowy figure approaching on horseback. It had slowed somewhat about fifty yards away, as if sniffing something wrong, but then sidled on up to the wagon, peered in, and paused, vaguely outlined against the whitish glow of the canvas top.

Lucas waited, hand on his gun. The figure cursed softly, sure now that he was alone. It headed on toward the river, every broken twig and stumbling step serving to pinpoint his location. Lucas followed. Downstream he heard the soft sound of a branch rubbing against coarse cloth, then the muffled sound of hooves along the bank. Gliding silently through the trees, he outstripped the slow-moving rider. He knew who was riding the horse. He waited for him to pass. He could only hope he would go back up the trail. He could hear the horse distinctly now. Soberly he considered what to do. He didn't want a fight unless he could be sure Tucker was safe. He squatted low in the brush, partially concealed by a tree trunk, his eyes never wavering from the spot where the rider would clear the woods.

Frank Parcher rode up the trail and passed within a few yards of him. Lucas had followed up on a minute but nagging thought, a fragile suspicion that his wilderness sense had told him to pursue, and his hunch had been right. The scout from the other train had come to spy. Lucas had no doubt that Frank Parcher was one of those men who carried all his brains between his legs, and that sooner or later he might have to kill him.

Eleven

At dawn they moved out. It was a strange group that followed Frank Parcher: each in their own wagons were the Taylors, the Collinses, and Rafe Blanchet, with the Taylors' Negro boy leading a string of six horses. Frank's lengthy description of the hardships and dangers that awaited them had completely discouraged four families, and they had pulled their wagons into Brownwood the morning Lucas Steele's train had left without them. Frank set a killing pace and, as he knew they would, three more wagons broke down the first day and were left behind. The settlers in the limestone house made them welcome, and with promises of help to start homesteading in the area they were content to settle there.

Frank had accomplished what he'd set out to do with relative ease. Now he only had to keep the three remaining wagons together in order to justify his position as their leader. They would catch up with Lucas Steele's train and would be able to keep pace with it.

Frank thought about the redheaded woman and the way she had warmed him when he looked at her. She reminded him of a puma or a wildcat, and he was sure she would fight like one. He would wait and, when the time was right, he would snatch her and head for the wild, desolate country in Mexico. He would tame her, break her for riding like he would a wild mountain pony. He thought of her naked beneath him, her mouth opening to him. He would take her slowly, savoring the warmth and scent of her, then he would devour her. . . . His mind told him to stop thinking about her for now; he was just torturing himself.

When they reached the Colorado, they retrieved the raft Lucas and Tucker had used earlier in the day and had left on the far side. Frank and Collins poled the raft with the help of Blanchet and young Jeremy Taylor. The Negro, Poppy, handled the horses. It was a smooth, fast crossing, thanks to the ready conveyance.

Five days after camping beside Pecan Creek, the three wagons topped a rise and saw the supposedly abandoned buildings of Fort McKavett. Located on a high bluff overlooking the San Saba River, the stone buildings looked anything but empty. Steele's wagon train was lined up alongside the barracks buildings, and the flag still flew from the flagpole in the center of the parade ground.

Frank led his wagons to the rear of the parked train and called a halt. A soldier came out of one of the buildings and directed the black boy to turn the stock loose inside a pole corral behind the barracks. He informed Frank that Captain Doyle wished to speak with him.

While Frank was talking to the soldier, his eyes roamed the compound for the redheaded woman. He caught a glimpse of her walking with the small honey-haired woman and had to force his eyes away from her. This was the woman who would ride with him when he headed south, the woman who would fill his nights with excitement. She would be afraid of him at first, but she would come to respect his superior strength. He was proud of that strength, and of his cunning ruthlessness and knowledge of the plains. He forced down his agitation at seeing her and headed toward the building the soldier had indicated.

Captain Doyle was seated behind a table, but rose and extended his hand when Frank walked confidently into the room. "Hello, Parcher. You know Lucas Steele and Buck Garrett?"

Frank glanced at the two men lounging against the wall. "I've heard of Lone Buck Garrett," he said in way of retaliation when neither man acknowledged his presence. If the implication was lost on the captain, it did not go unnoticed by Lucas and Buck.

Captain Doyle sat down and Frank stood in front of him, his feet wide apart in an arrogant pose, his back to the other men. The two facing each other across the table had little in common, and both of them knew it. They were both men of the plains, but it meant completely different things to each of them. Frank Parcher was the destroyer, James Doyle the protector. Frank waited for the captain to speak. Waiting was one of the things Frank did best.

"What happened to the rest of your train?"

Ordinarily Frank would have told him it was none of his goddamn business, but he'd decided to play the game.

"Well, captain, the folks got scared off when you tol' 'em 'bout havin' no escort west of Fort Stockton. Part of 'em stayed at Brownwood, the rest squatted with a homesteader a day's run away. Guess all that's left is me and them three wagons, and we're a goin' on to Californey."

Captain Doyle appeared to ponder this for a moment. Parcher hadn't told him anything he didn't already know, but it gave him an excuse to think. Buck Garrett and his own scout had already brought back this information, along with the report that Parcher was pushing the wagons beyond reason, resulting in the breakdowns.

"Mr. Steele has agreed to let your remaining three wagons join his train if they lighten their loads and exchange their wheels for some with heavy iron. Since Steele already has a scout," he nodded in Buck's direction, "you're free to turn back and regroup the rest of your train if they're still of a mind to make the trip." It was said. Now he would see how the other man reacted. For a time there was only the sound of the captain shuffling paper. When Parcher didn't speak, he added impatiently, "I understand you were already paid the money for the trip."

"And I'm a makin' the trip."

"We don't need or want your services," Lucas spoke up behind him.

Frank answered without turning to look at him. "I ain't offerin' any."

"You'll follow Steele's train?" Captain Doyle asked irritably.

Frank grinned. "It's goin' west. I'm goin' west."

James Doyle kept his eyes from the seething Lucas and fastened them on Frank. When he spoke his voice was abrupt. "Then you'd best get back to that bunch of greenhorns and get them ready for travel. I wouldn't bet a stack of cow chips on their chances of making it without Lucas Steele and Buck Garrett."

Frank grinned at the anger in the captain's voice. He didn't care doodly-squat for his opinion or anyone else's. He'd worked things around until they were finally going his way. He would be with the train until it reached El Paso. That was exactly what he'd set out to do when he left Pecan Creek.

"Goddamn!" Lucas swore as soon as Frank left them. "I don't trust that varmint any farther than I can throw a bull by the tail."

"He's not likely to try anything between here and Fort Stockton. It's after that you'll have to watch him. It's the three wagons he brought in that I'm concerned about," Doyle responded grimly.

"I'll give them until tomorrow to rest up and get in shape. Then it'll be up to them to keep up."

"Sounds reasonable to me. Thank you, Steele."

"Save your thanks. I'm not completely without

sympathy for those Louisiana farmers. It's Parcher that worries me. I'm telling you that if he gets to messing around with the women, I'll kill him quicker than I would a rattler," were Lucas's parting words.

The sun was hot as Lucas and Buck walked down the line of wagons toward the three at the end of the line. Stifling his frustration and fury, Lucas approached a tall, thin, sandy-haired man in neatly patched clothes and the heavy flat-heeled boots of a farmer. Reluctantly he held out his hand.

"Lucas Steele. I'm taking this train west. This is our scout, Buck Garrett."

"Rafe Blanchet, sir." The man's grip was firm, and his eyes looked steadily into Lucas's.

"How many in your party?"

"Only myself, sir. We buried my wife at Brownwood."

"Sorry, Blanchet." The man's look never wavered, and Lucas nodded. "You'll have tomorrow to get your wagon in shape if you're traveling with us. Captain Doyle will authorize a trade for two-inch wheels the army has stored here. Also, your water barrels can be exchanged for larger ones. Lighten your load by one third and check your food supplies so that you have a hundred pounds. Check the caulking on the water barrels and the bottom of your wagon. First and foremost, keep your place in line and stay away from the women. They're spoken for. I'm taking them to their prospective husbands. Is that understood?"

"Perfectly. Let me say I appreciate your letting us

join you. Frankly, until now I had my doubts that we would ever reach California." He glanced at Buck, who was looking into the wagon. Rafe reached in under the seat and brought out a brown and white pup that immediately started gnawing on his fingers. "I've only two left out of a litter of six. The mother was killed a few weeks back, and these two are the only ones to survive on what I could find to feed them."

"Looks like a good sheep-herding dog." Buck reached for the pup.

"It is. The mother was the best dog I ever had. She could pen a dozen sheep just by watching my hand signals." Rafe took off his dusty hat and wiped his forehead with the sleeve of his shirt. "I found her shot in the head lying right smack-dab in the middle of the trail. Someone must have mistaken her for a varmint. I don't see how they could have though; she never wandered far from the pups."

"What will you take for the pup?" Buck interrupted.

"It's according to what you intend to do with it. If it's for sport. . . ." He left his words hanging and his face took on a closed, guarded look.

"I'm not meanin' to use it to bait a cougar, if that's what you're gettin' at," Buck said curtly.

Rafe's face relaxed. "I had to know. It's been suggested."

"Well?" Buck disliked haggling.

"If it will be taken care of, you can have it. I'm feeding them corn bread and watered-down meat drippings."

"I'll pay a dollar."

"That's much too much. I'll settle for a hunk of meat from your next hunt."

Buck placed the squirming pup back down in the wagon. "I'll be back for him." He started to walk away, but turned back. "How well do you shoot?"

"That's the one thing I'm good at." Rafe's face creased into a smile. "Not so much with a handgun, but with my rifle I'll stand beside any man."

Rafe's smile told Buck he was younger than he had believed him to be at first. He was not as old as the expression he wore suggested. He was also better educated than could be expected of a farmer. They eyed each other for what seemed a full minute, then Buck finally turned away. He liked the man.

The Taylors were equally willing to do whatever was necessary to join the train. Alice Taylor gave her husband, Lucas, and Buck a reasonable time to talk before she stepped out of her wagon to join them in the shade. Neatly dressed in a bright cotton print, she was a large woman who appeared unbothered by the sun. But it bothered her more than she ever let show. Giving way to her feelings would be a sign of weakness, and Alice Taylor despised weakness. Coming to stand beside her husband, she offhandedly fanned her face to create what breeze she could with a silk fan she had brought with her from Philadelphia. Alice had made up her mind from the beginning of this trip that she would maintain the quality of life she was accustomed to. She had come from a house where imported glass windows let in the sunlight through Irish lace curtains, and where the food was served from china dishes and eaten with silver forks. She was a woman of property and intended to live like one.

Alice knew that her background had determined her character, had given her manners, gestures, attitudes different from those of the other women in the train. She knew this even as she knew she intended to fight this wild country. She intended to fight its ability to degrade a person and bring him down to the level of that disgusting man who had been hired to lead them. Alice's war with the world was a subtle one, one she never openly expressed. She was a quiet woman, a strong one, who knew her own mind. She was determined to get her family to California and to see them restored to a position of respect.

The decision to move west had been Alice's idea. There had been no question but that they had to move. After the discovery of mismanaged funds at the bank where her husband was a high-ranking officer, Philadelphia would no longer hold them. Her family thought she was foolish for standing by Daniel, even though he was innocent of any wrongdoing. Her close friends had suggested that the affair might blow over and that Daniel could return in time, but Alice knew that Philadelphia families had long memories for sins and short ones for virtues. Daniel didn't argue about taking his wife and son and moving west. He was going because one didn't argue with Alice, and because he knew Alice was right.

"My dear, come meet Mr. Steele and Mr. Garrett."

Daniel put his hand beneath her elbow and drew her forward. "Gentlemen, my wife, Mrs. Taylor."

"You can count on us, Mr. Steele. Whatever adjustments that have to be made will be made. What we lack in knowledge of this sort of travel we will make up in determination to cause you the least bother possible."

"Thank you, ma'am. I've outlined the requirements to your husband. We pull out the day after tomorrow at daybreak."

"We'll be ready. Good day." Alice watched the two men walk away, and for the first time since they'd left the boat at New Orleans she felt they were in capable hands.

Lucas and Buck walked to the next wagon. They both had things to think about, thoughts and opinions of the people they had just left. There would be time enough to discuss them after they'd met the last of the people they would spend the next couple of months with.

Otis Collins leaned against his wagon and spit into the dust as they approached. With deliberate slowness Collins stood away from the wagon. His attitude was wary, suspicious. Lucas didn't offer his hand. Like Captain Doyle before him, he knew instinctively that the man had a chip on his shoulder and was just aching for someone to try to knock it off.

"You're Collins," Lucas said flatly. "I'll tell you what I've told the others. Lighten your load by one third, exchange the wheels on your wagon for some the army will trade, and check your food. One hundred pounds for each person in your wagon. Caulk your water barrels and the bottom of your wagon. You'll keep your position in line and stay away from the women."

A dull red flooded Collins's face. "You're doin' a powerful lot of orderin'," he snarled. "Who in the hell gave you the right to tell me what I'll have in my wagon?"

"Your damn wagon can sit right here as far as I'm concerned. But if you join this train, you'll do as I say and that's my final word."

"Otis?" A thin woman with a pinched face stood nervously at the end of the wagon. A girl of about six, the image of her mother, peeked out from behind her skirts.

"Shut up, Emma. This here's man talk." Collins spit again.

"But, Otis—"

"I said, shut up!" He darted a bitter glance at her, and the child disappeared behind her skirt. "All right," he said grudgingly to Lucas. "But I ain't ridin' tail and eatin' dust."

Lucas shrugged. "Then sit here, if you want. I don't care what you do."

"You ain't got no call to be a tellin' us what to do. We got our own scout."

"Then you and your scout can strike out on your own. As a matter of fact, I'd prefer it if you did."

"Otis!" The cry that came from the woman was almost a wail.

Her husband turned a furious face in her direction,

but before he could say anything Frank Parcher appeared from behind the wagon.

"Don't get in a sweat, Collins. Steele wants to move fast. We can oblige 'im."

"But Frank—"

"It's for the best, Otis. Now git to tendin' to what's got to be done."

Collins stalked away, and Parcher grinned at Lucas. "I can handle 'im. He'll be ready."

"He'd better watch his mouth." Lucas looked Frank straight in the eye for so long, the other man's gaze faltered and he looked away. Lucas spun on his heel and left him. Buck lingered with deliberation, looking over Collins's wagon and sizing up the scout again.

Frank's face grew ugly. "What're you lookin' at?" he sneered. "I ain't got no use fer . . . half-breeds. Why, I've got a notion to. . . ." His hand went to his gun.

"It's a bad notion, Parcher. But if you really want to die, just move that hand a fraction."

Frank stared at Buck. The man's face was wicked. He stood lazily, hands hanging, but he was as ready as a crouching cougar. Frank saw it and recognized what he saw. With a curse he swung out and walked away.

The evening meal was over and Tucker climbed into the wagon to write in the journal. It was hot and she wanted to hurry and finish the chore so she could make herself available if Lucas came by. There was a chance they could walk away for a few private minutes together. Her heart had soared on gossamer wings since the night they'd spent beside the Colorado River. She was loved, and she loved in return!

April 30.

Fort McKavett was officially abandoned by the army just a little over a month ago. However, the sutler is still here, as well as a few other workers. The camp was first named Camp San Saba because it is located on the river by that name, but later the name was changed to Fort McKavett in honor of Capt. Henry McKavett killed at the Battle of Monterrey in Mexico. There are stone barracks for eight companies, twelve officers' quarters, hospital, guardhouse, magazine, and large headquarters. It seems such a terrible waste to let the buildings go unused. Three of the wagons from the Louisiana train joined us. Tomorrow we will have a day to wash clothes, bathe, and rearrange our belongings. Mr. Steele says the hardest part of our trip is still ahead of us.

Tucker closed the journal and blew out the candle. It was hot under the canvas, so she stepped down from the wagon into the cool evening breeze. Laura was sitting on a camp stool. Tucker moved a box so she could sit beside her.

"It didn't take long tonight. Writing is easy if you have something to write about."

"Someday you'll have to read it to me, Tucky. Things seem to happen so fast, I'm afraid I'll forget some of them."

"Buck's coming this way," Tucker said. She was still somewhat uncomfortable about the attention he paid to Laura.

Laura turned her head from side to side, trying to pick up the sound of his footsteps.

"To the right," Tucker said softly, and her heart gave a queer lurch at the smile of pure rapture that came over Laura's face. Oh God, she thought. When the letdown comes, will she be able to bear it?

"Evenin', Laura. Ma'am."

"Hello, Buck." Laura held her hand out for Buck. Usually he touched it briefly and squatted on his heels to visit, and Tucker would find an excuse for moving away.

"Come walk with me." He saw instant disapproval on Tucker's face. How could he make her understand that he would die before he would give this small, wraithlike creature one moment of heartache? He could understand Tucker's concern, but there was no way to explain matters to her. His actions would have to speak for him.

Laura looped her arm in Buck's. Her hand slid down his forearm, and her fingers interlaced with his.

"With me out of the way, maybe Lucas will come talk to you, Tucker."

"Oh, go on off with you." Her voice was light, but the look on her face told Buck of her worry.

He looked into her eyes and tried to reassure her without speaking that this girl meant more to him than life itself. He was sure she didn't understand his feelings and that his look did nothing to ease her anxiety. Slowly, his steps measured to Laura's, he led her out and away from the firelight, past the watching eyes of the women resting beside their wagons. Laura floated along beside him, her head reaching just above his shoulder. He squeezed her hand.

"Does that mean we're alone, Buck?" Laura whispered.

"We're alone, *mi amor.*"

"How is it that you speak Spanish? What did you call me? Somehow I think it was . . . nice."

"Most of the people in California speak Spanish," he said quietly. He didn't add that he'd learned Spanish at an early age when he was cursed by the old Mexican he lived with. They came to the end of the compound and Buck stopped, picked up a stick, and swished it across the surface of a boulder before he grasped Laura by the waist and lifted her onto it. He sprang up beside her.

"What did you do before you sat me up here?"

"I moved a stick around over the rock in case a snake had curled up on the warm stone."

"Oh!" She shivered and moved closer to him. He took her hand and put his arm around her, fitting her into the curve of his shoulder. She snuggled against him.

They sat quietly, listening to the night sounds, content to be together. It was as if the two of them were alone in the world. Finally Buck felt compelled to tell her his thoughts.

"This feeling of peace. It's strange, the way you give that to me. It's as if it radiates from you." The arm holding her drew her closer. "What is this gift you carry around with you?"

"I'm not sure what you mean."

"Peace and contentment. I find it when I'm with you."

"I'm glad," she whispered. "I'm so glad."

She closed her eyes and leaned her head against his shoulder. Listen, she told herself. Listen to what he has to say, what he needs to say to you. Help him if you can. You may not ever be able to give him any more than this . . . to sit and listen to him and quietly love him. She lifted her hand and held it against his cheek. She ached to comfort him, to make up for any past sorrows. She told herself she mustn't cry, no matter what. Buck needed no more tears in his life. He needed sunshine and peace and love. She realized that his need for love, and his capacity for it, was great.

"You've not been happy." Her voice was low, filled with pain.

"I am now," he told her, his voice suddenly thick. "When I'm with you."

She was silent for a moment, sensing his need for this quiet time. She felt her breath catch in her throat when his fingers lifted her chin, felt her insides warm with pleasure as she allowed herself the pure joy of kissing and being kissed by him. Such a lovely feeling was unfolding in her midsection and traveling slowly throughout her body. She wanted it to go on and on. Warm, moist lips traced the line of her brow and delicately touched her closed eyelids. His lips were working their way downward, touching her cheek and the tip of her nose, then settling very gently on her mouth, where they moved with delicious provocation. Her mouth opened under the pressure of his, yielding, molding itself to the shape of his. A surge of pleasure rushed through her as his tongue explored the sweetness of her mouth, drawing a soft moan from a deep-seated passion she had not even known existed. Never before had she felt quite like this. Never had she known this melting, letting-go sensation that now invaded her innermost being.

Abruptly he seized her arms and held her away from him.

"God! My sweet, my beautiful Laura. I'm sorry! I never intended to do that!" His voice was husky with regret.

"No!" Laura reached for his face with her hands and stroked his cheeks with her palms. "Please don't be sorry. When you kiss me, I feel as if I never want to leave you. I know what you're feeling. How could you be drawn to a girl like me while we're out here on the prairie? Are you afraid I'll try to hold onto you, Buck? I won't. I promise I won't. Sometimes I'm bitter about what's happened to me. I won't pretend otherwise. Sometimes it's hard for me to accept the fact that because I can't see I'll never be a man's . . . true love." Her voice broke a little. "Give me this little time with you. I'm trying not to be selfish. I want to try and make you happy for a little while. Because I don't think you've had a really happy moment in a long, long time. Maybe I can give you that, at least." Her voice was earnest, almost pleading. "Leaving you when we reach our journey's end will be harder without memories of you to take with me. So don't you see," she whispered eagerly, "that's exactly what I'm doing! I want a thousand sweet memories to cherish when we get to California. I want to have them all stored away someplace inside me, so that when I'm away from you forever, I'll be able to take them out of myself, out of my heart, like little treasures. I can live that way, Buck. I can get through life that way. But . . ." she put her hands up to her face, "but I've got to have something to remember!"

"No!" Buck now said the word with the same fervor she had displayed. "I regret that you can't see, but you have much more than any woman I have ever known. You are perfect, *mi querida*. You are sweet, wonderful, wise beyond your years. It's me who's the problem. What I am. I'm not worthy of your touch, much less your kiss. I've seen everything, done everything. I've no family that claim me. I've been in Yuma prison—would be there still if a gut-shot man hadn't confessed to the crime I was convicted of. I'm what I am, Laura. A man who lives on the edge of decency, accepted only for the service I give."

"Oh, Buck! Like myself, you can't go back and

change what's been done to you. It's what lies ahead of us that's important. Let me be with you for this little while. Let me have my memories to store away," she whispered desperately.

He was silent for the duration of a few heartbeats. Then, with a small sound that came from his throat, he drew her to him and held her tightly against him while he buried his face in her hair.

"You've upset my life. You've made me feel things I never thought I would feel. But I must tell you how deeply I love you, how I want to protect and cherish you. *Sí, mi querida,* hold me tighter. Pull me into your heart, *mi amor.* You are *mi alma, mi vida.*"

Laura had a sudden soaring sensation inside her, as if joy had come like a dove flying in through an open window, startling and yet so lovely it was breathtaking. One of the things she could remember seeing was birds, and now they danced into her mind like music. She felt so much happiness she was giddy, light-headed, unable to think clearly.

"What did you call me? Oh, Buck! I must know what you called me."

"My love, my soul, my life," he whispered as he pushed the strands of long, blond hair from her face and kissed her damp forehead.

"Oh, yes," she said and brushed the warm hollow of his throat with her lips. "Buck, oh Buck," she whispered breathlessly. "I don't have those beautiful words!" Her lips parted and searched for his. "I can only say that I love you so much!"

"They are the most beautiful words I have ever

174 / Dorothy Garlock

heard, *mi amor.*" This wondrous feeling of being loved was worth everything else in the world. Every nerve in his body cried out for her, yearned to be united with her. They clung together, covering each other's faces with tender kisses that grew more intense by the second.

"Buck . . ." she said weakly.

"Don't talk, my love, just let me hold you." His voice vibrated with tender emotion. "Oh, my *querida*!"

She pressed her face against his shirt, not wanting him to see the spurt of tears that filled her eyes on hearing his tender words. She was aware of the heavy beat of his heart, and placed her hand over it. He laughed, a soft thrilling sound that came musically to her ears. She clasped her arms around his neck, and her lips found the pulse that beat at the base of his throat. A feeling of faintness seemed to sweep over her. She wanted to cling to him, to give him love, to shield and protect him. His arms tightened around her, and he cuddled her against him. They sat quietly as he stroked her hair.

Laura would have been content to sit there forever. They didn't talk, and his hands caressing her no longer made her feel shy; it seemed a natural thing to do. She placed her palm against his face, and he pressed his lips into it before he released her and slid down off the rock. He reached for her, and she trustingly gave herself up to him. He stood her on her feet and, with an arm around her, led her back toward the encamped wagons.

"I have a present for you," he said so softly she wasn't sure she'd heard correctly.

"A present?" Her attempt to speak was weakened by the depth of her emotion.

"Yes, a present." Buck laughed and placed her hand on the wheel of the freight wagon. "Wait here." He climbed into the wagon and brought out the pup. Its stomach was swollen with the meal it had been fed, and it was drowsy with interrupted sleep. "Hold out your arms. Be careful and don't drop it."

"What is it? Tell me what it is." Her whispered voice trembled with excitement.

"It's a pup. It'll make us a good sheep dog."

"A puppy?" Laura held the cuddly pup up to her face and looked as if she would cry. Her lips quivered, and she took a deep shaking breath. "Did you say a sheep dog for *us*?"

"Of course, *querida*. A sheep dog for us. For you and me."

"Oh, Buck, I wish . . . I wish. . . ."

"You wish you could see it, *mi amor*?" A huge knot began to form in his throat. He stared deeply at her stricken face and saw the sparkle of tears come to her eyes.

"Not the dog, Buck. You! I wish I could see you, just one time!" The cry was like the wail of a small wounded animal, and as he watched, tears slid down her face like summer rain.

Twelve

Tucker watched Laura walk away with Buck. Again she was filled with conflicting emotions. Part of her was glad for the diversion Buck's company brought to Laura's life, while the larger part of her was fearful that this taste of male companionship would cause her to be forever dissatisfied with life as a spinster. The image of her face the day she'd mentioned entering the convent floated through Tucker's mind. It was the sad, haunted look of lost dreams and pitiful resignation. Thrusting aside this memory, Tucker got to her feet. She'd have to talk with Lucas about this problem that troubled her.

She called out greetings as she walked past the wagons. She was by now on friendly terms with all the women, with the exception of Cora Lee. But even though the women accepted her and Laura, there was still something of a barrier there because she'd been hired as a teacher. It separated her from those going to California seeking husbands and, in their minds, elevated her to a certain superior status. This, too, posed a problem for Tucker, who now wished there was some woman friend with whom she could share her worries about Laura. Though she was not a joiner, nor accustomed to exchanging confidences with anyone other than Laura, she'd been eager for the camaraderie that she'd expected would develop in this isolated society of women with a common goal.

Lottie called out to her and she paused. "Lookin' fer Laura? She's all right. She walked off with Buck."

"Yes, I know."

"Then why've ya got that sour look on yore face? Ain't nothin' wrong with Laura a walkin' off with Buck. She ain't one of 'em goin' to a man in Californey. So there ain't no reason fer ya to git all het up 'bout Buck courtin' Laura."

There were times when Lottie's frankness was downright frustrating. "Buck isn't courting Laura. They're friends, and nothing more."

"Humph! Ain't no sech thing as friends 'tween a man 'n a woman. All he's a thinkin' 'bout is gittin' 'er in the bed, 'n all she's a thinkin' 'bout is gittin' hitched afore she gits under the blanket."

"That's your opinion, Lottie." Tucker turned to the brown-haired woman holding a small girl. "Is Betsy asleep already, Mrs. Shaffer?"

"She's tired out. She's lookin' forward to the bath in the river tomorrow."

"We all are," Tucker said and moved on.

She stopped to speak to Marie Hook and her son, Billy. The woman had loosened up somewhat and now seemed to welcome the few words that passed occasionally between them.

"Are you and Billy having a nice evening?"

"Fine, thank you. Billy has beaten me in two games of chess already." She smiled warmly at her son. "But there's another day coming."

The boy lowered his head and smiled shyly.

"The game is far too complicated for me, Billy. But some evening I'll play you a game of checkers," Tucker offered. Billy bent his head even lower in the face of this direct attention.

Marie gave Tucker one of her rare smiles. "I haven't won a game of checkers against Billy in over a year."

"Imagine that! He must be good."

"He is. He has great powers of concentration."

"Oh, Mama!" Embarrassment brought Billy to his feet, and he disappeared behind the wagon.

"He needs more contact with people. I'm hoping he'll get that when we get to California." Marie shifted dark, luminous eyes to Tucker. "He also needs male companionship," she said sadly.

"Yes, a boy needs a man to teach him certain things." Tucker's eyes wandered over the camp. "Is Cora Lee visiting with the new people?"

Marie lifted her shoulders in a noncommittal shrug. "Cora Lee is off and away every night. We don't pay any attention to her comings and goings."

"Yes, well, I must be going. Laura will be coming soon and I. . . ."

"It must please you to see how well Laura manages, Miss Houston. You've done an admirable job of teaching her to be self-reliant."

"It was a matter of two orphans trying to survive, that's all."

Tucker couldn't help but think there was something mysterious about this woman, but she had little time to reflect on it because at that moment Mustang suddenly rounded the wagon with a load of firewood in his arms. He stooped down and dropped the boughs, tossing a piece into the guttering flames.

"Howdy. Had a little extra firewood," he explained. "You ladies a likin' bein' in the fort? It's just 'bout like bein' in a town, ain't it?"

"Well, not quite," Tucker laughed. " 'Night, Mrs. Hook. 'Night, Mustang."

"If ya be a lookin' fer Laura, she walked off with Buck," Mustang called after her.

Tucker gritted her teeth. Did everyone in the whole camp know that Laura walked out with Buck? She headed for the freight wagons and the faint glow of a lamp coming from one of them. The moon had not yet risen, and the buildings that made up the fort were but vague outlines in the darkness of the night. As she approached the wagon, the light went out and a man stepped down.

"Lucas?"

"No, *señorita*. It is I, Chata."

"Do you know where I can find Mr. Steele?"

"*Sí.* He is with the *soldado*. There." He lifted his arm toward the dimly lit officer's building.

Tucker turned to retrace her steps. She was disappointed. She needed to be with Lucas, to feel the loved, protected feeling a few minutes in his arms could give her.

The restless stamping of the mules captured her attention, and she went to lean against the pole corral and look at the stars. She stifled a sigh and told herself that Lucas would come to her when he could. He had heavy responsibilities, and he would never let his personal preferences override his duty. The warm night, the stars above her, and the companionable sounds coming from the livestock all contributed to lull her into unawareness of anything except her own reveries.

The man approached silently, and when she noticed him she called out the name of the man in her thoughts.

"Lucas?"

The shadow that was the man moved forward and she realized it was too short to be Lucas's, and that it walked with a bouncing gait that wasn't Lucas's walk. Tucker wasn't alarmed until he walked right up to her. Against the star-studded sky his figure was a dark, menacing silhouette, but there was enough light to let her see the glitter in his eyes. She recognized the scout from the other train, Frank Parcher. He was hatless. A gun was thrust into the top of his trousers.

"I thought you'd never leave them wagons. You picked a right good spot for us to have our talk." There was a smile on the man's face as he moved it to within inches of hers.

Tucker backed away. "I've got nothing to say to you!"

"Mebbe. But I got a thing or two to say to you," he answered with a chuckle.

"Nothing you could say would interest me," she snapped in a cool, lofty tone, and spun on her heel to leave him. His hand lashed out and clamped to her arm.

"Yer goin' to hear it anyhow. Minute I clapped eyes on you I knowed we'd have things to say . . . 'n do . . . to each other."

Anger boiled in Tucker. "Get your hands off me, you . . . mangy polecat!" She jerked on her arm and his fingers tightened.

"Out here on the plains, purty gal, we don't foller rules like they do in town. If'n we want to talk to a gal, we grab 'er 'n talk."

"Let go of my arm or—I'll scream my head off!"

"Yer the purtiest thing I ever did see. Got spunk, too. Ya'll get to likin' my touch. You 'n me'll be spendin' lots of nights all by our lonesome." His voice was as unconcerned as if he were discussing cattle prices.

"You're sadly mistaken, mister, if you think I'd ever spend any time with you!"

"I ain't mistook, Tucker. Tucker." He repeated her name as though trying to taste it. "You'll come with me when the time's right. I ain't a doubtin' it. Now, I got no time to be a romancin' ya or makin' love talk. You'll mount up and ride with me when I say so. Ain't no sense in wastin' a woman like you on these clabberheads."

"You're insane! I'd die before I'd go anywhere

with you. And Lucas Steele would kill you quicker than he would a buzzard if you so much as looked cross-eyed at me or any of the other woman on this train," she flared, seething with anger.

"Ya think I'd wait 'round for *Mister* Lucas Steele to call me out all gentlemanlike?" he asked with a low laugh. "Not likely, gal. I'll be a watchin' ya, same as I been doin', 'n if'n I get wind that ya took the notion to tell him 'bout me 'n you, why I'll jist have to hightail it outta here, wait on up ahead, and pick him off with a shot in the head. 'N t'won't matter none what ya tell 'im, thar ain't no way on earth that man can be ready fer me twenty-four hours a day. So by a talkin', you'd jist be a diggin' his grave fer him. Not that I'd mind. . . . I'll still have ya in the end. Jist be a mite more trouble, that's all," he concluded blandly. He watched her the way a spider might watch a juicy insect getting tangled in its web.

"You mean you'd just shoot an innocent man from ambush?" she gasped. But even as she asked the question, she knew he would.

He was laughing openly now at her astonishment. "What's he to me? I've killed horses I knowed bet-ter'n him. What's he to me," he repeated, "that I'd let 'im stand 'tween me and the woman I want? Don't need that meddlin' kind of varmint 'round nohow."

Tucker felt herself go ice cold. The next instant she was burning hot, as a flush of fear raced through her body. She was trembling from head to foot, but she made an effort to keep her voice steady. "You're talking crazy." She shook her arm again and was surprised when he released it.

She walked past him, and he let her get about five feet away before he pounced. With the agility of a mountain lion and a single sweep of his arms he had her tight against him, her arms pinned to her sides. One of his hands covered her mouth and the other clutched at her breasts. Tucker's eyes were wide with terror as she helplessly searched the darkness, feeling the length of his torso pressed against her back.

"Jist remember, what passes 'tween you 'n me is ours. Say one word to anyone and I'll drop that wagon master faster'n he can blink from any hill or clump of trees he passes. 'N that ain't all, purty woman," he rasped through the coppery tendrils that now clung damply to her temples. "That boy what sits by his maw would make a fine, easy target, too— if'n ya decide to be difficult, that is. Bang! Right between the eyes. Ever seen brains a splattered all over?"

Tucker stood numb and still while he whispered this litany of horrors into her ear. Oh, my God! He was serious!

"Then there's that little blind gal. . . ." Tucker's blood froze at the mention of Laura. "You can't keep a watchin' out fer her all the time. Why, ya don't even know where she is right now. Might be you'll lose sight o' her fer a few minutes . . . 'n might be when you find her, she'll be a layin' gut-shot in the trail," Parcher continued his grisly monologue. "I'm a givin' ya yore choices."

Tucker stood riveted, quaking with sheer terror. He was holding her so tightly she could feel the gun in his belt digging into her ribs.

Parcher chuckled harshly and pulled open her bodice with one swift tug. His hand now closed over a firm, bare breast. "Yer my woman. Yer the one I want. Not a used-up one, or a squaw like my pa had. Understand?"

Tucker shuddered but nodded numbly.

"You won't be forgettin' 'bout that gut-shot gal now?" he reminded her softly as he ran his hand down from her bosom to her pelvis and jerked her buttocks up tight against him. He made a few grinding motions with his hips against her before he abruptly released his grip and stood holding her arm and staring down at her.

Somehow Tucker managed to fasten her bodice, and the instant his hand left her arm she stumbled away into the darkness.

Frank leaned against the rail and chuckled. She was everything he'd thought she would be. Sensible when it was called for, and fiery when mad. He'd wanted to throw her to the ground and satisfy himself right then and there, but he knew she was a woman worth waiting for. Their time would come. And when it did, they'd be far away, with no one listening but himself, the coyotes, and the wolves. He could feel the throbbing strength of his swollen manhood, and he found himself yearning for it to be sheathed in the redheaded woman.

* * *

Cora Lee stepped from the shadows and stood before Frank. She had been watching him and the teacher, but from such a distance that she hadn't heard what they were saying. She stood looking at him with her hands resting on her hips, desire growing in her like a living thing. She'd hoped the scout wouldn't throw the teacher to the ground and rape her; she hoped he'd save himself for her.

She knew what she needed; she needed the full weight of this powerful man upon her, making love to her. The need that was coursing its way through her, throbbing in her head and knotting her stomach, had to be satisfied. She knew it would be the moment Frank placed his hands on her waist and drew her toward him. He spread her dress where she had opened the neckline provocatively, and lightly pinched the erect nipples that strained against his hands. It was not important to Cora Lee who this man was, or if she even liked him or not. She knew she had to have him.

Frank took her hand, and they moved from the pole corral, dodged around the night guard, and turned into the brush alongside the river bank. He walked rapidly, ignoring the branches that sprang back to strike Cora Lee as he passed through them. He found the place he sought and turned to her.

"Take your clothes off," he said abruptly as he lifted his hands to slide his suspenders from his shoulders. Cora Lee moved over and molded herself against him, but before her arms had reached his neck he pushed her away. "Take your clothes off," he repeated.

He watched her silently as she struggled out of her dress. When she stood naked before him, he lowered her to the ground and fell on top of her. His swollen shaft sought the wetness between her legs, and he immediately plunged into her. She moaned and arched against him, reaching, grabbing.

Surprised by the look of lust on her face, he felt his desire ebbing. Damn the bitch! He slapped her with his open hand. Instinctively her clenched fist came up, and she struck him a blow alongside the head. A wave of sexual excitement swept him, and he slapped her again. Cora Lee began to fight him in earnest. She suddenly realized what was happening to her, and she was frightened by it.

The stabbing shaft between her thighs tore into her, causing her body to arch up against him helplessly. She tried to expel him from her body, but it was no use. She couldn't move as he drove deeper and deeper inside her.

In her own confused way, Cora Lee had believed she could find a solution to her obsession with Lucas Steele by turning to another man. She knew now that the man she had turned to was cold and ruthless. He knew her weakness and was using it to degrade her while he satisfied his own lust.

He battered her with long, hard thrusts until her aching bones felt as if there were no padding between them and the hard ground. When he finished he quickly removed himself from her.

Of all the lovers she had ever known, he was by far the most brutal. He had not said one word to her except to tell her to take off her clothes. He had shown no appreciation for her willingness to lie with him, nor admiration for her beauty. Most important, he had not even tried to carry her to the point of ecstasy where she could rest knowing the thing was done, her need satisfied.

Frank hitched up his suspenders and squatted on his heels to watch Cora Lee. She was a good-looking woman, but a mite too horny for his taste. He had deliberately finished with her before she reached satisfaction. She was still hot, still panting for it. He would play her along, keep her that way, let her stew in her own juices for a while. Then he'd give her the plowing of her life, and after that she'd be eating out of his hand.

"Tell me about the redheaded woman."

"What do you want to know?" she snapped as she began to dress.

"Is she Steele's woman?"

"Would it matter to you if she was?"

"Answer me, goddammit, if'n you don't want a busted mouth."

"She's not his woman. She'd like to be, but I got ideas about that," Cora Lee muttered.

Frank grinned. "Fancy 'im, do ya?"

"None of your business," she flung at him.

He laughed. "Play yore cards right 'n we'll both get what we want," he suggested conspiratorially.

"And I suppose you'll deal the hand," Cora Lee

said doubtfully as she pulled her knees up under her skirt and held them tightly.

"My game," he said softly. He reached out a hand and rubbed the back of it across one of her still sensitive nipples. "Tomorrow night. Here. I'll give ya a real good time." His tone was subtly different, almost gentle.

Cora Lee didn't answer. Miserably she realized she didn't need to. Frank knew his own power, and he knew she would be there. She sat in the glade for a while after he left her. She still needed someone to satisfy her tonight.

She got to her feet, straightened her dress, and smoothed back her hair. She would find someone to help her, someone to release her from the strain of the trembling demands of her body. It would have to be one of the soldiers, one young enough to cope with the fires that consumed her.

The moon was up and the wagons stood out clearly against the skyline. Cora Lee stood at the far end of the corral and watched as the night guard was changed. The men talked in low tones for a few minutes, and then the soldier going off duty started walking in her direction. Cora Lee waited until the replacement had turned his back and walked to the far side of the corral before she stepped out into the path.

"Evenin', soldier. You goin' off duty?"

The soldier stopped. He had known she was standing there, but he hadn't mentioned it to the replacement who had come to relieve him. After several hours of night duty his eyes were adjusted to the darkness, while the other man had just come from lighted barracks. It had been months since he had talked to a woman alone, and the temptation to do so was irresistible.

"Evenin', ma'am. You ort to be careful 'round here at night. You could be mistook for a horse thief. Somebody could shoot you by accident."

"But you didn't shoot. You knew I was here."

"Yes, ma'am."

"Now that that's cleared up, can we walk?"

"We ain't suppose to have nothin' to do with the womenfolk, ma'am. The captain would strip the hide off me if he caught me."

Cora Lee laughed softly and took his arm. "We'll have to make sure the captain don't catch you. I'm lonesome, soldier. I know a little place where we can go and talk."

He hesitated. "I don't think I ort to, ma'am."

"My name's Cora Lee. What's yours?"

"Dabney. Private Casper Dabney."

"You're not on duty, Casper. Wouldn't you like to be with me for a little while before you go back to the barracks? I bet there isn't a man in your company who wouldn't give a month's pay to be in your shoes right now." As if by accident she brushed her breasts against his arm and heard his swift intake of breath.

"But the captain said—"

"Oh, poo on the captain! He wouldn't turn down the chance to walk out with me." Cora Lee laughed lightly. She could see his resistance fading as she knew it would. "Come on, Casper. I've had my eye on you for quite a spell." She let her hand wander up his chest to his neck. He was trembling violently. "Don't you want to be with me, Casper?"

"Yes, ma'am. It's only that the captain—"

"He'll never know." She took his arm, drew it around her waist, and placed his hand just beneath her breast. "There's a place back here by the river where we can . . . talk."

Fifteen minutes later Cora Lee was lying on her back in the clearing. The young soldier had spent himself almost the moment he'd touched her. She had known he would, but she also knew the resilience of the young, and within minutes she had him aroused again. Now she lay quietly, rolling her head back and forth as the ecstasy she craved built within her.

"Private Dabney! On your feet!" The voice rang with command.

The soldier jerked away from her, and Cora Lee's eyes flew open. Oh, God, no! Please . . . just a little more time! But she knew it wasn't to be. She had to do something, immediately, to improve her situation. She rolled over as soon as the boy left her and began to sob.

Private Dabney hastily arranged his clothes while the sergeant picked up his rifle.

"You're under arrest, private."

"Sir, I—"

"Oh, sergeant." Cora Lee got to her feet, holding the bodice of her dress together with both hands. "I'm so glad you came. He . . . that soldier made me. . . ."

"You don't have to be a tellin' me nothin', ma'am. I got eyes."

"Then you could see—"

"Go back to your wagon," he ordered with no pretense of politeness. "Get movin', private."

"I didn't force her, sir." The enormity of what was happening and what Cora Lee was accusing him of struck Casper like a thunderbolt. He held back and turned pleading eyes on the woman. "Tell him, ma'am."

"Tell him what?" Cora Lee said harshly. "That you dragged me here and threw me down? That you . . . that you . . ." Her voice trailed away in a pitiful wail.

The grizzled old sergeant stood looking at the woman and then back at the private. Would the younguns never learn? And this'n had the makings of a damn good soldier, too. Did the foolish lad not know he was just about thirty minutes away from gettin' shot for rape? He prodded him in the back with the rifle, and they moved toward the corral. Cora Lee sniffed a few times and followed. Inside the fort the sergeant stopped and jerked his head toward the wagons.

"If'n yer a wantin' the whole camp to know 'bout this, you'll come to the captain and make charges. If'n ya don't, you'll go on back to yore wagon and keep yore mouth shut. I don't need to be a tellin' ya that!"

Cora Lee hesitated. This was something she hadn't expected. The sergeant was giving her a choice. She looked into his face and saw the hard, unsympathetic look in his eyes. He knew she hadn't been forced.

Would he say so? Would he forget what he'd seen and let the private go? She nodded her head, and he understood what she meant. She turned toward the darkened campsite, and the two soldiers proceeded toward the officers' quarters.

Thirty minutes later Sergeant Malone opened the door of the captain's quarters and called to Private Dabney.

"Come in, private."

Casper entered the room on legs that were weak with fear. The last thirty minutes had been the most difficult of his life. He knew the penalty for rape, and he knew the captain would not hesitate to carry out the punishment. He squared his shoulders and saluted smartly. He would take his punishment like a man, but, oh, God, what about his ma and sweet Martha Rose waiting for him back in Louisville? Would his disgrace be a reflection on them?

"At ease, private." The captain leaned back in his chair and looked steadily at him. "I'm disappointed in you, Dabney. I thought you were made of better stuff. One thing in your favor is that you waited until you were off duty to dally with the woman. She said you forced her. Did you force her, private?"

"No, sir."

"Have you talked with her before?"

"No, sir."

"What fatal charm do you have, private, that you meet a woman and she lets you bed her within minutes of your meeting?"

"I . . . don't know, sir."

"You were ordered to stay away from the woman on this train, private. Do you know the penalty for rape?"

"Yes, sir."

"Do you doubt that I will hesitate to have you shot?"

"No, sir."

"Do you know what is standing between you and execution at this moment?"

"No, sir."

"It's Sergeant Malone. He saw the woman intercept you, saw you walk away with her. When you didn't return, he followed and observed your . . . activities. He said if rape was committed, you were the one who was raped."

Casper's face turned from white to brick red, and he swallowed repeatedly. Silence filled every corner of the room. The captain looked at him long and hard. Casper felt compelled to say something.

"Sir, I . . ." He gulped and tried desperately to find words.

"Yes, private?" The captain was not going to make it easy for him.

"I . . . didn't force her."

"That's already been established, private. You disobeyed orders by dallying with her. You were in a hell of a position to defend this fort lying on your face with your britches down. Had the sergeant had a mind to, he could have put a knife in your back. Were you so desperate to have your ashes hauled that you would risk death, private?"

"No, sir."

Captain Doyle got to his feet. "We're a company on the move, Private Dabney, or you would be confined in a guardhouse. Instead, your sentence will be twenty lashes, punishment to be carried out at once. You'll have tomorrow to recover. The day after, if you are unable to sit a saddle you will be left behind to face court-martial." The captain's voice was brisk. If he felt any sympathy at all for the young private, he hid it well. "Sergeant Malone, you and I and Lieutenant Crossly will carry out the punishment. I want no word of this to leak out to the troops or to the civilians. Understand?"

It was past midnight when four men rode out from the fort and headed back down the trail they had covered the day before. Buck heard the faint sound of the horses' hooves and wondered at the secrecy of the late-night mission. Curiosity gnawed at him, and he quietly got to his feet and bridled his horse. He led him out of the fort and swung up onto his back, Indian fashion. About a mile out the ears of his horse rose, flicked a time or two, and stood straight up. Buck slipped from the sorrel, tied the reins to a tree, and went cautiously into the brush.

The sound of steady slaps guided him to a clearing. A man's hands were tied to a limb above his head. He was stripped to the waist. Sergeant Malone was applying the whip. Captain Doyle was counting the lashes. The other man was holding the soldier's shirt. There was no sound coming from the man being whipped, although Buck knew well the agony he was suffering. This sort of punishment was dished out regularly by the brutal guards at Yuma Prison. Buck had been on the receiving end of the lash enough to know that Sergeant Malone was not applying the whip enthusiastically. Yet each lash seemed to break across the clearing like the snapping of a branch. When the captain's count passed fifteen, Buck knew the count would go to twenty. He waited.

The count reached twenty, and the captain reached up to cut the man down. The sergeant sprang to catch him, and they lowered him gently to the ground.

"Careful," the captain cautioned. "Let's get him on his horse, belly down, and take him to my quarters."

Buck was back in his bedroll when the men returned to the fort.

Thirteen

May 2.

We left Fort McKavett at daybreak. All the women, with the exception of those in the three wagons that joined us two days ago, are in britches as Mr. Steele ordered at the beginning of the trip. Captain Doyle and his company of men are escorting us as far as Fort Stockton. When we stopped for nooning, Sergeant Malone asked if one of his men could rest for a while in the back of our wagon. His back was injured, and he was having trouble staying in the saddle. He was a very young soldier and was grateful to be lying down. We crossed over a trail today that was mostly sandy and covered with wild sage. Tonight we are camped again beside the San Saba River.

Tucker sat with her feet toward the small fire she had built, not because the evening was cool, but because Billy had brought the firewood and she felt she needed the light to push back the darkness. It had not been an enjoyable day. They were traveling on the fringe of the rolling foothills, and at times they passed over naked rock or plains barren of any growth. The trail was sandy, and the wind, hot and constant, burned her face as her mind grappled with the events of two nights before.

In the light of day it had seemed as if none of it had happened. She and Laura had spent their free day with Lottie and Mrs. Shaffer. When the women went to the river to wash, Tucker had made sure she and Laura were in the midst of them. She had not seen Frank except from a distance, and today he had ridden beside the last wagon in line. She dreaded the day it would be their turn to take up position at the end of the train.

The puppy could not have come at a more opportune time. It kept Laura occupied for most of the day, so she didn't intrude on Tucker's reveries, which consisted of trying to figure out what to do about Frank Parcher. She considered telling Lucas, but immediately discarded the idea. She knew that if Lucas or Buck or anyone else began to act in the least bit suspiciously or tried to call Parcher out, Frank would follow up on his threats. He could get away at the first whiff of danger and strike at any time along the trail. And she was sure Frank would kill not only Lucas, but Laura and Billy, too. She couldn't let that happen! It seemed hopeless. Unless. . . . New resolve began to glimmer in the back of Tucker's mind. Perhaps she should start thinking about eliminating Parcher herself. . . .

"What should I name him, Tucker?"

With great effort, Tucker brought her mind back to the present, and to Laura sitting across the campfire from her with the dog in her lap.

"I thought you'd decided on Browny."

"I don't want to call him Browny just because he's a brown dog. I want to call him something special."

"Well, what do you think is special?"

"I can remember seeing blue sky and blue flowers. I'm sure they're the ones you call prairie bluebells. But I can't call a boy dog Bluebell!" She giggled happily. "But I could call him Blue. What do you think of that name, Tucker? I can call him Blue. Here, Blue! Here, Blue!" She tried out the name for sound.

"Sounds good to me. I don't think you'll find another brown dog named Blue." Tucker was making a show of humor for Laura even while her thoughts were grim.

Oh, Laura, Laura. What will become of you if I have to leave you? The words battered against Tucker's troubled brain. Who would take on the burden of caring for a blind girl? Buck is the only man she's ever spent any time with, Tucker thought wretchedly. He's enjoying her company now, but what if that pleasure palls when the novelty of the experience wears off? There's Lottie; she isn't likely to be snapped up quickly in the rush for brides in Coopertown. But Lottie will have all she can do to take care of herself. What if Laura had been right? What if the convent were the final step? Tucker groaned inwardly. Let something happen, God, please let something happen to stop that evil, disgusting Frank Parcher.

While she sat wishing for divine intervention, Lucas and Buck appeared from between the wagons. After lifting his hand to his hat brim in greeting, Buck went to squat on his heels beside Laura, his fingers reaching out to fondle the ears of the pup. Tucker's eyes clung to the steely gray eyes Lucas focused on her face. She got to her feet and without a word went to the end of the wagon and around to the other side. Lucas followed.

In the darkness they melted into each other's arms. She clung to him as if she were drowning. He felt so good! He held her close, and she nestled her head against his shoulder.

"I've missed you," she breathed, gripping him tighter. She wanted to hold on to him, make sure he was real.

"What's the matter, sweetheart? You're shaking."

She raised her head and laughed a little. "I'm glad to see you, that's all."

He put his cheek to hers. "Your face is hot. Did you wear your hat today?"

"The wind kept blowing it off." Say something she thought. Say something that will keep him with you for a while. "I came looking for you the first night we were at the fort. You were with the captain. Lucas, it's just been an awful day!" Immediately she hated herself for complaining.

He kissed her, his lips lingering hungrily on hers.

"Today was just a sample of the trail ahead, sweetheart. You'll get toughened to it."

"It wasn't that! It's just that . . . I'm worried about Laura." He stopped her words with gentle kisses.

"You worry too much about Laura. Why not worry about me and how much I want to be with you and how I find every excuse to ride back so I can get a glimpse of this bright fiery hair." His hands moved up her back to fondle her tumbling curls and she found herself silently praying, Oh, God, don't let anything happen to him.

"I do worry about you, Lucas. Be careful, darling. Please be careful!"

He pulled away from her and tried to look into the face she kept hidden against his shirt. "What brought this on?" He gave a small laugh. "I won't say I don't like it, though. It's been years since anyone's worried about me."

"I don't like that scout from the other train," she blurted out, and then wished desperately that she hadn't.

"Don't worry about him. If he so much as looks at you, I'll horsewhip him." He hugged her to him with infinite tenderness. "He hasn't bothered you, has he?" he asked, suddenly wary.

"No," she said hastily. "I just don't like him."

"I'm watching him. So are Buck and Captain Doyle. If he rides up to your wagon, we'll know it. Now what did you mean about being worried about Laura?"

She hesitated. This really wasn't the time she

wanted to bring it up, but as long as she'd already done so she would have to follow through.

"It's her and Buck." She leaned into him, grateful for his strong arms. "Laura has never been alone with a man before. She's so happy now, but I feel it can't last. I'm afraid for her. I'm afraid her heart will be broken."

"What you're saying is that you think Buck will use her and cast her off, isn't it? I've known Buck for a long time. He'll not hurt Laura. If I had thought there was even a chance of it, I would have put a stop to his walking out with her. Buck is a lonely man, but he's a fine one. I'd bet my life that he'd give his own before he'd see any harm come to Laura. So, my little worrier, you can forget about them and worry about me."

"Oh, Lucas, I love you. I love you so much!" She whispered the words and sought his lips with her eager ones.

The kiss lasted a long time while his hands molded her curves to his angular frame. She could feel his powerful body tremble, and she was achingly aware that he wanted her in the same way she wanted him.

"I've dreamed of hearing you say that for years," he said huskily. "Someday I'll show you why."

"How about now?" She nibbled on his ear, then nipped it playfully.

"I'd rather do this." He kissed her hard. It was such a luxury to hold her. It had been days since he'd held her, felt her. As she melted into the kiss, he suddenly pinched her bottom in retaliation for her nips.

"Why, you . . . you . . . you'd better watch out or . . . I'll give you a black eye!" she threatened in the face of his chuckles. All her fears had fled to the back of her mind. This was now. She would store up all this to last until she could be with him again. "I wish there were some place we could go to be alone." How brazen she had become! Had she really said that? She concealed her face against his shirt.

"Don't be embarrassed, sweetheart. I want it, too." He smiled at her sheepishly. "I find it hard to think of anything else."

"Oh, you!" she said, her eyes like twin stars shining up at him. "We can wait, Lucas. Come to me when you can."

"I'm learning things about my Tucker Red. She *can* be sensible when she wants to be." He kissed her nose. "I don't care if every single person on this train knows that you belong to me, I still can't court you like I want to. Your safety and that of the other women has to be my main concern right now. But after we get to California, we'll have a lifetime to be together." With one finger beneath her chin he lifted her face so he could look into her eyes. "I'm paying your way, and Laura's, to California, because when we get there you're not teaching anybody's kids but ours." Even in the darkness he could see her eyes brimming with tears. "You've carried the load for the two of you long enough. It's my turn now."

"What can I say?" she whispered shakily.

"Say the thing I most want to hear," he prompted

gently, and his thumbs wiped the tears from her cheeks.

"I love you. Love you."

"That's my Tucker Red. Now don't bite me and ruin it all," he teased.

She laughed softly and snapped her teeth at him. "You're crazier than a drunk hoot owl!"

"Maybe so, woman. But stand still and let me kiss you. There may be a long dry spell before I can do it again."

Buck's observant eyes saw Tucker's shoes and Lucas's dusty boots move close together when he glanced beneath the wagon. Seconds later they had moved away into the darkness. He had known for some time that Lucas was in love with the teacher. He was glad for his friend. Lucas had been lonely.

It bothered Buck that the girl he had given his own heart to was not aware, not really anyway, of the difference between a white man and a breed. How would she feel if she ever regained her sight and saw for herself why he wasn't considered a white man? He watched Laura with the pup. Would she turn from him in disgust? He refused to think about it and reached out a hand to squeeze hers while pretending to pet the dog.

"A soldier rode in our wagon this afternoon. Sergeant Malone asked if he could. Tucker said he lay on his stomach. Blue curled up beside him."

"I knew about it. I told the sergeant you wouldn't mind. The boy was feeling poorly. I've made a collar for Blue," he said, trying to change the conversation before she started asking questions about the soldier. "It'll fit for a while, then I'll have to make him another one. I fixed a thin strip of hide, too, so you can tie him to the wagon when you let him out. That rope you used today would hold a mule."

Laura laughed. "It was all Tucker could find." The smile left her face. "Tucker's been awful moody lately. I think she's worried about you and me, Buck."

"Has she said so?"

"No, but I can tell. Tucker doesn't have to say anything. We've been together so long I can tell by the sound of her voice when she mentions your name. Don't be mad at her, Buck. She cares about me, so she looks after me like a mother hen. We've had only each other most of our lives."

Buck watched her face in the flickering firelight. Always the corners of her lips were tilted in a smile. Her face had the peaceful, happy look he had seen on a statue of the Madonna in a mission in California. He didn't know what to say, so he said nothing and somehow he knew she understood.

Laura reached out her hand and miraculously found his. "But we know, don't we, Buck? We know that Tucker has nothing to worry about. I'll tell her tomorrow."

"Do you want me to tell her?" He gripped her hand tightly.

"No. I'm a grown woman now. It's time Tucker felt free to turn loose of me and find a husband and have children of her own."

"She may have found him already."

"I know. She's in love with Lucas."

"He's a good man. Best I know."

"Tucker deserves to be happy."

"And you, *mi querida*?"

"I will be," she said firmly. "Blue. Blue, where are you?" She tugged on the leash and the pup came bounding into her lap.

May 3.

This afternoon we entered a wide valley that stretched for miles. On each side of us lay rolling hills topped with glossy evergreen and skirted with oak and mesquite. A herd of tawny antelope darted out of the tall grass and headed for the trees at our approach. It was a breathtaking sight, one that was hard for me to describe to Laura. Flowers of every color grew everywhere: paintbrush, bluebonnet, buttercup, and dandelion. It is hard to believe a day's journey could take us out of the barren plains and into this beautiful valley. But it was easy to see how the change in surroundings lightened the hearts of all the travelers after bearing up, without complaint, under the constant hot winds, parching sun, and unbroken glare of the dusty trail. This is a vast and lush land, full of surprises.

May 4.

This day went more quickly than most. We passed the mouths of narrow valleys, or canyons as Mr. Steele calls them. The farther west we go, the more dry draws we cross, none of them marked on the map. We seldom see homesteaders, but judging from the obvious signs, there are large herds of cattle. Game is also plentiful. Almost every night Mustang cooks an antelope. The meat keeps better when cooked and gives a good smoked flavor to beans and stew.

May 5.

Although this is the last night out before we reach Fort Lancaster, the wagons are drawn into a tight circle and a heavy guard is posted. Some of the women finally complained about the sameness of the food and wanted to go berrying and looking for dandelion greens, but Mr. Steele would not permit it. We were told to stay within the circle of wagons. He promised we will have a chance to bathe and wash clothes when we reach the fort.

Tucker put the journal into the trunk and blew out the candle. She was tired. The journey was proving to be more of a trial than she had expected. She was pleased that Laura was taking it so well; but for herself, her body was aching as well as her heart. The daylong jolting on the wagon seat and the continual strain on her arms as she drove the sometimes stubborn mules brought a constant soreness to her shoulders and back. She propped herself up against her trunk and surrendered herself to her weariness for a quiet moment.

Laura walked with the pup almost every evening now. As she made her way around the inside circle of the wagons, there was always someone to call out directions to her. She had become acquainted with Rafe Blanchet and the Taylors. She talked with Rafe about the mother of the pup, and while visiting with Mrs. Taylor had been offered a drink from a real glass.

"It was so thin," she'd giggled later, "I was afraid I'd bite a hunk out of it."

At first Tucker had tried to discourage Laura from taking these nightly jaunts, because she feared Frank Parcher might threaten or harm her in the way of a warning to Tucker. But after watching her a few times, she'd discovered that if Buck was not near by, Mustang, young Chata, and even the women—all fond of Laura—were watching out for her. So, knowing she needn't worry about her for at least an hour, Tucker leaned back and relaxed.

She dozed, but soon awoke with a start. The end canvas on the wagon had opened a crack and someone had slipped inside. The extra weight rocked the wagon and alerted her. Instant alarm brought her to her feet. Before she reached her full height, the man bore down upon her, knocking the wind out of her and crushing her against the boxes stacked along the side of the wagon bed.

"Ain't goin' to let out a peep now, are ya?" His hand was over her mouth. Stunned from striking her head against one of the crates, Tucker tried to focus her eyes. Her ears were ringing and her heart raced with terror. Her breath returning, she started to struggle trying to free herself, but he easily kept her pinned to the floor of the wagon. His hand moved a fraction, and she opened her mouth to scream. The sound that came from her throat was more like a grunt when it was cut off by a hand clamping down over her nose as well as her mouth. Just when she thought her lungs would burst, he brought his face close to hers and released her nose so she could breathe. She tried to turn away from his rank beneath.

"There'll be a time when ya can holler all ya want, purty gal. I like 'em to fight. But ya keep still now or I'll hafta squeeze the life outta ya." One hand fastened on her throat to demonstrate. "Hear?"

Almost faint with fear, Tucker nodded. He took his hand from her mouth.

"Get out of here!" she gasped hoarsely. "Lucas will come—"

"No he won't. He's helping round up some mules what got out—accidental-like." He was straddling her body, and he leaned his head closer to hers. Had she not been so frightened, the smell of him would have made her sick. "I ain't no fool, purty gal. I been a watchin'. When the blind gal walks the pup, the scout and ever'body else is busy watchin' that she don't walk into a fire or nothin'. They ain't a payin' no nevermind to you." One hand remained at her throat and the other began to roam her breasts.

Tucker stared at him with utter loathing, hating

him with every fiber of her being. Somehow the feeling of hate gave her strength.

"They'll kill you if they catch you here," she managed through bruised vocal chords.

"Worryin' 'bout me? I come to make sure ya knowed ya was my woman. I ain't a wantin' ya to fergit what I tol' ya down by the corral."

"I remember every word you said, you . . . varmint! You better know that I'll put a knife into your guts and twist it the first chance I get."

To her amazement he laughed. "I knowed ya was the woman fer me."

"I'll die first!"

"No, ya won't. You'll fight ever' step of the way. I got to be a leavin' ya, sweetie. But first I want me a little kiss."

As soon as his mouth was near enough, she sank her teeth into his lip with all her strength. He grabbed her hair and twisted until she let go. Before she could scream, he clamped his free hand over her mouth, snapping her head back against the floorboards. Excruciating pain shot through her neck. She could feel his hot breath on her face.

"So we's goin' to do us a little bitin', is we?" he muttered through gritted teeth. "I can do some of that, too, if'n I've a mind to." His big hand left her hair and plunged toward one of her nipples. His fingers closed over the tender flesh and he rasped, "How'd ya like fer me to bite one o' these purty little things?"

She tried to struggle, tried to kick him. His fingers and thumb found her jaws and he attacked her mouth with brutal kisses, all the while holding her so tightly she thought her bones would break. Her struggles were futile; his hold on her merely tightened. He finally lifted his head, and Tucker vaguely heard his dry laugh. She fought to keep the bile from rising up in her throat.

"Ya'll be the best little bit o' tail I ever had, purty gal." Tucker was so dazed by his attack she could hardly hear his words. "I'm a goin' ta leave, but you listen up good. If'n ya don't behave yoreself, that little gal'll die . . . slow like. It'd be right easy, Tucker gal, even easier 'n shootin' 'er. A mean rattler and a long stick is all I'd need. I'd flip that rattler in her lap while she's a sittin' with that pup, and she'd swell up like a toad and scream herself to death. Ain't purty. I seed it once or twice."

"You're not even human!" Tucker moaned.

" 'Nother thing! If'n I get to thinkin' you've blabbed to Steele, I'll just fade off fer a bit 'n they'll have a helluva time tryin' to track me. If'n that happens, remember, it'll be Steele first, then that boy what brings ya firewood, 'n then the blind gal. Then it'd be jist you 'n me, purty woman."

"Get out of here! You turn my stomach!" Tucker was surprised she was even able to speak.

"I'm a goin', but I'll be a watchin'," he whispered.

She didn't realize she'd been holding her breath until she let it out. When he was gone, she almost fainted with relief. She sat up, straightened her clothes, and pushed the hair back from her face. Her stomach churned as if she was about to be sick. She grabbed the towel she had used earlier to wash off the trail dust and used it now to try to wipe away her memories of this encounter.

After a while she slipped on a clean shift, spread out her bedroll, and lay down. With mounting distress she silently acknowledged that there was no place where she was safe from him. She could never be alone again unless she could do something about it. Too angry to give in to tears, but too rattled to sleep, she lay wide-eyed, thinking about what to do and listening for Laura to return to the wagon.

Fourteen

May 6.

The wagon train reached Fort Lancaster an hour past noon today. The fort was built around a large rectangular parade ground surrounded by twenty-five buildings that house two companies of soldiers. Located on Live Oak Creek a half mile above its junction with the Pecos River, the fort was established in 1855 to protect travelers on the San Antonio–El Paso Trail.

Sergeant Malone came by to thank Tucker and Laura for allowing Private Dabney to ride in their wagon. He lingered, telling them he'd been stationed at the fort in '55 when it was first built.

"Back then Comanches were meaner than steers with crooked horns. I'll be a tellin' you that for a fact. They had themselves a real love of hangin' pretty hair from their belts, ma'am. They'd a been after that red hair of yours like flies on a fresh cow pie, and the good Lord help anythin' that got in the way."

"That's comforting to know," Tucker said drily.

Sergeant Malone regretted his casual words and cursed himself for a fool. He tried to repair the damage in his poetic Irish way. "Smile fer me, me beauties, and forget the blatherin' tongue of a foolish old Irishman. You be truly the one thing of beauty in all this barren land. There'd not be a rose in all Killarney that'd match your smile. I be a tellin' the truth, now."

It was impossible not to laugh.

"And there'd not be another man in all Ireland who'd be needin' to kiss the Blarney stone more than yourself, Sergeant Malone." Tucker matched his accent perfectly.

The old sergeant's weathered face creased in a smile, and he slapped his dusty hat against his leg. "It takes a true Irishman to know when he's bested. Good day to you, lassies." The smile was still dancing in his eyes when he left them.

The train had come to a halt beside the creek and was stretched out between it and the fort. The women had the rest of the day to do their washing and to bathe in the clear shallow water. Tucker's and Laura's wagon was in position behind the grub wagon, which meant they would be last in line when the train pulled out again. Tucker's mind was working overtime trying to invent a logical excuse to keep from being near the Collins's wagon and Frank.

"I can hardly wait to get down to the creek, Tucker. Can we go now?" Laura prodded.

A heavy sadness crept into Tucker's heart. Laura

was so bubbly, so happy, and she herself had never been more miserable in her entire life.

"Let's see when Lottie is going and we'll go with her."

"We can go alone, Tucker. Buck said as long as we stay near the wagons we'll be all right."

"I still think we should go with someone. Oh, there's Mrs. Hook and Billy. Are you going down to the creek?" she called.

"Yes. Would you and Laura like to go with us? Lottie and Mrs. Shaffer will be down later," Marie Hook answered.

Relief was a tangible thing in Tucker's breast.

The creek bank was steep and lined with timber. Tucker climbed down with the dirty clothes and came back up the bank to help Laura.

"Go down backward on your hands and knees like you used to go down stairs when you were little. I'll stay below and guide your feet."

The water was clear and flowed over a bed of smooth pebbles. Billy waded out into the middle, sat down, and called to Laura. "Come out here and sit on the rocks. It's a good place to wash your hair, Laura."

Marie looked at Tucker, who nodded approval. "Come get her, Billy," she called.

Under Billy's solicitous guidance, Laura, with her britches rolled up to her knees, waded into the flowing stream.

"What caused her blindness?" Marie asked. The washing was done and spread on the bushes to dry. Tucker was rubbing her wet hair with a bar of soap.

"I don't know. She was six when she came to the farm. She had bruises all over her face and head. I think a terrible beating caused it, because she hadn't been blind for long."

"A blow to the head more than likely," Marie said almost to herself. "Has a doctor looked at her eyes?"

"Yes, but he was an old drunk and I don't think he knew any more about it than I did."

Tucker had lowered her head into the stream to rinse the suds from her hair and failed to see the pained expression on Marie's face.

"We're going over to the grassy spot, Mama," Billy called, pointing to the opposite bank. "I'm going to pick some of them flowers for Laura."

"*Those* flowers, Billy," Marie corrected. "Stay in sight. Don't go wandering off into the brush."

The ground on the other side of the creek was thickly carpeted with green grass and strewn with bright yellow dandelions. Laura, her hand on Billy's shoulder, waded out of the creek, her britches wet and her hair hanging to her waist in wet strings. Tucker, instantly nervous and alert, looked around. There wasn't another person in sight. She saw Marie's calm face and relaxed. The only sounds to be heard were the gurgling of the water as it splashed over the rocks and the happy voices of Billy and Laura.

The afternoon wore on, and more of the women came to wash. Marie and Tucker sat in companionable silence, drying their hair in the sun and watching the two in the meadow across the stream.

Tucker didn't see the wild, moss-horned bull when he broke from a clump of mesquite, but Marie did.

"Billy!" she screamed.

The huge longhorn trotted out into the meadow, stopped, then pawed the ground several times. The first thing Tucker noticed was the sun glinting off the tips of wide, sharp horns. The beast rolled its head and sniffed the breeze while white foam dripped from the corners of its mouth. Marie knew instantly that the bull had gone mad and was going to attack. Billy and Laura were a good fifty feet apart, Laura being closer to the bull. Frantically she waded out into the stream.

"Laura! Laura! Run! A bull! Run!"

It could have been the screams of the women as they realized what was happening, or just confusion because she couldn't determine where the command was coming from, but Laura started running in the opposite direction, toward the brush. She stumbled, fell, then got to her feet again.

"Tucker!" she wailed.

"Stop! Laura, stop! You're going the wrong way!" Tucker shouted.

"Tucker!" The plaintive cry came again.

Billy turned and, without a moment's hesitation, raced toward Laura. The bull, surprised to see so much movement, made three complete turns and braced its legs.

"Stand still, boy!" The order came harsh and loud.

Rafe Blanchet ran out of the stream from behind the bull. His pant legs were rolled to his knees, and he was shirtless. He waved a wet blue shirt above his head to attract the animal's attention. He darted past the bull and took up a position between it and Laura.

"Don't run, girl! Let me draw him away first, then you get her, boy, and hightail it across the creek."

Rafe kept on waving the shirt. "Yaw! Yaw!" he shouted. The blood red eyes of the bull followed his movements. Rafe danced to the right, holding the shirt in front of him like a cape, while shouting over his shoulder: "Move slowly, boy. Get the girl. When I get the beast turned, run for the creek."

Tucker's terrified eyes went from the half-naked man to the bull to Laura and Billy. The bull was charging now, quickly closing the distance between itself and the man. Rafe had moved in a wide circle, and Billy had reached Laura. With hooves pounding, its horns held low, the bull raced toward Rafe and hooked into the space where he had been just seconds before but had vacated as he leaped to the side. One of the bull's horns pierced the blue fabric as the animal reared its head, and the shirt was torn free from Rafe's grasp. The bull plunged on, turned, then stood shaking its head as if to clear its vision. The shirt hung down beside one ear, drool hung from its mouth in strings.

Rafe clapped his hands and shouted, trying to turn the creature once again. Tucker raced into the creek and grabbed Laura's arm, and she and Billy splashed through the water with Laura between them. Rafe hadn't dared to take his eyes from the bull and didn't know when Billy and Laura left the meadow.

"Yaw!" he shouted at the animal and clapped his hands. "You're an ugly brute!"

As if maddened by the insults, the bull lowered its head and charged again, missing Rafe's midsection by mere inches. Rafe turned and could see the boy and the girl scrambling up the opposite bank. Only the two women were standing in the creek.

"Run," he shouted while clapping his hands. "He'll turn your way if he takes a notion."

Tucker looked frantically around for a way to help. Her eyes found a man on a horse a short way downstream. His forearm was resting on the horn of his saddle as he sat calmly watching the scene. Frank Parcher!

"Help him," she shouted even as the bull charged again.

Rafe waited until the last minute before springing to one side, but a dagger-tipped horn pierced his pant leg and tore a gaping hole in his upper thigh. There was an instantaneous burst of pain, and he lost his balance and fell. Sensing that it had downed its foe, the bull whirled, then lowered its head to charge again. Rafe staggered to his feet, his leg almost collapsing under him, and waited. He knew he couldn't run, but he might be able to outmaneuver the beast, who was becoming madder with each passing second.

Tucker darted a glance at Frank. He hadn't moved. His eyes were riveted to what was happening across the creek. He hadn't made any attempt to take his rifle from its sheath.

When the bull charged, Rafe attempted to jump to

one side again, but he was hooked in the side by the sharp tip of the long horn and crumpled to the ground. Horrified, Tucker watched the bull approach, heard it snort. Rafe lay in an inert mass among the flowers. It wasn't possible that all this had taken place in but a matter of minutes; it seemed to Tucker the agony of suspense had been going on for hours.

The bull shook its head from side to side, and the blue shirt, still hanging from its horn, waved back and forth. It pawed the ground as it prepared to attack. Tucker sprang into action, yelling and screaming and waving her hands, trying to attract its attention, but its dazed red eyes saw only the body on the grass.

Vaguely Tucker registered the sharp crack of a shot being fired. The bull staggered, the momentum of its charge halted. The animal fell to its knees. Another shot was fired, and she glanced toward Frank. He still sat as unconcerned as before. She spun around to see Lucas standing on the creek bank, his rifle at his shoulder as he waited to see if the animal required another bullet to bring it down. The bull, its right horn buried in the ground, the shirt draped over its head, twitched its tail several times and flailed its legs helplessly before its frame shuddered and lay still.

Tucker was gulping in huge breaths of air as she started running toward the downed man, Marie beside her. They were halted by Lucas's sharp command.

"Wait!" He sprang down the bank and waded across the creek. Cautiously he approached the bull.

Tucker glared with hate-filled eyes toward the

place where Frank had sat and watched so uncaringly as the bull attacked. He had vanished from sight.

Lucas stood his rifle against the dead beast and knelt beside Rafe. Tucker and Marie reached him almost at the same time. Lucas turned the man over on his back. Marie fell to her knees and her hands began, immediately, to search for his wounds.

"Give me your knife," she said to Lucas without looking up. "We've got to stop the bleeding."

"You can use his shirt." Tucker started toward the dead bull.

"No! Don't touch it," Marie said sharply. "We can't risk getting any of that foam in the wound. I suspect the bull's got the crazy sickness." She took the knife from Lucas. "Go over and get that clean shirt of Billy's off the bush. The white one." Her orders were brisk. Tucker took off on a run to obey.

People were coming down from the fort. Tucker snatched the shirt from the bush, then called out to Mustang. "He's hurt bad. Bring something to carry him on."

Rafe was taken back to his wagon on a canvas litter. Marie had bound his wounds temporarily, but by the time they reached the wagon, Billy's shirt was stained a bright red. They lowered the tailgate and lifted Rafe up to willing hands that placed him on his bunk. Tucker and Marie stood together at the end of the wagon.

"We'll take care of him now, ma'am," Mustang said.

"No. I'll tend him." This came from Marie, politely but firmly.

"Ain't no call fer ya ta have ta do it. I been tendin' hurt critters since afore the Alamo."

"Mama." Billy tugged on his mother's hand.

"Go get my bag, Billy, and that pillowcase full of clean cloth." She looked straight into Mustang's eyes when she spoke.

"I already got it, Mama. The bandages, too." Billy held out a black bag, and Marie took it from his hand. "My mama was the best doctor in all Tennessee, Mister Mustang. If anybody can fix Mister Blanchet, she can."

Mustang's mouth moved as if he was going to say something, but no words came out. Tucker turned startled green eyes toward Marie. With the bag in her hand she was already climbing into the wagon.

"I'll need Billy. He knows what to do. But I'll need someone to help me lift Mr. Blanchet. Will you help me, Mr. Mustang? I'll need whiskey to wash the wound and, Tucker, will you ask Lottie to set some water to boil? And, Mr. Steele, any animal that eats on that carcass out there will surely go mad. I suggest that it be buried and rocks piled on the grave so it can't be dug up. And, oh, yes, tell the men not to touch it with their hands and to bury Mr. Blanchet's shirt with it." The orders were given so calmly and with such confidence that no one even thought about questioning her right to give them.

Laura, frightened and shaking, was standing

beside their wagon. Mrs. Shaffer and Betsy were with her.

"Are you all right, Laura?"

"I think so. Lottie went to get my shoes and our other things. Dora says Mr. Blanchet is hurt real bad. She says that Billy said his mother was a doctor and that she can help him. Can that be true, Tucker? I've never heard of a woman doctor."

"I've not heard of it either, but she seems to know what she's doing. Here's Lottie. They need hot water, Lottie. And Mustang said there's a jug of whiskey in the grub wagon."

"Thar's more than one jug," Lottie replied disgustedly. "I'll fetch it and we'll git water to boilin' and supper a cookin'. Tell that mangy old coyote he ain't to worry 'bout this end."

"Laura!" Buck came galloping toward them, his eyes on Laura who stood shaking and disheveled, her hands gripping the wheel of the wagon. Her hair, still wet, hung in golden strands with bits of grass and twigs clinging to it. She had rolled her wet britches down to cover her legs, but her feet were scratched and bleeding from the scramble up the steep bank. "Laura!"

Tucker thought she had never heard such anguish in a man's voice.

Buck jumped from the saddle and went to Laura. He took her by the shoulders and drew her to him. "Are you hurt, *mi amor*?"

"Buck! Oh, Buck, I was so scared!" Laura put her arms around him and clung to him tightly.

The eyes of everyone in the camp were watching as Buck held her close and whispered to her, his mouth close to her ear. A feeling of aloneness swept over Tucker. For the first time since she had known Laura, she had turned to someone else for comfort. Tucker's eyes swept the crowd. Some of the women had wistful looks on their faces, others wore broad smiles. Buck seemed not to care a whit that they were attracting attention. He reached around and let down the tailgate, then lifted Laura in his arms and sat her on the end of it. He bent down and took her feet in his hands.

"Madre de Dios!" he swore.

"I'll bring ya over some water, Buck," Lottie said. She handed Tucker a brown clay jug with a cork stopper in the top, and waved her on. "Ya better be gittin' back with this. Buck'll look after Laura."

As Tucker passed the Collins wagon, she looked over and saw Frank Parcher lounging against the side of it. Anger such as she had never known consumed her. She was carrying the jug, her finger in the small loop on the side, and she was tempted to smash it in his face. She slowed her steps but swung away a bit so she would not have to get too close to him.

"You didn't even attempt to help him! You . . . polecat! You're lower than a snake's belly," she hissed at him.

He grinned. "Why should I have? He warn't worth wastin' a bullet on. Now, me . . . I was jist a watchin' to see that nothin' happened to my woman."

"You're an animal!" Her green cat eyes sparkled

with rage toward this man who had made her life a living hell since the night he had come out of the darkness and grabbed her at Fort McKavett. With nostrils flared and her back rigid, she moved on. The soft laughter that trailed her made her want to turn and kill him.

The sun went down. Quiet settled over the camp. After the evening meal everyone gathered in small groups and talked about Laura's and Billy's escape from the mad bull and of Rafe Blanchet's bravery. Even the Taylors came up to the big fire to visit. Alice Taylor, a woman more liberal in her thinking than the others, was the least surprised to discover a woman doctor in their midst.

Tucker sat beside the cook wagon with the others. She refused to make the trip to the Blanchet wagon after dark and asked Dora Shaffer to take plates of food to Marie and Billy.

Buck bathed Laura's sore feet, and she put on the clean stockings Lottie brought to her. He picked the grass and twigs from her hair and fetched her hair brush. After the initial shock of seeing him do these intimate things, the women kept their distance and averted their eyes. When darkness came, he spread a patchwork quilt beneath a tree and carried her to it, setting her down so she could rest her back against the tree trunk.

"Is it dark, Buck?"

"*Sí.* It is dark."

"Then kiss me one time."

"One time? I could kiss you a million times, *mi*

bonita querida!" He said it in Spanish and repeated it in English. "My beautiful beloved."

Tears welled and glistened brightly on her lashes. Her heart skipped a beat. She thought she would choke with the effort of holding back the sobs in her throat.

"Don't, Buck. Please, don't."

"Don't what, beloved? Don't say that I love you and that I'll spend my life keeping you safe? I'll shout it if it will convince you that I mean what I say. Everyone knows after today that I love you. It's up to you, now, whether or not you accept me."

"I can't let you do it! I can't let you spend your life leading me around by the hand. You deserve more. Much more than a blind girl can give you."

He put his fingers lightly on her mouth and then ran them across her cheek and circled her ear. His hand cupped the back of her head, and he pulled her firmly against him.

"It's you who deserves more, Laura. You don't know what it means to be a breed. It means I'm not considered white by lots of people. And as my wife you won't be accepted either."

"That's so unfair! I don't care if you have Indian blood. I want nothing more than to be with you. But I can't help but worry that I'll be a . . . burden."

"I want you just as you are. You'll never be anything less than my love, the one person in the world I want to spend my life with." He inhaled deeply and let the air escape slowly from his lips. "I feel like I've been to hell and that this is heaven. I can't lose you!"

"I don't understand. Why did you choose me?" The thought in her head was transformed into words that came out of her mouth before she realized she was saying them.

"Believe me, *querida*, you are lovely! Not only your face, but your spirit as well. I'll be the luckiest man in the world if you accept me." He hugged her close and buried his lips in her hair.

Laura laughed with sheer exaltation. "Oh, I accept you, darling Buck!"

It was all Buck could do to hold in check the urges that flooded him and to keep himself from crushing her to him. Her face seemed to glow with her happiness, and her lips, sweet and softly parted, reached for his. His kiss was gentle, reverent, as though she were something infinitely precious. Her arms wound around his neck, and she snuggled against him. A whisper of a sigh escaped her as she leaned her head on his shoulder.

Lucas climbed into the neatly arranged Blanchet wagon. A lighted lantern swung from the crossbow as his weight on the heavy springs tilted the wagon bed. Marie had bedded Billy down on a pallet. She sat on a camp chair beside the bunk.

"How is he, Mrs. Hook?"

"I don't know, Mr. Steele. I don't believe he will die from his wounds. If he dies, it will be from something else."

Lucas didn't say anything, but looked at her

strangely. The silence dragged on, and finally he said, "I've never heard of a woman doctor."

Her face tightened. "No? Do you think we are not intelligent enough to be doctors, Mr. Steele?"

"I didn't say that. It just seems an unusual profession for a woman."

"You're not alone in your thinking." Marie looked down at the quiet face of the man on the bunk. "But I couldn't refuse to do my best to save Mr. Blanchet after what he did today."

"I see."

"No, you don't see." Her dark eyes flashed angrily. "You can't possibly begin to understand the prejudices against a woman who tries to do what is considered man's work. I was schooled in Scotland, married there, and my husband and I came back to America so I could help my fellow countrymen. We went to Ohio; the people refused to accept me. So we went to Tennessee. There was even more prejudice there. A pregnant woman died, and I managed to take the living child from her womb. Even though I saved the life of the child, they set fire to my house and killed my husband. Of course he was dead drunk at the time. A doctor himself, it gnawed at him that his wife was more capable than he was." Her spirited tone changed to one of resignation. "I'll not set up another practice in California, Mr. Steele, if that's what's bothering you. I'll marry a farmer and be a good wife to him as long as he makes a home for Billy." Her calm voice was back and her clear eyes looked directly into his.

"My job is to see that you get to California, Mrs. Hook. What you do when you get there has nothing to do with me. We move out tomorrow. Do you think we should leave Blanchet here at the fort?"

"No," she said quickly. "Don't leave him. Billy and I will stay with him and drive his wagon."

"One of the drovers can drive a wagon for a few days, but if it takes longer than that for him to recover, we'll have to leave him. I can't spare a drover after the army leaves us at Fort Stockton."

"Cora Lee can drive our wagon," Marie said stubbornly. "Billy and I will stay with Mr. Blanchet."

"You have no obligation to do any more for him than you have, Mrs. Hook."

"Oh, but I have. I won't know for ten to twelve days if Mr. Blanchet got the crazy sickness from the animal. If any of the saliva, the foam the animal was spewing, got into his wounds, he will surely go mad and we will have to . . . shoot him." Lucas's face registered his surprise. "It's true. We'd have to shoot him, or leave him chained to a tree to scream his life away. I couldn't do that to him after what he did for Billy and Laura."

"And there's a chance this will happen?"

"There is the chance. His wounds were bleeding profusely though, so I'm hopeful for his full recovery, but I refuse to leave him here where he would be in unsympathetic hands. Besides, I doubt if there is anyone here who is familiar with the disease."

"We'll do whatever you suggest. Do you want someone to ride with you?"

"No. Billy and I will be all right. I'd rather the others remained unaware of this waiting period."

"All right. Would you like for me to sit with him while you go for some of your things?"

"Thank you. I do need to get some of our belongings. I won't be long."

Marie climbed out of the wagon and braced herself to face the women now that they all knew she was one of those mysterious, alien things—a woman doctor. Tucker came to meet her and walked with her toward the cook wagon where it seemed everyone in the camp was waiting.

"How is he, Marie?"

There wasn't a sound while Marie made the announcement. Afterward everyone seemed to talk at once. If Rafe was a hero for saving Laura and Billy, Marie was a heroine for saving Rafe. The acceptance stunned her.

"How is Laura?" Marie asked after she got over her astonishment.

"Humph!" This came from Lottie. "Buck is seein' ta Laura. I suspect we jist might be a havin' us a weddin' afore we get to Californey."

Fifteen

Tucker looked back and saw Fort Lancaster fade into the early morning light. The large orange globe rising over the eastern horizon predicted a day similar to the last two: hot and breezeless. On a small knoll two does stood quietly with a buck at their side. A few morning birds called and flitted in the tall grass, unmindful of the wagons passing down the well-worn trail toward the Pecos River. They ascended a steep hill, then traveled across a prairie that led to the riverbank. This was the only point within miles where the banks were not high and rocky.

The ferry was run by a friendly man of indeterminate age who hid his surprise at finding so many women accompanied by so few men. The wagons were loaded onto the ferry two at a time, lashed down, and a man stood at the head of each team. Tucker and Laura were among the first to cross. Upon disembarking, Tucker drew up the mules and halted the wagon alongside the trail so the other wagons coming off the ferry could pass. She dreaded this day as she had dreaded no other. Alone with Laura near the end of the line with the Collins wagon directly behind her, she knew she would have to suffer Frank's presence before the day was over.

It was just past noon when the train strung out again along the trail. Laura had bombarded her with questions about what was going on and, although she wasn't in the mood to talk, the conversation made the hours pass more quickly. The only time she saw Frank was when she got out of the wagon to get Blue, who was getting his exercise at the end of his leash. Frank was passing, and before she realized who it was she looked up and met his leering stare. He hadn't stopped, and for that she thanked God over and over.

Laura was bursting with excitement. She relived each precious second she had spent with Buck the night before. She longed to include Tucker in her happiness but restrained herself. In the strange, unhappy mood Tucker was in, she might say something Laura didn't want to hear. So she decided to keep the precious secret to herself for just a little longer.

It was midafternoon when Frank rode up beside the wagon. Tucker looked up and there he was. He rode alongside, not saying anything, but staring at her with an intensity that sent a cold chill along her spine. After the first glance, she refused to look at him. And Laura, knowing someone was there, remained silent.

All afternoon Tucker had been careful to keep the heads of the mules as close as possible to the wagon ahead. Ordinarily two or three wagon lengths were maintained between wagons, sometimes as much as two hundred feet if it was dusty. She sat, ramrod stiff, refusing to acknowledge the man riding so close beside the wagon.

She didn't know which realization came first: the fact that Frank's horse had backed off and was no longer beside her, or that Lucas and Buck were riding toward them. Laura's keen ears picked up the sound of the approaching horses.

"Who was that riding beside us? And who's coming now?"

"It was the scout from the other train," Tucker said lightly as if it didn't matter. "And Buck and Lucas are coming this way."

"I hope they stop."

"So do I," Tucker said, and she'd never meant anything as much in her life.

"What are you trying to do, put those mules into Lottie's wagon?" Lucas's words were teasing but so close to the truth that Tucker had a hard time retaining her smile.

Buck maneuvered his horse around to come up beside Laura.

"Come ride with me, Laura. The land is flat and it isn't too hot."

"I'd love to ride on Dolorido. First let me put Blue in his box. When he's not eating, he's sleeping."

Tucker feigned composure so Lucas wouldn't suspect her fear of being left alone. He was watching her closely. Oh, God, she thought. He thinks I don't want Laura to be with Buck! If only I could tell him that I just don't want to be alone back here near that awful man!

"Reckon there's room for me on that seat, teacher? I'll drive the team for a while and give you a rest."

Tucker pulled the team to a halt long enough for Buck to lift Laura from the wagon and seat her across his lap, and for Lucas to tie his mount to the end of the wagon and climb up onto the seat beside her. When they were moving once again Lucas held the reins, and what was otherwise a miserable day was suddenly brighter. He slowed the mules and allowed a distance between them and the wagon ahead. It didn't matter to Tucker now.

"How are you, Tucker Red?"

"Fine."

"Is that all you can say? Fine?"

"Wonderful. Now," she said with her joyful heart shining in her eyes.

"That's my girl." His face broke into a smile and the creases she loved appeared on each side of his mouth. Then he became thoughtful. "You look tired, and you've got dark smudges under your eyes that haven't been there before. Are you sure you're all right?"

"I'm fine. I didn't sleep well last night. You know, after all the excitement of Laura and Billy almost getting killed by the bull, and poor Mr. Blanchet getting hurt, and finding out Marie was a doctor."

"Sure that's all it is? Sure it isn't Laura and Buck?"

Tucker's lips tightened stubbornly, giving her an

air of cool aloofness. "I don't think Laura will listen to anything I say about that now."

"Buck wants to marry Laura." He said it simply and quickly. Tucker drew in a quick breath.

"I never thought about him wanting to marry her," she admitted slowly. "I know he likes her a lot. He didn't make any bones about that yesterday."

"He not only likes her, he loves her. He wants to marry her and take care of her for the rest of her life, just as I want to take care of you."

Tucker was silent for a long while. "Laura is young and beautiful and . . . untouched. I can see how Buck would fall in love with her, but after a while he may get tired of having a blind wife to lead around."

"Are you sure you're not against this because Buck has Indian blood?" He was staring out over the empty plains.

She was shaken by his words because they were so close to the truth—not of a personal prejudice, but of the facts of life. "In Arkansas half-breeds don't mix with whites, they mix with Indians. I don't know how it is in California. I've got to be honest, Lucas, I'm worried about Laura's future with Buck."

Lucas slapped the reins against the mules' backs before he spoke. "They don't mix with whites in California, either," he said sadly. "Rather, they don't mix with some whites, and Buck's grandfather was one of them. He's a stubborn old Dane who came out on a trading vessel many years ago, got a grant from the Mexican government, and improved on his land. His only child, a daughter, fell in love with a half-breed and ran away with him. When the old man found them, she was pregnant with Buck. As soon as the child was born, he was put with a Mexican family to raise. Buck is one-quarter Indian, not even half." He paused as if to emphasize the statement. "For many years the old man refused to have him on the ranch, but allowed him to go to the convent school to be educated. At the school Buck realized what he was and that he was considered an Indian. So he went to the mountains to live with them. It was there that my father and I met him."

"His mother didn't want him?"

Lucas shrugged. "If she did, she didn't have the courage to stand up to the old man."

"What happened to his father?"

"Buck doesn't know, but he suspects he was shanghaied and sent off to some foreign place."

"Is his grandfather still living?"

"He was when we left California. He sent for Buck just before we left, but Buck refused to go to him."

"And his mother?"

"I don't know if she's still living or not. A few years back I went with Buck to the ranch and waited while he rode up to the house to see her. He was gone for about a half hour."

"And?"

"He never said a word and I didn't ask."

Tucker's thoughts whirled in confusion. She couldn't allow her sympathy for Buck to cloud her judgment as to whether or not he was right for Laura. "Where will they live?" she asked after a while.

"Buck wants to find a good place and build a little ranch. We both do. It'll take a lot of hard work and there'll be lean years, hard years, but I figure we'll make out. Are you afraid of that, Tucker? I never figured on living in a town."

"I want to be wherever you are, Lucas," she answered quietly.

"Don't you think Laura feels the same about Buck?" he asked gently.

"I guess so. No, I know so, but that doesn't mean he's the best man for her," she said stubbornly.

The afternoon wore on. Enormous white clouds piled high overhead and rode along on the high winds from the south, making patches of shade race below them to give welcome relief from the bright glare of the sun. The land rolled gently, barely enough to make a difference, and at times one could see for miles.

"I wish you could ride with me every day," Tucker said wistfully.

"You'd soon get tired of my company."

"I could always start an argument," she teased.

Lucas chuckled. "We had plenty of those when we first met. I thought you were the prettiest woman I'd ever seen—and the contrariest. I still think you're pretty."

She reached over and pinched his arm. He captured her fingers.

"I wonder what those mules would do if I kissed you."

"They're not even looking this way, silly."

He planted a lingering kiss on her lips, and she let her head rest on his shoulder.

Much later, when she saw Buck bringing Laura back to the wagon, she said, "I wish we didn't have to be back here at the end of the line."

Lucas glanced at her quizzically, but said nothing for a while. "Tonight when we circle, you pull up and I'll have Mustang change places with you."

"Won't that be a little too obvious?"

"Who in the hell cares."

The week it took the train to reach Fort Stockton was the longest, most miserable week of Tucker's life. Always conscious when Frank's eyes were on her, she was careful never to be alone, and she went into the bushes with Lottie, Marie, or some of the other women to relieve herself. When it came time to eat, her tight throat almost refused to allow the food to pass. She lost weight. The britches she had made were now hanging on her slender hips, and she tied a sash about her waist to hold them up.

Laura, on the other hand, was blooming. The winds and the weather had sharpened her simple beauty, aroused her senses, and her love for Buck had transformed her from a girl into a woman with all the natural womanly desires. He came each evening to sit with her for a short while, and Tucker took this time to write in the journal, knowing Frank Parcher would keep his distance as long as Buck was there.

Fort Stockton was like an oasis in the desert. The wagon train came off the hot, dusty plains and stopped beneath a cool, thick canopy of oak trees. That evening Buck took Laura for a walk, and Tucker took her journal to the cook wagon and made her entry by the light of the cook fire.

May 18.

We have been on the trail a little over a month, and late this evening we reached Fort Stockton. The fort is built of limestone and adobe and was opened in March of this year, 1859. There is a large flowing spring here, according to Sergeant Malone. It is the only one for hundreds of miles. The Comanches have always considered this their territory, and I can't help but feel a little sad for them that they are no longer free to come and go from this place. When we pull out of here, we will be on our own. Captain Doyle and his men will be stationed here permanently. We will be traveling the stagecoach road and from time to time will pass the lonely stage stations. I wish to God we knew what lay ahead.

Lucas had plenty to worry about. He had been able to find only three men whom he considered suitable to sign on for the trip west; he needed four. The mules he'd traded for were not as young as he would have liked them to be. Otis Collins was pestering him to stay over a few days at the fort, and Marie Hook had told him Blanchet was running a fever.

Behind all this was the knowledge that Tucker was not the same spirited girl who had come in on the Fort Worth stage with a defiant gleam in her eye and her chin tilted in stubborn resistance. She insisted she wasn't sick, but he'd noticed that she ate very little and that her features were becoming more sharply etched due to weight loss. The green eyes he'd found himself languishing in were no longer bright, and her soft, ripe lips that he ached to taste with his own quivered with a forced smile.

Could it be she was having conflicting thoughts about joining her life to his? Could it be she was sorry she had been so hasty in declaring her love? She seemed to be reconciled to Laura's marrying Buck, even glad at times, so that couldn't be what was bothering her. He would have to give her more rein, he decided, make it easier for her if she wanted to back out of her promise to marry him. But, oh, God, he thought, don't let that be what's eating at her! First things first, he told himself sternly. Right now I've got to get this train moving.

Mustang, with Lottie's help, was stacking the new supplies in the freight wagon. Lucas started his tour of inspection there.

"Did you get what you needed, Mustang?"

Lottie answered. "Yup. We bought up the last of the dried peaches 'n apples. You shoulda seed that critter's eyes pop when Mustang dangled the silver afore 'is face."

"That right, Mustang?"

Mustang spat into the dust. Before he could speak, Lottie did. "Yup, that's right."

"If you need more help in getting the wheels greased, Mustang, sing out."

"He ain't never goin' to git nothin' done a lolly-gaggin' 'round here," Lottie said stoutly.

Mustang threw up his hands. "Them's the only words ya spoke all day what's worth a hill of beans." He jerked his tattered hat down over his eyes. "I'll just leave this fixin' to ya, Lottie. It's woman's work nohow." He made his escape.

"Humph!" Lottie said. "Men don't know straight up 'bout 'rangin' food stuff."

"You're right, Lottie," Lucas said with a twitch of a smile. "I'm depending on you to keep your eagle eye on Mustang," he warned as he moved down the line.

"I'll do it, Lucas. I'll keep my eye on this end."

Marie was sitting on a camp stool beside the Blanchet wagon. Billy was walking away with Rafe's brown-and-white pup tugging on the end of a leash.

"Evening," Lucas said. "Looks like Billy's quite taken with the pup."

"Yes," Marie said quietly. "He's enjoying Mr. Blanchet's company, too."

"How is he?"

"His wounds are healing nicely. He sat on the wagon seat for a while today. He's very proud," she said with one of her rare smiles. "It galls him not to be doing for himself."

"I can understand the feeling. Is he still running the fever?"

"A mild one. It's not unusual in his case."

"Mustang is coming around to grease the wagon wheels."

"That's kind of you, Mr. Steele. Mr. Blanchet has been worried because he's unable to do it. He appreciates your allowing the drovers to help with his mules, too."

Lucas waved aside the thanks with a flick of his and. "And . . . the other?"

"Six to eight days will tell for certain."

"Send Billy for me when you know for sure. I hope to God it won't be necessary, but if it is, I'll take care of things from there on, Mrs. Hook. You've done more than your share as it is."

"Thank you. I was hoping you'd say that. To do what would need to be done would go against everything I've ever been taught or believed in."

Lucas looked into steady, dark eyes and saw great strength of character there. He hadn't paid much attention to her before. Now he realized that the California farmer who took this woman for a wife would be a very lucky man. His respect for women as a whole had increased tenfold since the beginning of the trip. There was not a one among them who had not been willing or able to carry her own weight. Even Cora Lee, who resented Lottie's orders, drove her own wagon and cared for her mules.

"We'll pull out at first light as usual. From here on we have to make every mile count." Lucas started to leave, but turned back. "I understand Collins gives you some jawing from time to time." She raised her brows, but said nothing. "Chata has eyes like a hawk, with ears to match," Lucas explained.

"It's nothing I've not had before, Mr. Steele. Billy and I realize that ignorant, narrow-minded people exist, and that their prejudices are their problems and not ours."

Lucas stood shaking his head in bewilderment. "Mrs. Hook . . . *Doctor* Hook, you amaze me. Good evening."

"Evening, Mr. Steele." Marie watched him leave, her dark eyes smiling, her usually solemn face for once relaxed and almost happy. Then the worried look returned to her face as her thoughts returned to Rafe Blanchet. She had never met a man who was so understanding, who had such varied interests and such a thirst for knowledge. What a terrible waste if such a man had to be . . . destroyed.

Lucas stopped at the Taylor wagon. "Are you folks still of a mind to leave with us in the morning?"

Alice Taylor, looking as cool and neat as if she had just stepped from the porch of a manor house, waited for her husband to speak. He looked at her first, as he always did. She ignored the look, as usual, trying to force him to take the initiative, hoping he would show some forcefulness.

"Yes, of course," Daniel Taylor said. "That is, Mrs. Taylor and myself . . . have talked it over, and. . . ." His voice trailed away and he looked at his wife. She was busy taking a handkerchief from her pocket. "We're going with you, Mr. Steele, although Collins is urging us to break off and wait here for another train." His voice was firm with determination.

"Glad to hear it, Taylor. I'm pleased to have you with us. You've got a good boy there in Jeremy, and in the black lad, Poppy, as well. The sutler's got a good stock of goods if you need additional supplies."

"Mrs. Taylor and Jeremy took care of that while Poppy and I greased the wheels."

There was actually a note of confidence in the man's voice. Lucas's gaze crossed that of Alice Taylor. She was looking at her husband with quiet pride on her face. I've learned more about women on this trip, he thought, than I'd have learned in a hundred years. Here was another woman worth her salt.

"How is Mr. Blanchet this evening?" Alice pronounced her words distinctly in an eastern accent unfamiliar, but not unpleasant, to Lucas's ears.

"Doctor Hook tells me his wounds are healing." It was only the second time he had referred to the woman as *Doctor,* and he was surprised how easy it was.

"She's a remarkable woman. She told me she was educated at the school of medicine in Edinburgh, Scotland. Our doctor in Philadelphia was trained there, and he spoke of the difficulty of being accepted due to the long list of those seeking admittance. We are fortunate to have her with us."

"I agree. Well, I must press on. Good evening, ma'am, Taylor." Lucas lifted his hand to his hat in deference to Alice, and walked away.

Collins had pulled his wagon a little away from the others. The outfit, like the man himself, was unkempt, from the tattered canvas that covered the wagon to the rickety stool his wife sat on beside it. The entire setup was just short of a shambles.

"Evening, ma'am."

Emma Collins looked up at Lucas and then away. She was holding her little girl on her lap. The child was sleeping with her head in the crook of her mother's arm. "Evenin'."

He barely heard the woman's voice. Her face was pinched, and from the corner of her mouth a snuff stick protruded and a small dribble of dark brown streaked her chin. She fanned her sleeping child with the brim of a faded sunbonnet. Lucas was about to ask for her husband when he heard the man behind him.

"You wantin' somethin', Steele?"

Everything about the man irritated Lucas, from his belligerent attitude to his homespun britches that refused to come up to the middle of his globelike belly and hung sloppily beneath by the grace of wide suspenders. He gave them a tug now, as if by doing so he was expressing his independence.

"I hear you want to stay here and wait for another train. We're leaving in the morning. Good luck to you, and to you, too, ma'am." Lucas saw the numb expression on the woman's face and felt sorry for her.

"Hold on, Steele! Ain't nothin' been decided on yet. Me 'n Taylor 'n Blanchet is in this together. I reckon we got a say comin' as to when we pull out."

Lucas rocked back on his heels, wanting nothing more than to plant his fist in the man's face.

"Taylor and Blanchet have had their say, Collins. And as far as I'm concerned, you've had yours. I only stopped by out of respect for your wife. Now I've got more important things to do than stand here jawing with you."

When Lucas turned his back, Collins's hand fell heavily onto his shoulder. Lucas spun around. His fist lashed out and landed squarely on Otis's jaw. It was purely a reflex action. The big man's head jerked to the right, and he staggered back several steps before he could regain his balance. By that time Lucas had covered the distance between them and had grabbed the front of his shirt.

"Don't you ever put your hands on me again, you worthless varmint, or I'll tear your head off!" The look on his face would have been warning enough for a sensible man, but Otis Collins was not a sensible man.

He lowered his head like a bull and gathered himself to charge. Lucas smashed a fist into his stomach, then shoved him away and hit him in the face. Collins staggered, but plunged on. As he rushed in, he swung his hamlike fist, but Lucas's punch was faster and caught him on the mouth. He rocked back on his heels and spat blood. Wild with fury he rushed in again, but Lucas sprang out of his way like a cat and hit him with such force that it hurled him into the dust.

Collins rolled over, got first to his knees and then slowly to his feet. Lucas stood waiting, spread-legged, his face a mask of impassivity.

"You ain't heard the last of this," Collins said thickly.

"I'm listening."

"You had no call to hit me."

"Mister! Mister, please. . . ." Mrs. Collins was on her feet trying to balance the child in her arms. The little girl was crying soft mewing sounds. "My Maudy is sick."

"Shut up and stay outta this, Emma."

Mrs. Collins moved determinedly toward Lucas, ignoring her husband. "She's got pains in her belly. I want that . . . woman to doctor her."

"No! Ain't no witch woman gonna lay a hand on my youngun! I done tol' ya that, Emma." Collins's voice was alive with vindictive hatred, and he stared hard at Lucas.

The woman seemed to wilt, then suddenly braced herself and turned on him like a spitting cat.

"You sidewinder, you! You let my baby die and I'll cut yore guts out. You ain't nothin' but a big old loudmouth good-fer-nothin' that ain't got no brains atall! If that woman'll doctor my Maudy, you'll let 'er. You hear me good, Otis Collins, if Mr. Steele'll ask and she's willin', you'll lift no finger agin 'er!"

"You shame me, woman, by goin' agin me, and I'll strip the hide off ya!"

"You lay a whip on me 'n I'll shoot a hole in ya big 'nuff to drag a mule through," she spat.

It was all the woman could do to hold onto the child. She was writhing in pain and her bare feet, reaching to her mother's knees, were trying to get a hold so she could double up.

"Please, mister!"

Agonizing shrieks tore from the child's throat.

"Come on, Mrs. Collins. I'm sure Doctor Hook will help her if she can." He took the child in his arms.

Lucas saw Frank Parcher come out of the darkness and lay a restraining hand on Collins's arm. "Calm down, Otis. Let the woman see if'n she can get the youngun eased. Ain't goin' to do no harm."

"If'n ya think it's best, Frank."

"It is, Otis. And it's best all 'round if'n we leave outta here with the train come mornin'."

Sixteen

May 21.

We are camped two days out of Fort Stockton. There is nothing but bald prairie all around: not a bush or a tree, not a stick of wood, not even a buffalo chip. The Collins wagon is still with us. When the train pulled out from Fort Stockton, it fell in behind the last wagon. We are traveling on the stagecoach road. It isn't much of a road, but it's better than rough prairie. We passed one stage station— just a square hut made of adobe with a corral behind it—and a man and a boy there waved to us. Our scout rides far out each day; we seldom see him or the wagon master. They scarcely even take time to eat the evening meal. There is more tension now that we are without the army escort, but everyone seems to be in good spirits. As for me, I am so weary that I find maintaining this journal increasingly a chore.

The time of day between sundown and dark

passed quickly on the prairie. Long bars of red streaked the sky and pink-tinged clouds hung low on the western horizon. The air was turning cool as it can on the prairie without a hint of a breeze stirring. In the camp, firelight flickered. The smell of woodsmoke and cooked meat hung in the air.

Tucker and Laura walked the short distance to the Blanchet wagon. Rafe and Billy were engaged in a game of chess, and Marie sat quietly watching. Rafe got to his feet.

"Please," Tucker said quickly, "don't let us interrupt your game. We brought our quilt and thought we'd just sit for a while." Actually it had been Tucker's idea to go visiting. Laura would have preferred to wait beside the wagon in case Buck found the time to come by.

"It was certainly a hot dusty day," Marie commented when the quilt was spread and the girls were settled on it.

"I keep thinking about that cool water in the creek by Fort Lancaster," Laura said with a small laugh.

"I don't like to think of that place at all." Tucker's voice was edgy. "I don't imagine Mr. Blanchet does, either."

"I don't know about that, Miss Houston. Because of that bull I got to know Doctor Hook and Billy. And . . . think of Billy. He could have gone through life believing he was the chess champion of the world."

"You don't beat me every time." Billy's bashfulness seemed to have disappeared.

"Not yet," Rafe teased. "But give me a few weeks and it will be a different story."

Tucker pulled her knees up under her skirt and held them tightly as she watched the man and the boy. Her eyes went to Marie's face. She was watching them, too. She's pretty, she's lonely, and she's sad, Tucker thought. She turned her attention to Rafe, studied him. His eyes are dark, she thought. Lucas's are light. This man is tall and thin. Lucas is tall and thin, too, but there's a difference. It's the way Lucas carries himself. She turned to see Marie watching her.

"Is the little Collins girl all right now?" Tucker wanted to say something to get her mind off Lucas and away from the heavy feeling of doom that was constantly with her.

"I think so. The little thing hadn't had a bowel movement in over a week. All she eats is biscuits. Mr. Blanchet was kind enough to let me give Mrs. Collins some dried fruit. I explained to her that the child needs greens and fruit occasionally.

"I'm surprised Mr. Collins allowed you to doctor her," Tucker said with a trace of scorn in her voice.

"I don't think Mr. Collins had a choice."

Marie and Billy had been sleeping under the wagon. Tucker's glance found the neatly made cot on its short legs, the pallet beside it, and the canvas side curtains ready to be dropped to the ground for privacy. She wondered about Rafe's wife and how she could have become so depressed she would take her own life. She'd had a comfortable wagon and a good man to take care of her. What more had she wanted?

The night was close about them and there were no stars to be seen. The camp was quiet. Most of the women were tired and had gone to bed early. Only the men getting ready to go on guard duty stood beside the chuck wagon drinking the strong black coffee. Even Marie and Billy and Rafe were preparing to call it a day.

Tucker exaggerated a yawn and a heavy sigh. "Shall we go to bed, Laura?"

"You go ahead, Tucky. I want to wait up a while longer."

"I doubt if Buck will come tonight, Laura. Come on to bed." Tucker tried to keep the impatience out of her voice.

"He said he would, and he will," Laura insisted. "You go on to bed."

"I'll wait with you." And I hope to God he doesn't come and take you away, she added silently to herself.

"You sound tired, Tucky. Go on to bed. I'll be all right."

"I said I would wait." Irritation crept into her voice, and she hated herself for it. But she wouldn't get into that wagon alone, she vowed. She couldn't!

"Is there some reason why you won't leave me out here by myself? You have before."

"Well I won't now. Oh, please, Laura. Let's not talk about it."

When Buck appeared out of the shadows, Tucker's heart jumped so hard she thought she would faint.

She was grateful for the darkness that hid her frightened face.

"Evenin'."

Laura got to her feet. "I knew you'd come. I told Tucky you would."

Buck didn't tell her that his reason for being away from the train so much was due to his surveillance of a ragtag outfit that was trailing along behind them. He didn't know yet if they were actually trailing them or just poking along, but he was certain they could have caught up and passed if they'd wanted to. He didn't like their looks and had said as much to Lucas. But that was today and this was tonight, and he was going to enjoy being with Laura while he could.

"It was a far piece to ride. I thought you would've gone to bed by now."

"Have you had your supper?"

"No, *mi amor*. Come and sit with me while I eat."

Tucker felt sick. For days she had managed not to be alone so Frank couldn't get to her, and now Laura was going to leave her.

"Now you can go to bed and not worry about me," Laura said over her shoulder. She walked away with Buck, her hand tucked securely in the crook of his arm.

Not worry! Not worry! Oh, God, Laura! Suddenly her knees began to tremble, then the muscles in her legs shook uncontrollably. Stumbling back to her own wagon, she moved a stool away from the wagon about ten paces and sat down. It was a long time before she could think coherently. This was the best place for her, she decided. Frank wouldn't dare come near her out here in the open. She was a fool not to have a weapon of some kind to defend herself. Come morning, she vowed, she would get herself a long-bladed knife even if she had to steal one.

It was very still. Nothing moved. On her right she could see the faint winking eye of the campfire, and the shapes of men squatting around it. She began to feel a little easier. She reminisced about Fort Smith. On a summer evening there would be lights along the streets, and people would be sitting in porch swings talking while others strolled along the sidewalks. There might be music and laughter and, for some, trips to the emporium for bits of lace and thread.

Far off a coyote howled and brought her back to the present. It was a lonesome sound. Her eyes sought the shapes of the men around the campfire. Although nothing stirred and she heard not another sound, for some reason she felt a strange tension came over her that she fought with sudden desperation.

"Waitin' fer me, purty woman?"

Tucker froze with terror. She had seen nothing and heard nothing. Yet the voice reached her from the darkness directly behind her. She started to rise but sank down again, determined not to move from this spot.

"Get away!" she hissed. "Get away from me!"

"Surprised ya, huh? Ya figured to keep me away from ya by stayin' with somebody?" His laugh was guttural. "Ain't nobody goin' to keep me away from ya, purty gal. You're my woman."

"I'm not your woman! You can be sure of that!"

"Only ones what's sure of anythin' is the dead."

"That's what you're going to be if you don't leave me alone!" Tucker refused to turn around. She wished now she had moved the stool even farther from the wagon.

"I wouldn't be much good to ya dead." His laugh was causing the fright to leave her and smoldering anger to take its place.

"Get away from me or I'll scream."

"No, ya won't. They'd jist think yer loony and tie ya up. Ain't no cause fer ya to be hollerin' a sittin' all by yoreself in the dark. But if'n ya do, I'll have to start a watchin' that little blind gal. Wouldn't be nothin' atall to draw her off in the dark. It's all the same to 'er."

"You touch her and Buck will kill you."

"If'n I don't get him first. Wouldn't be no chore atall, what with him a ridin' off by hisself ever' day."

"What are you waiting for? Why don't you make your move and get it over with?"

"Ya gettin' anxious fer me, purty woman? You a wantin' to feel me a 'twixt them purty legs? I ain't in no hurry. I felt ya some 'n I know what I got comin'. It's worth waitin' fer."

Tucker was speechless with horror and outrage that he would stand in the dark and speak to her in such a way. She knew his hateful face was grinning that exasperating grin, and she longed to smash it to a pulp.

"Ain't ya got nothin' to say to that, purty thing?" It was the throaty chuckle more than the words that brought her thoughts into perspective.

She turned on the stool and faced the wagon. She could see nothing, but she knew he was there.

"Yes, I have something to say," she said quite calmly. "I am going to kill you. I was never so sure of anything in my whole life."

"That's the kind of talk I like from ya. You 'n me is goin' to make a good team. I ain't aimin' to—"

"That you, Frank?" A man's husky voice broke into his words. "What's takin' ya so long? I been a waitin' fer ya."

"I'm a comin'. Go on and I'll catch up."

"Ya better come. That high 'n mighty wagon master is gonna be a checkin' to see if'n we is on guard. I ain't aimin' to give him no reason to jump on me agin. Not jist yet, anyhow," Otis growled impatiently and stomped away.

"That wagon master won't be comin' to check fer a good while yet. That Cora Lee knows how to pleasure a man, jist like you'll know afore the summer's out. Ya sure ya want me to go, purty gal? Ya right sure?"

Tucker sat with her hands clenched, refusing to answer. She stared into the darkness where she thought he would be. Minutes passed and she knew he was gone, but he wanted her to think he was still there. How could he have been so sure that Lucas wouldn't come to see if he was at his assigned post?

She gritted her teeth, trying to fight down a wave of agonizing jealousy. Lucas wouldn't . . . not with Cora Lee. Yet even as her eyes closed tightly and her mind tried to reject the mental image of them together, a clear thought flashed into her consciousness and questions came flooding into her mind.

What had happened between her and Lucas that she should be so sure of the way he felt? Because they had spent a night together was no reason. She had given herself up to the belief that he was the man with whom she could be happy—yet she scarcely knew him! Even if she escaped Frank Parcher, and if she survived the trip to California, there was no chance of happiness if there was a doubt in her mind that Lucas was not everything he pretended to be: a man who wanted one woman, a home with her, children. If it could never be, it was better to know it now.

With a sensation of numbness, she got to her feet. She was no longer afraid of Frank Parcher catching her alone. There was only one thing on her mind. She had to know!

Tucker went directly to the campfire where Mustang was making more coffee. He had filled the pot with water and stood swishing it around to stir up the old coffee grounds before adding a handful of fresh ones.

"Where can I find Lucas, Mustang?"

"He ort to be a comin' in soon, missy."

"I want to find him now, Mustang. Please . . . tell me where he is."

Something in her voice made the old man look at her closely in the flickering light. Something must have happened; first Cora Lee and now this one.

"Well . . . go past the freight wagon and out onter

the plain. He ort to be out 'bout a hundred paces. If'n ya don't see 'em, ya'll see his horse."

"Thank you." She turned on her heel and left Mustang shaking his grizzled head.

At the freight wagon she turned. Her eyes were now accustomed to the dark. She put one foot before the other counting the paces. She heard the restless movements of the horse before she saw its dim outline. It was riderless. A few more paces and she saw the distinctive shape of Lucas's hat. As she watched, he moved around to the front of his horse. He was not alone. Cora Lee was standing close beside him and the murmur of their voices reached her. She couldn't distinguish their words, but Cora Lee's happy little laugh was unmistakable.

Then it was true! Tucker stood stunned. If she had been hit with a fist, the blow could not have been more staggering. Dumbfounded, she watched Cora Lee move a little away from Lucas, then close the space between them. She saw Lucas take her arm, and she realized how hopeless her love for him was. Desperately she had held onto the hope that Frank was lying. But how could she not believe her own eyes?

"Go on back, Cora Lee," Lucas was saying. "I'll come by your wagon in the morning."

Lucas's words reached Tucker, and she knew the only thing she could do now was to save her pride. Silently she spun around and retraced her steps. She walked past Mustang with her head held high.

"Did ya find him, Tucker?"

"No. I'll talk to him tomorrow. Good night, Mustang."

Tucker reached her wagon and leaned weakly against the frame. Somehow she knew Cora Lee was walking down the line toward her, and that she knew Tucker had seen her and Lucas. Not for anything was she going to get into the wagon and let the woman think she was afraid to face her.

"Evenin'," Cora Lee sang out. She stopped and, slowly, like a cat stretching, she lifted her arms above her head. "Ahhhhh," she sighed, "there's nothin' like visitin' with a man to relax you before goin' to bed." She swayed suggestively. "You don't mind, do you? It ain't like you two was goin' to get married or anythin'."

Tucker tried desperately to come up with a suitable reply while thinking, how will I ever live down the humiliation?

"Mind? I should say not! I'm not wanting a big belly when I get to California. I'm going to get a rich landowner and play queen over the peasants," she flung back.

For a moment Cora Lee was taken aback. "You mean you don't care?"

"Care? Why should I care? Lucas is someone to amuse myself with while we're on the trail, but I want more than a trail boss when I get ready to settle down," she plunged on blindly.

"Then there's no reason to be wasting your time with me." His voice came with the suddenness of a gunshot from beside her.

Tucker had been so engrossed in her effort to keep Cora Lee from knowing her heart was breaking that she hadn't heard him approach. Her nerves already strung taut from the incident with Parcher, and her composure nearly shattered by her discovery of Lucas and Cora Lee together in the darkness, Tucker now experienced an inner explosion that left her helpless and numb in the face of this final assault on her emotions. Strangely, like a sudden and unexpected death, the break was made without her feeling in the least involved in it.

"Well, I wouldn't exactly call it a waste," she managed to say. Oh, God, she thought. How can I sound so calm? My life is over!

"Well, I would," he said softly into the quiet night. There followed a silence filled with anguish. It was broken by Lucas's terse words, "Come on, Cora Lee, I'll walk you to your wagon."

"Sure, Lucas. Do you have more guard duty tonight?"

"Not until early morning." He took Cora Lee's arm, just above the turquoise bracelet, and they walked away.

" 'Night, Tucker," Cora Lee called over her shoulder.

Tucker stood dumbstruck, too shattered by what had just happened to be able to do anything about it. Then she quickly pushed herself away from the wagon and, lifting her chin, drew her breath in sharply and deeply in a struggle to regain control of herself. From far off, softly at first, but with a sound that swelled on the slight breeze, came the howl of a coyote. Carried on the night air, it was a sound of desperate loneliness that echoed in her own heart. She climbed into the wagon, lay down on the pallet, and rested her head on one arm, letting the other cover her eyes.

"Oh, Lucas," she whispered softly into the quiet. "How can it end this way? And why can't I stop loving you?"

Although she would have denied it a few weeks ago, Tucker realized now that she hadn't really been convinced Lucas had fallen in love with her. It had all happened too fast . . . been too easy. If she knew one thing, it was that nothing in life came easy. The problem was with her; she had believed what she'd wanted to believe. And it had been wrong. All wrong. She had given him her virginity, and yet she knew nothing about him except what he had told her himself. She had believed him because there was something big and strong and sure about him. She had the feeling there was nothing anywhere that could frighten or disturb him. He was a man who knew his strength and her weaknesses and had used them to lull her into believing that he loved her.

Even Frank Parcher is more honest, she thought to herself. He is what he is. He wanted her and had told her he would kill to get her. She couldn't expect any help from Lucas now. Now it was strictly between her and Frank. She was going to have to kill him, she thought with renewed resolve.

Trying to keep at bay the pain in her heart that she

knew could cripple her, Tucker began to plan from that moment on. The thing to do was to remain quiet, yet to calculate and make preparations. Tomorrow she would search Lottie's trunk for a gun or a knife, and she would conceal it on her person. If she failed to find one, she would steal one from the chuck wagon. Once this decision was made, her mind began to click. She would play along and let Frank think she was going with him, but hold out until every other chance was gone before she left the security of the train. She knew that what she would do then would have to depend upon the events of the moment. But the very fact that she had a plan at all gave her a feeling of strength. She only wished it would fill the hollowness she felt inside her.

She heard the soft murmur of voices at the end of the wagon and knew Laura had returned. Presently the flap lifted and Laura stepped in, moving with sure steps around Tucker's pallet to her own. She removed her britches, slipped out of her shirt, and lay down. Tucker watched her in the soft light of the moon that had come up over the front of the wagon where the canvas was folded back to allow the breeze to circulate.

"Are you asleep, Tucky?" Laura whispered in case she was.

Tucker almost didn't answer. "No, but just about," she finally said.

"I felt bad about leaving you alone tonight. I wish you could have been with Lucas. Maybe tomorrow night he'll come and walk out with you."

"I don't think I want him to, Laura." The words were out, and Tucker knew she should be glad she had been able to say them. Didn't she want her affair with Lucas to be behind her, now that it was over?

"What do you mean?" Laura raised herself up and leaned on a bent elbow. "What do you mean?" she repeated.

"Just what I said. I'd rather not walk out with him. I don't . . . love him, and I don't want to encourage him."

Laura was stunned by this news. She and Tucker had always confided their innermost thoughts to each other. Tucker had told her of the beautiful experience she and Lucas had shared the night they were stranded across the river. She hadn't gone into intimate details, but had wanted her friend to know that when the time came for her, it would be wonderful, beautiful. They had whispered in the night and had talked for hours while the wagon rolled across the endless prairie about the life they would have in California with Buck and Lucas. And now this. . . . It was as if all the beautiful dreams had suddenly vanished.

"Are you sure?" It seemed to be all Laura could say.

"Sure as sin," Tucker said in what she hoped was a casual manner. Her wounds were too fresh to speak of them, even with Laura. And she didn't want to intrude upon Laura's happiness.

"Well," Laura said quietly and lay back down, "you should know your own feelings, I guess." In the silence that followed she asked, "Is that why you've been so edgy lately? You've been trying to make up your mind?"

"I didn't have much trouble making up my mind," Tucker said firmly. "Make no mistake about that. But I guess I have been edgy trying to think of a way to tell you," she lied.

"You needn't have worried that I wouldn't understand, Tucky. Anything you do will always be all right with me. It's just that . . . I'm so sorry." Tears were sliding from her sightless eyes and down beside her nose, dropping onto the arm where she rested her cheek.

Tucker flopped over onto her side. "Oh, well," she said indifferently. "You know the old saying . . . easy come, easy go. I think when I get to California I'll find a rich landowner, preferably one who's old and sick." She laughed lightly, pleased that it didn't sound too forced. "We'd better get to sleep. Morning will be here before we know it." And feigning exhaustion, she lay wide-eyed, dreading the sleepless night that stretched ahead.

Seventeen

The day was unbearably hot, but the wagons were moving toward mountains whose purple shadows seemed to reach toward them with the promise of cool breezes and relief from the relentless sun and ever-present dust. For an hour of lonely riding there had been no life apparent on the desert. Now the inevitable buzzard soared overhead, knowing that sooner or later all things on the desert would die and that he had only to wait for his food.

They followed a tortuous route. This was the mean country Lucas had talked about at the beginning of the trip. It was a baked and brutal land, sunblistered and arid. The trail snaked its way through prickly pear and cat's-claw, and around them stretched vast rolling plains of sand, rock, and cactus.

The sun ascended, and sweat trickled down Tucker's neck. The bodies of the mules became dark with moisture. They traveled in silence while the sun grew hotter as it rose higher in the sky. The swaying, bouncing motion of the wagon seemed conducive to drowsiness, and Laura dozed, her hat pulled over her face.

Tucker took off her hat and ran her fingers through her hair to loosen it from her scalp. She had spent a sleepless night, her mind refusing to let her body rest. This morning while Laura was having breakfast, she had searched Lottie's trunk and found a two-edged knife with an eight-inch blade and a lightweight handle. It was exactly what she needed. She had strapped it to her thigh with a scarf and cut a hole in the pocket of her trousers so she could reach it easily. She touched it now. It was hot and heavy against her leg, but comforting, too.

They nooned beside a dry draw. The mules were grateful for the rest and stood patiently in their harnesses while Tucker and Laura carried them each a bucket of water. The air was very still, the sky impossibly clear. Tucker walked toward a small mound of rocks and, after a glance around for snakes, sat down and turned her face toward the mountains. She realized with a start that she loved this country. In spite of everything, she was glad she and Laura had signed on to come west. Her homesickness of last night had been a fleeting thing.

Lucas skirted the wagon and rode toward the rocks. His first impulse was to retreat. As disheveled as she was, Tucker was lovely. The sun glinted in her red hair and made it shine against the blue of the sky. She appeared fragile, small, and . . . lonely. Fragile and lonely as a black widow spider, he reminded himself, and rode up to her with unfeigned impatience.

"Put your hat on. Do you want to get sunstroke?"

The clipped words brought her head around to stare into his unshaven face and steady unblinking eyes. His tight lips created hard lines around his mouth. He sat in the saddle in a deceptive slouch, but she knew him well enough to know that every nerve, every muscle, was alert and taut.

Tucker got to her feet, standing well away from the horse. "Of course. I forgot."

"Wait!" he said as she turned to move away. It seemed as if the word was pulled out of him.

Tucker shook her head slowly. "I've nothing to say to you." She looked at the ground, feeling empty and sick.

"I've got something to say to you. You asked me how come I felt I'd known you for a long time. Here's the reason." He threw a small bundle to the ground near her feet. "I realize now she was probably just some whore from a brothel in New Orleans—nothing a man could build dreams around. Keep it. You two belong together." Savagely he glared into her quiet face, his jaw muscles working as he fought to control his anger and hurt.

He whirled his horse, the sand kicked up by its hooves sprinkling the package that lay at her feet. He rode away wishing he had never laid eyes on Tucker Houston. When he was thinking about that damn woman, he wasn't thinking about getting this train through to California, and he wasn't thinking about Rafe, who could go mad any day and have to be killed. He wasn't even thinking about the renegades following along behind the train. He was sure they were renegades; he couldn't figure any other reason for four white men, three Mexicans, and a Negro to be together. He cursed himself for a fool and put the spurs to his horse.

Tucker stooped to pick up the bundle wrapped in doeskin. When she straightened up again, her vision blurred and she swayed dizzily. The sun, she thought. I've got to get out of the sun. She took the package to the shade of the wagon where Laura sat patiently fanning herself with the brim of her bonnet and holding the end of Blue's leash while the pup frolicked on the ground.

"Was that Lucas?" They had scarcely exchanged a dozen words all morning.

"Yes. He told me to put on my hat."

Tucker went to stand at the end of the wagon and quietly folded back the doeskin from the small velvet box. She pushed the small catch and the lid sprang open. The face staring up from the portrait in the box startled her. The woman had her green eyes, her red hair, and was about her same age. She was beautiful and expressive, with a hint of vulnerability; a woman who had the capacity to feel things deeply and to be hurt to the same degree. Did she look like this woman?

Suddenly things began to make themselves clear in her mind. Lucas was in love with the woman in the portrait, and because she had the same red hair and green eyes he had been attracted to her. He hadn't loved the flesh and blood woman. He loved the woman on this miniature. Tucker sighed deeply. Regardless of what he had said, this woman was not a whore. The purity of her spirit was reflected in her slightly mischievous eyes and in the honest, forthright curve of her lips.

Tucker wished for a mirror so she might compare her face with the one in the portrait. Unconsciously she put her hand to her hair and pushed it forward. The woman's hair was arranged neatly in the pompadour style, and there was lace at her throat. Tucker took her hand from her hair, slightly embarrassed by her foolish gesture. This was a woman of style and quality, something she would never be. She closed the box and rewrapped it in the doeskin. Sometime before their final parting, she would return it to Lucas.

The day went slowly, but it went. The sun marched relentlessly across the sky and disappeared over the western edge of the world. When only a faint glow remained in the sky, the wagons circled for the night. Tucker, with Laura's help, unhitched the mules and a drover took them away. The light had dimmed to twilight by the time the evening meal was ready, and to darkness by the time it was eaten.

Laura sat beside the wagon with Blue straining at his leash. She was quiet and for once ignored the pup's wish to walk around the camp. Tucker looked at her with a twinge of uneasiness, but not even for Laura could she forgive and forget what Lucas had done. Throughout the day she had thought about it, and about other times when Lucas had been with

Cora Lee and how Cora Lee's eyes followed him. No woman brazenly sought out a man without some encouragement, she concluded. There was no possible way she could rationalize Lucas's actions.

"Do you want to walk, Laura?"

"I don't believe so, Tucker. I'm awfully tired."

"Then I'm going to bed. Are you coming?"

"In a little while. I'll let Blue run, then I'll tie him in his box under the wagon."

Tucker climbed into the wagon and stretched out on her pallet. With the knife under her pillow she felt brave. Fear was the least of the emotions consuming her. When the time came, she would know how to deal with Frank Parcher. The emotion that held her in its greedy grasp was loneliness. She had lost Laura to Buck and Lucas to Cora Lee. No. The last thought was not quite right. She had not lost Lucas; she had not had him in the first place—she'd only thought she had. She envisioned herself in the years ahead always teaching someone else's children in some remote valley in California, belonging to no one and no one belonging to her.

Laura came to bed and left the back flap of the canvas open so the breeze could pass through. She didn't speak, and Tucker watched her silently. Laura took her hair down and brushed it before plaiting it again. Tucker put her hand to her own tangled hair. She hadn't bothered to brush it when she went to bed. Laura lay down, and Tucker stared out the end of the wagon. For a few moments her thoughts were still, then she drifted off to sleep.

She was awakened suddenly. There was a moment of silence, then the sound of hooves on the sunbaked ground beside the wagon. Crouching behind the wagon seat, she peered out but could see nothing except the moonlight shining on the canvas of the wagon ahead. Then she saw that the mules were being brought to the sides of the wagons and staked. It was one of the new drovers who staked the mules beside their wagon; she could see him plainly in the glow of the moon. Tucker moved to the back of the wagon and looked toward the grub wagon. There was a cook fire keeping coffee hot for the night guards, and, as she watched, men passed silently between her and the fire.

She went back to her bed, but sleep had escaped her. Slowly the night passed and the darkness turned to beige. A quail sent out an inquiring call, and somewhere across the prairie another responded. Morning had come at last.

Tucker was brushing her hair when Lottie stuck her head into the back of the wagon.

"Yer awake, are ya? Dress yoreself in a skirt 'n put on yore bonnet 'n roll down yore sleeves. Hurry it up and come on our. We'uns is 'bout to have us some visitors."

"Visitors?"

"Injuns, varmints! . . ." Lottie turned and spat snuff juice out of her pursed mouth.

"Indians?" Tucker echoed.

"Come on. Git to hightailin' it," Lottie said crossly and disappeared from sight.

"What is it?" Laura whispered.

"Lottie said Indians." There was disbelief in Tucker's voice. "She said to put on a skirt. I'll get one for you." She raised the lid of the trunk and lifted out the first two she came to. "Here," she thrust one into Laura's hands. "Hurry."

Minutes later they joined the excited, frightened group beside the grub wagon. Lucas was standing hatless beside Mustang. He lifted his arm for silence.

"We've crossed paths with a bunch of Apaches going north. There're about forty braves and they've got women and children with them, so they are not a war party. They camped not two miles from here and they'll come calling before sunup."

"You knowed they was thar and never told nobody!" Collins complained.

"Shut up, Collins, and listen." Lucas turned his angry gaze on the man and all other eyes followed. "The trouble with you is that you're always talking. And while you're talking, you're not learning a damn thing!"

Lucas raised his arm again to silence the murmur that followed his chastisement of Collins.

"I said they're not a war party, but that doesn't mean they won't take everything they can get their hands on. And it doesn't guarantee they won't lift hair. Now listen. Buck's been scouting them and this is what he suggests we do. I go along with it. Some of the drovers are going to mix with you women like you were families. The rest are going to scatter out with their rifles in plain sight. Indians respect a show of strength. Act scared and they'll take everything we've got and our scalps, too. Has anyone got a Bible? We're going to put on a show."

"I've got one," Rafe said.

"Get it and a black coat and hat if you've got one. You're going to be a Bible-spouting, fire-and-brimstone preacher leading these pilgrims to the Promised Land. Now move. We don't have much time."

Marie looked at Rafe with worried eyes, but nodded her head approvingly. "You can do it if anyone can," she murmured.

"Now they're going to come charging in here to see if we've got backbone," Lucas said when Rafe left. "They think differently from us. Show fear, and they'll think you're lower than a snake's belly. Pay them no mind! Don't any of you turn a hair! And you men—draw a gun or fire a rifle before I give the word and I'll kill you where you stand."

Rafe came through the crowd in a black coat and flat-brimmed black hat. He had a large book in his hand.

"It's a history book," he grinned. "It's bigger and looks more impressive than my Bible." He stretched his neck out of the scratchy collar. "God knows I'm no minister of the gospel, but it seems singing is called for."

"Good idea. I don't care if it's 'Oh, Susanna' or 'Polly-Waddle,' but make it loud." Lucas looked beyond the crowd and nodded his head. "Start now, they're coming."

"Sing 'Rock of Ages'!" Rafe shouted.

Rock of Ages, cleft for me, let me hide myself in thee.

"Louder," Rafe yelled, "louder!"

Let thy water and thy blood, from they wounded side which flow, be of sin the double cure, save from wrath and make me pure.

Tucker stood holding tightly to Laura's hand. She felt a presence beside her and looked around to see that Frank had moved very close to her.

"Ain't gonna let no goddamn Injun git my woman." He spoke the words loud enough for her to hear over the singing. She ignored him until he took hold of her arm. She jerked it away and brought the heel of her shoe down as hard as she could on his instep. She could feel the contact it made with the bone, and she heard him curse.

The sound of pounding hooves and shrill yells came from behind them. Tucker could feel her face go pale. The thundering hooves suddenly halted, and dust drifted toward and over them.

"Read!" Lucas spoke sharply.

Rafe's voice trembled at first, then strengthened. *"There is a God who presides over the destinies of nations and who will raise up friends to fight our battles for us."* He shouted, raising his arm dramatically. *"The battle, sir, is not to be strong alone; it is to the vigilant, the active, the brave. And again, we have no election!"* Rafe could smell the sweating horses moving behind him, but he continued to read, *"What would you have? Is life so dear or peace so sweet as to be purchased at the price of chains and slavery?*

Forbid it, Almighty God! I know not what course others may take, but as for me, give me liberty, or give me death!" His heart was pounding and he was perspiring, but he turned and faced the Indians. "Greetings, brothers," he said calmly and gestured at the ground around him, indicating that they should dismount and stand before him.

The wagons were ringed with Indians on restless ponies. They had rough-hewn faces and shoulder-length hair. They wore breechcloths and leggings and twisted bands of cloth wrapped around their heads. It seemed as if all sound stopped the moment Rafe finished speaking. The riders stopped their yipping and held their mounts still. The only sound was Blue's playful puppy barks as he strained against his leash. Curious dark eyes stared at the white people gathered before the black-clad man.

A hawk-nosed brave edged his pony forward and waved his coupstick in the air. "We want food! Tobacco! Meat!"

"No!" Buck seemed to materialize out of thin air. He stood beside Rafe, his feet spread, his arms folded across his chest. "No!" he repeated. "We will not give an Apache brave meat. Apache braves are great hunters! Let them hunt meat."

The brave's eyes turned on Buck, measuring him. Buck stared him in the eye, his left hand close to his gun belt. Lucas stood beside the wagon, his rifle cradled in his arms.

"We can take what you have," the brave said harshly, arrogantly.

"What we have is not worth the warriors who must die to take it. Come if you must, but sing your death songs first and prepare your squaws and your papooses to starve on the long trail to your land in the north, for many of you will die."

He took his gun from the holster and held it in the crook of his arm.

"Mustang," he said quietly, "lift the food bags out of the wagon. Do it slow. Chata, Lottie," he spoke a little louder, "show the rifles . . . don't shoot for God's sake, just show them." The rifle barrels came out of the ends of nearby wagons. Mustang began to pile bags of food on the ground in front of Buck.

"We have little food," Buck said. "Less than what we need to get to where we are going. But we will share it with your squaws and papooses. Apache warrior should hunt his food," he said contemptuously.

The warrior waved his hand over the country from which they had traveled. "There is no game."

"Can not the Apache warrior range far? We pass through this land in peace. We have killed three antelope." He held up three fingers Buck waved his hand to the people behind him. "We do not want your papooses to be hungry. This food is so your children will not cry in the night. We have no war with the Apache, who are brave men and great warriors."

There was silence.

Rafe spoke suddenly, "Go with God!" He raised his arms, holding the history book over his head. "Go! Walk with the Great Spirit. He will bring the rain, the buffalo, the elk."

The hawk-nosed Indian dismounted, and without any sign from him, four others followed. He directed them to pick up the bags of food, then he stood before Buck, his legs spread, his arms folded across his chest in much the same way Buck was standing.

"I will barter for the woman with the hair like fire."

There was a gasp from one of the women standing beside Tucker, and she felt every eye turn toward her. She had seen the dark eyes of the brave pass over her, but he hadn't given any indication that he was paying any more attention to her than he was to any of the others. She felt Frank become instantly tense. She said quietly to him: "Make a move and Lucas will kill you. Then I won't have to." She kept her eyes straight ahead.

Buck was surprised, but his face and voice didn't register the feeling. "The woman with hair like fire is not mine to trade."

The Indian stared into his eyes. "Whose woman?"

"My woman," Lucas said, moving over to stand beside Buck.

"One pony." The Indian's eyes fastened on Lucas's face.

Lucas shook his head.

"Two pony, one dog."

Lucas seemed to hesitate. My God, Tucker thought, this must be a dream! They were actually talking about trading her!

Finally Lucas said, "She is weak, she cannot skin

a deer." He lifted his shoulders indifferently. "She is lazy. But her hair is worth much."

The Indian considered this. "Is she good on the blanket?"

Lucas lifted his shoulders again and glanced over his shoulder to where she was standing beside Laura. He faced the Indian again and rubbed his chin with his fingers, deliberating. "On her belly."

A snicker came from Collins, and Tucker thought she would faint from embarrassment.

"No papoose?"

"No papoose," Lucas said sadly with a slump to his shoulders.

The Indian's dark eyes moved to Tucker and glittered with contempt before returning to Lucas.

"One pony," he said and his expression changed to arrogance.

"One pony for a woman with hair like fire?" Lucas retorted scornfully. "Take off your bonnet, Tucker," he said over his shoulder.

"I'll do no such thing!" she spat at him.

"Three ponies, two dogs," Lucas said firmly.

"No!" The curve of the Indian's lips spoke his contempt for such a price for a worthless woman. He turned and vaulted to the back of his pony. He gave Tucker another disgusted glance and raised his hand. He raced away, his warriors following, leaving only dust behind.

It was several seconds before anyone moved. When they registered that the Indians were gone, they all started talking at once.

"Harness up," Lucas said sharply. "Let's get the hell out of here."

Tucker's face was white and she was trembling. Yet she managed, by dragging Laura along behind her, to reach Lucas. In front of the whole assembly she brought her foot back and kicked him, as hard as she could, on the shin.

"If I were a man, I'd kill you!" she hissed.

Lucas winced when her foot made contact. "You sure as hell aren't a lady!" His scorn cracked like a whip across her pride and his steely blue eyes pinned her glance.

"You wouldn't know a lady if one jumped out of the bushes and bit you," she snapped.

He looked down at her with cold eyes narrowed to mere slits, and his voice was cutting. "Run along and play your games with someone who's interested. I've got work to do."

The gasp this time came from Laura, and Tucker suddenly remembered her presence. She turned her back on Lucas.

"Come on, Laura. We don't want to keep the great man from his duties." Tucker led Laura away with as much dignity as she could muster.

Billy Hook reached Rafe and took a history book from his hand. "You'd make a good preacher man, Mr. Blanchet."

Rafe had removed the heavy black coat. His shirt was soaked with sweat. He mopped his brow with a handkerchief. "No, Billy. I'd not make a preacher man, or a medicine man, either. Wheeeee . . . I was scared to death."

"You didn't show it, Rafe," Lucas said. "You did fine. It was pretty smart of you to speak up when you did."

"Would they have killed us?"

"It's hard to tell. Indians are notional. They like a display of force and a good show. We gave them both. Buck had them figured pretty well. They think a lot of their children, and he played on that."

The sun was now up over the horizon. The sky had hazed over and a wind had come up. Sudden gusts kicked up sand and flapped the canvas tops.

Marie came to walk with Rafe and Billy. "You were magnificent, Mr. Blanchet. You may have missed your calling."

"Don't tease me, Doctor. There were moments when I couldn't even see the printed words, and the only thing that saved me was a cantankerous old headmaster who'd made me memorize Patrick Henry's speech as a punishment."

Marie laughed. "Then we should give three cheers for that headmaster." They reached the wagon, and Rafe began to hitch up the team. "Are you feeling all right, Mr. Blanchet?" Marie asked casually.

"I don't feel quite top-notch. I still get a little pain in my side, but that's all." Rafe grinned. "I don't want to get well too fast and lose my part-time driver and my chess partner."

Marie brought up one of the mules, and Rafe backed it into the traces. In her mind she clicked off the days since the bull had attacked him. She and Billy could have returned to their wagon several days ago, and she wondered what Rafe was thinking about their staying on. Three more days. If only he can get through three more days without stomach cramps or fever! He's such a kind and understanding man, she thought, in a world where there is so little kindness and understanding.

May 23.

Today, three days out of Fort Stockton, we encountered our first Indians. According to our scout, Mr. Garrett, they were Apaches on their way north after spending the winter months in the mountains of Mexico. They were not a war party, but they were fierce-looking people. We were instructed by the scout and the wagon master to put on a show of bravery, and, to their credit, every man, woman, and child performed admirably, with no outward signs of panic. Mr. Garrett finally bargained with the Indians and, after much haggling, gave them bags of food. We did not see the women or children, but we did see marks across our trail made by the travois they pull behind their horses.

Eighteen

The mountains were still ahead, low on the horizon and faintly purple in the distance. Tucker stared at them now, soaking them in, because by late afternoon the train would be heading into the sun and it would be impossible to see them. The morning went quickly, and they nooned beside a brushy gully. Tucker helped pick up sticks and twigs to store in the tarp slung under the grub wagon.

During the afternoon Tucker and Laura drowsed on the wagon seat. The heat was affecting them, the heat and the hours of sitting and riding with nothing to look at but empty, barren land. Long before noon the visit from the Indians had been exhausted as a topic of conversation. After Laura's outburst as they had walked away from Lucas—"He ought to be ashamed of himself; I don't think I'll ever like him again"—nothing more was mentioned about him or his part in the tableau. Laura rehashed the part Buck played, and Tucker had to admit that Buck had handled himself admirably.

The wagon ahead picked up speed, and Tucker

had to use the quirt on the mules to keep pace. They were moving along quickly by the time Lucas, riding down the line, reached them.

"Buck checked out the way station ahead. If we move right along, we'll be able to camp there tonight." He spoke crisply without looking directly at Tucker, touched his hand to the brim of his hat, and moved on.

The stagecoach way station was a simple two-room adobe cabin run by a man and his wife. When the wagons were circled and the stock watered and staked for the night, Lottie came by to ask if Tucker and Laura would like to walk over to the cabin with her to invite the couple to supper.

The woman was obviously thrilled to have other women to talk to, even for a short while. She proudly showed them the station. The large room was for feeding the hungry stage passengers, and occasionally its long tables were placed against the wall and used as beds. There was a huge fireplace with cast iron cooking utensils hanging from hooks on the facing beam. The smaller room was the private quarters of the stage keeper and his wife.

"Doesn't it get lonesome?" Tucker asked as they headed toward the wagons.

The woman's laugh was rich and warm. "Oh, Bill and me is glad to see people come, and we're glad to see 'em go. Bill and me won't be lonesome, long's we got each other." Her voice was full of tenderness. "We took this job so we could work together and be together. It's home."

Supper over, the men sat beside the fire and the women moved away and regrouped. Tucker and Laura sat on the fringe and listened to the talk. The woman from the way station had exciting stories to tell about passengers who came through on the stage.

"Well I tell you, this woman what came in on the stage was a livin' sight. Bill says I ain't ort to be talkin', but sakes alive, she was the prettiest thing I ever laid my eyes on, and sweet talkin', too! She had a woman with 'er who did for 'er, and she weren't no slouch herself. It just so happened that the stage laid over. Well now, 'bout this woman, the other'n called her Madame Ge-neen, or somethin' like that. She was a French girl from Bordeaux, she said. I kinda got all flustered, knowin' I was havin' such highfalutin company for supper, but the little gal pitched right in, rolled up the sleeves on 'er fancy dress, and made up a batch of the lightest biscuits you were et, and to top it all off she made milk gravy. Now this was the madame a doin' all this. The other'n sit in a chair like she was queen of somethin' or other. But soon as the meal was et, we knowed who held the whip. The madame said, cool as you please, 'Get up off your ass, Josephine, and clean the table. Me and these folks is goin' to have us a little card game.' Well . . . the driver, the guard, and a man passenger played cards with that woman 'til way in the night and she cleaned 'em out. She sure did. Now, my Bill, he said he thought. . . ."

Buck had come up silently behind Laura and put

his hand on her shoulder. "Want to take a walk, or listen to this?" he asked softly.

Laura's smile was for him alone. "Need you ask?" she whispered.

He helped her to her feet and they walked out into the darkness. Tucker felt the vacant feeling in the pit of her stomach expand to include her heart as she watched them go. She was losing everything so fast!

The evening was comfortably warm and alive with soft night sounds coming from the camped train. A wayward cloud scudding past released the captive moon that now shone on the man and the woman walking so close together that their two shadows made one.

"Now?" Laura asked softly.

"Now." He stopped and took her in his arms. Laura lifted her face upward. He kissed her lips softly and nuzzled her hair, breathing in the sweet fragrance of it. Her arms went around his neck and he kissed her again, his parted lips savoring hers for a long, blissful moment as his hands roamed over her back and around to tenderly capture her small firm breasts. Her cheeks grew warm and flushed with the pleasure he aroused in her as his thumbs teased the soft nipples into excited peaks.

"I've missed being with you these last days," she whispered.

"No more than me," he murmured in her ear. "Oh, love, I long to grab you up and run away to the highest mountain, where I'd have you all to myself."

Laura moved to press her trembling mouth upon

his. "Buck," she breathed against his lips. "I still can't believe that you love me." Her hands fluttered over his face. She traced his eyebrows with her fingertips and moved them down to his nose and across his cheeks. "Your face is so smooth."

He laughed softly and nipped at her fingers with his lips. "Do you think I would come to my beloved with whiskers that would scratch her soft skin? I scraped them off with my knife."

She laughed, tipping her head back until her hair fell past her hips. She slipped her hand inside his shirt and rubbed his smooth chest, reveling in the warm feel of his body. She held her mouth up to his, and there was a soft union of lips and tongues as their mouths parted and clung with wild sweetness that held still the very moments of time. Clasped tightly to him as if he would draw her into himself, Laura felt the thunderous beating of his heart and heard his hoarse, ragged breathing in her ear. His hand moved down her back with hungry impatience and pressed her hips tight against him.

"*Querida,* my virgin *querida,*" he whispered. "I should not be rough with you . . . but when I hold you I cannot help myself. I long for you every waking hour." He smoothed her hair back and traced his mouth along the column of her throat.

"I'll not break apart. I want to be treated like any other woman," she said with her lips pressed to his hair. "Buck . . . sometimes I want us to . . ." she hesitated, "I want us to love each other like . . . a man and a woman love each other. Tucker said it's wonderful, beautiful, with the man you love."

Buck took a deep shuddering breath. "Laura! There was never a woman to compare with you! You say these things to me while we stand in this place, when I would give my life to love you in just such a way."

Laura placed a trembling hand across his lips. "Not your life, darling. Never say that!"

He kissed her soft palm, her slender fingers, her wrist. His gentleness brought immeasurable tenderness to her breast. She lay her head against his chest and encircled him with her arms.

"You're an angel, my beloved," he whispered softly. "When you lie beside me, soft and warm, letting me love you as I long to do, it will be as my wife." He raised her head with gentle fingers so he could watch her face. "When we get to El Paso I'll find a priest to marry us, and then you will be mine for all time."

The import of his words reached into her mind, and she held herself away from him.

"Are you sure you want to do that?" Her question hung in the air and she held her breath.

"More than I ever wanted anything in my life." His voice deepened and there was no doubt of his sincerity.

There was a deep silence between them. Presently, with his arm encircling her waist, they began to walk again.

"Something has happened between Tucker and

Lucas, Buck. Tucker says she doesn't love him, but somehow I think she does. She's feeling miserable, and I can't talk to her anymore. It's as if she's pushed me away."

"Lucas is as cross as a bear with a sore tail," Buck said, reflecting on what Laura had said. "He had no call to do what he did this morning. He could have simply told the brave he'd take sixteen ponies, and that would have put a stop to any trade talk."

"I feel guilty being so happy when Tucker is so downhearted," Laura said wistfully. "Wouldn't it be wonderful if they would marry and live near us in California?"

Buck took his time replying, first bending to kiss her forehead. "Only if they are in love, sweetheart."

"Do you think Lucas loves her?"

"I thought so, *querida*. But I cannot tell what another man feels. I only know how I feel!"

Laura stopped, lifted her arms, and wound them closely around his neck. He bent to kiss her lips.

"Don't worry, *mi amor*. What is to be will be. I waited for you, looked for you, yearned for you . . . and you came to me. Perhaps it will be the same with your friend. She will find her love." Strong, careful fingers moved aside the long golden hair, and his mouth pressed warmly, hungrily to the slenderness of her neck. He cradled her against him, and she clung tightly, her eyes closed. Her heart almost stopped, then raced so wildly she was left breathless. Buck lifted his head at last and gently kissed her closed eyes.

"We must go back now, *mi amor*. But I wish the time would go fast so that we can be together all night, every night."

The camp was quiet. Mustang stood holding the coffee pot, gesturing to see if Buck wanted a cup. Lucas sat on a chunk of wood near the dying fire. Buck squatted on his heels, and Mustang filled his cup.

"You taking third watch?" Buck asked, keeping his eyes away from the light of the fire.

"Yup. I figure if we're to get visitors, it'll be then," Lucas said, knowing full well it was unnecessary conversation.

"Why do you figure Parcher is behaving himself?"

"I've been wondering about that. I can't find a thing to fault him for. He seems to keep Collins pretty well in line, too. Stands his watch and rides tail. Still don't trust him."

"He's got a mean streak a mile wide," Mustang said. "I ain't got no use for him atall."

"He's mean, but small-caliber mean. When he makes his move, he'll act alone. I don't see any connection between him and what's following." Buck threw the rest of his coffee into the fire and stood up. "I'll hit the bedroll. I plan to ride out a couple hours before daylight."

"Surprised, you'd leave that little gal long 'nuff to ketch a wink," Mustang said with a sly glance at Lucas.

"What do you know, old man?" Buck grinned.

"It's been many a year since a pretty girl looked at your ugly face."

He walked away and it suddenly occurred to him what he had said. *Looked at your face.* Laura, his love, had never looked at his face. Would she have fallen in love with him if she could have seen him? Or would she have shied away and never given herself a chance to know him? Even as he asked himself the question, his mind was rejecting the idea. It was a possibility he could not bear to think about.

Lucas shook the last of the coffee dregs from his tin cup and set it on the chuck-box shelf at the end of the grub wagon. Mustang had gone off on some errand, so he was alone with the glowing embers. He looked up at the stars. They were brighter than usual, and there wasn't a single cloud in the sky. Even the silver moon wouldn't be up for another hour or so. There was only the unbroken darkness and the loneliness.

He leaned on the wagon and let his gaze wander over the camp. It touched every wagon, still and silent. In each one of them there was someone who could turn to someone and share what they had seen or done during the day: how the country looked, how tired they were, how scared they'd been when the Indians had arrived. But there was no one for Lucas Steele, wagon master, to turn to. Last night and all day today loneliness had crept into his bones like an ache. Tucker Houston's words had pierced him like fangs, and they'd left their venom to work into the wound. Why couldn't he quit thinking about the damn woman? In anguish Lucas whirled away and walked outside the circle of wagons.

At first he didn't know where he was going. Then, off on a ridge, he could see the silhouette of the man on watch. A hundred yards away he called a soft "haaloo" and received an answer. He approached and saw Chata waiting, his bedroll on the ground. He'd been half sitting, half reclining, his rifle beside him.

"Something wrong, *señor*?"

"Nothing wrong. I'll take this watch. You go back and get some rest."

"*Sí, señor.* You would use my rifle, no?"

"Your rifle? Oh, yes, thank you, I will," he muttered distractedly.

"My horse is staked right there," Chata pointed. "I leave him."

"All right."

The young Mexican walked toward the camp. Lucas stood still, wondering how in the world he had come to do such a stupid thing as to walk out of camp without his rifle. He silently cursed himself, then began to walk back and forth. What was he going to do? How was he going to get that redheaded witch out of his mind? From the moment he'd set eyes on her in Fort Worth, she had crept into his bloodstream like a poison. She had driven him to torment her today! Even a savage Indian had seen her beauty and been fascinated by it. Hair like fire! Fires of hell are more like it, he thought angrily. His leg still ached where she had kicked him. He'd wanted to slap her at the time, lash back at her somehow, but he knew he'd already made a big enough fool out of himself. He also knew that Buck disapproved of what he'd done. Hell, he knew himself when he was doing it that it was wrong! He stared with tormented eyes toward the darkened wagon train and suddenly saw the shape of a woman coming toward him.

Damn! He said nothing as she approached him in the darkness, and he made no move toward her. She came to within ten feet of him before she spoke.

"Lucas?"

"Cora Lee. What the hell are you doing out here? I could have shot you."

"But you didn't." She laughed softly, remembering these words from another night, another place.

"No, I didn't. But another man might have."

"I knew it was you. I watched you leave camp and saw you come here."

"You followed me? Why?"

"I wanted to be with you." She came close to him and placed her hand on his arm. "Talk to me for a little while, Lucas. I get so lonely."

"There're plenty of people back there for you to talk to," he said sharply.

Cora Lee twisted around and sank down onto the bedroll. Lucas looked down at her and reached to take her arm and pull her to her feet.

"Please sit and talk to me?" Her voice had a husky catch in it.

He ran his hand over his face. He didn't want the girl here, but he didn't want to hurt her feelings. Yet she was interrupting his thoughts. This was a night he needed to spend by himself; he didn't want to waste it with her.

"I checked the axletrees on your wagon this morning, Cora Lee. There's no reason to think they're going to break, not on this flat prairie anyway."

"I know that. It was just an excuse to come talk to you." She pulled on his hand. "Sit down for a minute."

Lucas looked down at her. She was a pretty woman. Pretty to look at, but that was all. She didn't have any more brains than a flea. God help the farmer in California who gets her for a wife, he thought as he sank down on his haunches to tell her, quietly and firmly, to leave.

Cora Lee took the move as a sign of acceptance and reached out to stroke his hair. Lucas jerked his head away, but before he could get to his feet her arms were around his neck and she was pressing herself against him.

"Stay and love me, Lucas." She pulled open her unbuttoned bodice and large ripe breasts, gleaming white in the darkness, pressed against his face when she rose up onto her knees. "I can make you feel things you've never thought of feeling, Lucas. Stay, darling! Stay and let me do all the things I've been wanting to do to you."

Dumbfounded by her attack, his mind went blank. The force of her weight against him almost toppled them both over onto the bedroll. In spite of himself he felt a sexual excitement. He'd never been accosted by a woman before. Cora Lee moved and her mouth, open and wet, came down onto his own, and her hand, gentle at first, then with persistent, skilled fingers, worked its way to his belt buckle.

Lucas had the feeling he was being devoured, raped.

"My God!" He pushed her away and got to his feet. "My God!" he said again.

Cora Lee lay back on the bedroll, her breasts fully exposed. With deliberation she began pulling her skirt up inch by inch from her ankles. "Come on, darling," she crooned softly. "Come to me. Don't you want me?"

Lucas stared at her: her white face, her white breasts, her disheveled dress. Tucker's earlier accusations leapt unbidden into his mind. His thoughts began to gather into some semblance of order. Cora Lee had been pestering him about one thing or another ever since she'd joined the train. She'd been at him about the wagon, or the mules, or some other piddling worry that he'd put down to woman's ways. Now this! Why, she was nothing but a whore!

"I sure as hell *don't* want you! Get on your feet!" He spat the words angrily. She lay looking at him, saying nothing. "Get up!" He was about to jerk her to her feet, when he heard the soft signal come from behind him.

"Haa-loo." It was Buck's call. They had used it for too many years for him to be mistaken about it now.

Lucas reached down and jerked Cora Lee off the bedroll and onto her feet. "Fix yourself," he hissed.

He turned his back to her and raised his hands to his mouth to give an answering call.

Seconds later Buck, running noiselessly in his knee-high moccasins, was beside him. Eyes that could see in the dark had told him from fifty yards away that there was a woman with Lucas. She stood beside him, her breasts barely covered. Lucas turned on her viciously.

"Get the hell out of here, Cora Lee, and tomorrow get your things together. I'm leaving you at Fort Davis. I'll pay your way back on the stage or you can stay there. They've got need of a whore," he said harshly, his stupefaction and self-recriminations overpowering him.

"I love you, Lucas," she said with tears in her voice. "I've never said that to another living soul, but I'll say it to you. I love you." She walked away with none of the proud arrogance she usually displayed.

Lucas waited until she was well away from them before he turned to Buck. "Well?" he demanded through gritted teeth, as if daring Buck to mention what he'd just seen and heard.

"That outfit that was comin' down the trail behind us went sneakin' by. They're ahead of us now."

"All eight of them?"

"Yup. The drover you got from Fort Stockton—Valdez—he heard 'em and woke me. We watched 'em. They made a deep circle when they passed and went a half mile before they put spurs to the horses. Got good horses."

"You think they'll wait ahead?"

"Not likely. They're wantin' to beat us to Fort Davis."

"If we get an early start tomorrow, we'll make the fort by sundown."

"I'm going to trail that bunch and make sure they don't double back," Buck said.

"About that woman, Buck, I . . ." His voice trailed off.

"None of my business what you do, Lucas," he said abruptly. "I got to get goin' if I'm goin' to do any stalkin'." He loped back toward the camp leaving Lucas feeling frustrated and angry.

Nineteen

The day began like any other day, with everyone hopeful that the train would get the early start Lucas had counted on. Mustang banged on the iron pot, the signal that breakfast was ready. The smell of bacon and woodsmoke and boiled coffee hung in the air. The women straggled out of the wagons, their shirts tucked into the makeshift britches and their hair screwed up in tight knots atop their heads. The men had already eaten and were bringing up the mules.

"Now git to gittin'," Mustang urged. "Quit a flappin' yore jaws so we can git a movin'. We'll be in Fort Davis afore nightfall where thar's trees 'n shade 'n cool creek water."

Laura and Tucker took their bacon, corn bread, and coffee back to the wagon. Since the mules were already hitched, the two gulped their coffee hurriedly, expecting the call to move out to come at any moment. But nothing moved, and the mules began to get restless. Annoyed at the delay, Tucker was thinking a few uncomplimentary things about the wagon master when he came riding by.

"Have you seen Cora Lee this morning?" His lively mount danced and pawed the ground.

Tucker tossed her head. Her loose hair billowed wildly, and her tormented eyes ignited. "Have you lost her?" she asked in a voice dripping with bitter sarcasm.

Lucas pulled up on the reins cruelly, and his horse stood still. He glared at Tucker. "I don't need any of your waspy remarks. Have you seen her or not?"

"No! What's more, I don't care if I never see her again!" Tucker flung at him.

"Goddammit!" he swore as he put his heels to the horse.

"What could all that be about?" Laura asked.

"I don't know. I suppose Cora Lee has wandered off."

"I don't think it's very nice of her to keep us waiting."

"There are all kinds of people out here, Laura, and many of them are not nice." There was a cynical edge to her voice.

"I can only think of a few, Tucky. 'Most everyone is nice to me."

"That's because—"

"I'm blind," she interrupted.

"That isn't what I was going to say and you know it," Tucker snapped. "Everyone is nice to you because you're good and sweet and nice to them!"

It was getting lighter. The morning sun streaked the sky. Tucker leaned out to see if the lead wagon was getting ready to pull out. All she could see was

Lottie standing with her hands on her hips. As she watched, Lucas rode up, dismounted, and tied his horse to the wheel of the grub wagon. Soon Lottie was banging on the iron pot.

"Come on, Laura. The great man is going to make a speech."

"Oh, Tucky. Don't poke fun so."

The group that gathered at the wagon was at first irritated, then concerned.

"We can't find Cora Lee Watson," Lucas told them bluntly. "Her things are still in the wagon. I don't think she would have gone off on her own without taking extra clothes. If any of you have seen her this morning, speak up." He waited and no one spoke. "All right. This is what we'll do. We'll turn the stock loose inside the circled wagons for you women to watch, and the mounted men will spread out and look for Cora Lee."

Tucker took Laura back to the wagon as the drovers herded the horses and mules into the enclosure. She felt empty and apprehensive, and the words she had spit out at Lucas came back to haunt her. She hadn't meant them literally.

Lucas was worried. He strongly suspected that he and Buck were the last ones to see Cora Lee. He couldn't get her words or the dejected slump of her shoulders as she'd walked away from them out of his mind. He gathered the men together and directed them to fan out and ride in a widening circle around the camp.

The sun was well on its way across the sky when

Lucas saw Buck coming in and rode out to meet him. Buck's horse was lathered, its sides heaving from a long run. He had waited miles up the trail for the train to catch up, and when there was no sign of it after a reasonable time, he had put the spurs to Dolorido. He hauled up on the reins, bringing the spirited sorrel to a rearing halt.

"What's wrong? Why aren't you moving?"

"One of the women is missing," Lucas answered.

"Which one?" Buck demanded sharply.

"Cora Lee. She hasn't been seen since last night."

Silently thanking God that it wasn't Laura, he directed his attention to the problem at hand. "Did you check the stage station?"

"She isn't there. My God, Buck, we may have been the last to see her."

Buck swore and wiped the sweat from his face with his sleeve. His dark eyes searched the landscape, then came back to Lucas's set face.

"That woman smelled of trouble," he commented.

"Do you think she would have just walked off into the desert?" Lucas suggested.

"No tellin' what a woman like her would do, but I don't think so. If she was goin' to leave, she'd 've taken a horse. Is one missin'?"

"No," Lucas grimly confirmed.

Buck sat quietly for a moment. He watched the women guarding the stock, the restless mules hitched to the wagons, the small spiral of smoke rising up from a newly made fire. Finally he said, "Look there."

Lucas followed his pointed finger and saw the buzzard circling lower and lower in the sky. "Oh no. Do you think . . . ?"

"There's only one way to find out."

They found her, almost a mile away, under a small clump of bushes. The buzzard flew into the bushes and then away as they approached. The sight was sickening. Cora lee lay sprawled, her head at an odd angle, her mouth agape, her eyes already picked out by the buzzard.

The men slowly got off their horses. Lucas felt ill. He went to the body and placed his hat over her face. Buck searched the ground around her. It was slightly sandy, and the wind had erased any sign of anyone else having been there.

"She either walked or was carried here. No horse been here lately," Buck observed. "Looks like she was shoved under the bushes. That would account for her head bein' all lopsided."

"Someone killed her," Lucas murmured.

"She sure as hell didn't walk out here, crawl under the bushes, and die," Buck commented drily.

"Who would have done it?" he asked disbelievingly. Lucas's eyes pinned Buck's. "Last night she wanted me to take her, but I wouldn't have touched her with a ten-foot pole. I've never had a woman come on to me so strong. Not even a whore in Socorro acted the way she did."

"I've heard of women like her. I'll say this because it might ease you some: she came on to me, once, too. I think it was somethin' she couldn't help. Somethin' like a sickness."

"I hate to take her back this way."

"Yup, but it's got to be done."

Lucas bent over the crumpled body and buttoned the front of her dress all the way up to her throat. A spasm of guilt shook him. Her words kept going through his mind: *I love you. I've never said that to another soul.* He took off his shirt and wrapped it around her head and upper body.

"I'll get on my horse. Hand her up."

Lucas rode down the trail with Cora Lee's body cradled in his arms. The women, gathered in a group, waited silently at his approach. He rode into their midst.

"She's dead," he announced. In the shocked silence that followed, anger flooded him. Who would do this? Parcher? Collins? The new men he hired on at Fort Stockton? Taylor? The Negro boy, Poppy? The only ones he could be absolutely sure of were Buck and Rafe and Mustang. Rafe had been with Marie—or had he sneaked out in the night? He found himself forced to question all possibilities.

"Will some of you women take care of her?"

For a moment there was silence, then Marie said, "Take her to her wagon, Mr. Steele. I'll take care of her."

"I'll help." This came from Lottie, and there were sighs of relief among the rest of the women.

"Mustang, ride over and tell the man at the stage station what happened and find out if there are any graves nearby. We'll bury her near someone if we can." He surveyed the group before him with cold, interrogating eyes. "You women get yourselves ready for burying," he ordered crisply. "And you men—I want every one of you to go fifty paces beyond the freight wagon and wait for me."

Buck and Lucas rode to the end of Cora Lee's wagon. Buck let down the tailgate and climbed up. He took the body from Lucas, who immediately rode off, and placed it on the straw mattress.

"Ma'am, it's not a pretty sight," he said to Marie Hook, who waited there. "Buzzards," he added in the way of explanation.

"Thank you for telling me, Mr. Garrett. I'll be all right."

Buck left her there and went to tend to the loose stock.

The rest of the men were waiting for Lucas at the spot he'd designated. Storming up to them on his black horse, he immediately accused: "That girl was murdered! I know goddamn well she didn't just walk out there and die!"

Collins began to sputter.

"Quiet!" Lucas shouted, his fury bitter in his mouth. He felt incredibly weary, but his anger goaded him on, "You, Collins! You're so anxious to talk, we'll start with you."

"Wh—what'd ya mean?"

"Just what I said, you fool! You had an early watch, then what did you do?"

"Ya got no call to talk to me like that, but I'll tell ya anyways. I took my ol' woman to bed."

"Will she swear to that?" Lucas shot back.

"She better, or I'll beat the livin' daylights outta 'er." He snickered, but no one else laughed.

"Parcher?"

"Why're you pickin' us out, Steele?" Frank's lips were curled in a sneer. "I don't have to tell ya nothin', but I will. I stood my guard, then rode over and played cards with the stage keeper."

"All night?" he pressed.

"Most of it."

"Valdez?" he directed to one of the new men.

"*Señor* Buck say to me and Chata to watch men who trail behind. We go, *señor.*"

"Gazares?" he asked another.

"We with Cutler, *señor.* We watch, we sleep."

Lucas called on each man in turn, and each spoke up with a logical alibi. Finally Lucas dismissed them and admitted to himself he was making no headway. Hell . . . he didn't even know what had killed the girl!

Cora Lee's grave was dug beside those of two cholera victims from an earlier train. Lucas carried her there dressed in her best gown and a fancy fringed shawl. Lacking a coffin, she was wrapped in a blanket Marie Hook had taken from her own trunk.

Tucker and Laura, dressed in their best out of respect for the dead, stood on the edge of the group surrounding the grave. Rafe led the singing. Tucker was surprised how many of the women knew the words to the hymns. They sang out as if it were something they could do for Cora Lee. Mr. Taylor, attired in a dark suit and sweating profusely in the hot sun, read the Scripture.

During the reading Tucker became conscious of Frank Parcher standing close behind her. She moved as far away from him as she could without dragging Laura with her. He followed. She was forced to stand and suffer his hand against her back. When the singing started again, he leaned closer and whispered in her ear: "Gonna be a heap o' horny men a missin' the little split."

Stung with embarrassment and indignation that he would make such a remark at the girl's burial, Tucker bridled. The unfeeling swine! She gritted her teeth and envisioned him in the grave instead of Cora Lee. Her control was about to give way when Frank moved. The next instant Buck was beside Laura, looking over Laura's head toward Tucker. Had he seen Frank speak to her? Was that the reason he'd moved up beside them?

The service ended, and the women went back to the wagons. In spite of the fact that Cora Lee had made no effort to get to know them, had exchanged but a few words with most of them, there was not a word of criticism spoken against her, even though most of the women were aware of her nightly wanderings. It was pity they were feeling for her, pity and guilt for not having made a greater effort to understand her.

Now that the burying was over, the question in everyone's mind was how did she die? Shock had temporarily kept fear at bay, but now the shock was wearing off and the realization that one among them was dead was making itself felt. In their wagon, folding and putting away their clothes, Laura voiced what Tucker had been asking herself.

"It's scary, Tucker. Who do you think killed her?"

"I wish I knew."

Tucker was totally drained. She felt as though her body had been pummeled and her mouth washed out with sand. She didn't dare voice what was floating around in her mind. *I don't know who killed her. I don't want to know for sure. There's one man capable of killing like that, and I don't dare accuse him. Had Cora Lee crossed Frank in some way? Was he playing the same game with her that he's playing with me?*

The sun was directly overhead when Lucas rode down the line to speak to Marie Hook. She was in the wagon she and Billy had shared for a while with Cora Lee. Lucas dismounted, and she climbed down to stand beside him.

"I'll drive the wagon. Billy will stay with Mr. Blanchet. I've explained to him that Mr. Blanchet may come down with a sickness and what he is to watch for. He's a sensible boy."

"I wanted to talk to you about that, Doctor Hook. If you'd rather stay with Rafe, I'll get one of the drovers to drive this wagon."

"It would be too obvious, Mr. Steele. It's best we do it this way. We have three days after today before we can be reasonably sure Mr. Blanchet will be all right."

"It's a lot to put on Billy."

"Being the son of a woman doctor, Billy has had to grow up fast. I can rely on him."

"Thank you for helping with Cora Lee. Do you know what killed her?"

"Yes, I know." Marie's dark eyes swept a circle around them. She waited a few seconds, as if to brace herself for what she would say. When she spoke her voice was objective and well-regulated. "This will be harder for you to hear than for me to say, Mr. Steele. Men, as a rule, shy away from this type of conversation with a woman. But bear in mind that I am a doctor. In Scotland we were conditioned to deal with almost every situation imaginable. I assure you I am not in the least embarrassed by what I must say."

"Say it, Doctor."

"I have suspected for some time that Cora Lee was a nymphomaniac. That is a medical term meaning a female with an excessive sexual desire. Few people in this country are even aware that such a thing exists. The desire that drove Cora Lee toward sexual fulfillment is comparable to a drunkard's craving for alcohol. She was a pitiful thing."

If Lucas was shocked by her words, he hid it well.

"But . . . what killed her?"

"She died from either a powerful blow over the heart, or because something covered her mouth and nose and she couldn't draw air into her lungs. Possibly both. When we removed her clothes, I found the places where she had been struck. I also found semen, fluid ejected by men during sexual intercourse, on her thighs and on her stomach."

Marie could feel the anger radiate from the man beside her, but there was more and she would tell it all. "Because of Cora Lee's nature, it would be easy to assume that she willingly went out there with some man. And possibly she did. But that was where her willingness ended. Mr. Steele, from the bruises on her arms and body, the condition of her clothing, and the signs of her struggles, it was obvious that she was painfully violated—brutally raped, beaten, and left to die."

"My God!" Lucas's face had turned a dull gray beneath the brown put there by the sun. "My God!" he said again.

"I know it's a shock to hear this, Mr. Steele," Marie said gently. "But there are many different kinds of people in this world. Some of them are monsters who do unspeakable things to women."

Lucas marveled at the calmness of the woman standing beside him. "Thank you, Doctor, for telling me." He touched his hand to his hat brim and mounted his horse.

The train started after the noon meal. Lucas took the same position he had taken every morning since their departure from Fort Worth. Riding off to one side of the trail, he sat his horse and watched the whole train take shape. After the wagons were strung out, he rode at the head, seeing nothing but the endless miles where nothing moved but the wind.

That night they camped in the foothills of the Davis Mountains. The wagons were drawn into a tight circle among pine trees. The stock was watered and picketed nearby. As darkness closed in, the call for supper rang out. The women gathered for the evening meal. Everyone was quiet. There was a fearful nervousness throughout the group. Even Lottie had little to say as she dipped the rich stew into the bowls. Most of the women, including Tucker and Laura, sat near the big cook fire to eat. It was as if the death of Cora Lee had drawn them all closer together.

Emma Collins was a troubled woman. She was also a woman of few words. The only pleasure she had in life was Maudy, her little girl. And for that child she would fight to the death. She wanted as much for her child as Mrs. Taylor—who ate on china plates and drank from tall, thin glasses—wanted for hers. Emma had long ago accepted the fact that her husband was a cruel, stupid man incapable of providing her with even a comfortable existence. But with the advent of this trip west, it had seemed to her simple mind that fate had lent a hand, and that she would find in California all she had ever dreamed of having for Maudy.

Emma was aware that Otis had changed since the night in Fort Stockton when she had defied him and taken Maudy to see the woman doctor . . . and when Lucas Steele had so easily beaten him to the ground.

He'd gotten moodier, meaner, if that were possible. He now rose in fury whenever she or Maudy crossed him in the slightest way. Today he had slapped the child, knocking her backward over the wagon seat, because she had whined for a sugar tit.

All through the afternoon he had sat on the wagon seat, brooding and angry, talking only to Frank Parcher when he rode up beside them. Emma had seen him in these moods before, and she feared what was coming. He would find an excuse to whip her.

She prepared supper, and Otis and Frank came to eat it. They sat before the fire nursing their mugs of coffee. Emma and Maudy got into the wagon. Maudy crawled into her mother's lap, and Emma rocked her in the creaky old rocker that had belonged to her mother.

"Papa's mad." Maudy put her arms around Emma's neck.

"He ain't goin' to hurt ya, lovey," Emma promised. "Mama ain't goin' to let him hurt ya."

"Papa's got a pretty," Maudy said suddenly, as if to cheer up her mother.

"Mama's got one, too. It's you, lovey."

"Papa's got a real one though. Wanna see it?" Maudy slid from her mother's lap and went to the chest where Otis kept his things. It was his private place; Emma never dared to open it. She felt a stab of fear now as Maudy lifted the lid. But the fear was magnified ten times when she saw what the child pulled out of the box.

"Lovey!"

"Ain't it pretty?"

"Oh, Maudy! Give it here. I'll hide it in my pocket. Don't tell Papa we found it."

"Can I have it, Mama? I peeked and saw Papa put it in the box."

"We'll see, lovey. It's time for ya to get to bed. Lay down and I'll tell ya 'bout when I was a little girl and my papa made me a swing. It went so high I felt like a bird."

The few minutes it took Maudy to fall asleep were among the longest of Emma's life. Finally, when the child was sleeping soundly, she got up and opened the chest again. It had been years since she had lifted the lid, and she still remembered the whip on her back the last time she had bent over it. Now, strangely, she wasn't afraid of the whip. She dug deep in the chest and found her father's six-shooter. She held it and spun the chamber to see if it was loaded. Emma knew about guns. She was raised on the frontier in Arkansas, where life was hard and death was sure for those who couldn't protect themselves. She put the gun in the waistband of her skirt and pulled her loose shirt over it. Then she sat down to wait. She knew as sure as her name was Emma that before long Otis would call her and tell her to walk a ways from the wagon.

Emma sat in the chair and reflected on how little all this meant to Maudy at her tender age, and on how it had been her own father's dirt farm that was sold to buy this wagon. She looked at the hands that had raised Maudy, worked hard on the farm, driven the mules, chopped the wood, cooked the food, and . . . covered her face to ward off the blows from Otis's fists.

"Emma! Get out here!"

The call had come.

She went out the front of the wagon, climbed over the seat and down over the big wheel. Her glance swept the camp. The fires had died down, and the camp was quiet. Everyone had turned in for the night, all comfortable and cared for. . . .

"Move out. I wanna talk to ya."

She stepped over the wagon tongue and walked toward a cluster of trees. Deep within her, Emma was sure, as sure as a woman could be, that if she crossed Otis one too many times, he would kill her. Then what would become of Maudy? She would have to fight! That was the answer. This time she would fight for herself and for Maudy! She was not at all sure she would win—she had precious little experience in standing up to Otis—but she knew this battle must be won here and now. She reached the trees and stopped. "This fer 'nuff?" she asked.

Otis stopped, then moved forward a few more steps. Emma stood her ground, her face lifted, calm, proud of herself for once in her life . . . but frightened, too.

"Steele's goin' to be nosin' 'round askin' 'bout whar I was last night. He's goin' to pin that gal's killin' on somebody, and it ain't goin' to be me. If'n he comes a smellin' 'round, you tell him I was in bed all night. Hear?"

"But you warn't, Otis. You know that."

"I ain't said I was. I said ya tell him I was!"

"But you warn't."

"Goddammit, woman! Yer due a whippin', 'n yer gonna get it if'n ya don't heed what I'm a tellin' ya." Otis jerked the whip out of his belt, and Emma backed off a few paces.

"I done tol' ya at Fort Stockton, Otis Collins, that I ain't takin' no more whippin's."

"Oh, ya ain't, is ya?"

"You killed that gal, Otis."

Her words stopped the arm that was raising the whip.

"What'd you say?" he said slowly, threateningly.

"You killed that poor girl."

"Ya don't know what yer a sayin'. That 'poor gal' warn't nothin'! Even you is more'n what she was, Emma. She'd screw anythin' that walked!"

"That warn't no reason to kill 'er."

"I ain't sayin' I killed 'er."

"No. I'm a sayin' it. Maudy saw you puttin' that pretty green bracelet she was always a wearin' in yore box. I got it right here in my pocket."

At first Otis was stunned. He seemed to be rooted to the spot where he stood. Then he took a deep breath, his chest heaving. He was actually trembling with fury. It was a full minute before he could speak.

"Ya let that snot-nosed brat get in my box! I'll kill 'er!" His jaw was thrust out, his huge body hunched to spring on her.

"No! You ain't goin' to hurt Maudy."

"I ort to a killed *you* and not that slut! Leastways she done some good fer me! Got sassy, she did. Sassy and snotty, like yer gettin' sassy and snotty!" His voice was low, hard, laced with icy rage.

The whip snaked out and cut Emma across the face. The pain held her motionless for a second. Her first reaction was to run back to camp. She spun around. The next lash caught her across the shoulders and back, cutting into her like a knife and almost throwing her to the ground. She stumbled to regain her balance. Otis was in a frenzy, putting all his strength behind the whip. Emma fumbled for the six-gun in the waistband of her skirt and suffered one more biting slash from the whip. When she turned, she had the gun in her hand. Otis never even saw it. She fired, and fired again.

The shots sounded like pops in Emma's ears. Then there was silence.

Otis had been flung backward and lay sprawled on the ground. Emma stood holding the gun ready, knowing that if he so much as moved she would shoot again. The blood from the slash on her face rolled down over her mouth, but she didn't notice.

When she was sure Otis was not going to get up again, she staggered over to a tree and clung to its trunk. Her head whirled, her stomach churned. She closed her eyes, leaned over, and vomited.

Twenty

May 25.

I have already written about the murder of Cora Lee Watson and the shooting of her killer by his wife. Tonight I will mention that Otis Collins was buried near the spot where he died, with only the men who dug his grave present. Mrs. Collins had been brutally whipped by her husband before she shot him. Everyone has been terribly shaken by these events, but more of people's hidden strengths are emerging, and I think we are all drawing closer together in mutual need and respect. We are fortunate we have Doctor Hook, who took care of Mrs. Collins's injuries and gave her a potion to make her sleep. Mrs. Taylor took over the care of Maudy Collins until her mother is recovered.

We arrived in Fort Davis in the middle of the afternoon. It is a large fort spread out in the mouth of a canyon about one-half mile south of Limpia Creek. The fort was named for Jeff

Davis and was put here to protect travelers from the Apache and Comanche Indians. It is the closest thing to a town we have seen since we left Fort Smith. There are many buildings, barracks, shops, officers' quarters, and even quarters for officers' families. We would like to linger here for a day, but Mr. Steele is determined to move on in the morning.

Something happened just before the train reached Fort Davis that Tucker could not record in the journal. Not at this time, anyway. But it was tremendously important to her, and the relief she felt was so acute as to be both a pleasure and a pain.

The air was clear, no clouds spotted the sky. It was pleasant sitting on the wagon seat with a small breeze fanning their faces. The mules walked easily on the ribbon of trail that ran through the green grass. Here the grazing was good, there was plenty of fuel, and the spring-fed creek was clear and cool. The mountains filled the western sky. The desert lay behind them—and beyond the mountains ahead of them—but this was now, and Tucker and Laura were enjoying it.

Frank Parcher rode up beside the wagon. "Hello, purty woman."

His gaze took in the angry flush that came to Tucker's cheeks and the venomous flash of her green eyes when they flicked toward him and then away. He had not spoken to her within anyone's earshot since that first day he had ridden out from

Brownwood to meet the train. Tucker ignored him and unnecessarily snaked the whip out over the backs of the mules. Sensing the tension, Laura remained quiet.

"I'm goin' to be a leavin' ya when we get to the fort. I ain't goin' to be gone fer long." Tucker looked straight ahead. "Ya goin' to miss me, purty woman?" he asked with a chuckle. "I'll be missin' seein' that purty hair a shinin' in the sun and watchin' ya movin' 'round in the light of the fire." He rode alongside without taking his eyes from Tucker's face. "Nothin's changed, purty gal, nothin' atall. We'll be meetin' up again, ya can count on it. I'm a waitin' man . . . a man what waits till the time is right. Don't ya be forgettin' all the things I tol' ya." He glanced over his shoulder and then back to Tucker's set face and rigid back. He laughed. "I swear, if you ain't the beatinest woman I ever did see! Yer mad as a hornet and I ain't done nothin' . . . yet. Wal, so long fer now, purty woman."

He wheeled his horse, cut between the wagons, and rode out across the prairie. Chata, leading a string of mules, moved up even with the wagon but stayed far to the side. He was looking at Tucker when she glanced at him, and she knew the young Mexican boy had deliberately pulled up beside them when he saw Frank beside their wagon. She was beginning to wonder how much the men knew about Parcher. She smiled at him and waved her hand, receiving a flashing smile in reply.

She turned to see a frown on Laura's face. "That was the scout from the other train, wasn't it? I don't like the way he talked to you. What did he mean? Has he talked to you before?"

Tucker laughed. For once lately it was not forced—she actually felt like laughing. Parcher was leaving the train! Oh, thank God!

"He thinks he's irresistible to women, that's all. I don't pay any attention to him," Tucker bubbled.

"But he's talked to you before. You never said anything about it."

"I'll swear to goodness, Laura! It really wasn't worth mentioning. It wasn't important at all. I'd like to forget I ever saw the . . . snake!"

"See there? I could tell you didn't like him. Are you afraid of him?"

"Him?" Tucker scoffed. "What can he do to me?"

"I don't know, but I don't like him. I don't think Lucas would like for him to be talking to you like that."

Not even the mention of Lucas could dampen the wild, sweet relief in Tucker's breast.

"I'm sure not telling him about it, and I don't want you to tell him either, Laura. I can take care of myself, and you, too, if I have to."

"I still think he should know. He could protect you from that man."

"Oh, flitter! He didn't protect Cora Lee from Otis Collins."

"That's not fair, Tucker. We all know that Cora Lee wandered at night and didn't pay any attention to what anyone said."

"Let's don't talk about Cora Lee, and let's don't

talk about Frank Parcher. Let's just be glad we're off that desert."

Lucas led the train down the Overland Trail right through the center of Fort Davis. They passed the quartermaster storehouse, the cavalry stables and corrals, stone barracks, and a long line of officers' quarters with small kitchens built behind them. Everyone stopped their work to watch the train pass.

Tucker was beginning to believe they were never going to stop when Lucas called a halt at the far edge of the fort. Then she realized that they had reached a good spot, rather secluded, and that they would be free to wash in the creek without an audience of lonesome, woman-hungry men watching.

"Isn't it wonderful to be clean again?" Laura was able to say a short while later. She was toweling her hair. The women were taking turns squatting in the stream in their shifts and bathing while the others stood watch. Now, with their britches and shirts washed and hanging on the side of the wagon to dry, and with cotton dresses covering their clean bodies, Laura and Tucker stood on the bank to guard while the rest of the women bathed. Comradeship had deepened among them since the death of Cora Lee. It had truly started back when Laura and Billy had been rescued from the bull. And now the bond was extended to include Mrs. Collins and Mrs. Taylor.

"Will you be all right for a while if I go down and help Mrs. Taylor with Maudy?" Tucker asked solicitously.

" 'Sakes alive! I'll be fine. Go on and don't worry about me," Laura assured her friend.

To Laura's trained ears, even the tone of Tucker's voice told her that something had happened to ease the strain her friend had been under recently. She hadn't had that light, familiar tone for several weeks. They hadn't discussed Lucas since that terrible night in the wagon when Tucker had said she didn't love him. Laura held out hope that the breach between them could be patched. She would talk to Buck about it. Tonight I will be with my darling Buck, she reminded herself happily. I am surely the luckiest girl in the world!

That evening supper turned into a rare treat, with bread and sweet cakes purchased from the fort bakery.

"You look awfully pretty tonight," Tucker said when Laura climbed out of the wagon after they had eaten.

"My beau is coming to call," Laura explained happily.

"So that's why you tied your hair back with your new blue ribbon."

Laura put her hands up and gave the ribbon a little tug. "Does it look all right?"

"Pretty as a fresh cow pie resting in soft green grass," Tucker teased.

"Oh, Tucky! You're crazier than a scalded cat!"

"Maybe so, but you do look pretty tonight."

"Thank you. Tucky, I haven't told you for a long time, but I do love you."

"I know that, you silly girl!" Tucker said lightly, thinking she had kept the emotional tremor out of her voice.

"You cry on me, Tucker, and I'll . . . hit you with something!"

"Back to your old tricks, Laura Foster? I'll take you down and sit on you!"

They were silent for a while after that. It had been a long time since they had felt like this. So much had happened to them since Tucker had first read the advertisement in the paper and had applied for the teaching job. Laura's future was now tied up with Buck's. Tucker was going to be alone again for the first time since she was eight years old.

Tucker couldn't bear the silence any longer. "I'm going to clean the wagon while you're with Buck," she said.

"Why don't you wait and let me help?"

"You've done your share of cleaning and fetching wash water. Tonight I'm going to clean."

It was after dark by the time Lucas had completed the hundred and one chores connected with the train. He was weary in both body and spirit. The horror of finding Cora Lee dead on the desert, the killing of Otis Collins, the strain of waiting to know if he was going to have to shoot Rafe Blanchet—all combined with the gnawing ache in his heart that had begun with Tucker's senseless behavior.

There was not a thing he could do about most of his problems, but there was something he could do about the one with Tucker. He could get things straightened out between them—or ended—once and for all. If he was convinced things were over between them, maybe he could get her out of his mind.

The first step was to bluntly ask Buck to keep Laura away from the wagon for a good long while. Buck showed a rare glimpse of his sense of humor when he said he planned to do that anyway, but not for the purpose of making the wagon master's courting easy for him. The next thing Lucas did was to pick up clean clothes from the freight wagon, walk down to the creek, and plunge in.

It had not taken Tucker long to clean the wagon. There was not much to do except shake out the bedrolls, dust off the trunks and boxes, and sweep the layer of dust from the floor. She did this and was about to step from the end of the wagon when Lucas appeared. Swiftly and silently he took her by the forearms and backed her into the wagon. She backed away in surprise, and he followed until she was cornered in the front of the wagon with no place else to go. Butterflies took flight in her stomach.

"What do you want?" she demanded.

"Sit down," he ordered. "I can't stand up straight in this damn thing."

"Then get out."

"Not on your life. Sit down," he said curtly.

Startled somewhat by the fact that this arrogant man thought nothing of entering her wagon without an invitation, she obeyed. He sat down opposite her, and in the close confines of the wagon his knees touched hers.

"I've had time to think. Not much, due to all that's happened the last few days, but one thing is clear in my mind, Tucker Houston, and that is that you're a woman who needs a strong hand." She started to interrupt and he said, "Keep quiet and listen." His eyes wandered over her tight expression with insolent freedom, "I don't know what game you're playing, but I know you're a liar."

Tucker felt herself go hot with anger beneath the stinging scorn in his voice and expression. Itching to hit him, she clenched her fist.

"Don't," he said, and she read the secret amusement in the depths of his eyes before they narrowed to mere slits of frozen light in the deeply tanned face. "You were lying. The things you said to Cora Lee were things you made up in an instant of anger over something she said to you. I don't want to know what made you say them. I just want you to know that I'll not put up with your childish attempts to pass me off as a plaything you used to amuse yourself." He spoke softly but distinctly, each word dropping into the ominous stillness like a cold, hard stone. He seemed to be deadly calm. "Do you understand what I'm saying?"

A bead of sweat appeared on Tucker's upper lip. After a moment she swallowed, and then her growing anger forced her into speech—reckless, almost stuttering, speech.

"You—you've got to be the most arrogant man in the world! Is it beyond your realm of thinking that I may have decided that I don't like you, that I want nothing more to do with you? I . . . don't want you in this wagon. Your job as wagon master does not give you the right to come in here uninvited. Did you come to get your picture back? Well, here it is!" She reached behind her, grabbed the doeskin package, and thrust it into his hands.

"Hush up!" He set the package aside and caught her wrist in fingers like iron bands. "You're going to have to learn to keep your tongue under control."

The command in his voice made her shiver, but pride forced her to defy him. "You won't be the one to teach me!"

Deep breaths lifted her firm breasts and shuddered through her lips as she fought for control. Even as she said the words, she knew she shouldn't have issued the challenge.

"You're going to stay in line from this night on, Red. I'm tired of fighting your fiery moods. One wrong step and I'll spank your bottom." He spoke with lazy calmness, but the threat was no idle one. "I haven't waited all this time to find you just to let you make my life miserable."

The words burned into her mind. He was thinking about the woman in the portrait again!

"I'm going to marry you, Tucker Red."

"I don't even look like her!" she blurted. "I don't look like that . . . whore!"

"She was no whore and you know it. And you do look like her, but that isn't the reason I'm going to marry you. I'm marrying you because I love you, not a picture, because you love me and need me, because there'll never be another man who can take my place in your life. You love me, Tucker Red!"

"I don't!" she sputtered.

With a quick jerk she was forced into his lap, and before she could catch her breath he had pinched out the candle.

"You are the stubbornest, most muleheaded, cantankerous woman I have ever met," he said decisively before he covered her mouth with his. In the far recesses of her mind she seemed to remember he had said the same words to her once before.

He took her lips in a hard, unyielding kiss, as if by his action he could use up some of his anger. She struggled, her pride refusing to let her lie docile in his arms. One hand moved to hold her head, and his arms held her trapped against his chest.

He raised his lips long enough to whisper: "Be still or, by God, I'll give you something to wiggle about!"

"No! Lucas . . . don't."

"I'm going to love you, Red," he said, his voice a throaty growl.

"No! Laura will—"

"Laura won't be back for a long time."

"You . . . planned this!" she yelped in shocked dismay.

"Yes, I planned this. I dreamed about this and I'm going to love you, even if I die afterward! And it's going to be a proper loving, Red. Take off your dress." His lips were moving over her face, and he raised her head to look into her eyes.

"You think that because I let you once that—"

"Don't talk that way," he said sharply. "Don't you dare dirty what we did back by the Colorado. Stand up and take off your dress or, by God, I'll tear it off."

She stood with her back to him and unbuttoned her dress. She knew she wanted him, and she would be proud to despite his taunts. She wanted him to love her tenderly, as he had once beside the Colorado, yet he was so fierce now she was almost afraid.

He was ready for her when she turned. She could see the glow of his nude body. He threw the bedroll down onto the floor of the wagon.

"Come here and kiss me, Red."

Pride fought desire. Tucker faltered. It shouldn't be this way, she thought, so deliberate, so unfeeling, anger and resentment causing him to do what love should have prompted. "I wish you . . . wouldn't."

"No, you don't. Come here." He pulled her into his arms and sank down onto the pallet.

His kisses were fierce, his mouth moist and firm forcing hers to open so his tongue could wander her soft inner lips before venturing deeper. Her breasts, with only the thin material of her shift covering them, were crushed against him, his thighs molded to hers. She trembled, trying not to feel, willing herself not to like what he was doing to her, but it was futile. Her flesh and blood, nurtured by her love for him, responded.

His skin felt satiny smooth, warm, and she stroked

his arm with her palm, sliding it over his shoulder to the muscles of his back. He shifted position and quickly drew her shift over her head and folded his arms and legs about her. His hands became wonderfully gentle, and it seemed that time, and with it her resistance, stretched into the merest gossamer, so that she made no effort to prevent him from touching any part of her with his hands or his lips.

"You are so beautiful," he breathed against her mouth, his voice thick yet full of wonder. His lips moved across hers slowly, as if afraid he would miss a tiny part. His fingers traced every nerve and plane of her form, touching her with the gentle control of a lover determined to give as well as receive pleasure. Tucker ached for him, heat gathering in the sensitive areas of her body and giving rise to an urgency that could only be appeased by the weight and driving force of his body.

He kissed her a long, lingering, wonderfully tender kiss and settled his body onto hers. Her palms smoothed his back and came to rest against his flat buttocks as they lifted and he reached down to grasp hers. This was love. His body, his being, wordlessly expressed the depths of it with painstaking tenderness and reverence. He gave of himself, and sensations swirled as two bodies united and became one. His mouth covered hers as a cry rose up in her throat, trapping it in his own, and love rushed in to meet the outpouring of their passion.

Eventually they were still. Her arm circled his shoulder, and his head rested heavily on her breast.

His half-open mouth turned to her skin, moist and warm. His face was damp. She smoothed the black hair from his forehead in a caressing motion. Gradually his taut body relaxed, and his mouth nuzzled the rigid nipples on her breasts. There was a strange quiet in both of them. She held him like a tired child, clutched fiercely to protect him from all the problems that plagued him. She stroked the back of his head, loving his weight, his warmth, and wishing she could keep him safe and secure here in her arms until they put this savage country behind them.

Lucas stirred, raised his head, and peered into her eyes. His own were filled with warm affection. He began to kiss her, lazily, thoroughly.

"You going to behave now, Red?" he asked in a loving, softly slurred voice.

"If I don't, will I get this punishment again?" Her hands roamed his torso from his shoulders down over his lean ribs.

He chuckled. "After I spank your backside." He cradled her against him and found her lips.

She was feeling happy and lazy and satisfied as his mouth caressed hers gently, firmly. A little noise came from his throat and, drawing her closer, gentility gave way to greed. He shifted his thighs, and tangible proof of his returning desire pressed against her.

"Damn! One sweet bite of you calls for another. I could dally with you all day and never get anything done."

"What'd be so bad about that?"

"You'd be pregnant before we got to California," he said between kisses.

"What'd be so bad about that?" she repeated.

He raised his head and looked at her with surprise. "You wouldn't care?"

" 'Course not. I want dozens of kids and . . . think what fun we'll have making them."

"Oh, Red," he murmured, his voice cracking, "don't ever scare me like you did. Be as ornery as you want, fight me if you must, but don't threaten to leave me or say you don't love me!" His voice was rough with remembered pain.

"I'm sorry, Lucas. Truly, I am. Someday when this wretched journey is over, we'll read the journal entries together and tell each other everything else that happened each step along the way." With her hands on his cheeks, she forced him to look into her eyes. "I've never loved this way before, and sometimes it's . . . painful," she whispered.

"It's a pain I wouldn't have missed for anything." His face changed with his happy grin. "You look a mess. Your hair is all tangled."

"You don't look so great, yourself. You need a haircut."

"Do you want to do it?"

"Sure. I've got some shears in my trunk."

"Come on, then." He got to his feet and reached down to help her up. When he straightened, he cracked his head on the wooden bow that held the canvas top. "Goddammit!"

Tucker laughed.

"Seems you laughed the other time I cracked my head, too." He grabbed her and, hugging her to him, playfully bit her on the neck. "Oh, Tucker Red . . . I just want to pull you inside of me and take you wherever I go."

"I'd be like a flea and you'd be constantly scratching. I'd rather be a butterfly and sit on your shoulder."

"Oh, no! You'd always be flitting off somewhere and I'd be spending all my time chasing after you."

Outside the wagon, in the light from the lantern, Tucker trimmed his hair. Members of the train passed back and forth as they visited with neighbors or just walked around enjoying the coolness of the mountain air. They smiled or called a greeting, but didn't linger. They knew the wagon master had taken the teacher for his woman. Two romances had blossomed already, and each woman on the train held out hope that she, too, would find romance in California.

Twenty-one

Tonight and for as long as he wanted her, Frank Parcher was certain the redheaded woman would be his. He hadn't planned on making his move until the train was closer to El Paso, where it was just a short jump over into Mexico. But waiting was no longer possible. He congratulated himself on his patience so far—and it had taken patience to stay with the train taking orders from Steele. Frank chuckled and took off his hat to wipe the sweat from his forehead with his sleeve.

He'd ridden out of Fort Davis at midnight last night. Resting now in the dappling shadow of a scrub oak, he glanced back at the second horse he was leading. It carried the plunder bags and the second saddle he would need to take his woman to Mexico. He was busy calculating how he was going to get her away from the train. He knew for certain that he was going to shoot Lucas Steele out of the saddle. It would be an easy shot, and so satisfying. His rifle lay in front of him across the pommel, its muzzle pointing down the slope, his right hand grasping it around the action, his thumb caressing the hammer.

Back at the fort he had stood in the shadows and listened to the talk there. He'd discovered he wasn't the only one interested in the train. A trainload of women would bring a right smart lot of money sold in the right place. A whorehouse down south would give as much as a hundred dollars gold for a white woman. He'd heard some drifters talking about how easy it would be to pick off the train, and he'd decided to hightail it out. No bastard was going to cheat him out of his woman.

Thinking about that woman was making him careless. He put his heels to his horse and moved on. It had been a good long time since he had skylined himself on the top of a ridge. If a man wanted to live in this country, he stopped with a background against which his shape could offer no outline. Frank never took a risk if he didn't have to, whether he suspected an enemy to be nearby or not. He had known men who'd skylined themselves, slept beside a campfire, took a step away from their weapons . . . they were dead now.

There was one worry that kept inching its way into Frank's mind—Lone Buck Garrett. Sooner or later he would have to tangle with that half-breed. With Steele out of the way, more than likely it would be Garrett to come after him and the woman. He thought on it. If Lone Buck kept to his usual pattern of the last few weeks, he would be a good five miles ahead of the train, leaving the Mexican kid to scout the rear. If the

Collins woman was driving her own wagon, the drover would be back with the mules, leaving the kid free to roam. But that didn't particularly bother Frank. Only Garrett did.

The day was hot and muggy, and from the looks of the clouds in the southwest a storm could be brewing. Frank grinned with satisfaction. A good crackling storm would be a help. Now he searched out a probable vantage point where he could watch for the train and not be spotted by anyone from below. He reckoned it to be a little past noon. He had made straight for the hills when he left the fort and had found a spot to catch a few winks and give Lone Buck time enough to move out. Now he figured to be between Garrett and the train, and it was time to turn his sights on Steele. One shot would knock him out of the saddle and another would finish him off. In the hubbub that followed, he'd ride in and get his woman. She'd come willingly once he turned his gun on the blind gal.

Below him and to the right was a clump of bushes and a boulder. He gauged its height and his own position, then glanced about for a place to tie the horses.

Buck left the camp an hour before dawn. The night was still close about and there were no stars. He rode cautiously along the dim trail and headed southwesterly toward the hills. He avoided the trail the wagon train would take come dawn and cut straight across country. It was lonely, rugged terrain where stunted cedars and gnarled oaks clung to the ridges of the canyon and where low spreading shrubs with hookline thorns could cripple an unwary horse.

Chata had been waiting for him when he'd returned from his walk with Laura. He had sent the boy to the fort to see what he could find out about the eight men who had circled the train a few days back and to see if he could find out what Parcher was up to. He had known that no one was likely to pay any attention to a skinny Mexican kid hanging about.

Buck allowed himself a chuckle. The stupidity of some people! They were so busy looking at what was on the outside of a man's head, they paid no attention at all to what was on the inside.

Parcher had bought a horse and saddle and enough supplies for several weeks. The eight renegades had bought whiskey from the sutler and had camped outside the fort. Chata had not been able to get close enough to hear much of their talk, but he had heard enough to know the men were aware of the train of women and of how much a white woman would bring at a bordello in Mexico.

While he'd hashed over this information with Lucas, Buck had sent Chata back to watch Parcher. Parcher was the immediate danger; he was about to take action. So far the others had just talked. When Chata returned with the news that Parcher had ridden out, Buck and Lucas talked over their own plan of action and Buck lay down for an hour's sleep.

Now, with an eye to the sky and the probable storm that was brewing, Buck approached a rise in the ground where a stream dipped through a cut. He dismounted. While his horse drank its fill, Buck looked over the rise and studied the slope with a skeptical eye. Buck's mind had been sharpened and his senses honed by years of frontier living. He knew the mountains and how to live in them. No cat could move more quietly, no hawk had a keener eye, no deer was more alert. The Indians had taught him to live by his senses, and his senses told him that he was now midway between Parcher and the train.

Some distance ahead the valley narrowed before it widened out and finally opened onto the plains. If Parcher was waiting, he would be in that place.

Buck climbed into the saddle, crossed the stream, and pushed on, keeping near the trees. He did not head for the likely spot of ambush, but above it. He watched the sky for birds startled into flight and his eyes methodically swept from side to side, taking in every clump of brush, every outcropping of rock. He watched the sorrel's ears. He had cut his horse out of a wild herd whose ancestors had survived for genera-tions by being alert to danger. Self-preservation was bred into the animal. Buck worked his way along the upper level of the hillside, riding in and out of the trees, weaving a careful path.

He was emerging from behind a stand of spruce when he saw movement down below. He pulled up on the reins, and his horse stood perfectly still. He kept his eyes glued to the spot and saw the movement again. The sorrel's ears came up one at a time, flicked, and stood straight. Buck slid carefully from the saddle. What he had seen was the back of a horse, its tail swishing at the flies that tormented it. Looking carefully, he discerned a second horse. How far away? A quarter of a mile?

A small, open grassy spot lay before him. Farther down stood a clump of brush. To reach it he would be visible for no more than a few seconds. On the way down, he pulled a handful of tender grass. He paused behind the first clump of bushes he reached before he moved to the second, then started down the slope on an angle opposite the one he had been using. Using infinite care and keeping close to the cover of the brush, he approached the two horses from the front so they would see him and not be startled. Moving to their heads, he allowed them to take the grass from his hand. From this position Buck knew there was only one place Parcher could be waiting.

Buck took his gun from its holster and checked the load. He felt for the knife tucked in his belt at the small of his back. He squinted his eyes under the brim of his hat and studied the terrain with care, measuring the distance. It had been a long time since he had been quite this cautious. Nothing must happen to him now. His life had suddenly become very precious to him— ever since the small, golden-haired angel had come into his world.

He knew he shouldn't do it, but he allowed himself a moment to think of Laura. When he thought about her, it was like breathing clean, fresh air after being locked in the sweatbox at Yuma Prison. Sometimes the most important thing in a man's life came at the most unexpected time, he reflected. It had been that way with him. He hadn't wanted to come east with Lucas to take the women back to Coopertown; but knowing that Lucas needed the money to start a spread, he had agreed. Now no hour of the day passed that he didn't think of Laura. She was always with him. He hadn't believed himself capable of feeling this all-consuming love for another person.

Buck squatted down beside the waiting horses. They had accepted his presence and stood patiently swishing their tails. He chewed thoughtfully on a stem of grass and considered Parcher's position. It was well-chosen. The horse behind him stomped a restless hoof against the turf. Buck hoped the sounds of the horses would account for any noise he might make in his approach. A man of great patience, Buck was patient now. He waited for a sign from below. Movement! The movement was there and then it was gone. He waited, and there it was again: Parcher was moving to rest his back against the boulder. He had settled himself with his rifle across his knees.

As he watched and waited, Buck again allowed his thoughts to drift to Laura. In his reverie, he shifted his weight only a fraction, but it was enough to dislodge a cluster of pebbles near his foot. The stones tumbled noiselessly down the grassy slope. Buck, silently cursing himself, held his breath, waiting for them to lodge somewhere. But one pebble continued to roll and bounce, picking up speed until it struck and glanced off the boulder concealing Parcher with an unmistakable ping.

Parcher was instantly alert, lurching into a crouch but careful to stay within the protection of his rocky shelter. His rifle poised, he scrutinized the slope, peering cautiously in every direction. Buck was still hidden, scarcely breathing. After ten minutes of waiting and watching, Frank cautiously took a few steps out to make sure he was alone. He watched his horses standing unperturbed, swishing their tails, occasionally stamping a hoof, and, concluding that nothing was amiss, he settled back into his niche to watch for the train.

Buck waited almost half an hour, then slipped through the grass without a sound. About a dozen feet from Parcher he stood up and rested his hands on his hips. "You waitin' for somethin', Parcher?"

Buck watched the man's back stiffen, his head suddenly thrust forward in surprise, but Parcher made no other move. He was trailwise enough to know that, if he did, he was as good as dead. Buck waited, letting his silence work on the man's nerves. Finally, as he knew he would, Parcher began slowly to get to his feet.

"I'd be careful with that rifle if I were you."

"I ain't no fool," Frank growled as he turned.

"I'd say you were. Not even a half-wit greenhorn would lay himself out as open as you did." Buck could see that his taunt hit home when Parcher's fingers tightened on the rifle.

"Say yer piece. I'm movin' out."

"Just one of us is movin' out, and I figure it's goin' to be me."

Frank's legs spread and his shoulders dropped. "Ya think I'll jist stand here and let a stinkin' Injun shoot me?"

"You won't have any say in it." Buck's voice was quiet and he appeared to be relaxed, as if they were having a casual conversation. "I'm going to shoot you, Parcher. For Mrs. Blanchet."

"What? Who tol' ya 'bout her?" he growled. Backed into a corner as he was, the man looked wolfish. His face was dark, his eyes hard and cruel.

"Taylor's boy, Poppy. He watched you rape Mrs. Blanchet in the bushes, but slaves don't talk about white folks to other white folks. They only talk to Mexicans and . . . Indians."

"Niggers, Mexes, and Injuns! There ain't a hair's diff'rence a'tween 'em!" Frank sneered.

Buck grinned, his gaze on Frank's face. When the man was about to make his move, Buck would know it by the look in his eyes.

"I'd say from the looks of your plunder and that second horse, you wasn't plannin' to trail alone, Parcher. Was good of you to give me two good horses instead of one." Buck waited, giving Frank's anger a little more time to stiffen him up, before he gave his final jibe. "By the way, did you hear that Lucas Steele has taken one of the women for his own? The pretty teacher with the flaming red hair is his woman now."

Frank's eyes narrowed, and Buck ducked to the side as he fired. Two guns boomed at once. Frank's shot went wild; Buck's found its mark. Frank was flung back a half dozen steps. His rifle flew out of his hands as he grabbed his side. Buck crouched, waiting.

Frank writhed on the ground. He let out a cry and suddenly dug his heels into the turf, trying to push himself away from the spot where he'd fallen. Buck spotted the head of the big rattler as it swung around, startled from a doze when Parcher fell almost across its length. Its rattle quivered in warning, but Frank was unable to move away.

"Kill it!" he screamed. "For God's sake, kill it!"

"Why?" Buck asked calmly as he walked over to pick up Frank's rifle. "It's only trying to protect itself."

Clutching his wound, Frank tried to roll over to get away from the snake, but his movements only lured the creature in for the kill. He lay on his back and lifted his head, helplessly watching death close in on him. As he saw Buck standing by—motionless, looking on, not helping—the image of another such dance of death darted unbidden into his mind. He relived with sickening clarity the drama of a man being gored by a bull, while he himself sat watching unconcernedly. He let out a shuddering gasp as the rattler sank its fangs into his arm.

Parcher's face was white and twisted. Buck walked over and looked down at him. "For Mrs. Blanchet, and anyone else whose life you've ruined."

Frank's mouth opened wide and his eyes became wild. "Don't leave me like this! Leave . . . my gun!" he whimpered.

"So you can shoot me in the back?" Buck looked

upon him with cold, dispassionate eyes. "Too bad you won't have to suffer as long as you deserve to. The snake took care of that."

"Shoot me," Frank pleaded. "Shoot me. Ya'd put a horse outta its misery."

"A white man might, an Indian might not. I'm a breed, Parcher. Think on that while you wait for the buzzards to circle. It was a breed who did you in."

Buck walked back up the slope carrying the rifle. He heard Frank calling—pleading at first, then cursing. Without looking back, he shoved the rifle into the saddle scabbard and mounted Parcher's horse. Leading the spare mount, he rode up the incline, untied his own sorrel, and looped its reins over the saddle horn.

"Come on, boy. Let's get back to the wagons." He took up the lead rope, whistled for Dolorido to follow, and headed down toward the Overland Trail.

For some time Lucas had realized that this particular valley they were passing through was perilous. The slope rising from each side of the trail offered cover. It was the perfect place for an ambush. He wished to hell Buck would show up.

He was riding beside the lead wagon when he heard the shots. There were two of them, and they came so close together they could have been mistaken for one. But Lucas knew there were two as they barked hoarsely two, maybe three, miles away. He listened anxiously and scanned the landscape. There was silence and his anxiety grew. What was done was done, he told himself, and he couldn't do a damn thing about it but wait and see who came down out of the hills.

Up ahead the hills seemed to retreat. He wanted, suddenly, to get there as soon as possible. He shouted to Mustang to whip up the mules and pointed to the open country ahead. He wheeled his horse and rode down the line urging each driver to keep up. The wagons went lumbering by, the women driving the teams, calm and composed, doing what had to be done. They accepted the orders without the least sign of panic, and the train picked up speed.

At the end of the line he saw a rider coming at a dead run. It was Chata. He was leaning low in the saddle and didn't slow up until he reached the end wagon. Then he drew up sharply, his horse rearing high.

"They come, *señor*!"

"Are they trying to catch up?"

"They come fast, *señor*."

"Did they see you?"

"No. I do what *Señor* Buck say."

"Then we'll run for it and get as far out into open country as we can. Ride tail, Chata, and if it looks like they're going to charge us, fire two shots."

Lucas shouted to the drovers leading the strings of mules to move out ahead. The last wagon in line was a freight wagon. The driver shifted his cud of tobacco and nodded in assent to the curt instructions to stay behind but keep up. The Taylor wagon was next. Lucas wasn't sure how the man would react under pressure. "We got eight renegades coming up fast behind us. We're heading for open country in case we have to stand them off."

"We'll keep up," Taylor shouted, then to his wife, "Get the rifle, Alice."

Taylor's boy, Poppy, was driving for Emma Collins.

"Can you shoot, boy?" Lucas asked when he came alongside.

"No, sah." The boy's eyes became large with fright.

"Well, I can!" Emma called out and started climbing, painfully, over the wagon seat.

"Keep up! Keep up!" Lucas shouted to each of the drivers.

At Tucker's wagon his eyes clung to her white face. The breeze created by the fast-moving wagon had blown her hat off, and her hair was a cloud of fire floating behind her. She glanced at him and back at the mules.

"Giddap! Get moving, ya blasted, worthless, crow bait!" she shouted, and Lucas couldn't hold back and grin that creased his serious face. The whip snaked out smartly and flicked the rump of a mule. Lucas looked and looked again. It was Laura's hand that held the whip! She sent it cracking out over the backs of the mules again. Tucker glanced at Lucas and saw him grin. She pursed her lips in a kiss. He returned the gesture. God! What a pair, he thought, and moved on.

The train that had stretched over a quarter of a

mile closed up to half that distance. Lucas scanned the landscape for signs of Buck. They were nearing the place where the valley opened upon the plains. Another mile would be as far as the mules could run. That should bring them well out into the open.

Lucas had almost reached the front of the train when he heard the two warning shots. Wheeling his horse, he raced back to see Chata motioning frantically. A group of horsemen, spread out, were charging the train at full gallop.

To run would invite disaster, for there was no place to run to. Lucas knew there was only one defense against a mounted attack: the circle. It had proven itself time and again against any number of raids when Lucas was freighting with his father.

Yelling like an Indian, he pushed his horse into a lunging run and raced for the head of the train. "Circle!" he shouted. "Circle the wagons!"

Mustang caught the sound of his voice and swung his team to the right. Conditioned from their many nights of making camp, the others followed. The frightened teams swung wide, but they followed Mustang's lead. The drivers tried desperately to keep their seats on the jolting, bone-bruising ride across the rough prairie.

Shouting like a wild man, Lucas raced from wagon to wagon shouting instructions. "Keep up! Keep up! Tighter! Pull 'em in!"

Gunfire erupted from the end of the train. The fight had started. Lucas drew his six-gun and wheeled to face the charging renegades. He cut across open ground and fired. A horse went down, throwing its rider over its head. In an instant he shifted his gun to another target and fired, then fired again. The second shot winged a black-bearded man who jerked with the impact. Instantly he swung his mount and headed for Lucas. As they came abreast, the lean, hairy man raised his gun to fire, then threw his arms wide and toppled from the saddle. The frightened horse raced on past Lucas dragging the man face down over the dusty trail. A wagon raced by and Lucas caught a glimpse of Emma Collins in the back, her rifle at her shoulder, firing coolly and cautiously.

The panic-stricken mules continued to run although the circle had been completed. The drovers had turned the stock loose when the fighting began, and now the frenzied animals charged into the middle of the wild scramble around the wagons.

The attackers had initially split up, half charging one side of the train and half the other. Now they were further divided by the circle. Lucas took in his surroundings, searching for a target. Not one of the four inside the circle was still standing. He started to ride between the wagons to the outside when a mule was hit by a blast from a shotgun. The stricken animal went to its knees, the wagon tongue jabbed into the ground as the mule fell, the wagon jackknifed and turned over.

Something lunged up from the ground and jerked Lucas from the saddle. It was the man who had been flung to the ground when his horse was shot out from under him. The man was big, desperate, and fighting for his life. They grappled, rolling over and over in the grass, struggling, gouging. A rock-hard fist slammed against the side of Lucas's head. He held onto his gun. He felt something tear into his clothing, felt the bite of the knife in his thigh. He smashed the man in the face with his gun barrel.

As suddenly as it had begun, the fight was over. The entire attack, from beginning to end, had lasted no more than a few minutes. Two of the raiders turned tail and ran for the hills, leaving their companions, dead or dying, among the chaos they had created.

The shooting stopped after a few wild shots were thrown at the retreating enemy. The mules stood trembling in their harnesses, their heads hung low and their sides heaving. The violence had ended. People poured out of the wagons and ran to help those who were hurt.

Lucas stood over the unconscious renegade and shoved his gun back into his holster. He picked up his hat and put it on his head in a purely automatic gesture. He could feel the wetness of blood inside his clothing, and the ache in his head throbbed heavily. His eyes searched the area, and his heart began to pound with wild, desperate fear.

"Oh, God! Oh, God!" he muttered hoarsely and began to run.

The dying mule struggled in its harness beside Tucker's overturned wagon. She was on her hands and knees, numb with shock, her hair in wild disorder, her clothing ripped.

"Laura!" she called frantically. "Laura!" She looked up at Lucas when he knelt beside her. "I can't find Laura," she cried.

Twenty-two

Blue was whining. Tucker, on her knees beside the overturned wagon, could hear the forlorn pup.

"Laura!" She fought down the ugly taste of fear in her throat. "Laura! Can you hear me? Help me!" she cried. "Somebody help me."

Lucas cut the dying mule free of its harness and unhitched its teammate. People were coming from all directions in answer to Tucker's cries. They lined up alongside the wagon and lifted the heavy box. Blue came scampering out. Lucas crawled through the torn canvas and crushed boxes. He found Laura lying crumpled and still, the whip clutched in her deathly white hand. He grasped her carefully under the arms and pulled her free of the rubble.

Her face and head were bloody, her shirt badly torn. Tucker dropped to her knees beside her and grasped her hands, trying to squeeze life into them.

"Laura! Laura!" she screamed over the still, silent form. "Laura, answer me!" But there was no response. "Laura, wake up. Oh, Laura, don't die. Please don't die. You're not dead! You can't be!" she moaned. She tried to wipe the blood from Laura's face with her hands. "Laura!" she sobbed. "Please be all right."

Lucas felt weak and remembered his own wound. At first he had thought it was no more than a small cut; now he wasn't sure. He took a step to comfort Tucker and knew he was bleeding heavily. He paused long enough to take the kerchief from around his neck and tie it about his thigh. He took Tucker firmly by the shoulders and led her away sobbing as someone came to carry Laura to Marie Hook.

Fifteen minutes later the camp was in some semblance of order. Two drovers and Chata had been seriously wounded. Several others, including Mrs. Shaffer, were injured slightly. Four of the raiders lay dead and two were dying. Marie and Rafe, with Billy's help, had spread bedrolls beside Rafe's wagon and were caring for the wounded. Laura had been moved there and lay in Rafe's bunk with Tucker sitting beside her.

It was only a little past the middle of the afternoon and so much had happened! Lucas walked his horse around the circle and looked toward the southwest for the hundredth time. His anxiety for Buck was now overriding his other concerns.

Someone had started a fire and a slow finger of smoke was pointing upward. There was something so everlastingly normal about starting a fire and boiling coffee. How many times had he seen his mother start a fire and begin to cook when the first shock of disaster was over, be it a death, a storm, or a sudden accident. It was so simple, a lighted fire, yet it gave a man comfort and security.

Lucas shaded his eyes and watched the movement on the hillside. Minutes later the movement materialized into three horses, two of them riderless. One broke away from the others and raced toward camp. Soon Lucas recognized Buck's sorrel, riderless, and a sense of grief, loss, and anger rose up to consume him.

Then the rider leading the extra horse whipped his mount and they thundered recklessly down the slope. A wave of relief washed over Lucas. No man could sit a horse coming down a slope like Buck. He rode out to meet him.

"Damn you! You scared the hell out of me letting Dolorido come in riderless."

"What's happened here? I heard the shooting."

"Renegades charged us from the rear. That Parcher's horse?"

Buck nodded. "He won't be needin' it. Anyone hurt here?"

"Chata, Valdez, and Cutler were hit pretty bad. Others not so bad. We killed four, two are dying, and two ran off."

Buck started to ride past him. Lucas knew his eyes were searching for Laura. Goddammit, he thought. There's no easy way to say it.

"Buck, wait. . . . Laura was hurt. The wagon jackknifed and rolled over. . . . She was under it." Buck stared straight ahead and Lucas wondered if he had heard him. He spurred his horse and trotted up beside him. Buck sat stonily, his eyes shut. "She has several cuts on her head and she's scratched and bruised. No broken bones that Marie can find," he said, seeking to comfort his friend, but he was forced to add, "she's unconscious."

"Where is she?"

"In the Blanchet wagon. Tucker is with her."

Buck dropped the lead rope and slid from the saddle. He went to the end of the Blanchet wagon without seeing the wounded lying beside it. The canvas was folded back to allow the air to circulate. He looked in and saw Tucker sitting on a stool beside the bunk fanning Laura with a cardboard fan. Fear flooded over him like an icy wave.

He climbed inside. His heart contracted painfully at the sight of her scratched face and the deep gash on the side of her head. She was so pale, so still and so small. Her body scarcely showed beneath the sheet that covered it. A wet, bloody cloth lay against her forehead.

Tucker looked up with tearful, red-rimmed eyes. "She's been just like this. She hasn't moved," she whispered, and fresh tears rolled down her cheeks.

Buck looked down at Laura with bleak eyes and remembered the words she had whispered to him last night. *Hold me tight, Buck. Don't let me go.* Oh, God! If he could only hold on to her now and keep her from slipping away from him!

Tucker stood up and moved away from the bunk. "Do you want to sit with her for a while? I'll get fresh water and wash these rags." She piled the bloody rags in a wash basin.

Buck sat down on the stool and began to fan Laura with his hat. Tucker left the wagon. She wanted to be alone so she could cry freely. Cry for Laura, who had been so happily in love; cry for Buck, who looked so stricken; and cry for herself, because she felt she couldn't bear it if Laura should die and be left behind in a prairie grave like Cora Lee.

At sundown one of the raiders died and was taken away to be buried beside the others. Working tirelessly, Marie tended to the wounded. Her quiet, efficient manner instilled confidence in the others and she had only to ask for a basin of water, a clean cloth, or the whiskey she used to sterilize the wounds for someone to jump and put it into her hands. Rafe had proved to be quite handy with the patients. He helped to set Chata's broken arm as well as hold him while Marie probed in his side for a bullet. The injured men looked on Marie as almost godlike. Her decisions were not questioned. When she looked back on this day, she would recall it was the first time she had been accepted as a doctor first and a woman second.

"Marie." Rafe took her elbow and helped her to her feet. "I know I should call you doctor, but may I call you Marie, just this one time?"

"Of course. I call you Rafe."

"Go along to the wagon and get some supper. I'll be here and I'll call out if you're needed," he urged gently.

"I think I will." She smiled. "You and Billy can take care of things for a while."

She walked away with the smile still on her face. Oh, my dear Rafe, she thought. This is the final day and you're all right! I gave myself two extra days from the time you were attacked by the bull, and they have passed. Someday I'll tell you about it, but not now. It's too soon!

During the early evening the other raider died, but not because Marie had not done everything she could to help him. Lucas had to submit to having the cut in his thigh cleansed and stitched closed. Parts from the wrecked wagon that could be used again were removed, and trunks and boxes were restored to order. The evening meal was eaten. The camp settled down around a large campfire to talk about the raid and to wait for news about Laura.

Emma Collins had accounted for two of the raiders. She and Maudy now sat chatting with the other members of the train. It seemed the Louisiana woman had come alive now that the overbearing presence of her husband had been removed.

Alice Taylor sat beside her husband saying little. He had conducted himself admirably, in her estimation, and his own self-esteem had risen to the point where he was entering into the discussion freely. She was proud of him. She had always known that someday, somewhere, he would find himself. She believed he had found his place, here in the west.

Thoughts of Laura were uppermost in everyone's minds. She was much more than just a member of the train. Her courage, her confidence, and her cheerful disposition had earned her the affection of every man, woman, and child among them. Secretly each felt that if Laura with her sightless eyes could endure the hardships on the trail, they could, too. Marie did not build up false hopes about her recovery. She explained that Laura had suffered a stunning, damaging blow to the side of her head, and the swelling could cause injury to the brain. All they could do was keep her as still as possible and keep cold, wet cloths on her head to help hold down the swelling.

Buck sat beside Laura all through the night, moving aside only occasionally to make room for Tucker or Marie. Outside, firelight played shadow games on the white wagon covers. There was no shortage of firewood due to the wrecked wagon, and people moved around camp quietly as if by doing so they were in some way helping Laura.

The night was pleasantly cool. The storm that had threatened had moved to the south and the sky was clear. Far off a coyote serenaded the night with plaintive music. Buck's moccasins crunched on the gravel as he walked out from the wagon. The mules flicked their long tails and continued cropping the lush grass. These were familiar sounds. Buck's ears had learned to sort the sounds, to pick out the strange, different ones from among all the others. Now he heard only the low murmur of voices coming from the wagon where the center of his world lay fighting for her life. Never had Buck encountered an absolute defeat, one that he couldn't cope with or turn aside from without regret. It had simply never occurred to him that a woman would bring him to the point where, if he lost her, his life would be over.

He returned to the wagon and took up his vigil beside the cot. Leaning over, he kissed the still lips tenderly. Tucker couldn't bear to watch. He wasn't even aware he was whispering to Laura that he loved her . . . over and over.

The hours before dawn were the slow hours. The minutes seemed like hours, the hours like days to those who waited. Tucker and Buck waited together. Lucas slept in snatches on the bedroll he'd flung out beside the wagon. Marie and Rafe sat with the injured, at times nursing cups of hot coffee in their hands.

Morning finally came, and the camp stirred. There would be no traveling today. It didn't need to be said. The day would be warm and sunny, but a gentle breeze rippled the tops of the wagons and promised relief from the heat. A canvas shelter was raised over the injured men to shade them from the sun.

Lucas went to the end of the wagon and called to Tucker. "You're dead tired, sweetheart." He lifted her down from the wagon and she clung to him.

"She hasn't moved, not even once, Lucas," she said wearily.

"Lie down and get some sleep." He pressed her down onto his bedroll. "I'll wake you if there's any change."

Tucker lay down obediently and her exhaustion overcame her. She drifted off to sleep.

In the middle of the morning the stage passed. Lucas rode out to stop it and send word of the attack back to Fort Davis. Shortly after that he woke Tucker, and she took up the vigil beside Laura. Buck went to the water barrel and poured several dippers of water over his head, washed, and poured himself a cup of coffee. He went to the other side of the wagon and sat down, leaned his back to the wheel, and looked off toward the mountains. His eyes filled with tears that rolled down his cheeks unchecked. He sat there not caring how much he might be exposing his human frailty to anyone who happened to pass by.

Shortly after Buck left her, Laura began to move her hands restlessly. Tucker changed the wet cloth on her head and noticed that her lips were moving slightly and that she seemed to be breathing more deeply. A frown puckered her brows, seemingly from pain, when she moved her head suddenly. Tucker called out to Marie.

Marie bent over Laura and listened to her heart, then held her fingers to the pulse at her wrist.

"She may be about to wake up. Hold the pillows on each side of her head so she can't turn it."

Tucker moved to the head of the bunk and Marie took the stool. Together they waited.

"Oh," Laura murmured. She tried to lift her hand to her head and Marie gently intercepted it. "Oh, my head!"

The words were clear and they filled Tucker with sudden hope. Laura's eyelids quivered and she opened her eyes, shut them, then opened them again.

She blinked as if she was trying to wake up. Tucker started to speak, but Marie shook her head, so she remained silent. "Is the fighting over?" Laura asked suddenly.

"Yes, it's over," Marie said firmly.

"Tucky!" Laura's eyes flew open. "Is Tucker all right?"

Tears were rolling down Tucker's face. "I'm all right, you silly girl. But you scared me half to death!"

Laura's eyes remained wide open. She reached up her hands to grasp something. Marie took them in hers. A frightened look came over Laura's face.

"What is it?" she whispered. "What happened to me?"

Holding tightly to Laura's hands, Marie bent close to her face and peered into her eyes.

"Is it night?" There was panic in Laura's voice.

"What makes you ask, Laura?" Marie asked calmly.

"I don't know. It's different! It's not dark!" She was beginning to tremble.

"It's all right. Shut your eyes for a minute and open them slowly. Don't be afraid and try not to move your head."

"I'm afraid! I can see something! Am I dreaming? Am I dead?"

"Do you see something moving?" Marie moved her hand back and forth in front of Laura's face.

"Yes! Is it my hand?" The words came with a sob.

"No. It's my hand. I'll take it away. Now do you see anything?"

"I see white. Everything is white!"

"You're seeing the white cover over the wagon."

"I can see your face! Oh, Lord! Marie, I see your face!"

"Don't panic," Marie said calmly. "And don't cry. Tears will keep you from seeing. Lie still and blink your eyes."

Marie moved and made room for Tucker. Tucker grabbed Laura's hands. There was such a different look to the eyes that fastened on her face.

"Tucky! Oh, Tucky, I can see you! I really can. I can see your face and your hair like fire . . . you look like I thought you would only . . . prettier! Oh, I'm so glad I got to see you! Please . . . I'm afraid it will go . . . before I see Buck! I want to see Buck! Oh, Tucky, will it go before I see Buck?" Her voice was a wail of plaintive longing.

Tucker stumbled to the end of the wagon. "Buck!" she screamed. "Buck!" Her almost hysterical cries reached into every part of the camp. "Buck, come quick!"

Buck reached the end of the wagon in seconds, his face white, his heart pounding with dread. He was inside the wagon and on his knees beside Laura before Tucker could say anything. Laura's eyes were open and her hands reached for him.

"Laura! *Mi vida!* Thank God!" He held her hands to his lips.

"Buck! My darling Buck," she whispered. Freeing one of her hands she held it against his cheek. "You're . . . beautiful!" Buck leaned closer and looked at her eyes. "I can see you! Something wonderful has happened and I can see you!" She tried to smile. "Oh, Buck! I was so afraid it would go before I could see you!" Her lips quivered as if she would cry, but she held back and refused to let the tears dim what she was seeing. Buck's lips moved, but no words came. He looked at Marie and she smiled.

"She's right. Something wonderful happened. The blow she received today seems to have undone the damage she suffered long ago. I've heard of such a thing, but I never thought I would witness it."

"Will she be all right?"

"I think so. The fact that she came out of the coma so quickly means there was no permanent damage." Marie stepped out of the wagon.

Tucker bent down and kissed Laura's cheek. "Laura, I'm so happy. Oh, honey, it's so wonderful I can hardly believe it! I'm going to leave before I bawl. I don't want you to see me all red-eyed and sniffling." She kissed her again and hurried away.

Left alone with Laura, Buck gripped her hands and smoothed the wet hair back from her forehead, being careful of the wound on the side of her head. She smiled at him palely, her eyes open wide and clear—smoke-fringed blue eyes miraculously come back to life and seeing him, truly seeing him. He felt suddenly shy.

"Buck." Laura spoke quietly. "Everything seems so . . . strange." An age seemed to pass before she said anything more, an age of tense uncertainty for Buck. Her eyes were fastened on his face, steady and intently probing. "There were many things I wanted to see, but I wanted to see you most of all." She blinked, trying not to cry "It's been so long since I've seen a man, I pictured you as . . . older." Her lips quivered and she lifted her hand to his cheek. "You're so handsome! . . . I never thought I'd see your . . . dear face!" Buck didn't know what to say. "It seems like I don't know you, you're so beautiful," she whispered. "I think I want to shut my eyes and listen to you talk to me so I'll know it's you!" Her face crumbled, the effort to hold back the tears failed. "Now . . . I'm scared you won't want me, even if I can . . . see!" There was pain, anguish, pleading in her voice.

A growl of protest came from his throat. "Won't want you?" He bent and kissed her tenderly on the mouth. The kiss lasted a long time and was full of sweetness. "You're the only thing I have ever loved. I didn't know what love was until I met you. You are my heart—my soul—my everything!" His humbled voice vibrated with emotion.

"You're . . . sure?" she asked shakily.

"I was never so sure of anything in my life!" His voice was a soft purr of happiness, and he bent to kiss her again.

Laura closed her eyes for only a second. She wanted to look and look at him. Gently she lifted his face and cupped it in her two hands.

"Darling Buck, I'm just now beginning to believe that I can see," she whispered. "Oh, Buck! Just think . . . I'll see the mountains and everything between here and California. And Blue! I'll see Blue and . . . Lucas and Lottie, and . . . I'll see a tree! And . . . I'll see myself! Tucker said I was pretty, but I never believed her." She began to cry.

Sobs caught in Buck's throat. He swallowed repeatedly.

"You can believe me, *mi alma*! You are more than pretty. You are beautiful! When I first saw you, I thought you were the most beautiful thing I had ever seen. Even if you were not, you are my life. You will see everything with me beside you, loving you, taking care of you." He lowered his head, not wanting her to see the tears in his eyes. He kissed her gently again and again and whispered to her about the life they would share.

The day was spent in celebration. At intervals during the day every member of the train was allowed to climb into the wagon so Laura could see them. There was much laughter from tear-streaked faces as she greeted them and exchanged some bits of chitchat with them. Through it all she held on to Buck's hand as if he were the only solid thing in her reeling world. His face, weary and haggard only hours before, was relaxed and smiling. And his eyes, when they rested on Laura, were adoring.

The train would not move until Marie decided it would be safe for Laura and the wounded men to travel. With that in mind, the camp settled into a new routine. The stock was moved to fresh grass, wheels were repaired, bedding aired, wagons cleaned and rearranged. Laura and Tucker would take over Marie's wagon, and she and Billy would move in with Rafe. It seemed the natural thing to do.

Later that night Tucker and Lucas stole away for a few quiet minutes alone.

"Should you be walking on that leg, darling?" Tucker put her arm around him and lifted his arm to her shoulders.

"I'd walk on a stub to get out here alone with you," he said as he pulled her into his arms and kissed her for a long, exquisite moment. He raised his head and she saw the love glowing in his eyes. She felt as if she hadn't been in his arms for months, hadn't kissed him in years. This was the man she loved, the other part of herself. She snuggled her face into the curve of his neck so her lips were against his skin.

"I love you, you . . . wild man, you! I was never so scared or so proud as when you charged that . . . bunch of—"

"Bastards?" he whispered with a chuckle. "You can say it, just this one time."

She laughed and wrapped her arms around him, hugging him fiercely to her.

"Just one time?"

"As I've said . . . you need a firm hand, Tucker Red."

She looked into his face with undisguised hunger. Their love glowed in unspoken communication. Each could read what was in the thoughts of the other.

"I love you," she said suddenly, unable to hold the words back any longer.

Smiling into her sparkling eyes, Lucas ran his hand down her body in a soft caress. His wandering fingers found the buttons on her shirt and his hand slipped inside. Passion flared. He found her mouth, and his kisses became hot and bold.

"Talk, talk, talk! There's only one way to stop you," he said with tender rebuke. His mouth came down again and seized hers in a crushing, consuming kiss. "Good Lord, how I love you," he rasped.

Laughing with ebullient joy, she wrapped her arms around his neck. "I love you, too," she whispered against his lips. His hands came up to frame her face and he searched the depths of her eyes. She repeated the words with all the passion of a woman truly in love.

"I don't know if I can wait till we get to El Paso," he whispered between snatches of kisses.

"Why El Paso?"

"That's where I'm going to marry you. I want you in my bedroll so I can love you every night."

"What's wrong with soft prairie grass?" she whispered innocently.

"You mean . . . now?"

"Why not? You've already introduced me to the wicked pleasures of the flesh!" Her eyes twinkled to match the stars above. She gave him a cheeky grin.

"But . . . those damned britches!"

"You'd be surprised at how easily they come off."

"Then get to working on it, woman," he growled. "I can't wait much longer."

Epilogue

June 3.

Yesterday, June 2, 1859, we arrived in El Paso. The town is made up of small adobe houses, most of which lie across the Rio Grande River in Mexico. On the north side there are several settlements. Two days ago we passed Fort Quitman, but didn't linger because a company of soldiers offered us escort to El Paso. I record these events first, but they seem unimportant compared to the entries that will follow.

All those who were injured in the fracas one day out of Fort Davis have recovered. Laura Foster, who regained her sight, is doing well. She will continue to wear the smoked glasses Doctor Hook designed and Mr. Blanchet made for her.

Three weddings will be performed this afternoon. Laura Foster will wed Buck Garrett, the wagon train scout. I, Tucker Houston, will wed Lucas Steele, the wagon master. Doctor

Marie Hook and Rafe Blanchet informed Mr. Steele this morning that they also wish to wed.

I have to add a personal note here, because to those not on this journey, and perhaps even to us looking back someday, things may seem to have happened very quickly. But out here on the prairie, fighting for survival, each day stretches into forever, and life becomes more precious as it becomes more precarious. It gets easier, somehow, to distinguish the essential things in life from the unimportant.

July 14.

Almost three months from the day the wagon train left Fort Worth, Texas, it arrived in Coopertown, California. The little town is located in a lush valley between two tall mountains. Mr. Steele stopped the train for a day outside of town, and all the women bathed, washed their hair, and put on dresses, the first they had worn since the weddings in El Paso. The group was obviously excited after having traveled hundreds of miles through the wilderness in search of a dream. But they are all stronger, surer women now, with their hearts full of joy but with their feet planted firmly on the ground.

April 15, 1860.

This is the final entry in this journal. I have waited a year to record these events. When the prospective wives arrived in Coopertown, they were housed in barracks put up temporarily for that purpose. Several social functions were arranged in order for the single men in the community to meet them. There was no pressure put upon the women to choose husbands; however, within a month there was not an unmarried woman left in town. Emma Collins married a farmer who loved children. Mrs. Shaffer also married a man who accepted her child. It was believed that Mustang was in the running for Lottie's hand, but she married a big German who wanted to start a freight line. Coopertown gained a teacher in Rafe Blanchet and a doctor in his wife, Marie. The Taylors built a fine new house, and Mr. Taylor plans to go into the banking business.

Laura and Buck Garrett were called to the ranch of Buck's grandfather. The old man was frail and dying. Buck Garrett inherited the vast holding and is now a rich and influential man in California.

Lucas Steele and I, Tucker Steele, bought land next to the Rancho Lauralita, as Buck renamed his grandfather's ranch in honor of his wife. We are building a home. We have only a cabin at this time, but plan to have the two-storied log structure complete by the time our baby arrives a month from now. We see Laura and Buck often. Laura is looking forward to the birth of her own child in the summer.

We are planning a reunion of all the people who made the trip west with us. At the reunion I will read this journal and relate events that I have, so far, told only my husband.

Tucker Houston Steele
April 15, 1860
Coopertown, California

Please turn the page for

a sample from

SWEETWATER

A Dorothy Garlock original novel

To be published by Warner Books

in March, 1998

Prologue

Allentown, Pennsylvania 1884

Her throat tightened, and her mouth filled with the metallic taste of anxiety.

The frenzied hammering of her heart was so loud that she thought Uncle Noah must hear it as he stood beside her concealed in the hedge of bridal wreath bushes that edged the lane. She peered through the inky darkness toward the unlighted house that had been her childhood home.

"Something has happened or they'd be here."

"Patience, ducks! It's only an hour past midnight." Noah flavored his speech with expressions he had picked up during his travels abroad. "Tululla said Cass got the message."

"What if they were locked in their rooms?"

"Then I'll get on my trusty steed, jump the moat, and rescue the fair damsels."

"Be serious, Uncle Noah."

"I am, love. I'm just so sure that Cassandra can pull it off."

The one reassuring fact that penetrated the whirl of Jenny's thoughts was that her nine-year-old sister was far smarter than their half-sister, Margaret, or that disgusting religious fanatic she had married. The child had had two days to plan on how to get herself and four-year-old Beatrice out of the house and meet them at this place.

Jenny peered into the inkiness toward the house. *May the Lord forgive me for not coming back home sooner to see how my little sisters were faring.*

Two weeks ago, after receiving a letter from Tululla, the cook, Jenny had taken leave from the academy in Baltimore where she was teaching and returned to her childhood home for the first time since her father's death a year ago.

She had not been welcomed.

On their father's dying bed he had made his oldest daughter, Margaret, and her husband, Charles Ransome, guardians of his two youngest daughters and executors of their sizeable inheritance. Poor sweet Papa would have been heartsick if he had known what would happen to the business he had worked so hard to create and the treatment his young children would receive.

Charles ruled the house with an iron fist. The girls were severely and cruelly punished for the slightest infraction of his rules. The day after Jenny arrived, Charles had slapped Beatrice so hard for dropping food on the tablecloth that he knocked her from her chair.

More angry than she had ever been in her life,

Jenny had loudly and furiously rebuked her brother-in-law for his actions. When Charles had stood over Beatrice, refusing to allow Jenny to comfort the sobbing child, and ordered Jenny from the house, Margaret had stood by her husband.

According to Tululla, it was Cassandra who had borne the brunt of Charles's cruelest discipline. She was allowed to read nothing but the Bible and forbidden to give her opinion on any subject. One of her duties was to empty the chamber pots each morning and scrub them. When religious friends came to call, she was commanded to recite long passages from the Bible; and if one word was wrong, she was whipped with a paddle or a willow switch. Sometimes she was banished to sleep alone in the barn at night.

Jenny had been so outraged that, after leaving the house, she had immediately begun to plan for the girls' escape. She had called on her Uncle Noah for help he had been glad to give.

"Missy—" The whisper came out of the darkness.

Jenny whirled around so fast she bumped into her uncle.

"Sandy, you scared me."

"The buggy is down da road by dem willow trees."

"Thank you, Sandy." She put her hand on the young man's arm. "Is your mother all right? I don't want either of you to get in trouble over this."

"Ma say, 'do it for the girls.' Ma say this ain't a good place for Mister H's babes."

"I'll never be able to thank her enough for getting in touch with me. Sandy, if the girls don't manage to get out of the house tonight, we'll be here tomorrow night. Will you try to get the message to Cassandra?"

"Yes'm." The boy turned and disappeared in the darkness.

"Uncle Noah, what will Charles do if he finds out that Tululla and Sandy helped us?"

"He'll be madder than a wet hen, I'm sure. But Tululla's been running this house for a long time, and he knows that Margaret's incapable of doing it without her. The jackass is fond of eating, and Tululla is the best cook in the county. She'd have no trouble getting another position. The girls are the reason she's been staying on."

"And he does get work out of Sandy. He treats him like a slave, but not in Tululla's presence. Sandy has always been kind of . . . dim-witted, but he's harmless and devoted to the girls. Uncle Noah, I wish I could be sure that Charles will not be able to use the law to come after us when he finds out the children are with me."

"We've been over that, ducks. You're going to a place where the bloody bastard can't reach you. Meanwhile, the lawyers will be working for you to be given legal custody."

A half hour passed. The sky cleared and a few stars appeared. The night breeze turned cold. It seemed to Jenny that she had been standing here in the bushes forever, although it couldn't have been more than three or four hours. She backed against Uncle Noah for warmth.

"They're not going to get out tonight." She whispered the words sorrowfully. Then, at a rustle of leaves, she instantly became alert. "I heard something."

"Shhh . . . shhh—"

She turned her head to catch the sound and heard her name being called in a whisper.

"Vir . . . gin . . . ia—"

"Here I am, honey."

Out of the darkness emerged one small figure. Jenny's heart sank, but only for a moment.

Nine-year-old Cassandra, carrying her sister on her back, moved toward them. Jenny rushed to meet them, then stopped and gasped.

Both girls were stark naked.

"Oh, dear heaven!"

"Margaret takes our clothes away every night, 'cause she's 'fraid we'll run off."

"That's outrageous!"

"They locked Beatrice in the closet 'cause she wet her drawers. But I found the keys. I locked their door. I . . . locked all the doors. And I dropped the keys down the well. Oh, I hate them. I wish they were . . . dead!"

Jenny tried to lift Beatrice off Cassandra's back, but the little girl let out a choking cry and clung desperately to her sister.

"It's Jenny, Bea," Cassandra said gently. "Go to Jenny. We'll be all right now."

Jenny took the child and wrapped her in her cape. Uncle Noah, still sputtering obscenities in a foreign language, wrapped his coat around Cassandra, and they hurried to the waiting buggy.

6

Chapter One

Wyoming Territory

Virginia Hepperly Gray, her stomach churning from the rocking, lurching movements of the stagecoach, sighed with relief when it came to a jerking halt. She patted in place her dark auburn hair. adjusted the hat pin in the crown of her hat and pulled on her gloves.

The door opened. She took the hand offered by the driver, stepped down and surveyed the huddle of buildings that made up the town of Sweetwater. She had seen quite a few new towns on the way west, but none was as primitive as this. It was all very new to her—this raw, wild, sparsely settled country. But it was just the place for her and the two small girls who followed her from the coach with confused looks on their faces.

"I'm thirsty," the younger of the two whimpered as she had been doing for hours.

The woman controlled her irritation and reminded

herself that she couldn't fault the little one for complaining. The children had been under a terrible strain for a year, and it had been only two weeks since they had escaped from their home in the middle of the night. So much had happened to them in such a short time.

"We'll get a drink of water at the hotel . . . if there is one."

Standing beside her trunks, which had been dumped onto the split-log porch of the unpainted building that served as the stage station, Virginia was aware of the stares of the crowd. Her stylish dark-green blouse suit, trimmed with black satin strips around the lapels and the bottom of the skirt, marked her as different from the people lined up to watch the stage come in. Roughly dressed, whiskered men eyed her, but turned away when she sternly returned their inquisitive looks.

"This is a poor excuse for a town," Cassandra, the older child, said. "It isn't at all what I expected."

"It isn't exactly what I expected either, but it's perfect for us. We agreed on that before we set out on this journey. Remember?"

"I understand. They can't extradite us back to Allentown from a territory."

At times Virginia was in awe of this little half-sister who at nine years of age had such an adult grasp of their situation.

A man in a black serge suit emerged from the building. His coat was open, showing a gold watch chain stretched across a brocaded vest. His black boots were polished but dust covered. The men on the porch parted to make way for him. He eyed Jenny, and then the girls, with a frown before he carefully removed his hat.

"Mrs. Gray?"

"I'm Virginia Gray." Jenny, annoyed at the irritation apparent in his voice, grew even more so when he so limply shook the hand she offered.

"Alvin Havelshell, ma'am." Steely blue eyes went to the girls standing beside the baggage. "I didn't know you were bringing your children."

"Is there a problem with that?"

"No. It's just that I expected a much older woman . . . ah . . . not a young married lady with children."

"Are you objecting to the children?"

"Not at all, Mrs. Gray. . ."

"*Miss* Gray. I have never been married." Jenny was a tall woman. Even though she and Havelshell were of equal height, she managed to look down her nose at him and watch his face redden and his lips flatten in reaction.

"It's just that you're . . . not what I expected." The frown on his face drew his brows together.

"I have a copy of my contract with the Bureau of Indian Affairs. My attorney went over it carefully. It specifies nothing about age or marital status. Would you like to see it?"

"That won't be necessary." He spoke curtly and stepped out into the road to motion to the driver of a wagon to pull it up to the station porch.

While leading his horse to the water trough beside

the station, a dark-haired, clean-shaven man paused, as had every other person on the street to observe the scene on the station porch. He tilted his head and grinned. If the Indian agent had expected a docile maiden lady to take over Stoney Creek Ranch and Indian school, one he could either bend to his will or scare off, he was in for a surprise.

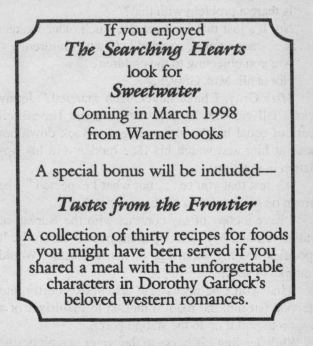

If you enjoyed
The Searching Hearts
look for
Sweetwater
Coming in March 1998
from Warner books

A special bonus will be included—

Tastes from the Frontier

A collection of thirty recipes for foods you might have been served if you shared a meal with the unforgettable characters in Dorothy Garlock's beloved western romances.